The Wild Adventures of Doc Savage

Please visit www.adventuresinbronze.com for
more information on titles you may have missed.

PYTHON ISLE
WHITE EYES
THE WHISTLING WRAITH
THE FORGOTTEN REALM
THE DESERT DEMONS
HORROR IN GOLD
THE INFERNAL BUDDHA
DEATH'S DARK DOMAIN
SKULL ISLAND
PHANTOM LAGOON
THE MIRACLE MENACE
THE ICE GENIUS
THE WAR MAKERS

Coming in 2015: THE SECRET OF SATAN'S SPINE

Also from Altus Press

The Wild Adventures of Tarzan

RETURN TO PAL-UL-DON

DOC SAVAGE
THE SINISTER SHADOW

A DOC SAVAGE ADVENTURE

BY WILL MURRAY & LESTER DENT
WRITING AS KENNETH ROBESON

COVER BY JOE DeVITO

ALTUS PRESS • 2015

First Edition — June 2015

DESIGNED BY
Matthew Moring/Altus Press

SPECIAL THANKS TO
James Bama, Jim Beard, Jerry Birenz, Condé Nast, Jeff Deischer, Norma Dent, Dafydd Neal Dyar, Doug Ellis, Elizabeth Engel, Walter B. Gibson, Henry Lopez, Dave McDonnell, Matthew Moring, Barry Reese, Ray Riethmeier, Anthony Tollin, Christopher Wood, Howard Wright, The State Historical Society of Missouri, and last but not least, the Heirs of Norma Dent—James Valbracht, John Valbracht, Wayne Valbracht, Shirley Dungan and Doris Leimkuehler.

COVER ILLUSTRATION COMMISSIONED BY
Henry Lopez

Like us on Facebook: "The Wild Adventures of Doc Savage"

Printed in the United States of America

Set in Caslon.

For Walter B. Gibson,

Without whom there might not be
any Shadow—or a Doc Savage....

The Sinister Shadow

THIS IS TO CERTIFY THAT I HAVE MADE CAREFUL EXAMINATION OF THE MANUSCRIPT KNOWN AS *THE SINISTER SHADOW*, AS SET DOWN BY MR. KENNETH ROBESON, AND DO FIND IT TO BE A TRUE ACCOUNT OF MY ACTIVITIES ON THAT OCCASION.

Chapter I

TOWER OF TREACHERY

THE SCRAWNY MAN was trying not to be noticed.

He was a doing a poor job of it. For the night was exceedingly black and the furtive individual was attired in white. Stains resulting from having prepared a recent meal, coupled with an outsized chef's hat stuffed into an apron pocket, bespoke his occupation.

Clutched tenderly to his sunken chest, he carried a dark object. It seemed quite heavy, for the lean individual lowered it to the neatly mown grass underfoot as he halted to listen. Crouched over it, he stabbed his gaze about, as if an unknown horror was about to pounce out of the murk upon him.

Early night traffic on the nearby residential New Jersey boulevard was a low murmur. Packed clouds high in the sky shut off the moonlight, making the walls of the palatial residence beside which the man crouched hardly distinguishable.

His ears detecting nothing further to alarm him, the nervous one gathered up the package. His clutch was careful, as if the contents required the most gentle of handling. He moved away from the huge house, avoiding ornamental bushes in a manner which showed he was very familiar with the grounds. A smooth path came underfoot. He followed it.

The path terminated against the door of a little white building. The door opened inward to the man's fumbling. He entered, lowered his burden to the concrete floor and closed the door.

A safety match made a low pop as he struck it, then filled the room with salmon-colored light. The place held a power lawn mower, a sprayer and diverse other tools used in caring for the elaborately landscaped grounds. Two windows had shutters on them. The man closed these before he turned on the lights.

Weak light bulbs on drop cords disclosed the object in the man's hands, which he had carried in a loosely folded newspaper.

A mist of perspiration on his pale forehead glistened in the glaring light. Giving the trousers of his cook's whites a hitch, he knelt beside the package, unwrapping it.

The object was a gleaming casket. Perhaps no longer than a dozen inches and a third so wide, it had been carved of some ebony wood making it appear as if it was a coffin in miniature. Gilt handles adorned the sides of this macabre replica casket.

These were constructed in the manner of latches, for the man carefully lifted these miniature fittings in a certain sequence, actuating an unlocking mechanism.

Lifting the lid, the man in white revealed an intricate mechanism; prominent within was a spool of tightly-wound steel wire. There was a tiny lever within the miniature casket, and setting the object on the concrete floor, the man in white knelt and flipped the switch.

Mechanism began toiling. From a concealed loudspeaker, a strange voice started to speak.

"Listen well, my pallbearer. This is your Funeral Director. Fail to obey my instructions to the letter, in an exceedingly timely fashion, and you will soon repose in a fine coffin very much like this one, but on a scale sufficient to encase your mortal remains."

There was a pause while the man listened, his face haunted by the words that smote his ears.

"This casket was left for you at exactly 7:30 p.m. You will have found it by the open window of your servant's room in time to receive this message before the appointed hour. At exactly 8:15, you will go to the tower room of the Cranston mansion where you work, pick the lock, and warm up the short-wave radio set housed there. You

will tune into the agreed-upon radio frequency, where you will receive further instructions. Do not fail, Pallbearer. That is all."

At that juncture, the wire stopped moving through the magnetic reproducer, and the device fell silent.

Restoring the lever, the man closed the tiny casket, resetting the tiny fittings in the reverse sequence with which he had opened them.

Wrapping up the unpleasant reminder of his employer in newspaper, the furtive one stowed the device in a shadowy corner of the tool house, where it would not be discovered.

Leaving the shed, he locked it, and slipped furtively back to the mansion by the servants' entrance. A thin sheen of nervous perspiration made his hollow face shiny. He noticed this in a hall mirror, and hastily lifted his stained apron, employing it to massage his features dry.

That task concluded, the man began moving through the mansion, making his way from the serving area to the second floor, creeping up the magnificent winding staircase, and working toward the attic area.

At the end of a gloomy hallway, a skylight showed a locked door; a brass padlock gleamed in the thin moonlight.

Slipping up to this, the cook—for that is what he was—removed a tiny pick from a trouser pocket and began fiddling with the padlock.

This operation took some time, during which fresh perspiration bathed the man's nervous features. Again the apron came into play, wiping his face clean.

Came a click. The padlock surrendered. The man eased in, pressed the door closed behind him, pick and padlock nestled together in a pocket.

Taking a wooden chair before a radio set, he warmed this up, watched indicator needles come to life, then dialed the set to a certain prearranged frequency.

Drawing the microphone closer to his lean lips, the cook started speaking.

"This is Pallbearer Creece," he whispered.

Silence mixed in with the buzz of static was the only response. Then a quavery voice announced, *"This is your Funeral Director. Give me your report."*

"Your plan is not going as expected, Funeral Director. Lamont Cranston intends to fight you."

"Bah! Brave words, but he is not in any way my equal. If he fails to accede to my demands, I will bury him without honor."

"There is an additional complication," husked the man addressed as Pallbearer Creece.

"Speak more distinctly that I may understand," demanded the querulous voice.

"In some manner, Cranston has learned who you are," the cook continued more clearly.

A grunt of shocked surprise came from the loudspeaker, then a brutal inquiry: *"How did you learn this?"*

"By listening to Cranston from my hiding place in the basement, through the furnace register of his study. He was talking to his lawyer, Sydney J. Palmer-Letts. Cranston told Palmer-Letts he had heard something which had revealed who you were. He was very careful when he gave the information. Had I not been standing directly beneath the study floor register where Cranston sat, I would not have overheard."

"False!" rasped the voice from the ether. *"Cranston cannot have learned who I am. It is not possible, for I am not known to him. Therefore, Cranston is mistaken. But who does he think the Funeral Director is? What name?"*

"He did not tell Palmer-Letts. Cranston said he could hardly believe his discovery, and would keep the information to himself until he was sure."

"Then you know nothing further?"

"No, but I have a hunch. I–I hesitate to voice it...."

"Speak, underling!" snapped the other harshly.

"Through the furnace register, I have heard Cranston listening to the radio."

"Yes?" prompted the other.

"He was listening to… *The Shadow!*"

A shocked silence followed that utterance. Static filled the tower room devoted to the short-wave set.

"That means nothing! Many listen to that infernal program."

"But as he listened, I heard him muttering, talking back to the voice coming over the air. Accusing him of being at the root of his problems."

"And you take this to mean what?"

"That Cranston thinks that *you* are The Shadow."

Cackling laughter greeted this assertion. It went on for some time, a ghoulish chuckling that brought goosebumps to the pale flesh of the nervous cook.

"So Lamont Cranston believes that he is being victimized by The Shadow," mused the querulous voice.

"It is only a hunch on my part," the cook said hastily. "Is he… I mean, are you—?"

"No, I am not that cursed creature," snapped the distant voice. *"The public does not seem to know who he is, or what arcane purpose motivates his activities. The police don't talk about him. His name hardly ever appears in the newspapers."*

The cook volunteered, "They say he is just a myth, kinda like the bogeyman. But I know guys who say they have seen him stalking about, moving in and out of the shadows like some damned black ghost."

"Never mind all that! It might serve my purposes if my future victims believe that The Shadow is their victimizer. Yes, that might do."

The cook licked his lips and muttered, "I'm kinda glad to hear that… glad you're not—The Shadow."

"What else did Cranston and Palmer-Letts talk about?" asked the voice from the short-wave set.

"About the demand for one quarter of a million dollars you made upon Cranston. Palmer-Letts saw the extortion notes you had me leave for Cranston to find, the first one making the demand, and the second promising him death if he did not pay up."

The Funeral Director emitted an ugly chuckle. *"And is he going to pay?"*

"Cranston said he would not, except as a last resort."

"He is going to depend on aid from the police, then?"

"No!" The cook's voice became somewhat puzzled. "Cranston encouraged Palmer-Letts to meet a man named George Clarendon, who has just arrived from Chicago and registered at the Hotel Thermon."

The voice of the Funeral Director lifted to a sudden shriek. *"George Clarendon! You say Palmer-Letts is to meet George Clarendon?"*

"Yes. Clarendon contacted Palmer-Letts prior to his arrival, saying that he wished to meet the lawyer about a confidential matter regarding Cranston. Palmer-Letts has gone to meet him, to learn what he could. Those were the instructions Cranston gave him. From what I could overhear, Cranston knew Clarendon from a club they both belong to. But Palmer-Letts seemed intrigued by some information Clarendon gave him. He seemed to think Clarendon could do a great deal more to help Cranston than the police."

Low mutterings came out of the radio set. The sounds were not words; nevertheless they conveyed clearly the fact that the Funeral Director was wildly excited by the name of George Clarendon. Indeed, there was more than excitement in the mutterings. There was a quality strangely like terror.

"LISTEN closely, Pallbearer Creece," the sinister voice said at last. *"The police have already proven helpless against us. We have murdered men who would not meet our demands, and in each case the police have deemed it the result of natural causes brought on by worry over*

the present terrible business conditions. So we have nothing to fear from them. But there was one power we do have reason to fear."

The cook, drinking in the harsh words, nodded his head vigorously.

"You know that my organization has been brought to perfection and nicely groomed for this great undertaking," the voice continued. *"I have understood that at some time we would have to meet and defeat this power. I even expected news of those inexplicable deaths in the papers would bring on the battle with this entity. So I am ready. Yes, I am ready for George Clarendon."*

"One man!" the cook chuckled hoarsely in relief. "What can one man do against us?"

"You laugh because you do not know what George Clarendon is!" The Funeral Director seemed angered by the chuckle. *"I do not laugh because I do know what he is. Nobody laughs at him, knowing that. Nobody but a fool. And I am not a fool. I know George Clarendon is the only force we have to fear in the world, the greatest obstacle to our securing fabulous riches and the domination of wealthy men through secret terror."*

The cook muttered a hasty apology to his master.

"Silence!" hissed the Funeral Director. *"Listen well!"*

Rapid, low orders came out of the short-wave loudspeaker. At the words, the treacherous cook's face became even more pallid than it had been. His scrawny arms and legs trembled until he could hardly control them. The flow of instructions ended with a thin demand inquiring if he understood, and when Creece said that he did, his teeth chattered until the words were hardly intelligible.

"You are very nervous about this—take care that you do not fail!" the voice quavered at him. *"The Funeral Director has a way of dealing with those who bungle his work—a word to the police will send you to the gallows for the murder of one of those men who supposedly perished of heart trouble."*

"I w-won't f-fail!" the cook faltered.

The sinister voice warned: *"Take care you do not! Others will attend to Palmer-Letts and this George Clarendon. And no one must fail. It is a battle for our existence we face. That is all."*

With trembling fingers, the cook turned off the short-wave set, in his mental anguish failing to restore the tuner to its former frequency.

Creeping back to the door, he slipped out—after first peering through a crack in the open door. Silently as possible, he replaced the padlock, clicking it shut, muffling the sound with his much-stained cook's apron.

With as much stealth as he could muster, the skulking cook slipped down the winding staircase, until he reached the first floor. Turning a corner, he almost collided with another servant.

"What are you doing out of your assigned area?" demanded Richards, the valet.

"N-nothing," returned the cook.

Richards studied him with steady eyes, and reminded, "You are new here, Creece. Mr. Cranston has many rules, and they must be strictly adhered to—to the letter. Do you understand?"

"I-I do. Of course I do."

"You have not been here but three weeks, Creece. If you hope to continue in Mr. Cranston's employ beyond the trial period of a month, you will remain in the kitchen area except when you are in your own private quarters."

"Yes, yes of course," the cook said agreeably.

Richards continued in a less severe tone. "Mr. Cranston has gone out and is not expected back until late. It does not appear that your services will be required this evening. Perhaps you might take the rest of the evening off."

"Yes, sir. I was planning to request that exact favor."

"It is no favor, Creece. Merely a convenience for all of us. I would have Stanley run you into town, but he is conveying Mr. Cranston to an important appointment."

"I understand, Richards. Thank you very much. Good night."

Greatly relieved, the cook made for the servants' entrance,

and slipped out into the night, intent upon his secret mission at the behest of his unseen master, the Funeral Director.

He walked several blocks in a northerly direction, found a certain street corner and paused by a cast-iron street light standard to light a cigarette.

As he smoked, a black car slithered up, drew close to the curbing. A most peculiar vehicle, especially to be abroad at this late hour.

For it was a flower car of the type seen at the long funeral processions for men of means. Instead of a rear seat, there was an open container bed where a profusion of white carnations had been arrayed.

The door popped open, and a rough voice demanded, "Are you Creece?"

"Yes, Lee Creece."

"Then get in."

With furtive haste, the treacherous cook calling himself Lee Creece stepped into the weird car, and clapped the door shut.

Motor muttering, the black vehicle powered away, intent upon executing the instructions of the mysterious Funeral Director.

Chapter II
THE EBONY HEARSE

THE HEARSE WAS as portentously ominous as it was black. And it was as black as Erebus. The funeral machine was long, its decorative rear windows were draped in black crepe, and on its hood stood the ornament of its manufacturer—a winged figure that might have represented the Angel of Death, but was not.

The dark machine slithered around a corner as it followed an equally ebony limousine. The limousine was working its way through midtown Manhattan traffic.

In the rear seat, a firm-faced individual lifted the mouthpiece of the speaking tube and addressed the uniformed driver in the front compartment.

"Stanley."

"Yes, Mr. Cranston."

"Is that hearse following us?"

"He has remained behind us for five blocks. But why would a hearse follow you, Mr. Cranston?"

Lamont Cranston did not answer that query. Instead, he rapped out a crisp directive to his driver.

"Attempt to discard him."

"Yes, Mr. Cranston."

The chauffeur depressed the gas pedal and the limousine lunged ahead. The trailing hearse seemed to follow suit, although it might simply have been taking advantage of the sudden opening in traffic.

The two vehicles wended their way through the evening streets for some minutes. The hearse stuck close behind the limousine.

"Stanley, take a roundabout route to our destination. That might tell the tale."

"Yes, sir."

Stanley spun the wheel, and his rangy frame rocked slightly as the limousine darted past a long touring car. In the rear, his passenger almost lost his balance on the swaying cushions.

Bearing heavily on the accelerator, the dutiful driver worked his elegant machine through the financial district, down into Chinatown, and then reversing course, back uptown.

Through it all, the intensely black hearse snaked in their wake.

Throwing frequent glances through the rear window, Lamont Cranston attempted to discern the features of the driver, but was unable to do so, except at such intervals where splashes of lamp light threw portions of the man's features into stark contrast.

Nothing useful could be determined thereby. The driver was hardly recognizable; moreover, he wore a billed cap, much like a chauffeur's, that prevented recognition.

"Definitely following, sir," said the chauffeur in a tight tone of voice.

"In that case, Stanley," said Cranston, "let us make haste to the Cobalt Club. Otherwise we will be late for my dinner engagement with Commissioner Weston."

In the front seat, Stanley nodded curtly, and wheeled the powerful foreign machine toward the sedate gentleman's club in the heart of Manhattan, pursued by the tapering white cylinders the hearse's headlights threw.

The chauffeur was evidently a conservative driver, since he made no extreme effort to shake the trailing hearse, yet by deft maneuvering, he slipped under the Seventh Avenue Elevated and, switching lanes, managed to shake the sinister trailing machine.

"Very good, Stanley," remarked Cranston with satisfaction. "Proceed to our destination."

A FEW minutes later, the limousine pulled up before the imposing edifice that housed the Cobalt Club and Lamont Cranston alighted, was greeted by the saluting doorman who flung wide the portal, and entered the foyer briskly.

While Stanley waited outside, the millionaire globetrotter walked to the grillroom and surveyed the tables, which had already begun collecting diners.

The Cobalt Club was no ostentatious night spot. Rather, it was an exclusive gentleman's club, with strict membership requirements. The general public was not permitted within its tasteful walls.

The *maitre d'* stepped up to Cranston and offered his apologies.

"Commissioner Weston told us to expect you, Mr. Cranston. Alas, he had no sooner arrived than he was called away on urgent business. It appears that a bank has been robbed on the East Side."

A frown touched the well-molded features of Lamont Cranston.

While the multimillionaire was digesting this morsel of disappointment, the *maitre d'* asked, "Will you still be dining with us?"

"Not tonight, thank you," remarked Cranston. "If Commissioner Weston returns, convey to him my deep regrets. We will have to dine on another occasion."

"Very good. Good night, sir."

Turning on his heel, Lamont Cranston strode from the grillroom, and returned to his waiting limousine. Entering the passenger compartment, he lifted the speaking tube to his firm lips and said, "The Commissioner has other business tonight. Home, Stanley."

Silently, the chauffeur sent the powerful machine purring

from the curb, piloting it in the direction of the Holland Tunnel, back to New Jersey. Turning a tight corner, he crossed a busy intersection—and passed into the blazing headlights of the mysterious hearse, idling at a red light.

"The hearse, sir," Stanley called out.

"Yes, I see it. We cannot let it follow us home."

As the sinister black machine turned into cross-town traffic, endeavoring to resume its trailing, Lamont Cranston was suddenly seized by an idea.

"Stanley, change in plans. Go directly to the Midas Club."

"Yes, sir," said the chauffeur.

Another gentleman's establishment, the Midas Club, was on the same order as the Cobalt Club, but somewhat more exclusive. Many of the latter's habitues were professionals who worked for a living, whereas the Midas Club tended to cater to the leisure class. One had to be a millionaire in order to qualify for membership. And no mere millionaire, either. A prospective applicant had to command five millions in personal wealth to qualify for membership.

Two blocks north, and three west is not a long distance in New York terms. But it was sufficient for Stanley to once again, with deft precision, shake the stealthy black hearse.

When the Cranston limousine pulled up before the exclusive Midas Club on Park Avenue, the trailing machine was nowhere to be seen.

The building was under twenty stories high—short for modern Manhattan—but it made up for it in its quiet ostentatiousness, a mark that suggested considerable sums had been poured into its construction.

Stepping out, Lamont Cranston leaned down and told his chauffeur, "Find a nearby place to park, and await me. I do not know how long I will be."

Stepping up to the entrance, Cranston pressed the door buzzer, and the flunky who answered studied his features with a lack of recognition.

"Are you expected?" he asked.

"I am not," returned Cranston crisply. Then, offering his card, he said, "Perhaps Mr. Brooks will see me regardless. Please convey my compliments to him."

The flunky accepted the card, eyed it, and immediately recognized the name of Lamont Cranston. The wealthy world traveler often made headlines for his globetrotting exploits. It was common to read that Lamont Cranston had gone to Africa on safari, or was exploring Madagascar for an extended vacation. It was not a vulgar fame, but those in the know knew who Cranston was.

He stepped aside and said graciously, "Step this way, Mr. Cranston. I will inform Mr. Brooks of your arrival."

There was a receiving room, but Lamont Cranston declined to take a seat; instead he paced with a restrained agitation.

Presently, an extremely well-dressed individual, carrying an elegant black cane, stepped into the receiving room and introduced himself.

"Brigadier General Theodore Marley Brooks, at your service, Mr. Cranston. To what do I owe the honor of this unexpected visit?"

"Speaking candidly, Mr. Brooks, I am in distress. I had a previous appointment with Commissioner Weston, but he has been detained on official business. I believe that I am being followed and, while considering what to do about the matter, I thought of you."

"Is this a legal matter?"

"It is. Yet, it goes far beyond the boundaries of the practice of law. I have an attorney of good reputation, who is presently looking into another angle of this problem. But I fear the situation into which I have tumbled requires more knowledge and expertise than he can provide."

"In that case, why don't you come to my quarters and we will discuss this."

Cranston nodded curtly. "Very good of you, Mr. Brooks."

The two men took the elevator to an upper floor, where the well-dressed barrister maintained an impeccably appointed apartment that cost more than many of the lofty penthouses of Manhattan.

A portion of this was given over to an office in which the fashionable attorney conducted some of his legal affairs. On the walls reposed a license to practice law in the State of New York, numerous plaques and civic awards, and in a prominent place hung framed in gold leaf a diploma from the Harvard Law School. Theodore Marley Brooks was reputed to possess the most astute legal brain ever produced by Harvard.

Waving the millionaire to a chair, Brooks took a high-backed leather chair, and uncapped a fountain pen with which to take notes. A legal pad sat on the green felt ink blotter.

"Now, Mr, Cranston, how may I help you?" he prompted.

While lighting a cigarette, Lamont Cranston considered where to commence his narrative.

"I should like to start at the beginning," he declared. "More than two years ago, I returned from abroad to discover that an impostor had taken possession of my New Jersey mansion. This impostor had managed by some artifice to make himself look like my precise double. So clever was he that even my household staff did not suspect that in my absence this bounder had been making himself at home as if he were I." *

"Did you call the police?"

Lamont Cranston shook his head somberly. "I fear not. For this man demonstrated to me that he knew the facts of my biography more clearly than did I. Moreover, he assured me that should I denounce him, he would turn me over to the police as the impostor—something he seemed supremely certain he could accomplish."

Lawyer Brooks regarded the millionaire with skeptical eyes.

"So you say this happened more than a two years ago? What has been the result of this fantastic impersonation?"

---

* *The Shadow Laughs.*

"This unknown individual allowed that, if I took extended trips abroad, there would be no trouble. Furthermore, when I chose to return, he would quietly vacate the premises, allowing me to live in my own house unmolested for limited periods of time."

Brooks' eyebrows shot up. "And you agreed to this?"

"I had no choice in the matter. This man displayed an almost supernatural confidence; moreover in his force of personality he was rather intimidating."

"Did this bold character threaten you with harm?"

Cranston shook his head. "Only insofar as I have related."

"I see." The attorney steepled his lean fingers. "What did your personal attorney say to this?"

"I have never revealed all of these particulars to Mr. Sydney J. Palmer-Letts. He deals in business and investment law exclusively. But he has tonight gone to meet a man named Clarendon who claims to possess some knowledge that may affect my situation. However, I began having second thoughts about that rendezvous. Hence, my thwarted dinner assignation with Commissioner Weston."

Lawyer Brooks studied his new client intently with dark eyes. "What brings you to this turn of events where you have decided to reveal these secrets to me?"

"I have recently returned from Afghanistan," asserted Cranston, waving his cigarette about. "And I have discovered on my study desk two notes, one demanding a quarter-million dollars ransom be paid to another party to be named. When I did not comply, a threat letter appeared on my desk, promising certain death if I failed to pay this individual's ransom."

"Who is this person?"

"The notes were unsigned, but they were of such a sinister character, I have come to suspect that this could only be the work of The Shadow!"

"The radio personality?"

"I frankly do not know whether the radio voice that has

captured the public imagination is the same personality as the one who has usurped my estate. But the latter is definitely known to me as The Shadow. Beyond that, I confess that I know little about him other than the embarrassing fact that he wears my face whenever he wishes."

"Audacious chap," remarked Brooks.

"Decidedly."

The two men sat in a silence as attorney Brooks digested this information.

Finally, the lawyer inquired, "Do you wish to retain my services?"

"I do," returned the millionaire. "But not for legal matters. At least, not just yet. I wish to hire you to make an introduction for me to the remarkable fellow who is known as Doc Savage."

"I see," mused the other, frowning.

Lamont Cranston matched that patrician frown with one of his own.

"Is this not acceptable to you? Simply name your price."

"It is not that," snapped Brooks. "It is just that I work with Doc Savage, and accepting a fee to bring this matter to his attention is not done."

The millionaire said, "I will be more than happy to pay a handsome fee to Doc Savage himself, for I understand he has a growing reputation as a philanthropist who handles the problems of others."

Attorney Brooks laughed shortly. "People do not yet understand the gigantic importance of Doc Savage's contributions to the world. But his work will go down in history as one of the greatest benefits to humanity ever witnessed."

"I have heard such things about this man," responded Cranston. "Even in the faraway lands to which I have ventured, they speak of Doc Savage's great deeds. He has unquestionably given more of value to mankind and to the world than anyone living. It is hardly conceivable, but his feats are equally miraculous in the fields of medicine, electricity, chemistry, geology, engineering—"

Brooks held up all of the fingers of one hand.

"There is a group of five men," he said. "Each is a master of some profession. One is an engineer, another a chemist, another an archeologist, another an electrical wizard, and one a lawyer. I am the lawyer of the group. In addition to being among the most learned men alive at their respective professions, each of these five is a lover of action and adventure."

Brooks now used the forefinger of his other hand to bundle the five fingers into a tight group and held them there.

"Let the forefinger represent Doc Savage," he remarked. "He is the man that binds the other five into a single unit. He is the only man who could hold five such geniuses in a group. He can do it because of the almost unbelievable fact that he is a far greater man at their own professions than any of his five companions. He is their leader.

"Doc Savage was trained from the cradle for one purpose in life. That purpose is to go here and there, from one end of the world to the other, looking for excitement and adventure, striving to help those who need help and punishing those who deserve it. A life purpose worthy of a wonder worker such as Doc Savage!"

Something like awe was in the attorney's voice as he spoke.

After absorbing this, Lamont Cranston offered, "The Shadow is rumored to be a power in the underworld, and may have an unknown number of hirelings in his organization. Fighting The Shadow is a job for a superman."

Theodore Marley Brooks' chiseled lips arched in a tight smile. "This is exactly why we are going to see Doc Savage. He is exactly that—a superman!"

"But do you know Doc Savage well enough to persuade him to help us against The Shadow?" queried Cranston anxiously.

"If I know Doc Savage, he will drop anything and everything to take a hand in this baffling mystery."

"It is settled then," said Cranston, crushing his cigarette out in an ashtray. "How soon can you introduce us?"

The attorney had been taking notes on the legal pad all during the interview, but now he capped his pen, and tore off the top sheet, after blotting it carefully.

When it was safe to do so, he folded the sheet and placed it in an inner pocket, then picked up his cane and took an expensive hat off a cherrywood coat rack.

"We will see Doc Savage immediately. I will ring him to expect us."

Lamont Cranston stood up, relief causing his tight features to loosen from worry.

"My town car is downstairs," Cranston suggested. "Let us take that."

MOMENTS later, they exited the impressive Midas Club. Lamont Cranston looked up and down the street, seeking his car.

Spotting it a block and a half away, he lifted one discreet hand, and the vigilant Stanley instantly brought the machine into life, its powerful headlights snapping awake.

The long black limousine pulled up smartly. Stanley stepped out, opening the door for his employer and, after clapping it shut, provided the same courtesy to the well-dressed barrister.

Returning to his driving compartment, the chauffeur slipped into traffic with smooth precision and wheeled the limousine in a westerly direction, toward Doc Savage headquarters.

Speaking into the acoustic tube, Lamont Cranston asked, "Stanley, has there been any sign of that dogged black hearse?"

"None, sir."

"Excellent." To his companion, Cranston remarked, "I do not know who is driving that hearse, but it smacks of the type of vehicle the sinister individual who calls himself The Shadow might utilize in his nocturnal prowling."

"A very astute observation," returned the attorney.

The two men settled down for the short ride across town, and although they were vigilant, they failed to notice the shiny black flower car which pulled into traffic several car lengths behind them, shielded from view by a clanging streetcar.

The queer flower car followed them with a stubborn discreteness.

Chapter III

SNATCHED

LEE CREECE HAD to bunch his bony fists to keep from biting his nails.

Seated beside the grim-faced hearse driver, he had been a nervous witness to the various attempts to locate the sleek limousine of millionaire Lamont Cranston. Twice they had spotted the powerful machine, and twice it had eluded them.

The hearse driver cursed volubly each time. His name, Lee Creece did not know. He introduced himself as Undertaker Desmond. No first name was offered.

In the illicit organization of the mysterious Funeral Director, Creece understood that there was a hierarchy. The captains and lieutenants immediately beneath the Funeral Director were known as Morticians and Undertakers. Below that were Pall-bearers, of whom Creece was a recent recruit. Below that station stood the lowly Embalmers and Gravediggers.

As the hearse hummed through the night, Creece kept his fear-stabbed eyes alert for signs of the Cranston town car.

"Looks like he's left the island," he ventured.

"Looks ain't nothin'," barked Undertaker Desmond. He was fiddling with the knobs of a short-wave set mounted under the dash. Static crackled from this.

Presently, an excited voice spoke.

"Mortician Fain to Undertaker Desmond."

Snatching up the microphone, the driver snapped, "Go ahead."

"Have located the Cranston machine. It's rolling along Fifth Avenue. Southbound."

"Maybe he's headed back to Westfield," Creece ventured.

"Shut up!" yelled the driver. "Stay with him. We're stepping up."

Abruptly, the hearse executed a squealing turn and flung about, diving into the opposite lane, dodging a multitude of taxis and slamming for Fifth Avenue.

Auto horns honked and brayed. Drivers shook fists out of side windows. Somewhere a traffic cop's whistle skirled irritatingly.

"If we get pulled over, we'll never be able to explain ourselves," stammered Creece.

"Shut your trap. If you're gonna work for the Director, you'll need to grow some hair on your chest."

The hearse ran two red lights arrowing for Fifth Avenue. Taxis dodged.

The driver rode his horn, and pedestrians and motorists alike showed a natural deference to the ominous machine.

From the short-wave loudspeaker, a voice exploded.

"Hell's bells!"

Creece blurted, "What is it? Did you lose them?"

"No, but they're pullin' up before that tall skyscraper."

"Which one?"

"The one where Doc Savage has his headquarters."

Lee Creece felt droplets of perspiration pop out on his upper lip. "Doc Savage! I didn't sign on to tangle with *him!*"

"Never mind that now." Into the microphone, Undertaker Desmond hissed rapid instructions.

"Cut him off. Ram him if you have to! But keep them from going inside until we get there."

"Right!" came the terse reply.

The hearse driver now became a madman. He floored the gas,

and sent his ungainly machine booming along, cursing and hitting the horn with frantic force.

Tires squealing and smoking, the funeral machine pulled onto Fifth Avenue just north of the tallest skyscraper in the world, a marvel of architectural engineering rearing up over one hundred stories high.

"There's a blackjack in the glove compartment," bit out the driver. "Grab it."

"What for?"

"What do you think what for? We're going to crack some skulls!"

Fumbling in the receptacle, Lee Creece found the sap and felt its dreadful weight. It was the hue of liver and rattled with close-packed buckshot.

AS THE LIMOUSINE drew up to its destination, Lamont Cranston instructed, "Pull up here, Stanley."

The auto slid smoothly to the curb, and the chauffeur smartly exited the driver's compartment to open the rear doors.

He never reached the handle.

A black automobile lunged out of traffic and slammed into the limousine's blunt trunk, causing the town car to jounce wildly on its springs.

In back, Ham Brooks exploded. "Jove! What was that?"

A boil of men surged out of the black machine and surrounded the limousine. Scarred knuckles drove in, and connected with Stanley's chin, rocking his head back and throwing his gray cap into the gutter. With an astonished grunt, the chauffeur went down.

Rough hands seized the door and flung it wide. Those same hands reached in and yanked Lamont Cranston from the upholstered leather interior.

"Guy, you're coming with us!" snarled one.

Cranston choked, "Unhand me!"

"You had your chance, Cranston," the man said grimly. "The chief wrote you exactly what you could do—or else. You didn't. So it's the—else!"

Cranston insisted, "You are making a mistake."

"The hell we are! You're about the sixth one, and we ain't made a mistake yet. Come on."

Lawyer Brooks had a reputation for being quick-witted, as well as a man of action. He displayed those attributes now.

Shoving out of the long machine, he separated his slim cane, revealing it to be a rapier of excellent steel.

It was no gentleman's affectation. For he lunged at an incoming man, and scratched him on the nose. The blade left a thin red line, but the man's eyes immediately crossed, his long legs getting into a tangle as his knees folded.

The man dropped, overcome by a sticky substance that had been applied to the blade that morning, as it was every morning. The compound was a powerful anesthetic, and could drop a large man in seconds, as it did here.

Wheeling around, Brooks went in search of another victim.

Before he could reach the ruffian who was manhandling Lamont Cranston, a gleaming black hearse roared into view, screeching to a slewing halt, and out came two additional men. Reinforcements.

One clutched a blackjack in one hand. He charged in. Ham danced up to meet him.

The sight of the slim blade seemed to unnerve the attacker, for his eyes went wide and he suddenly began backpedaling.

Emboldened, Ham closed with the erstwhile attacker.

Something in the latter snapped, for he halted and drew back one hand. He let fly.

The blackjack flew a short distance and collided with the dapper lawyer's forehead, dropping him in his tracks. His slim blade went flying. The blackjack wielder had to duck, lest he be impaled.

"Whew!" exclaimed Lee Creece. "I got him!"

"He almost got *you!*" barked the driver.

The latter had in his hand a snub-nosed .38 revolver. He jammed the destructive end ahead of him as he raced to the tangle that was Lamont Cranston and his would-be abductor.

"One side, guy!" snarled the driver, separating the two. For Cranston was showing that he knew how to use his fists. His assailant's face was fast becoming raw.

Clubbing the weapon, the driver brought the walnut butt down onto the well-hatted head. Once, twice. A third blow proved unnecessary, for the millionaire immediately became an elegant pile on the pavement.

"O.K., snap to it," bit out Desmond. "We'll dump them in the hearse."

The instruction did not have to be repeated. Every man still on his feet picked up Lamont Cranston and lugged him to the hearse. The rear receiving door was flung open and the man was unceremoniously thrown in.

"Now get that damned Gravedigger."

The unconscious lackey was gathered up and made to join Cranston.

"What about this other guy?"

"Leave him."

"But he's dressed swell. Maybe we can ransom him, too."

This caused the Undertaker to give the fallen lawyer a second look. Seeing that he was faultlessly attired, Desmond growled, "Not a bad notion. Grab him up."

This was snappily done and the hearse doors closed. Speedily, men deployed to their respective vehicles.

In all, not five minutes had transpired since the initial attack, and the startled crowd had scattered, fearful of gangland bullets. For the passersby quickly realized that the men who had been abducted were no doubt being taken for the dreaded and invariably fatal "ride."

They were wrong, but it did not matter. The fast-acting kidnappers were not challenged, and their funeral vehicles quickly melted into night traffic, running one behind the others, then separating.

Back at the towering skyscraper, a uniformed guard, exiting the building, caught some of the commotion.

Seeing a man he recognized as "Ham" Brooks being loaded into the back of a hearse, he did not hesitate. He kept going, pushing the revolving door all the way around until he was deposited back in the modernistic lobby.

Rushing to a lobby telephone, he called into the receiver, "Get hold of Doc Savage! This is an emergency! One of his men just got snatched. By a damn hearse, no less!"

Chapter IV

THE WONDER WORKER

A BRONZE DESK telephone reposing on an ebony table inset with ivory, rosewood and other rare inlays buzzed twice before a hairy hand reached out to snag it.

The hand brought the handset to a mouth so wide it might have been an accident of nature. The visage around it rather resembled a well-worn catcher's mitt that had been twisted into an approximation of a Neanderthal's homely countenance. Twinkling eyes were small and sunk in pits of gristle under low-hanging brows. Fists had pounded a modest nose into submission.

"Doc Savage headquarters, Monk speakin'," said the owner of the mouth in a squeaking voice, one very much like that of a small boy.

"Mr. Mayfair! This is the captain of the guards. Gus in the lobby reports that there has been an altercation outside. Mr. Brooks appears to have been kidnapped!"

"That fool shyster! I mean—what do you mean?"

"I saw only part of the altercation. Hoodlums in two black cars accosted a limousine outside the building. There was a fight. Then, Mr. Brooks and another man were thrown into the back of a hearse. The hearse and another car drove off rapidly."

"A hearse, you say? That don't sound right."

"I saw it with my own eyes."

"I'll be right down," barked the speaker, slamming down the

receiver. He stabbed an office annunciator and began talking into it.

"Doc! Gus just called in an alarm. Ham pulled up in a limousine, then two cars full of toughs waylaid him. The guard captain says they dumped him and the other guy in the back of a funeral hearse and took off."

"Take the regular elevator to the lobby. I will follow directly," said a voice of remarkably restrained tonality.

"Gotcha," said Monk, tearing out of the reception room as fast as his bandy legs could carry him. He had the short blocky build of a Congo gorilla—barrel chest, narrow hips and a hammered-down red-bristled skull squatting between rolling musclebound shoulders almost bereft of a neck. He would not need to stoop very much to go about on all fours. His burly arms were freakishly elongated, and ended in rusty fists that would have done a caveman proud.

Lunging out into the plain-looking corridor, Monk sprang for a passenger elevator, jabbed the call button impatiently with a thumb, and climbed on board when the elevator door rolled aside to admit him.

Pressing the button marked Lobby, he sent the lift shooting downward. This was a modern elevator, so it dropped eighty-six stories in a remarkably short period of time, without requiring any change in elevators. Many of the lifts in this, the tallest skyscraper in New York, were designed to carry passengers to a certain floor, after which they switched to another bank of elevators—the original designers not having defeated the problem of building an elevator mechanism which could carry a cage up all eighty-six floors.

This particular elevator had been designed by Doc Savage himself, and therefore needed no transfer.

When the cage jarred to a halt on the lobby level, Monk shoved out of the still-opening door, and was momentarily astonished to see that Doc Savage had beaten him to the ground. His blocky jaw sagged comically.

There was no mistaking Doc. He was a colossus in bronze, standing fully a head taller than anyone else as he moved through the modernistic lobby space toward the front entrance doors like a well-oiled machine. His dark bronze hair lay atop his fine-featured head so closely it might have been welded there. Most unusual were his eyes. They were filled with golden flakes, seemingly as fine as sand, which possessed the arresting property of continuous motion. It was as if each was a tiny whirlpool opening into some other realm where gold glinted with animate life.

It was not magic that allowed the big bronze man to beat the hairy one to the ground. Doc Savage had designed a special elevator for their private use, which had been dubbed the super-speed elevator. It dropped like a lead plummet, frequently throwing the passengers off their feet with the incredible velocity with which it operated.

Doc had merely sent the cage dropping at its fastest speed, which was nothing short of breathtaking, beating the regular lift.

Catching up to the bronze man, Monk commented, "Looks like a crowd gatherin' out there."

Doc nodded wordlessly, and pushed through the revolving door, Monk following close behind.

The turning door deposited them out onto the sidewalk, and the bronze man made a beeline for the limousine whose rear trunk had been bashed in.

A patrolman was down on one knee, attending to a man in chauffeur's livery, who appeared to have been knocked out.

The gray-uniformed driver was slow to come around. His eyes were half open, but they did not show comprehension. A purpling bruise on the point of his chin explained his condition.

Monk grunted, "Someone bopped him good."

Doc Savage bent to one knee beside the chauffeur, took his chin in one large bronze hand, lifted it, began studying the man's injuries.

The patrolman was saying, "I heard a commotion, and came running. I found him this way, Mr. Savage."

The fact that the cop addressed the big bronze man with such a mixture of familiarity and deference spoke volumes of the reputation of Doc Savage in New York City. It was no secret—in fact it was well known—that Doc carried special credentials from the police commissioner himself, which stated that he held the rank of honorary police inspector.

Thus the bluecoat's cooperative attitude.

From a pocket, the bronze giant extracted a small capsule, which he promptly broke under the chauffeur's nose. It contained a potent stimulant, more powerful than the conventional smelling salts. One whiff of the brew, and the chauffeur's eyes were popping open and he began struggling with his wits.

"What happened here?" demanded the bronze man.

The driver said groggily, "I was conveying Mr. Cranston and Mr. Brooks to this address when we were attacked by unknown assailants. One crowned me before I could see the other men."

"Lamont Cranston?" inquired Doc.

"Y-yes. Mr. Cranston is my employer."

Doc nodded.

The driver looked around, and asked weakly, "Where is Mr. Cranston?"

"Abducted," replied the bronze giant.

A low groan issued from the chauffeur's lips.

"Blazes!" squeaked Monk, ambling over. "I found Ham's cane lying on the sidewalk, in two sections. Ain't any way that fussy shyster would ever leave it lyin' around like that. They musta knocked him out, too."

Doc Savage stood up, and made a circuit of the limousine, flake-gold eyes studying the sidewalk. In short order, he had a clear picture of the sequence in which events transpired, beginning with the ramming of the vehicle conveying Lamont Cranston and Ham Brooks.

The bronze man took special pains to study the pavement. Here and there, he knelt. Removing an atomizer from his coat, he sprayed such spots as interested him.

Miraculously, the reagent he applied brought into visibility portions of tire tracks previously invisible to the unaided eye. The bronze giant committed the tread marks to memory. Very quickly, he had developed a mental picture of the kidnap cars, knew that they were luxury automobiles. One was doubtless the reported hearse. The other was shorter, and suggested another unusual type.

Standing up, Doc looked around.

Monk began accosting passersby, demanding, "Did anybody see this? What happened here?"

The lobby guard spoke up at that point. Gus gave a precise description of the two machines—the ebony hearse and the equally sable flower car.

Monk growled, "That sounds kinda goofy."

Other passersby began chiming in, adding to the account. Monk listened intently, and very quickly it became clear exactly what had happened.

At that point, an official limousine pulled up, and out stepped a short, brusque individual whose florid face was adorned by a close-clipped military mustache.

Monk eyed the new arrival and remarked to Doc, "Looks like the Commish himself."

Doc Savage strode over to meet the new arrival. "Commissioner Weston."

"Doc," said the Commissioner brusquely. "What is going on here?"

The bronze man gave a succinct account of the incident, after which the Commissioner made a face and blurted, "I had a dinner appointment with Cranston, but was summoned to the scene of a purported bank robbery."

"Purported?"

"It proved to be a false alarm. Faulty wires triggered the

burglar alarm, but it took almost a half hour to ascertain the mistake." Eyeing Stanley the chauffeur, who was now on his feet, Weston demanded of him, "Tell us everything that happened here!"

Stanley managed to do a credible job of recounting all that he had witnessed, but it had taken place with such blinding speed, after which the shaken driver had been knocked out, that his report added little to the existing details.

"Ham Brooks was conveying Cranston to see me," interjected Doc. "But I do not know the nature of his business."

Looking around, Weston made a harrumphing sound in his throat, and declared, "Whatever his business was, it seems to have brought about this unhappy state of affairs."

Doc stated, "Lamont Cranston is a good friend of yours, I understand."

Weston nodded firmly. "I had the impression something was troubling him when he made our dinner date. Blast it that I was called away!"

"Sounds like Cranston got the notion to visit Ham when you didn't show," inserted Monk.

"That is about the size of it," said Weston, fuming. "Lamont Cranston is an important man in town. Once this fiasco lands in the newspapers, there will be a press riot."

Doc Savage said, "Cranston had just come from the Midas Club, where Ham Brooks lives. Why don't you put out a dragnet for the hearse and flower car while Monk and I see what we can discover at the Midas Club?"

"I will do better than that," interposed Weston decisively. "I will drive you over there personally, while my driver radios the orders to Headquarters."

They left Stanley the dazed chauffeur in the hands of the patrolman, and climbed into the official limousine.

NOT fifteen minutes later, sirens howling, Commissioner Weston's car pulled up in front of the Midas Club, where they were admitted without question.

Exiting the elevator at an upper floor, they were let in by Ham's valet, who had the restraint not to ask any questions. But the manservant's eyes were worried.

Doc Savage entered the missing lawyer's private office first, flake-gold eyes scrutinizing everything in the room before crossing the threshold. Nothing appeared to be out of place, nor had the bronze man expected any such thing. The kidnapping had taken place elsewhere.

Doc went immediately to Ham's desk, and took the leather chair.

Monk ambled over to join him, while Commissioner Weston examined the law degrees on the wall, which proclaimed the missing barrister to be an alumnus of Harvard. Ham Brooks was unquestionably the most notable attorney in New York State, if not the world.

Small eyes searching the fastidiously neat desktop, Monk squeaked, "Not a durn clue, dang it."

"On the contrary, Monk," stated Doc Savage. He brought the legal pad closer, and examined the blank top sheet.

During a lifetime of training for the work that he did now, Doc Savage had studied under many tutors and educators. These specialists had ranged far and wide in their areas of expertise. He had learned the art of swimming underwater for great distances without surfacing from the pearl divers of the South Seas. A famous ventriloquist taught Doc to throw his voice. There were many others. All were masters of various arts, from woodcraft to lock picking.

During one sojourn, the bronze man—then a mere lad—had spent weeks in a school for the blind wearing a blindfold night and day. This exercise had been designed to sharpen his other senses, in order that he could operate in absolute darkness unhampered. During this retreat, he had also learned the Braille system of reading raised dots by which method the blind are able to read.

This and similar exercises had sharpened Doc's sense of touch. Running his metallic fingertips across the blank top sheet, the bronze man detected letters. Some of these he could read after a fashion by tracing them, but the process was slow.

Taking out a small atomizer, Doc sprinkled this across the top sheet, depositing invisible iodine vapor, which was commonly used by police scientists to bring out latent fingerprints.

In this instance, oils deposited by Doc's exploring fingertips were revealed as a thin, brown coating.

When the legal pad was restored to the desktop, the indentations made by Ham's impeccable handwriting stood out, starkly white against the brownish paper. In this fashion, the impressions were rendered readable.

"Would you look at that!" muttered Monk. He should not have been so impressed. The simian fellow was one of the foremost industrial chemists living.

This explosive exclamation brought Commissioner Weston hurrying over. Peering over Doc's broad shoulder, he studied the writing.

The notation was brief, as if Ham had been writing a memorandum to himself. The note began with a simple question:

> Who is The Shadow?
> What is his interest in Lamont Cranston?
> What is the purpose of his audacious imposture?

Reading this, Monk remarked, "The Shadow! I heard of that guy."

Commissioner Weston snorted, "A myth! There is no such person."

"Well," grumbled Monk, "a lot of people think there's somethin' to him. There's a swell bunch of rumors swirlin' around the name of The Shadow. What makes you think he ain't real?"

"My best detective, Cardona, insists that he is, but I've expressly forbade him from mentioning the name of The Shadow in official reports."

Doc Savage asked, "Why is that, Commissioner?"

Impatiently, with a trace of irritation, Weston explained, "Reports of The Shadow are so nebulous that his activities could be ascribed to anyone—or no one. Without anything concrete to go on, I will not have my official records cluttered up by the name of a nonentity."

"What about the voice broadcasting over the radio calling himself The Shadow?" asked Doc.

"Precisely my point!" exclaimed Weston. "The man on the radio is merely an actor, playing a part. He could hardly be the figure of terror that haunts the underworld's imagination, now can he?"

"Possibly not," agreed Doc.

"So," expounded Weston, "if the man on the radio is one Shadow, then the rumors abounding in the underworld must be another—if not more than one other. We have had so many reports of such a creature that it sometimes seems as if there are ten or twenty interlopers going by that name."

"I see your point," said Doc. Returning to the matter of the message at hand, he added, "From these notes, it appears that Lamont Cranston came to Ham Brooks with concerns about The Shadow, whoever he might be."

"Perhaps," said Weston grudgingly. "But we have no more to go on in the mystery of The Shadow than previously. While it is obvious Brooks referred to such a being, exactly which Shadow does his memorandum refer to?"

Monk suggested, "Since Ham is missin', along with Cranston, why don't we just round up every Shadow we can lay our hands on?"

"Excluding the radio actor, I presume," Weston said archly. "Or would you rather the police make of themselves a laughingstock by hauling in your radio actor on suspicion of being the notorious Shadow, whose features no one has ever seen?"

Monk made a face; he had no answer to that.

"We might," Doc Savage interjected, "repair to your official car and see if the dragnet for the hearse and the other vehicle has borne any fruit."

"At least one person is talking sense," huffed Weston. He stalked off.

When Doc Savage and Monk Mayfair caught up with the police official outside, the latter was conferring with his uniformed driver, who wore police blue and polished brass buttons.

"Tell them to keep searching," grumbled Weston.

"No luck?" asked Doc.

Weston shook his head angrily. "My men are scouring the city streets and there is no sign of any hearse or flower car."

Monk muttered darkly, "Looks like a doggone dead end."

Doc Savage suggested, "We might run over to the Cobalt Club. Lamont Cranston apparently went there before coming here, and he might have mentioned something that will give us an indication of his troubles."

"An excellent idea," said Weston. "I have missed my dinner and I am famished."

Chapter V

MURDER THAT SUCCEEDED

GEORGE CLARENDON SAT in the living room of the Royal suite at the Hotel Thermon. The Thermon was one of the most expensive hostelries in Manhattan, or even in New York State, and the Royal was its finest suite.

George Clarendon was studying several score of the newspaper clippings spread on the table. A tall, wiry man, his shoulders were slightly stooped and his face was pale, strikingly devoid of all emotion. It was a strange face, one startlingly like a death mask. Only the eyes seemed alive; and they were unnaturally so—deep, piercing, glowing with a queer, hot light, as if they were burning coals.

His white hands moved to turn the clippings, but otherwise were as still as his weird face. The fingers were long, slender, with highly polished nails.

He was attired in the quiet good taste befitting a man who could afford a hotel suite such as this. Only millionaires patronized the Thermon.

The newspaper clippings all had to do with the deaths of wealthy men in greater New York. In every instance, the body was found with no witnesses to the victim's demise. Autopsies had determined simple heart failure as the cause of death. The police had decided that each man had succumbed due to worry over financial conditions. Nowhere was there mention of a breath of suspicion that the men had been murdered.

The telephone buzzer whizzed softly. George Clarendon

answered the instrument, listened to the clerk downstairs, then said in a low, well-modulated voice:

"Sydney J. Palmer-Letts—tell him to come right up."

The phone was a continental type, transmitter and receiver in one piece. George Clarendon replaced it slowly.

He did not touch the pile of newspaper clippings, but moved to the open window and stood there, apparently staring down at the street traffic far below. Several minutes passed.

A faint shuffling noise sounded outside the door. It was very low. A rapid, firm knock followed.

"Come in—the door is not locked," called George Clarendon.

Nothing happened. Whoever was outside did not obey the summons.

George Clarendon whirled from the window, crossed the floor swiftly and listened at the door. He called again: "Come in!"

He received no answer.

His slender fingers moving with a flashing speed, Clarendon took from somewhere in his clothes a mechanism shaped vaguely like a straight-stemmed pipe. The stem portion was very thin and long. He thrust it through the keyhole of the door and pressed an eye to what would have been the bowl if the mechanism had been a pipe.

Reflected by mirrors and enlarged by magnifying lenses, the ingenious instrument permitted Clarendon to see the entire corridor outside. The mechanism was nothing less than a small and highly efficient periscope.

After George Clarendon had studied the hallway a moment, the periscope disappeared inside his garments. He opened the door.

The corridor was empty, except for the body of a man lying on the carpet before the door. He was a short man with black hair and a face which, although rather plump, looked intelligent.

George Clarendon's piercing eyes went alternately bright and dull, like coals fanned by some vagrant breeze, as they ran over the form. Then, bending, his long, pale hands lifted the fellow as lightly as though he were a pillow. He bore him into the room and shoved the door shut with a foot.

He lowered his burden and his strange eyes raced over the recumbent form. The short, dark-haired dead man wore a wristwatch. Initials were engraved in the band.

They were: "S. J. P-L."

Slender, pale fingers slid inside the man's coat, over his heart. They came away slowly, having detected no pulse.

The man poised over the body as second after second ticked away. His strange eyes glowed with their weird lights. Hovering there, he gave an impression of great power, of unlimited capabilities, almost as though he were an unnatural being. Too, there was an uncanny, phantom quality about his crouched form.

Truly a remarkable man, this George Clarendon.

GEORGE CLARENDON strode to the light switch near the door and fingered it. The bulbs in the ceiling fixture extinguished, although a reading lamp on the table still shed a fat funnel of luminance. A moment later that also went out.

Silence saturated the room, a sepulchral quiet very much like that of a tomb. No sound broke it.

But suddenly a flashlight ray licked out. The beam was thin and intensely bright. It swayed around the room like a taut white string, centering upon the table.

A sheet of paper appeared in the light as if by magic, then a fountain pen gripped in a long, slender hand. On the third finger of the hand a weird gem, a fire opal, caught the bright beam of the flash and cast eerie red reflections.

The pen moved, forming words which stood out on the paper in a script blue as violets. They were:

The initials on this man's watch show him to be Sydney J. Palmer-Letts.

He was murdered.

How?

Why?

The pen hesitated, then rapidly wrote the answers to the two questions. The strokes were rounded and bold, as if they told perfectly obvious facts.

Palmer-Letts was murdered by a poison gas, which left him to all outward appearances the victim of a heart attack.

He was murdered to keep him from talking to George Clarendon.

Who did it?

The pen stopped writing and hung above the paper. Then, while it poised there, the written words mysteriously disappeared from the paper. They vanished completely, as if some invisible genie had washed them away with a magic eraser. Those first written were first to vanish, the others fading out rapidly. When the paper was entirely blank, the pen wrote again—another answer.

Palmer-Letts was murdered by the same emissary of evil which had slain other men and made it seem as if they perished of heart failure.

He was murdered by the Funeral Director.

The pen and the hand remained motionless until that writing also vanished. Then they withdrew from the light. The flash extinguished.

Tomb-like silence again impregnated the room. It was broken by the faint breath of a sound the door made in opening. Outlined against the subdued lights of the rich corridor, a shadow was suddenly visible. It was a fantastic patch of murk, deeply black, possessing a vague quality of reality, but at the same time strangely shapeless.

And lying against the shadow, as if it were suspended in midair, was the lifeless form of Sydney J. Palmer-Letts.

The shadow floated into the corridor, the body moving with it. The door closed behind it without the visible aid of human hands. Down the passage a few yards the fantastic blot of gloom moved, stopping near the elevators. The body of Palmer-Letts lowered to the rug.

Seemingly absent of corporeal substance, as though a moth flitting about the corridor lights made it, the strange shape flowed back.

A moment later, the door of George Clarendon's room opened and shut.

The lights, coming on in the room, revealed only the tall, wiry, slightly stooped figure of George Clarendon. He slowly gathered the clippings from the table and tucked them in his wallet. Then he picked up the telephone.

"You announced a Mr. Sydney J. Palmer-Letts a moment ago," he told the clerk downstairs. "I am wondering what became of him?"

The receiver made scratching words. Evidently, they were a puzzled question.

"No," said George Clarendon in answer. "He is not here."

He replaced the phone on a stand and seated himself in a chair. Possibly five minutes elapsed before an excited shout came from the corridor. The body of Palmer-Letts had been found.

George Clarendon went into the hall, betraying just the proper amount of surprise at sight of the dead man. He assisted the bellboy who had discovered the body, carrying it down the stairs to the mezzanine floor lounge. They placed the corpse on a divan, covering it with a long white tablecloth.

The bellboy hastily called the hotel physician.

BEFORE George Clarendon entered his room half an hour later, he had stood by and seen the doctor examine the body of Sydney J. Palmer-Letts and pronounce him dead due to heart failure. Palmer-Letts had collapsed in the hallway, a moment after leaving the elevator, the doctor thought.

And Clarendon had soberly agreed that it did look like that was what had happened. He then repaired to his suite.

George Clarendon brought up short just inside his room.

An object stood on the table—a thing which had not been there before. Somebody had placed it there while he had consulted with the doctor!

The thing was a miniature black casket, a box slightly less than fifteen inches long and possibly half that wide. It was cunningly wrought, in every way made to resemble a tiny bier, down to the silver fittings.

George Clarendon stared at the ominous thing a moment, then moved swiftly from one room to another of his suite, searching. He found no one concealed there. Whoever had bought the black coffer had not remained.

Going back to the sitting area, George Clarendon stood looking at the object.

Carefully, he lifted the casket, and a distinct click came. Astoundingly, the object began speaking in a man's querulous tone.

The voice spoke to him.

"You have seen the Funeral Director reach out for one who opposed him!"

At the sound of the hissing words, George Clarendon betrayed no surprise. It was as though he had not heard them.

The menacing voice seemed to wait for him to speak. It met with disappointment, for Clarendon was silent.

"Sydney J. Palmer-Letts died as a warning to you, George Clarendon!" crackled the voice. "A warning for you to leave New York City and return to Chicago, from whence you came. You will do this at once!"

No words came from George Clarendon's lips. He did not move.

The voice from the black casket suddenly became agitated.

"I mean what I say!"

George Clarendon remained mute.

The voice continued reedily. "You see, I do not belittle your ability, George Clarendon. For I know who you are. You have accomplished remarkable things in your peculiar way, but always against men who had but a vague idea of how great you really were. Some of the fools did not even believe you existed. I know what power you have. Yet I do not fear you. I am confident, for my reach is greater than yours."

George Clarendon remained motionless, silent.

"I know who you are!" the Funeral Director snapped. "But you have no inkling of my identity. Such deep knowledge is beyond you. Nor will you ever be able to uncover it!"

An emphatic pause followed that statement.

"You—George Clarendon—are *The Shadow!*" gritted the menacing voice.

GEORGE CLARENDON had not spoken since entering the room. His strange face had shown no emotion. His weird eyes had betrayed neither curiosity nor fear. He merely stood and surveyed the black box as dispassionately as he would have studied a buzzing insect.

He did not speak now, but stepped swiftly to the light switch and clicked the illumination off.

An instant later, a thin flash beam stretched across the room like a silver thread. A hand, the weird gem on the third finger casting mysterious reflections, appeared in the beam as they probed the surface of the shiny black contrivance.

The long, pale fingers ran swiftly over the miniature casket. The back came off the thing, disclosing intricate mechanism within.

Revealed were a number of miniature vacuum tubes, bundled batteries, and a length of steel wire wound about a tiny spool substantially longer than a common spool of thread.

As easily as the average man would fathom the simple machinery of a child's toy train, the marvelous brain working in the darkness above the flashlight solved the secrets of the black box's uncanny ability to speak.

For the box housed a clockwork mechanism in which a magnetized steel wire ran through a reproducer, which was a means by which voices were recorded for playing back. The voice from the black box was nothing more than a recording made earlier.

The sinister person who called himself the Funeral Director could have recorded it at an earlier hour for the purposes of warning George Clarendon from further action.

The secrets of the black box laid naked, the narrow beam of the flashlight extinguished.

A low, terrifying sound pervaded the room. It was a laugh, a laugh so unreal and sinister that a chance listener, had one been near enough to give ear, could not believe the sound emanated from a human throat. Like the voice of some fantastic monster of midnight, it trailed away into nothingness.

The Shadow had laughed. And the room was silent, the very air within it seeming saturated with fear at the sound.

Chapter VI

MACABRE THREAT

THERE WAS LITTLE to be learned at the Cobalt Club, Commissioner Weston discovered when he brought Doc Savage and Monk Mayfair into the exclusive establishment's austere confines.

Only the *maitre d'* had spoken to the missing multimillionaire, and he was forthright in his denials.

"Mr. Cranston was informed that you had been called away, Commissioner," insisted the *maitre d'*. "Whereupon, he immediately left the premises."

"Did Cranston seem disturbed?" demanded Weston.

"I would describe his demeanor as disappointed," supplied the *maitre d'*. "Evidently, he looked forward to dining with you, Commissioner," the flunky added hastily, lest he be misunderstood.

Weston nodded brusquely, and scrutinized the grillroom a trifle wistfully. It was full of diners consuming their evening meals.

Turning to Doc Savage, he said, "There is nothing to be learned here, unfortunately."

"A visit to Cranston's New Jersey mansion might be in order," suggested Doc.

Weston looked momentarily nonplussed. His genuine concern for his missing friend aside, his stomach seemed to be in charge of his impulses.

"Why don't you remain here, while my associates and I visit the Cranston mansion?" suggested Doc.

"Nonsense! I will have Detective Cardona drive out there and make inquiries. We will dine here in comfort and await his report. You will be my guest, for I have recently been presented with a courtesy card, which makes me an honorary member of the Cobalt Club."

Doc said politely, "Monk and I have already eaten, and I would like to speak with the household servants personally. If you do not object," added the bronze man.

Weston seemed momentarily torn. Finally, he said with a trace of exasperation, "Very well. If you are dead set on driving out there, we will pick up Cardona and go as a group."

A flicker of an unreadable expression touched the bronze man's metallic and normally inscrutable countenance. Eyeing Doc, Monk recognized that the bronze man would prefer to act alone. Inasmuch as his close friend Lamont Cranston had gone missing, Doc could hardly refuse the police commissioner.

They walked out into the night and reclaimed Weston's official car, whose driver took them to police headquarters, and collected Joe Cardona.

Cardona was a stocky, swarthy-featured detective first grade who had come up in the ranks from Little Italy. Taking a stubby cigar out of his mouth, he nodded in the direction of Doc Savage and Monk Mayfair and told Weston, "I just learned of the dragnet out for the hearse and the flower car. Strange vehicles for pulling off a kidnapping snatch."

Doc Savage said, "The growing rash of wealthy men who have perished inexplicably is becoming worrisome."

Weston glowered. "There is nothing to it! Heart attacks—each and every one of them. Doubtless some of them were prompted by the present difficult business conditions."

Doc did not contradict the Commissioner, but said instead,

"Nevertheless, it is a remarkably troubling number of similar deaths."

"This is to be expected," insisted Weston. "Many of these men were under great strain, having lost portions of their fortunes in the Crash."

Doc Savage said nothing, as the official limousine slipped into the Holland Tunnel, to emerge on the other side, in New Jersey.

It was a longer, more comfortable ride north to the Westfield estate of Lamont Cranston.

The dwelling was isolated, but surrounded by a substantial wrought-iron fence. The house was palatial but otherwise un-remarkable, except perhaps for its lone attic tower, which seemed a little out of place.

The driver stopped before the gate and opened it, permitting the official car to slip through.

Alighting at the curved driveway entrance, they were met by Richards, the Cranston valet.

Richards recognized both Commissioner Weston and Doc Savage, although he had never met either man.

"I am sorry, gentlemen, but Mr. Cranston is out for the evening," volunteered Richards by way of greeting. "I understand that he was to dine with you, Commissioner."

"I was called away," retorted Weston gruffly. "Cranston has run afoul of kidnappers, I'm afraid."

Richards was too well-trained to respond with anything other than a murmured gasp and a sudden paling of his well-scrubbed features.

Cardona inserted gruffly, "Line up the household staff. We need to get to the bottom of this pronto."

Richards stood aside, allowing entry.

They entered the mansion, and Doc stated, "Cranston's chauf-feur, Stanley, was not abducted along with the others. He de-scribed being accosted by an unknown number of men arriving in a hearse and a flower car, such as would be found in a funeral procession."

This statement was not posed as a question, but it was clear what the bronze man's declaration intended.

Richards protested, "I knew nothing about this. Mr. Cranston simply went out for the evening, as is his habit."

Cardona interjected, "Was your boss showing any signs of being troubled?"

Richards said hastily, "Not that I am aware. Of course, Mr. Cranston does not confide in me. He is very private, and keeps his own counsel."

"Has anything been brewing out of the ordinary then?" pressed Cardona.

Richards searched his memory by staring at the ceiling. "He did meet with his attorney, Mr. Palmer-Letts, earlier in the day. That is the only visitor Mr. Cranston has entertained of late."

Doc asked, "Do you recall any behavior that was out of the ordinary, no matter how minor?"

Again, the valet searched the ceiling as a way of gathering his thoughts and recollections.

"Well," he said slowly. "This probably does not matter, but in recent weeks Mr. Cranston has been listening to a certain popular program on the radio, which I thought peculiar."

"What program?" asked Cardona eagerly.

Richards looked slightly abashed. "That very strange and sinister program that everyone is talking about of late. The one in which a nasty man speaks in a sneering voice and laughs like a demon."

Cardona was too good a detective to put words in the valet's mouth.

"Who is that?" he prompted.

"I believe," admitted Richards, "the voice calls himself The Shadow."

"Blazes!" blurted out Monk. "There's that spooky name again!"

Weston barked, "Blather! We know nothing more than we did before!"

So it appeared, until Doc Savage said quietly, "I would like to examine the radio over which this program was heard."

Both Commissioner Weston and Detective Cardona looked to the bronze man with frank disbelief.

"What do you expect to find in a radio?" asked Cardona.

"Exactly my question," chimed in Weston. "Pardon my frankness, Savage, but yours is a preposterous request."

Nevertheless, the bronze man repeated his request.

"Very well," said Richards. "Follow me then."

Richards escorted the party to the dark-paneled study where Lamont Cranston had a console radio sitting in a corner. It was an expensive set, able to pull in radio stations around the globe. It was also capable of listening in on the police short-wave band, the Coast Guard band, and other official radio frequencies.

Doc Savage examined this radio closely, without touching it.

"Anything funny?" questioned Cardona.

"The set is tuned to Station WNX," declared Doc.

Monk growled, "That's the station that big noise broadcasts from."

Cardona grunted. Weston made a harrumphing sound deep in his throat, but offered no comment.

Turning to Richards, Doc asked, "Has Mr. Cranston received any letters in the last few days?"

"Yes, of course," returned Richards. "Mr. Cranston is an active correspondent. He receives mail daily."

The valet appeared puzzled. That puzzled expression grew concerned when Doc Savage requested, "We should like to examine any recent correspondence."

Now Richards' voice grew openly aghast. "You wish to read Mr. Cranston's personal correspondence? I doubt very much he would appreciate that, gentlemen."

Weston inserted, "Tut-tut. We are not interested in his private correspondence, except insofar as he may have received demands from the gang who kidnapped him this evening."

This was a different matter, of course. The very proper valet struggled with his conscience, then relented. "Very well," he said stiffly. "Since this is a police investigation, I am forced to permit this indiscretion. But when Mr. Cranston returns to the security of his home, I trust you gentlemen will speak on my behalf. For I could be summarily dismissed for acceding to what you request."

Weston said sharply, "Cranston would want us to do everything in our power to track him down and rescue him from his kidnappers."

With a sigh, Richards went to a taboret, and removed a small key, with which he unlocked a desk drawer.

Cardona took control at that point, riffled through a number of envelopes whose return addresses did not appear to be suspicious. The millionaire was in the habit of restoring folded letters to their original envelopes, and storing them that way.

The ace detective began passing around these envelopes for the others to peruse.

Doc Savage examined the return addresses, but did not bother to peer within. He handed those envelopes to Monk for that purpose.

Instead, the bronze man reached into the drawer and began feeling about, probing above the receptacle.

Sensitive fingers found paper that crinkled and, reaching in further, Doc Savage removed two sheets of paper which had been affixed to the underside of the desktop with adhesive tape.

Hearing this commotion, Cardona came over, grunted, "What did you find?"

Doc Savage read the first sheet of paper and handed it to Cardona, then perused the second.

Cardona bit off a pungent oath. "Extortion letters!" he exploded.

The others crowded close, and these letters were passed around.

Cardona said, "The first one demands a quarter million dollars, and the second promises certain death if the first demand was not met."

Monk said, "Sounds like Cranston didn't cough up any dough. That's why they snatched him."

Doc Savage said, "Undoubtedly this was the matter he was going to bring to your attention over dinner, Commissioner."

Weston's face reddened. "Confound it! I wish I had been there to meet him. None of this fuss would have happened otherwise."

Monk added, "Cranston probably went to Ham in order to ask for your help, Doc."

Doc nodded somberly. "All the pieces appear to fit," he stated. To Richards, he said, "These letters are not stored in envelopes. This suggests they did not arrive in a sealed condition."

Richards looked blank. "I do not know what that means. But Mr. Cranston is a man of meticulous habits."

Doc stated, "Perhaps these letters did not come by ordinary mail."

Cardona interjected, "Beside yourself and Stanley, what other servants work in this house?"

"For the moment there is just the new cook, Creece."

"Where is he?"

"I gave him the evening off since Mr. Cranston would not require dinner to be served," replied Richards.

"How long in Cranston's employ?" clipped Doc.

"Just a few weeks."

"What happened to the previous cook?" demanded Cardona, eyes growing interested.

"The poor soul suffered a heart attack," supplied Richards. "It was quite unexpected. He was a bit on the young side to succumb to such a fate."

"Heart attacks again!" exclaimed Monk.

Weston swallowed his grumble of complaint. "Did you notice anything unusual about this cook?"

Richards did not have to search the ceiling for the answer to that query. "Why, yes. I found him coming down from upstairs earlier this evening, where he is not supposed to trespass. It was another reason why I gave him the night off. He seemed nervous."

Cardona asked, "What's upstairs?"

"The master bedroom. The upstairs study, and above that, there is the wireless room."

"Wireless room?" asked Doc.

"Yes. Mr. Cranston has a hobby of listening to short-wave radio broadcasts. He is often up there, although sometimes Mr. Burbank enjoys the privilege."

"Who is this Burbank?" demanded Cardona.

Richards looked momentarily perplexed. "I fear I do not know exactly. Mr. Burbank is a young man who comes and goes with Mr. Cranston's permission, and uses the radio room from time to time. I've not seen him in many months, either."

"Take us to this radio room," directed Doc.

They followed Richards up the winding staircase, past the second floor into the commodious attic area, and finally to the locked door of the solitary tower.

Doc Savage noticed the brass padlock and took it up in metallic hands. Shiny scratches showed around the keyhole.

Monk recognized their meaning.

"Someone picked that padlock, and I don't mean maybe."

Cardona shouldered in and took a hard look.

"Where is the key?" Doc asked the valet.

"I do not know," replied Richards. "I am not privileged to open this door."

Wordlessly, the bronze man took a slim chromium tool from a pocket and began manipulating the lock. It surrendered so swiftly that Detective Cardona took his cigar out of his mouth and let out a whistle of pure astonishment.

Weston eyed him reprovingly.

Doc entered, the others crowding in close behind. The room was square, small in a cozy way, paneled in yellow pine.

The radio set was of the "ham" radio variety, a twenty-meter rig. It could potentially be used to speak to anyone on the globe who was in possession of a set of comparable range and power.

The bronze man eyed the dials and noted the frequency to which the short-wave was set. It was at the far end of the band.

Warming up the set, Doc listened.

Static crackled from the loudspeaker. They waited for something more, but it never came.

Picking up the microphone, Doc Savage spoke.

"This is the voice of The Shadow."

The sounds emanating from the bronze giant's lips were not his usual tones. He had essayed a fair semblance of the radio voice that had captivated America for many months now.

After a pause, a querulous voice rejoined, *"The Shadow! I see you have survived my little present. I fail to fathom how you discovered my secret radio frequency, but have a care. I am not to be trifled with. For I am your Funeral Director."*

Doc managed a passable sardonic laugh, at which point the transmission went dead on the other end. Static returned.

Thoughtfully, Doc Savage turned off the set.

"What was that all about?" demanded Cardona, stabbing at the set with his stubby cigar.

"Call it an experiment."

"Well, it produced strange results," Weston snapped. "But what does it mean?"

"It means," remarked Doc Savage, "that the cook employed this set to communicate with the author of this kidnapping plot."

Weston glowered. "Why did he call himself your Funeral Director?"

Monk answered that by snapping his fingers and saying, "Could be that explains the hearse and flower car!"

"It might, at that," agreed Cardona, nodding wisely. "But not much else."

They filed out of the piney radio room, and made their way to the ground floor, where the valet awaited them.

Turning to Richards, Cardona asked, "When is this cook due back?"

"I did not set a time for his return, but it should not be long."

"We cannot wait all night," snapped Weston, thinking possibly of his growling stomach. "I will ask the New Jersey police to take the fellow into custody upon his return."

"A waste of time," suggested Doc. "Having accomplished his task, the cook is unlikely to return at all."

The truth of the bronze man's opinion was evident. No one challenged it.

But Weston availed himself of the telephone to make his request that Lee Creece be picked up for questioning. The fact that he offered no physical description to go on seemed not to bother the police official at all.

Reluctantly, they returned to the waiting limousine where the uniformed driver was excited.

"Commissioner, you are needed back in New York."

Weston's military mustaches bristled. "Confound it! What is it now?"

"A prominent lawyer has been discovered dead at the Hotel Thermon," explained the man.

"Ham!" blurted out Monk, jaw dropping.

"No," corrected the driver. "His name was Sydney J. Palmer-Letts. He appears to have died under mysterious circumstances."

"Palmer-Letts!" exclaimed Cardona. "Isn't that the name of—"

"Yes," supplied Doc Savage. "He is Lamont Cranston's attorney."

"You mean—*was*," grunted the unsentimental detective.

As they piled into the official car, Monk Mayfair complained, "This case keeps gettin' screwier and screwier."

No one contradicted the hairy chemist.

Chapter VII

THE CRIMINOLOGIST

THE MEDICAL EXAMINER was already in attendance by the time Commissioner Weston's official limousine rolled up the green-awninged entrance to the Hotel Thermon just shy of ten o'clock that evening.

There was a morgue wagon waiting at the curb, which caused Monk Mayfair to remark, "Big night for corpses."

They entered the lobby and the hotel manager bustled up to warn that, if they were not guests, they could not be permitted to enter, owing to a delicate matter that the police were investigating.

Cardona flashed his badge and said, "This is Commissioner Weston. These other gentlemen are with us."

"Be my guest, Commissioner," said the manager hastily. "Your officers are upstairs in the mezzanine with the—er—remains."

They mounted the stairs rather than take the elevator.

A sheet had been draped over the body of Sydney J. Palmer-Letts, which reposed in a divan. Cardona knelt beside the low tent and lifted the linen to reveal the dead man's face. It was rather grayish in cast.

Doc Savage also knelt and, inasmuch as his specialty was medicine, the other deferred to him.

"Looks like a heart attack," commented the M.E.

" 'Looks like,' sounds unscientific," retorted Cardona.

"Merely expressing a medical opinion."

Glancing to the bronze man, Cardona asked, "What's your hunch?"

"Outward signs indicate heart attack, but that would be a preliminary opinion, of course," declared the bronze man.

Cardona nodded, half satisfied. Evidently, the ace sleuth had more confidence in Doc Savage's opinion than he did of the medical examiner's. The bronze man was known as "Doc" because his first and greatest training was in medicine.

"Regular epidemic of heart seizures," muttered Monk, studying the dead man's ashen features. "This bird is about the fifth suspicious one."

"What was he doing here?" Cardona demanded of a thick-set man standing off in one corner, whom he recognized to be the hotel detective.

"Visiting a guest," the house dick responded. "He had just been announced. Was on his way up to the room, but keeled over before he got to the door."

"What's the guest's name?" asked Cardona, writing in his notebook.

"George Clarendon."

"Clarendon!" exclaimed Weston. "Great Scott! I know him! He has been absent from New York for over a year now. Where is he?"

"Up in his room."

"What number?"

"Two-sixteen," supplied the hotel dick.

Rushing to the house telephone, Weston demanded to be connected to Room 216 after identifying himself to the man who answered the insistent ring.

"Clarendon? Ralph Weston here. I see that you are back in town."

The receiver had good tonal quality. The smooth voice of George Clarendon could be discerned distinctly.

"Yes, Commissioner. I arrived from Chicago only last night."

"I have just arrived, and would like to discuss the matter of poor Palmer-Letts with you."

"I have been expecting such a call, but hardly imagined that the Commissioner himself would be the investigating party," said Clarendon. "Come right up."

Weston hung up. He turned to his ace detective.

"Cardona, you remain with the body. Savage, would you be good enough to join me? I suspect you would be interested in meeting George Clarendon. He is rather in your line. Calls himself a criminologist."

Doc Savage told Monk, "Remain here."

"Gotcha, Doc."

Together, the bronze man and the police commissioner went in search of an elevator.

GEORGE CLARENDON opened the door in response to the police official's brusque knock.

In contrast to his earlier irritability, Ralph Weston brightened at the sight of his old friend.

"Clarendon! Delighted to see you after all this time, old man. Where have you been keeping yourself?"

George Clarendon's penetrating eyes did not come to rest upon Ralph Weston's stolid face. Instead, they locked onto the metallic countenance of Doc Savage, standing slightly behind him like a tower of well-tailored muscles.

The bronze giant was in the act of rising to his feet, having plucked something from the corridor carpet and pocketing it surreptitiously.

Unaware of this, Weston turned and said, "Please pardon my lapse in decorum. Permit me to introduce to you Clark Savage, Junior, better known as Doc Savage. Savage, this is George Clarendon."

Clarendon put out a long-fingered hand on which sparkled a gleaming ring. They shook hands briefly and firmly.

Clarendon stood aside. "Step in, gentlemen. Your arrival is rather timely."

"You mean untimely," Doc countered. "As is the untimely demise of your visitor, attorney Palmer-Letts."

"Yes, very regrettable," said Clarendon, motioning them to be seated.

As the men settled into comfortable chairs, Weston began his interrogation. There was no question that it was that.

"First, Clarendon. Pray tell me why you have not been in your usual haunts these last many months?"

Clarendon regarded the two men impassively.

"As you know, Commissioner, during my recent New York sojourn, I had rather the reputation of a playboy."

Weston laughed briefly. "You did like the nightspots, and had the means by which to indulge your appetites."

"Overindulge, you mean," corrected Clarendon. "For the constant round of celebratory pursuits eventually caught up with me. They began to pale. I found myself less and less interested in the nightclubs, or even in the comfortable companionship to be found at the Cobalt Club. You might say I became more sober of mind."

"The times have had that precise effect upon many of your class," prompted Weston.

As he talked, Clarendon's piercing gaze frequently rested on Doc Savage, whose inscrutable features regarded him in return without apparent suspicion. The flake-gold eyes continuously whirled, as if the brain behind those orbs was thinking deeply.

Masking the move with one hand over the other, Clarendon slid his ring around so that the fiery gemstone was concealed in his palm. If the quiet bronze man noticed this artifice, he gave no outward sign.

"I became more and more absorbed in the problem of crime," continued Clarendon. "This city seemed to have more than its share and, for a time I operated a clipping service in which I retained an unemployed crime reporter to compile interesting articles on unsolved crimes. I found, however, that the most interesting criminal depredations were taking place in cities other than New York. Specifically, Chicago attracted me with its recent history of mobster rule."

"You are referring, of course, to the Capone reign?" prompted Weston.

"Quite," returned Clarendon. "I began to fancy myself something of a criminologist, so I relocated to Chicago to pursue my interests there."

"Rather abruptly," said Weston pointedly.

"Virtually overnight," agreed Clarendon. "And while I had some small success in the Windy City, no great fame attached itself to my activities. I confess I became somewhat homesick for Manhattan, hence my recent return."

Doc Savage interjected, "Why was Sydney J. Palmer-Letts visiting you?"

George Clarendon met Doc Savage's scrutiny with his own frank regard; his solemn face was unusually composed.

"Attorney Palmer-Letts," said Clarendon, "rang me up and asked for this meeting. He did not say what it was about, but it seemed very significant to him."

"And how does he know you?" asked Doc.

"Through a mutual acquaintance, a fellow member of the Cobalt Club, Lamont Cranston."

Weston nodded vigorously. "Palmer-Letts was Cranston's attorney." To Clarendon, he shot a keen glance. "Did he mention Cranston by name? Do you believe his concern had to do with Lamont Cranston?"

"He did not," said Clarendon. "At least, not in so many words. The name of Lamont Cranston came up only in passing."

There was a pause during which nothing was said. Below the hotel room windows evening traffic was settling down to the busy murmur that characterizes New York City at night.

"Why do you ask about Cranston?" inquired Clarendon.

Doc Savage answered that. "Lamont Cranston was abducted earlier this evening, along with an associate of mine, an attorney named Theodore Marley Brooks."

If the two men expected the features of George Clarendon to portray or betray shock or surprise, it did not come.

There followed a chilly silence, then Clarendon spoke.

"I know that name," he mused. "Harvard man."

Weston inserted, "We have just come from Cranston's mansion, where we discovered several demand notes. An unknown criminal has been attempting to extort Cranston out of a quarter million dollars, and Cranston, having failed to meet his demands, fell victim to a kidnapping plot. Lawyer Brooks just happened to be conveying Cranston to a meeting with Doc Savage to discuss the matter."

"Have you any clue as to this kidnapper's identity?"

"None whatsoever," Weston said flatly.

Doc Savage interposed, "His man, Richards, has told us that in recent days Lamont Cranston has become fascinated by the radio personality known as The Shadow. There is a possible lead in that direction."

"Bosh!" snapped Weston. "The criminal in question is no more The Shadow than am I!"

George Clarendon was strangely silent. Under his hooded brows, his keen eyes sparkled.

At length, he spoke.

"Excuse me if I fall into my recent role of criminologist. But I cannot help but to connect the skeins that seem apparent to me. Of late there has been a rash of wealthy men succumbing to heart attacks. Some of these individuals appear to be rather young to meet such a premature demise. And now Sydney Palmer-Letts has also fallen victim to an inexplicable heart seizure."

Doc Savage said, "Is this what brought you from Chicago?"

A slight smile traced itself across George Clarendon's lips. "Very astute, Savage. I can see how you came by your reputation.

Yes, reading newspaper accounts of this outbreak of heart failures compelled me to look into the matter. Unofficially, of course," he added, inclining his head in the direction of Commissioner Weston.

"The New York police welcome any assistance tendered by an upstanding citizen such as yourself," Weston returned graciously.

Doc Savage asked, "Have you formed any theory?"

"I confess that it is too early for that, having only arrived last night. But now that I hear the account of Lamont Cranston's troubles and, knowing the fate of poor Palmer-Letts, I am beginning to entertain a thought that some or all of the heart attacks are induced by some insidious means."

Weston interjected, "Since you yourself are a man of means, you would do well to guard yourself. Lest you fall into the category of a future victim."

Clarendon gave a half laugh, almost a chuckle. It was without humor. "Almost no one knows of my return to Manhattan," he assured them. "I doubt very much that I would be at risk."

"By tomorrow," lectured Weston, "the events that transpired at this hotel will be in the morning newspapers. Virtually all of Manhattan will know that George Clarendon is back in town."

"I shall take that warning under advisement, and I thank you for it," intoned Clarendon graciously.

That appeared to conclude the interview, for Weston abruptly stood up and said, "Please keep yourself available for further questioning."

Clarendon nodded somberly. "I have told you all that I know. I wish there were more."

"Now that that is settled," said Weston expansively. "Would you care to join me at the grillroom of the Cobalt Club? I have not had my supper, and I would enjoy hearing of your Chicago endeavors."

"I regret that I must decline," returned Clarendon suavely.

"For this unsettling evening has rattled my nerves, and I seem to have lost my appetite. I intend to turn in early."

Doc Savage said, "Before you do, you might want to close your hotel room window. It is getting rather chilly."

"Ah, yes, I will," said Clarendon. "I confess that I needed some bracing air. The shock of the news of Palmer-Letts' unfortunate demise has affected me in a queer manner. Now that I learn that Lamont Cranston has been kidnapped, my brain is in a whirl."

Doc's steady gaze came to rest on a dark object on a table.

"That is a rather unusual knickknack," he remarked.

"Isn't it?" countered Clarendon coolly. "It was present when I arrived. I have been unable to open the lid, and do not think it a jewelry casket. I suspect that it may be a music box."

"In the shape of a coffin?" asked Doc.

"Perhaps it is an antique. Were not many music boxes of an earlier vintage fashioned as curiosity pieces?"

Without asking permission, the bronze man lifted the item and examined it carefully, noting its workmanship and heft.

"I see no key with which to wind it," he remarked.

"Perhaps it was misplaced by a previous guest of the hotel," suggested Weston.

"Good point," said Clarendon. "Now if you gentlemen will excuse me, I must retire for the evening. It has been a difficult day."

Doc Savage lingered briefly, thoughtful eyes still examining the unsettling thing; then he replaced the small black casket on the table. His metallic features were thoughtful.

George Clarendon saw them to the door and asked, "Have you no clue or trail to the present whereabouts of Lamont Cranston or the attorney Brooks?"

"Every path has led to a dead end," supplied Weston. "We are hunting for a hearse and a flower car, if that means anything to you?"

"It does not," said Clarendon. He grew thoughtful. "But I may have a tip for you both."

"Tip?" said Doc Savage.

"Yes." The criminologist's firm lips compressed. "During my New York days, I often ventured down to some of the less savory dives, where the criminal element convenes. There, I made the acquaintance of many a valuable informant, of the type you might refer to as stool pigeons. One in particular stands out in my mind. His actual name I do not know, but he is renowned throughout the underworld as Spotter. This Spotter seems to have an ear out for anything brewing among denizens of the underworld. If you can find him, he may give you a clue to the kidnappers you seek." Clarendon added pointedly, "I understand further that he has knowledge of this mystery being known as The Shadow."

Doc Savage asked, "Where can Spotter be found?"

"In virtually any unsavory spot, I would say. Try the Black Ship first. If Spotter is not there, he might be discovered at a dive called the Pink Rat. Or Red Mike's. Or, for that matter, at Black Pete's. Good luck to you both."

"Thank you, Clarendon," said Commissioner Weston in farewell. "I trust I will see you at the Cobalt Club sooner than later."

"Definitely sooner," promised George Clarendon, closing the door.

He listened at the panel as the two men departed and, after the elevator doors had slid shut, he went to a black valise. From this the criminologist extracted a long sable cloak, along with a wide-brimmed hat of similar hue.

These donned, he became a funereal shape in the middle of the room. A black-gloved hand reached out and clicked the light switch. The room became as dark as a bat's cave.

In that absolute darkness, a chilling laugh whispered out.

It was the laugh of The Shadow!

Flowing like a river of ink, the spectral figure went to the hotel-room window and slithered out of it despite the fact that the window stood sixteen stories above the sidewalk.

No eye perceived the darksome form trickling down the fire escape like a black spider negotiating a tangled web. Thereafter, his flitting course was untraceable.

Chapter VIII

BLACK SHIP BRAWL

THE COLD CORPSE of Sydney J. Palmer-Letts was being loaded into the morgue wagon when Doc Savage and Commissioner Weston reached the hotel lobby.

"We're about finished up here, Commissioner," Detective Cardona reported, closing his notebook and pocketing it.

"Very well, Cardona. If nothing more needs to be done here, you will find me at the Cobalt Club, enjoying a late repast."

Turning to Doc Savage, Weston asked, "I would appreciate being apprised of any clue of significance you uncover as you search for your man, Brooks."

"Of course," said the bronze giant.

With that, Weston hurried out to his official car, which pulled away swiftly from the curb.

After he had gone, Monk turned to Doc Savage and undertoned, "I'm glad to be rid of that stuffed shirt. How he got to be commissioner of police I'll never know."

Doc Savage said, "Weston has his qualities."

"He hides them pretty good!" barked Monk. "Want I should mosey down to the Black Ship and poke around?"

"You do that. I may join you later."

Furrowing his sloping brow, Monk asked, "You got something up your sleeve, Doc?"

"If you need to reach me, I will be in my laboratory."

Before they could depart, Detective Cardona sidled up and spoke to Doc Savage.

"Now that the Commissioner has left, there's something I want to say."

Doc regarded him steadily. "Go ahead."

"Weston has his own ideas about The Shadow, and I have mine," Cardona vouchsafed. "I've seen him. There have been times when he's gotten me out of jams. Bad jams. Get me?"

"You are saying that The Shadow isn't all bad?" squeaked Monk.

Shrugging his shoulders elaborately, Cardona admitted frankly, "I don't know if The Shadow is good or bad. Or both. But a lot of bad actors have come a cropper because of him."

Doc Savage stated, "If The Shadow is a rising power in the underworld, he might simply be eliminating rivals."

Cardona reached up and scratched his head thoughtfully. "I thought of that angle myself. But somehow I don't think that's the true picture."

"In your opinion, what is?" inquired Doc.

The thoughtful expression on Detective Cardona's swarthy face tightened. At last, he sighed, "Only The Shadow himself knows...."

Monk stuck a stubby thumb into his barrel chest and said, "Is that right? When we catch him, it will be just too bad for The Shadow."

"*If* you catch him," murmured Cardona. "No one has nabbed him yet. Not cop nor crook. Nor ever seen his face. But he's done plenty for this town, stuff that doesn't land in the newspapers, because Commissioner Weston won't let any hint he's real get into my official reports. Believe me, I've left out plenty."

"Thank you, Detective Cardona," said Doc Savage, taking his leave.

Outside, the bronze giant hailed a cab, and Monk grabbed another. They went their separate ways.

By this time, it was eleven o'clock.

MONK MAYFAIR took a taxicab to his Wall Street penthouse, and changed into even more sloppy clothing than was his normal attire. Doffing a loud green jacket, he donned a black-and-white striped jersey sweater calculated to enable him to blend in with the unsavory crowd.

A knit cap such as seamen wear half-smothered his rusty bullet of a head and, with his much-scarred features, the homely chemist looked like a typical specimen of the underworld as he pushed into the smoky cellar interior.

The Black Ship was a disreputable dive located, appropriately enough, by the waterfront. The *slap-slap-slap* of water against pilings reached all the way to its sawdust-floored interior.

The dilapidated building might have been erected back in the days when New York was called New Amsterdam. It leaned like an old ship falling into ruin. The exterior was painted black, and there was an old-fashioned wood sign that hung over the door. Dull with age, a silhouette of a black clipper ship was embossed on its cracked board.

If this had been an earlier day, the Black Ship might have been called a tavern, or a saloon or even a grog shop from which unwary sailors were shanghaied. Now it was a speakeasy, one the authorities tolerated after a fashion, since the new U. S. President had legalized the sale of beer.

Shoving in, Monk made his way through the crowd, who were talking in furtive whispers. Cigarette smoke fouled the air, making faces difficult to see in the unmoving tobacco haze.

Sidling up to the bar, he accosted the barman and demanded a beer.

When a sudsy mug shot back at him, Monk muttered darkly, "I'm lookin' for a guy."

"Which guy?" demanded the barkeep.

"Don't know his real name," growled Monk. "I hear they call him Spotter."

"Spotter! What do you want with *him*?"

His squeaky voice tougher than normal, Monk growled, "That's my dang business. Now cough up. I don't know what the bozo looks like. Is he here?"

The barkeep looked around, and gave the faces in the gloomy atmosphere the once-over.

"No soap. Don't see him. Try the Pink Rat across town. But make sure to pay me first."

Monk slid a silver dollar across the scarred bar top and husked, "There's a ten spot and maybe more in it for you if you tell me what this Spotter looks like."

The barkeep hesitated. The look of naked avarice that came into his eyes told he was tempted. The crooks' code of silence that branded any man as a rat who talked loosely of a fellow underworld denizen tangled his normally talkative tongue.

Seeing this, Monk muttered, "I can make it twenty."

"Let's see the twenty," the barkeep said grudgingly.

Monk fingered a twenty-dollar bill from a pocket and slapped his hirsute hand down with the bill peeping out.

The barkeep looked over the hand, and gathered it up swiftly.

"Cough up," barked Monk.

The barkeep leaned over and breathed, "Small guy. Scrawny. Wears a peaked cap. Doesn't hardly shave but once or twice a week. His eyes are sharp—sharp like a rodent. Spotter sees everything, but nobody hardly ever sees him. Get the picture?"

"What's he do?"

"Whatever will fetch him good coin," returned the barkeep vaguely. "He works around, but ain't attached to any mob. Get what I mean?"

"Yeah," said Monk. "Sounds like a freelancer."

The bartender chuckled roughly. "That's a nice word for it!"

"Got any more for me?" pressed the hairy chemist.

"Spotter works as a kind of combination lookout and spy. He's good at fingerin' them that gets put on the spot. Know what I mean? That's all I got to say. Now drink up. Next one's on the house."

Monk's small eyes gleamed. "Sure that's all?"

"You heard me."

"Maybe, just maybe, this Spotter guy has another name," suggested Monk.

"I doubt his mother named him that!" the barkeep chortled. "Not any more than that big radio noise everyone is petrified of was born The Shadow."

"The Shadow," muttered Monk. "There's a bird I'd like to meet some day."

"Is that so? Birdie Crull said that very thing, or something close to it. But then The Shadow landed on him. Landed hard. Birdie took one of The Shadow's slugs in the gut. They loaded him into a Black Maria for a one-way trip to the boneyard, they did. But Birdie didn't die. He got out of town a day after the medicos patched him up. Happened not far from here. A regular customer until that day, Birdie was. Talk is The Shadow later caught up with him. He's croaked now, Birdie is. That damned Shadow never gives up when he goes after a guy." *

Just then a tough lifted up from a scarred table, sidled up to the bar and took a seat next to the disguised chemist.

This light-haired fellow possessed the broad physique and rugged features of a man who worked with his muscles. Out of the corner of his mouth, he undertoned, "Did I just hear you mention The Shadow?"

"Yeah, I did," growled Monk. "What's it to you?"

"Just this," grunted the new arrival. "I'm gunning for The Shadow."

"Is that so? That's tall talk. What's your name?"

"Cliff Marsland. What's yours?"

---

* *The Living Shadow* & *The Shadow Laughs.*

"Call me Ape. That's all—just Ape. Are you saying The Shadow is real?"

The other nodded, "I seen him. I've traded bullets with him. I may have nicked him, too. He's real, all right. I'm not talking about the bogeyman on the radio, either."

"What's The Shadow's racket?"

"That's the problem. No one knows. Any more than they know who is under that wide slouch hat of his."

"Slouch hat, huh?" gruffed Monk. "What else does he look like?"

"Hard to tell. Wears a long black cloak, bundled up high so it covers his mouth. He always keeps his mouth covered. Figure that out."

"Anything else?" prompted Monk.

"From what little I could see of him, he has eyes like burning coals. Hypnotic, they bore right through you like a matched set of hot pokers. Another thing, he's got a sharp nose. Like a hawk. That's what he looks like—a human hawk with wings black as midnight."

"That don't tell me much, but thanks," said Monk. "What do you know of another bird named Spotter?"

Marsland shrugged elaborately. "Smallfry. Underworld hang-er-on. Does jobs of a certain ratty type, know what I mean?"

Monk grunted. "That's what I hear." Then, he added, "I'm lookin' for this Spotter."

"Why?"

"I think he'll lead me to The Shadow if I lean on him right."

"In that case, you and I should be pals. I want to be led to The Shadow, too."

"Know what this Spotter looks like?"

"Yeah, I do," allowed Marsland. He looked around slowly, reported, "No sign of him here. But we might find him over at the Pink Rat."

"Then what do you say we ankle over there?" suggested Monk.

"Finish your beer," said Marsland.

"I ain't especially thirsty," replied Monk, slipping off the stool.

They stepped out into the night, and Marsland said evenly, "There's a shortcut out of this neighborhood through this alley."

Monk hesitated. The alley was almost supernaturally dark.

A crafty gleam coming into his small eyes, he said, "Sure. Lead the way, Marsland, ol' pal."

Cliff Marsland stepped forward, and entered the alley, which virtually swallowed him.

Moving slowly, the apish chemist followed gingerly, one hand slipping into his striped jersey.

Monk was reaching for a special pistol he had shoved into the waistband of his khaki trousers. He had no sooner gripped the steel butt when there came an abrupt clatter, and the hairy chemist was unexpectedly tripping over a clutter of steel ash cans that had been shoved in his path.

He had been half expecting an ambush, but not of this type. Monk went down, and as he yanked his pistol free, a splash of dry coal ash slapped into his face, followed by the hard muzzle of an automatic pressing into the side of his blunt skull.

"Hold it right there!" warned Marsland. "I don't team up with just anybody. I need to know your bona fides. Who do you work for, or with?"

"What makes you think I do?"

"Anybody looking for The Shadow is cruising for trouble—either making or avoiding. Now which is it?"

"Just a second while I get this dang ash out of my peepers," sputtered Monk.

The automatic's cold steel muzzle pressed closer to Monk's temple.

"No tricks," warned Marsland, blue eyes hardening.

"How can I pull anything wise after you blinded me?" barked Monk hotly.

The heated defy seemed to make perfect sense, so the cold steel muzzle withdrew.

Climbing to his feet in the dark, Monk used one hairy paw to swipe at his blinking eyes, while he kept his supermachine pistol behind his back, out of view.

"Where the heck are you, Marsland?" he complained.

"To your left," replied the other.

That was when Monk Mayfair swung about and uncorked the controlled fury of his supermachine pistol. It emitted a short moan like the bass string of a bull fiddle being sawed. Its terrible reverberation filled the alley. Stuttering muzzle flashes lit up the dingy spot.

The sputtering light showed Cliff Marsland as a burst of slugs stitched across his chest, driving him backward.

The underworld crook went down, his weapon unfired.

Holstering his pistol, Monk confiscated the automatic, shoved it in a pocket, and gathered up the felled criminal.

Slinging him over one shoulder, the hairy chemist lugged him out into the sickly yellow lights of the city night, and lifted one hand to hail a passing taxi.

"You're not Spotter," he growled, "but maybe you'll do in a pinch."

Such was the reputation of the neighborhood that no one emerged to investigate the commotion. Stray slugs hurled in gangland scrapes had felled more than one inhabitant of this zone of skullduggery. Nor did any police uniforms show under the dim streetlights. Patrolmen avoided the spot, not being immune to gangster lead.

As the apish one piled his burden into a taxicab, one shifty figure did emerge from the shadows.

"That's Cliff Marsland," he husked. "Wonder who that big monkey is what's snatched him?" The furtive one grinned yellowly. "Somebody will pay good coin for this dope."

Sliding into the smoky confines of the Black Ship, the wizened individual went in search of anyone who would pay for the information he had fortuitously gleaned.

The barkeep looked up and barked, "Hey, Spotter. You just missed him."

"Missed who?"

"Guy what wanted to chin with you. Said his name was Ape."

Spotter bustled up to the bar, and began whispering.

"You got it backwards, Louie. I didn't just miss him. I just missed gettin' glommed *by* him." Spotter lowered his voice to a nasal whine. "I just glimmed the bird hustlin' a guy into a hack, and the guy was out cold!"

The barkeep whistled. "Recognize either one?"

Spotter shook his head vehemently. "I don't know who that human gorilla was, but the other gazebo was Cliff Marsland."

"Looks like this was your lucky day, Spotter."

"My luck," muttered Spotter, looking about craftily, "starts when I can turn what I saw into silver shekels."

A FEW minutes later, the wizened underworld spy sidled into a pay telephone booth at an all-night drugstore. Getting the operator on the line, he asked for a certain number.

After two rings, a voice responded.

"Undertaker Desmond speaking."

"This is Spotter. I'm makin' my rounds and just came from the Black Ship. There was a guy name of Ape who was askin' after me when I wasn't there. When I pulled up, I spotted this same guy dumpin' Cliff Marsland into a cab. Took off with him. Worth anything to you?"

"No. We are interested in only two things: The Shadow and a man named George Clarendon."

"Yeah, yeah," returned Spotter nervously. "You already gave me the dope on Clarendon. That's why I'm makin' my rounds. I just been over to the Pink Rat, and down at Red Mike's before that. No sign of him."

"Keep looking, Spotter. The big boss will pay plenty for a line on this Clarendon."

"Tell the boss I'm doin' my level best. I won't let him down. Never have."

With that, the connection was terminated and Spotter strolled out into the night. As he walked along, his shifty eyes veered to every shadow. Some made him shiver, but none bothered him. Still, a few were so long and dark, like streaks of coal, that when passing headlights impelled them into life, Spotter jumped.

Shadows made him nervous that way.

Chapter IX

UNDER THE BLUE LIGHT

IN A WINDOWLESS chamber somewhere in the heart of New York City, soft footfalls whispered against a sable rug.

A Stygian darkness dominated the unknown space. Unseen hands reached up and turned on the hanging light. Instantly, a blue funnel was created, disclosing a desk whose top was a polished black.

Little of the room could be seen in the spectral blue light. For the walls were black, as was virtually every article of furniture in the unfathomable space.

The man seated behind the polished ebony desk also wore black. A black cloak was draped over his shoulders. A shapeless slouch hat sat atop his head, its wide brim throwing his features into further shadow.

Removing this hat, the solitary figure placed it on the desk and lifted from a hook a set of earphones, which he clapped over his ears.

Even bereft of the face-concealing hat, little could be seen of this personage's features, for the crimson collar of his cloak shielded that portion of his face directly beneath a jutting, hawk-like nose.

Speaking into a microphone on the desk, the weird figure pronounced a single word: "Report!"

A calm voice returned, "Mann delving into backgrounds of

recent heart attack victims. He reports irregularities in their backgrounds."

"What manner of irregularities?" whispered the being in black.

"Rumors of shady dealings. Unsavory associations. Nothing proven. Victims otherwise not connected to one another."

A knowing laugh disturbed the darkness. Then the eerie voice spoke again.

"Further instructions to Marsland. Abandon previous duty. Search for any sign of Cranston and Brooks, or knowledge of their kidnappers, in underworld."

There was a pause.

"To Burke and Vincent. Seek suspicious black hearse and matching flower car believed to be involved in Cranston abduction."

"Instructions received."

The light on the wall went dark, hands at the desk took up a sheet of paper and began to write.

> Unknown extortionist has targeted Lamont Cranston. Attorney Brooks was caught up by accident. Perpetrator does not realize the connection between Lamont Cranston and George Clarendon. Believes one to be The Shadow, but does not suspect the deeper truth. Evidence suggests that the Funeral Director has crossed paths with The Shadow before. Electrical distortions created by the wire reproducer make his voice difficult to distinguish clearly.
> Known suspects:
> Diamond Bert Farwell[*]
> Ezekiel Bingham[*]
> Isaac Coffran[**]
> Spotter[***]

These words were written in blue ink that was very vivid when first applied to paper, but quickly faded into nothingness.

---

[*]   *The Living Shadow.*

[**]   *The Eyes of The Shadow.*

[***]   *The Shadow Laughs!*

After the last name disappeared, long slim hands made a mark, underlining one of the names. Had anyone been present in the sanctum of The Shadow, they would have not known which name had been underlined, for it had already disappeared. Soon, the underlining also vanished, leaving the white sheet entirely blank.

In the darkness relieved only by the eerie blue light, the strange being called The Shadow laughed softly and faintly.

Then it penned a single phrase.

The Shadow knows!

The laugh returned, rising in the demoniacal mockery, promising dire things for the perpetrator, whose identity the being of midnight had already deduced.

Chapter X

INFERNAL DEVICE

THE MIDNIGHT HOUR had come and gone. City traffic hum had died down to a muted mutter, punctuated by an intermittent honking. Doc Savage was working in the largest room of his skyscraper headquarters.

The setup, which occupied most of the eighty-sixth floor, consisted of the reception room—the smallest of the three rooms—a scientific library unrivaled in all the world and, lastly, the most fabulous portion. This was a laboratory that was the envy of scientists around the globe.

Only one other scientific workshop in the world exceeded this one in completeness. That was the great secret laboratory Doc Savage maintained by the Arctic in a retreat he called his Fortress of Solitude. There, the bronze giant spent weeks toiling on scientific discoveries that were often a generation ahead of the present time. A young fortune had been expended in assembling both. But Doc had spared no expense.

Deep in remote Central America mountains lay a lost valley, a chasm on the floor of which dwelled descendants of the ancient Mayan civilization, a people shut off from the world. In this valley was a fabulous deposit of gold, the greatest mines of the old Mayan civilization. Doc had befriended these people long ago. There was a radio receiving set in the valley. Doc had but to broadcast a few words in Mayan at a certain hour each seventh day, and a week or so later, a burro train of bullion would appear mysteriously from the mountains with funds to be deposited in his account in the national bank of the Central American republic of Hidalgo.

The process that occupied the bronze giant's attention at this late hour did not require any vast apparatus, however. Doc had been subjecting the monogrammed handkerchief that had been purloined from the scene of Sydney J. Palmer-Letts' unexpected demise to a battery of chemical tests.

For this procedure, the bronze man had cut the handkerchief into quarters, subjecting each piece of fabric to a different regimen.

He tested for poisons, acids, and other dangerous residue.

Each of these tests took time, and at intervals Doc Savage went to a phone in the chemical section of his great white-tiled laboratory to check up on the progress of the search for the missing Lamont Cranston and Ham Brooks.

"No progress to report," informed Detective Cardona.

"Call me directly at this number if anything turns up," requested Doc.

The bronze man hung up and returned to his tests. He had examined one fragment of the fabric under a machine called a mass spectrometer, which produced lines of colored light indicative of any chemicals that might have impregnated the fabric. The results had been puzzling, so the bronze man had taken a different piece of the handkerchief and was attempting to discern what had produced such unusual results.

Previously, he had prudently declined to sniff the handkerchief, lest there be any dangerous deposits. Now, with his tests suggesting a perplexing chemical residue, the bronze man carefully lifted a piece of handkerchief and inhaled the air carefully, without directly sniffing the fabric.

A lifetime of scientific training had produced an acute set of nostrils. The routine of daily exercises rigorously adhered to included the bronze man inhaling different vials of scents while blindfolded, and correctly identifying the contents of each tube. After years of doing this, the bronze man could successfully detect the difference between brown sugar and refined cane sugar, or any other similar substances, by olfactory sense alone.

The silken handkerchief smelled peculiar. Doc thought he detected some familiarity in the odor, but could not identify it perfectly. But it was enough. Enough to determine that the handkerchief had been subjected to something unusual, causing chemical odors to adhere to the fabric.

At this point, a rather sickly individual burst into the laboratory.

"Got it!" announced the new arrival.

"Bring it here," directed Doc.

The individual who crossed the immense space was rather slender, not very tall, and possessed a forehead that bulged out so much it seemed to arrive seconds before he did. His ears stuck out from the sides of his head like sails. He was very pale.

This was Thomas J. Roberts, familiarly known as "Long Tom." He was the electrical engineer of Doc Savage's group of assistants, and looked as if he spent much of his life tinkering with vacuum tubes and insulated wiring in a dank cellar. In point of fact, Long Tom had become a millionaire by inventing things in his private laboratory deep in a former wine cellar which he maintained. Had he been born a generation earlier, Long Tom would probably have invented the light bulb.

Long Tom placed an intensely black object on a glass-topped table. He had wrapped it up in a newspaper, which he now unfolded.

Revealed was the miniature black casket which had formerly reposed on a table at the Hotel Thermon, where George Clarendon resided temporarily.

"Any trouble?" inquired Doc.

Long Tom shook his head, which was pale of hair as well as flesh. "I waited until almost midnight, then I picked the lock of the hotel room. I used one of our infra-red flashlights to find this thing in the dark."

"You did not disturb Clarendon?"

"He wasn't there," returned Long Tom flatly. "I didn't hear any breathing, and put my ear to his bedroom door. Just to be sure, I set the infra-red torch on the floor and peeped through the keyhole with the special goggles. The infra-rays penetrated the bedroom. The bed was still made. No sign of Clarendon."

Doc Savage remarked thoughtfully, "Clarendon insisted that he was retiring for the evening."

"Must have changed his mind," offered the slender electrical wizard. "He also left a window open, so it was fairly cold in there."

"Did the window overlook a fire escape?"

"It did. But you'd have to creep down sixteen stories to reach a back alley."

Doc Savage said nothing further, but studied the black casket, turning it over and over. He discovered that the underside seemed to possess a small door. But he declined to open it.

Long Tom eyed it with pale eyes, and mused, "Could be an infernal device."

Doc said, "Let us see what the fluoroscope reveals."

Taking the casket over to another device in the electrical section, the bronze man warmed up a fluoroscope similar to that found in major hospitals. While Doc kept it for experimental purposes, it was also useful for examining suspicious packages, for more than once the bronze man had discovered a bomb which he then had to dispose of carefully, sent by determined enemies, of which there were many in the criminal underworld.

The fluoroscope screen revealed a nest of complicated apparatus, as well as a spool of wire.

"Could be a detonator," Long Tom suggested.

Doc shook his head. "No, it is more of the order of a magnetic recording device."

Removing the casket, the bronze giant took it back to the glass-topped table and, knowing it was now safe to do so, opened the back.

It was possible to work the spool so that the magnetic wire could be rewound and played again. Doc Savage did so.

The tiny device ran on batteries. Doc managed to get it working. The spool began revolving, and a querulous voice commenced issuing from the casket.

The two men listened intently.

The aged voice droned on, and suddenly there came a different sound. A sharp hiss.

Reacting with blinding speed, Doc Savage backpedaled, simultaneously gathering up slender Long Tom in his mighty arms.

He had taken the precaution of standing well back of the casket when the voice began speaking; conceivably this saved their lives.

For no sooner had the hissing ceased, than the bronze giant and his slender burden were standing in the cubicle that resembled a soundproofed radio broadcasting booth. Doc slammed the door shut behind them. Setting Long Tom back on his feet, the bronze man actuated controls, which caused great ceiling fans to whir, and began drawing the noxious gas safely out of the laboratory.

The booth was entirely airtight and gas-proof.

Long Tom demanded, "Booby trap?"

Doc nodded. He watched the threatening vapor turn into a haze, which was lifted ceilingward, and patiently waited for it to dissipate.

This took some twenty minutes. Indicator lights came on, showing green. This told the bronze man that sensitive instruments arrayed throughout the laboratory were giving the all-clear. The last of the gas was gone.

Stepping out of the booth, Doc strode over to the casket, and saw that much of the interior works had melted—the result of whatever combustible agent had generated the gas. This portion of the mechanism was so tiny that the bronze man had failed to recognize its significance. The fact was that one or more of the so-called "peanut" vacuum tubes had been dummies, and doubtless contained the chemical to produce the gas.

Long Tom studied this and remarked, "Pretty clever. Looks like it was designed to release the gas when the message was played."

Doc Savage shook his head. "No. It was designed to do that when the message was played a second time. For it was clear to me that the spool had already run once before."

Doc found some delicate tools, and began removing the spool, saying, "It should be possible to replay the balance of the message on another machine."

They were setting up the spool on a device of Doc Savage's own invention when Monk Mayfair came bowling in, literally dragging a man behind him.

The man was out cold and Monk had him by the collar of his coarse sweater. Dragging had caused the unconscious prisoner to lose one shoe.

The bronze man turned, asked, "What have you brought home now?"

Monk grinned his broadest and said, "I tried to get a line on that Spotter down at the Black Ship. No soap. This here mug started talkin' big that he was gunnin' for The Shadow and could take me to Spotter. Instead, he tried to waylay me in an alley. It didn't work out so good for him."

Monk released the man's sweater with the result that the insensate one's thick skull banged into the parquet floor.

Long Tom asked, "Who is he?"

"Said his name is Cliff Marsland—probably a torpedo."

"We will interrogate him when he wakes up," advised Doc. "First, we have a recorded message to study."

Setting up the wire, the bronze man flipped the lever, and the wire recording continued from the point at which it had ceased.

When it reached the point where the querulous voice proclaimed that George Clarendon was The Shadow, no one spoke a word.

THEN, after a few moments, a strange sound drifted slowly from nothingness to audibility—a sound that was a trilling, low and fantastic, difficult to describe because it bore close resemblance to almost no common sound. Monk and Long Tom exchanged glances, knowing that the trilling was the small unconscious thing which Doc Savage did in moments of mental excitement.

When the nebulous tremolo had at last ebbed into nothingness, the bronze man said, "George Clarendon will bear looking into."

Monk asked, "Think he's really The Shadow?"

"The voice on the wire seems certain of it," stated Doc. "But that assertion hardly constitutes proof."

Long Tom tugged at an oversized ear. "Might explain why he made excuses, and then scrammed from his hotel room. Could be he had dirty work to do."

Doc Savage declined to respond to that. He picked up Cliff Marsland and set him on a wooden chair, which had stiff armrests, as well as a number of buckles and straps. It looked a little like a crude electric chair.

The bronze giant began strapping the unconscious gunman into the chair, and requested, "Monk, fetch some truth serum."

"Gotcha, Doc," said the simian chemist, grinning in anticipation.

Monk sauntered to a cabinet and charged a hypodermic syringe, then returned with an amiable expression on his homely features.

"Here it is, Doc."

The bronze giant accepted the syringe; he had already rolled up one of Marsland's sleeves. He injected the man, then waited fifteen minutes.

When the prescribed period of time was up, indicating that

the serum had taken hold, Doc broke open a stimulant capsule under Marsland's nose, causing the man to shake his head like a dog coming out of a nap.

The mobster looked around groggily and asked, "Where am I?"

"A long way away from the dark alley you tried to slug me in," grunted Monk. "Looks like the tables got turned, huh, guy?"

Marsland eyed the hairy chemist with no particular interest.

"I'm not talking," he said flatly.

Doc Savage informed the man, "We have just administered truth serum to you."

Cliff Marsland made his face hard, but the light that came into his eyes was anxious.

Doc began questioning him.

"Who do you work for?"

"Whoever hires me," the gunman said flatly.

"I will ask again: who do you work for?"

Cliff Marsland was a stubborn fellow. He also possessed a strong will. Normally the truth serum would have penetrated his resistance by now, but he was fighting it in some fashion.

Doc Savage knew it was just a matter of time, however, before the rugged hoodlum succumbed to the potent chemical flowing through his bloodstream.

He switched tactics. "Do you know a personage calling himself The Shadow?"

Marsland hesitated. "I have heard the name."

"Do you know him personally?"

Now the man's hearty tones became slurred. "Yes," he said with difficulty.

"Who is he?"

"I do not know."

"Who does know?" pressed Doc.

"I don't know anyone who knows who The Shadow really is."

"When did you first meet him?"

"In France. During the war. He was going by another name, but I don't remember it...."

"You joined up with The Shadow during the war?"

"No... when I got out of stir, a year or so back."

Monk decided to insert himself into the interrogation at that point.

"Talk turkey, mug. What's your connection to The Shadow?"

"Work for him. Handling the strong-arm stuff."

"Now we're gettin' somewheres," said Monk.

Doc Savage inquired, "Is The Shadow behind the recent rash of mysterious deaths by heart attack?"

"I do not think so."

"Is The Shadow a criminal?"

"I do not think so," repeated Cliff Marsland.

"Do you know a man named George Clarendon?"

"Never heard of him."

"Could he be The Shadow?"

"Don't know," said Marsland in a mushy voice.

"Do you know who the man calling himself the Funeral Director is?" asked Doc.

"No."

As the questioning went on, Marsland became more and more groggy and his responses shorter and less understandable. The strength of the truth serum was such that this was a side effect of its potency.

Abruptly, Doc Savage broke off the interrogation.

"Long Tom, call police headquarters and see what you can learn of a former convict named Cliff Marsland."

Long Tom rushed off to the library to make his call in private.

Doc Savage related the events that had occurred before Monk's arrival.

"Let me see the spectrogram results," the hairy chemist requested.

Going over to the machine, Doc Savage turned it on again and they studied the bars of light. Each with its own meaning.

Monk stated, "I'm thinkin' that Palmer-Letts was killed by a gas that brought on the sudden heart attack."

"That is my surmise," agreed Doc. "But the exact constitution of a gas that would produce such a drastic effect escapes me."

Monk grunted, "That don't mean it can't be formulated. We've seen weirder stuff than that in our time."

"Agreed," said Doc, switching off the spectrometer.

Long Tom rejoined them, saying, "They know about Marsland down at Headquarters. A few years back, he did time in Sing Sing for murder. Talk is he may not have done it, though. He might have been covering for a sister who had a boyfriend who did the deed."

"So Cliff Marsland might or might not have been guilty of the crime for which he served time?" suggested Doc.

"That's it in a nutshell," snapped Long Tom.

Doc Savage pondered this morsel just a few moments.

Presently, he said, "Regardless of the truth, Marsland appears to be a common gunman for hire. We will make arrangements to send him to our College for rehabilitation."

Monk grinned broadly. "With pleasure. After what that crook tried to do to me, he needs to be straightened out, but good."

The apish chemist went to find a telephone.

Long Tom asked Doc, "Are you going to tell Commissioner Weston that George Clarendon is The Shadow?"

Doc shook his head. "Not without further proof. Our chief concern remains Lamont Cranston and Ham Brooks, as well as the strange master mind calling himself the Funeral Director."

Long Tom rubbed his jaw thoughtfully. "It doesn't look like the Funeral Director is The Shadow, since he threatened the person he thinks is really The Shadow."

"While we can conclude nothing definitive about that wire

recording, our activities must be concentrated on uncovering the truth behind these interconnected mysteries."

Ambling back from the library, Monk announced, "A special ambulance will meet us down in the basement garage. I'll take Marsland over there, and make the swap."

"Do not delay, Monk," said Doc. "We have a great deal of work before us."

"Right."

Chapter XI

THE SHADOW ORDERS

IN THE DARKNESS of his hidden sanctum, The Shadow lifted the telephonic headset to his ears once more.

A voice spoke in response: "Burbank speaking."

"Report."

"No new reports from field agents. Marsland overdue to report."

"How long overdue?"

"Over an hour."

"Where was Marsland at last report?"

"At the Black Ship, listening for rumors pertaining to the missing men, Cranston and Brooks," stated Burbank.

"New instructions for Burke. Proceed to the Black Ship. Discover what has happened to Marsland."

The blue light went out.

Twenty minutes later, the tiny light flared anew, signaling a call.

The voice of The Shadow again reverberated in the darksome space.

"Report."

"Burke reports that Cliff Marsland was seen leaving the Black Ship in the company of an unidentified individual. A crook named Spotter is claiming to have seen this individual loading the unconscious Marsland into a taxicab."

"Describe the individual."

"The individual stands five feet tall, is red-haired, weighs approximately two hundred and fifty pounds, and possesses the general characteristics of a human gorilla."

The laugh of The Shadow came again. It had an interested quality.

"Instructions," he intoned. "Proceed to Doc Savage headquarters and tap his private telephone."

"At once."

The light went out again. And in the darkness, The Shadow laughed briefly. Then he arose, donned his shapeless black hat, and clicked off the blue light.

In the resulting murk, the rustle of unseen curtains could be heard, but that was all. The Shadow had departed his sanctum.

Chapter XII

DECOY

MONK MAYFAIR HAD finished trussing the unconscious Cliff Marsland for the trip upstate, ready for bear him to Doc Savage's private elevator and down to the sub-basement garage. There, to hand off the prisoner to the ambulance attendants who were due at any minute.

The ambulance concern was owned by Doc Savage himself—one of the many enterprises which he had rehabilitated at the start of the present business depression.

The men who drove it were sworn to secrecy. They would convey Cliff Marsland north to the wilderness section of upstate New York far, far from any habitation.

Doc Savage maintained a secret institute, known only to his inner circle. It was in the nature of a hospital and sanitarium, for the criminals the bronze man captured were not turned over to the police, but instead transported to that hidden place.

There, their crooked brains were operated upon by a team of surgeons schooled by Doc Savage. In this manner, memories of their evil pasts were wiped away. Then they were set upon a course of reeducation, and taught how to reenter society as decent human beings. Also, they were taught a worthwhile trade, and to hate crime.

Upon graduation from this criminal-curing "College," they were sent out into society to make their own way. Many of these men had been career criminals and even worse. But humanitarian that he was, Doc Savage did not believe in prisons or execution. Only in rehabilitation.

As Monk finished with Cliff Marsland, the hairy chemist threw the burly man over one sloping shoulder and entered the reception room.

"All set, Doc," he announced. "Any word on Ham and that swell, Cranston?"

"The police are out in force, but there is no news."

Monk made an astonishingly monkeylike face.

"You don't suppose they might've killed them?"

Doc shook his head. "They had ample opportunity when they attacked the limousine. No, their intent was clearly and manifestly to kidnap Lamont Cranston."

"But Ham wasn't part of their plan, was he?"

"No. But I have released a statement to the press to the effect that Ham Brooks is a valuable member of our little organization and that we will not rest until he has been found."

Monk brightened. "I get it. You want the Funeral Director to demand a kidnap ransom from you?"

"That is my plan. We will see if he takes the bait."

"O.K. then. Marsland's all set to go. Has the ambulance arrived yet?"

"Not as yet."

Suddenly, a light flared on the impressive Oriental table at which Doc Savage sat. An ivory inlay glowed red. That it was more than a mere decoration was evident by the eerie trilling that emerged from the bronze man's parted lips briefly.

"What is it?" grunted Monk, depositing Marsland into a comfortable chair rather unceremoniously.

"This indicator light is tied into the telephone system. When the circuit is interfered with, it illuminates."

Monk picked up the receiver, listened to the hum of electrical current emanating from the diaphragm and said, "Workin' fine."

"The indicator light is designed to alert me when our phone line is tapped."

"Tapped!" burst out Monk. "Who could pull that off?"

"Someone very clever," said Doc Savage, standing up. He considered the situation briefly, then picked up the telephone receiver.

Dialing a number directly, the bronze man reached the ambulance service he controlled.

"Change in plans," he told the answering attendant. "Have the ambulance meet us at the Hidalgo Trading Company warehouse on the Hudson River. The man Marsland will be handed over to you there."

"Yes, Mr. Savage," replied the other.

The line went dead.

Monk studied the bronze man and said, "You never mention the names of our future graduates. You want the party listenin' in to know that we have Cliff Marsland."

"I do," admitted Doc. "I want you and Long Tom to drive to the Hidalgo warehouse and meet the ambulance there."

"You think they're gonna jump us there?"

Doc inclined his head. "Either that, or follow you to the College. We must not allow that. Lead them astray, and endeavor to capture them. But do so in a manner that will raise no fuss. We cannot afford to let any aspect of our secret institution come to light."

"Gotcha, Doc," said Monk, lifting Marsland back into his burly arms. "I'll take this bozo downstairs right now. Tell Long Tom to shake a leg."

TEN minutes later, Long Tom Roberts joined Monk Mayfair in the sub-basement garage where the simian chemist had already deposited the sleeping Cliff Marsland into the trunk of a sedan.

Slamming the lid down hard, Monk said to Long Tom, "Get in. This could be quite a ride."

Long Tom took the passenger seat complaining, "I would have been here sooner, but some nosy-nosy reporter was pestering me for an interview."

"Must be new in town," snorted the hairy chemist. "Most scribes know Doc Savage and his crowd don't give interviews to the press."

"Said his name was Clyde Burke. With the *Classic*."

"That rag! That's the yellowest tabloid in the city. He has some nerve!"

Monk got the car in gear, and it rolled smoothly up the ramp, where the garage door lifted in response to a radio signal emanating from the dashboard.

The machine pulled out onto the sidewalk, and paused while small-eyed Monk looked one way and Long Tom Roberts glanced in another.

Neither man noticed a rather frail figure detach himself from a clot of shadow adjacent to a parked delivery truck.

Moving very low so as not to be seen, he climbed the bumper at the rear of the car, clinging to the tire carrier, his head down, hat stuffed into a coat pocket.

As Monk Mayfair pulled into the post-midnight traffic, he had no inkling that he had picked up an additional passenger.

The homely chemist drove west several blocks, in the direction of the Hudson River, and was soon approaching a long concrete building that sat on piles over the water, looking from a distance like an old steamship pier now fallen into disuse.

"Keep your eyes peeled, Long Tom," Monk said tightly.

"You don't have to tell me twice," retorted the slender electrical expert.

They were so intent on scrutinizing the old pier ahead that as they slowed down, they failed to notice a man drop from the rear-mounted tire carrier and lie flat on the pavement without moving, in an effort not to be seen in the rear-vision mirror.

The former passenger was very practiced at lying still. Neither Doc Savage associate noticed him as they rolled away.

Picking himself up off the street, the frail-looking individual pulled his shapeless hat out of his coat pocket and used it to broom dust and grit off his dark suit coat.

Setting his hat on his head, he peered around in all directions and noticed an all-night lunch wagon, which overlooked the warehouse destination. He headed in that direction, discovered a pay telephone inside, and made a hurried call.

"Burbank," said a methodical voice.

"Burke reporting. Followed Doc Savage car to destination. Old warehouse on Hudson River."

"State address."

The man provided the address, after which he was told, "Await arrival of supporting agent."

The line went dead.

Hanging up, the frail-limbed individual selected a seat at the counter that made him very conspicuous to anyone approaching the warehouse.

Chapter XIII

MARSH MAYHEM

TEN MINUTES LATER, a telephone rang in a room high in the Metrolite Hotel, situated in downtown Manhattan. A young man possessing clean-cut features and a powerful build answered it.

"Harry Vincent speaking."

"This is the telephone company testboard," a voice murmured. "We have had some trouble with the circuits tonight and wished to make sure calls now *go to* your instrument satisfactorily. Damp air from the ocean ruins the efficiency of some of the instruments. Just as a *street* which is coated with *black* ice can imperil even a sturdy *phaeton*, so, too, can frost on the wires affect sound transmission. Does your telephone work perfectly?"

"Yes," replied Harry forthrightly. "The telephone seems to be functioning all right."

Hanging up, he repeated the five emphasized words under his breath:

"Go to street black phaeton."

Orders from The Shadow!

The Shadow! That name was coming each day to bring more and more stark, mad terror to the hearts of evil-doers whenever it was mentioned. The Shadow was not exactly a detective. He was not a criminal. No one knew just what he was, any more than they knew what motivated him.

For no one knew who The Shadow was!

Even Harry Vincent did not know. And he had never met

anyone who did know the identity of that fantastic master of the darkness.

The Shadow was almost a nonentity, an uncanny being who existed in the person of as many men as the occasion required. An unbelievable expert at make-up and quick-change, The Shadow assumed the personalities of others at will. At times, Harry Vincent had been almost convinced this mysterious personage could be several men at once. But always, The Shadow seemed no more real than his name—a shadow.

Yet The Shadow was a being of fabulous resources. All who came into contact with him learned that. Harry Vincent was beginning to believe that there was nothing The Shadow could not do. The Shadow never sold his services for money. He worked only on cases in which the mystery was so deep that the police often did not even realize there was a mystery! And the manner in which he solved crimes was uncanny.

Harry jerked his thoughts back to the business at hand. He had been instructed by the mysterious Burbank, The Shadow's contact man, to look into the disappearance of well-known clubman, Lamont Cranston, and attorney Ham Brooks. But so far all his legwork had failed to pick up a trail.

With this latest directive, straight from The Shadow himself, he wondered if his nebulous master had discovered something significant.

Departing the hotel, Harry Vincent veered left along the street, traveling at a swift pace. At the first corner, a block away, he turned left again.

An automobile was parked there. It was the open type of machine much in favor among the more affluent residents of Manhattan—a low, powerful phaeton. The color of the car was a subdued black, a hue calculated to make it inconspicuous.

The door was unlocked. Harry entered.

Affixed to the dash was a blank envelope. Harry undid the flap and removed the sheet of stationary within. Unfolding it, he discovered letters inscribed in a brilliant blue ink. The message was in a code Harry had previously memorized. Deciphered, it read:

DRIVE TO HUDSON RIVER WATERFRONT. PIER 40. LOOK FOR BURKE. ENGLISH JOHNNY'S. LOCATE MARSLAND.

After he had absorbed the written instructions, the letters faded away.

Further instructions from The Shadow!

Harry took the wheel. The phaeton leaped away, the exhaust a loud hiss.

He piloted the machine west, in the direction of the Hudson River.

The car pulled past a driveway that serviced a long covered shed pier. Evidently, it was a warehouse.

Harry coasted the open machine to a silent stop on the side street a block from the ancient pier structure. He left it, and covered the rest of the distance on foot.

There stood a lunch wagon. It was one of those portable structures which somewhat resemble a streetcar. It was none too clean.

A sign announced:

ENGLISH JOHNNY'S LUNCH ROOM

Clyde Burke occupied a stool inside, a glass and a bottle of milk on the scarred counter before him. Burke was a man not yet thirty years of age, with firm, well-molded features which indicated long experience. He lacked Harry Vincent's powerful build, being light in weight and almost frail. Yet his actions were those of a man who loves excitement.

Burke was another agent of The Shadow. One of many, not all of whom Harry was acquainted with. Clyde was a newspaperman and had been associated with The Shadow's organization some time, Harry knew. Burke was a good scout.

Harry Vincent took a stool adjacent to Burke and ordered a

bottled beverage. He showed by no sign that he knew the reporter. However, drawing out a cigarette, he fumbled through his clothing as though unable to find a match.

Clyde Burke supplied the match. Harry thanked him and made a remark about the weather. Thus, they began a conversation without the lunchroom waiter or other customers being aware that they had met before.

"I have been able to watch the warehouse from here," Burke said in a low tone. "See it—through the window above the cash register?"

Head tilted back as though to enjoy the smoke from a cigarette, Harry threw a glance through the grimy window.

The warehouse was a low, wide-flung structure painted a somber hue. One end rested on pilings over the water. On the front of the building was an old, faded sign, faintly discernible:

HIDALGO TRADING COMPANY

"Instructions are to watch for Cliff Marsland. Doc Savage captured him."

Vincent stifled a whistle of astonishment. He had heard of the Man of Bronze. Who had not?

"What kind of place is it?" Harry asked softly. "You been able to find out?"

"I made a remark to the waiter about the queer sign," Burke replied. "He's a talkative cuss. He said that he never sees much activity, except that every so often an airplane or a power launch would come out of the river side. He thinks it's some kind of private seaplane hangar."

"Must be where Savage keeps his fleet," said Vincent. "Do you think Cliff is still there?"

"Well, he must be. No automobiles have left the place. And no boats, either. I've watched and listened carefully."

"Let's look the place over," Harry said grimly.

Finishing his drink, Vincent left the lunch car.

A moment later, Clyde Burke joined him in a puddle of gloom where no street light shed illumination.

BREATHING their thanks that the street was so gloomy, they advanced on the old warehouse with the disreputable air about it.

"There's a door on the side," Clyde explained. "They unloaded Cliff there and took him inside. I dropped off the tire carrier when I saw they were near their destination."

Through the oppressively dank and odorous night, they crept. The murk along the side of the ramshackle warehouse took them in. Ears pressed against the sheet-iron door detected no sound.

Burke considered. His orders from The Shadow had been to protect Cliff Marsland. Nothing had been said about the method. That, Clyde knew, was up to him. When The Shadow gave orders, they were to be obeyed implicitly, without question, but when there were no orders, The Shadow's agents used their own judgment.

Harry and Clyde were conferring over an appropriate course of action. They were still considering when Burke heard a sound.

An unmarked ambulance pulled up, coasting to a stop. A man got out.

There was a sign on the white sides, but it was difficult to read in the dark.

The men walked up to the sheet-steel door and depressed the button buzzer.

"Look!" breathed Clyde. "The door is opening!"

A platter of sickly light spilled across the rough cobbles as a door swung wider. Men appeared. Several of them. They were carrying out an unmoving form wrapped in a coarse horsehair blanket. A man, apparently unconscious, or bound and gagged!

"Cliff!" gasped Clyde Burke. "They're moving him!"

Harry Vincent drew his automatic, tense with determination. He and Clyde advanced. Then they were brought up shortly.

More men had come out of the warehouse. These carried stubby machine guns and it was evident from the bulging of their coats that they wore bulletproof vests.

"It would take an army to whip that gang!" Harry breathed disgustedly.

The blanketed form, which Vincent and Burke were convinced was Marsland, was placed in the white ambulance parked beside the warehouse. The white-coated ambulance attendants returned to their seats. The engine burst into life.

Harry and Clyde Burke retreated hastily—and not a moment too soon, for the headlights of the ambulance splashed on the spot where they had been standing. The machine drew slowly away from the building.

"Come on!" hissed Harry. "We'll trail them!"

Haunting the darkest portions of the thoroughfare, they raced to the phaeton Harry Vincent had parked. Starting the engine and swinging the long car into the street occupied only a second.

"There they go!" grunted Clyde.

The rear lights of the ambulance were possibly two blocks away. The fact that there were two of the glowing red points, one tail lamp on each rear fender, would make trailing the big machine simpler, if they later lost sight of it.

Harry wheeled the phaeton in pursuit, keeping well in the wake of the ambulance.

"Now if we could just see The Shadow!" Clyde remarked hopefully.

Vincent confessed the same desire. As resourceful as the two agents were, their mysterious master seemed omniscient and all-powerful.

THEY encountered no such being, however. The big machines flung along the darkest, most deserted thoroughfares in the city. Keeping careful track of their route, Harry realized they were circling to avoid the night traffic of the business section.

The ambulance led them through the Holland Tunnel and

into New Jersey, then turned north onto a highway. The machine increased its speed as it passed into a sparsely settled area.

There was some night travel on the highway, enough of it that Harry felt he was justified in hoping that the men in the ambulance would not discover they were being trailed.

Just to make that even less of a possibility, Clyde chose a moment when the machine was out of sight around a curve to climb out on the fender and hang his coat over one headlight. In the intensely dark night, the single headlamp, which still spilled luminance ahead, would give the phaeton an entirely new personality.

Later, Clyde retrieved his coat and returned to the front seat. Curious, he threw the beam of the spotlight on the roadside.

"Whew!" he ejaculated. "Look what we're getting into!"

Careful not to take his attention off his driving for long, Harry Vincent glanced about while Clyde manipulated the spotlight.

They had entered a marsh! A stark sea of salt grass swayed in the moonlight. Open leads reflected pale moonlight. Swamp oaks appeared here and there, like solitary sentinels with twisting Halloween arms.

Under the headlights, the gray concrete took on the aspect of a glabrous serpent squirming beneath the whistling tires of the phaeton. Or so it seemed to Harry, after he looked at the weird repulsiveness of the marsh pressing in on the crooked road.

"Looks like the Hackensack Meadows," remarked Burke.

"Wonder where they're bound for?" Vincent puzzled.

That query answered itself almost at once. The twin tail-lights of the ambulance ahead veered off and melted into the marsh.

Harry dared not turn off the headlamps and creep forward. The risk of blundering off the road and into boggy marsh was too great.

However, he did bring the car to stop and shut off the engine while they listened. Far ahead, they heard the moaning exhaust of the machine they pursued.

"They've sped up!" Burke vouchsafed. "The driver certainly must know this road to travel at that clip!"

Harry Vincent set his foot heavily on the accelerator. The phaeton leaped forward, rocking along the crazy meanderings of the narrow trail.

As they raced along, sudden headlights sprang into life, blinding them.

Surging out of concealment, the ambulance charged, its bumpers gnashing and clashing with the auto's unprotected rear like some voracious monster of steel.

The phaeton spun crazily, the steering wheel jerking out of Harry's tight grip.

The next few moments became a wild blur as the long machine swapped ends and tilted off its complaining tires—a mad whirl which finally ended with a disagreeable splash.

Then there was silence.

Chapter XIV

DARK SHADOWS

THE SIDE DOORS of the hapless phaeton had sprung their locks, and flapped wide as the long machine toppled off dry ground. Clyde Burke was thrown against his door, and flopped out. But Harry Vincent, thrusting out a clutching hand, kept him in the machine. A man in that mucky salt marsh would be as helpless as a fly in syrup. If the car did not sink at once, they would have something solid underfoot. Possibly they could jump and reach the road.

The blunt radiator grill hit unseen water with a mucky splash. Headlamps went instantly dark. Front wheels and radiator ducked beneath the surface. The shock crashed Harry Vincent against the windshield. The glass was of the non-shatterable variety and it caved under his weight like cardboard, but did not cut him.

Burke emitted a loud, pained grunt.

"You hurt?" Vincent demanded anxiously.

"I'm not crippled!" Clyde snorted. "But I'll carry a map of this dashboard on my face for a month!"

Breathing an order for Clyde to follow, Harry dug a flashlight out of a door pocket, then scrambled on the springy top of the phaeton.

He dashed the cone of light from the flash against the road.

"This is not so bad!" he exclaimed in relief. "We can jump that distance easily!"

Taking as much of a run as the tilting top of the automobile would permit, Harry launched his form into space. His feet came down on the solid roadway. Then he held the light for Clyde Burke's jump.

Burke did not have quite as much agility. He landed a yard short, plunging to his waist in the cold brine. Extending an arm, Harry hauled him bodily to safe footing.

"Phew!" Clyde complained. "This mire smells—!"

His words ended in a loud bark of surprise and pain.

Simultaneously, the flashlight was knocked from Harry's hand. An avalanche of human forms descended on him, bore him to the earth.

Doc Savage's men had jumped them!

Harry clawed into a coat pocket, seeking his automatic. A couple of men fell across his legs and tangled there like muscular pythons. Others enveloped his arms, pinioning his wrists, preventing him from completing the action.

Fists began striking his jaw, his throat, and other spots. A seeking hand fished into his coat pocket, produced the gun, and began applying the hard butt to his skull.

Thus stunned, Vincent was in no mood to resist the ropes that began winding around wrists and ankles.

He could tell by explosive grunting nearby that Clyde Burke was receiving the same rough treatment.

With mad wrenchings and jerkings, Harry tried to burst free of his bindings. The effort was barren. Someone kicked him in the midriff with terrific force and he collapsed, paralyzed with agony.

A white beam of light burst from an electric lantern one of their captors held. Squinting in the dazzle, Harry determined the men numbered nearly a dozen. A group had been hiding here in wait for them! He also saw Clyde Burke was bound as securely as himself.

Rough hands seized their helpless limbs and packed them along the narrow, twisting road, deeper into the marshy morass, treading on high ground to avoid the waving, knee-high salt grass. Harry noted that not a single vocal order had been given.

Their captors trudged forward amid ominous silence. But the quiet was not shared by the marsh about them. For the air was filled with the high-pitched chirring of crickets. The night was cool, so their sound was slow and steady, not frenzied and excited as it would have been on a hotter evening. Summer had given way to the Fall, and the nights had been successively cooler.

As they were forced along to an unknown destination, moonlight painted the stranded phaeton with a gleam like silver, especially on the trunk which jutted up out of the marsh water.

The door of the machine opened. Seemingly of its own accord. Apparently, no one got out. But an instant later, the darkness nearby seemed to stir as though it possessed life.

No eyes witnessed this oddity, but if they had, they would naturally have assumed it was the trick of lunar light and shadow. It was that kind of night.

Moments later the shadow seemed to flit after the retreating men. It would have been difficult for any eye to have followed this shifting fragment of murk. But the dancing black goblin of a form appeared to be trailing the others.

HARRY VINCENT and Clyde Burke were escorted to a sizable shed that stood in the middle of nowhere. It possessed a leaning, ramshackle aspect.

As they were prodded toward it, Clyde remarked to Harry, "At least it's standing on dry ground."

"Yeah. I had visions of being tossed into the marsh to drown."

One of their captors spoke for the first time. "Shut up!" he ordered.

That was all. No one else offered threat or comment.

They were taken into the shed, and made to sit down at gunpoint. There was a litter of tools and ropes in the shed, and these latter were used to tie them hand and foot. Some burlap bags were scavenged, shook free of dust and dry saw grass, and jammed down over their heads, obliterating vision.

"Sometimes," Burke told Vincent, "wise guys who are about to be blotted are treated this way."

Straining his bonds, Harry husked, "If they wanted to rub us out, they would have done it back in the marsh."

"Maybe," muttered Burke. "Maybe."

The sound of the door being closed, and a hasp scratching into place came next. This was followed by the click of a padlock snapping shut.

A rough voice said, entirely without cruelty, "Someone will be along for you two before morning."

That was all. The soft clump of their footsteps trudging away followed, diminishing until the slow chirp of crickets entirely obliterated it.

Harry and Clyde shifted around on the dirt floor and endeavored to put their backs together in hopes of helping one another untie their fetters. The ropes were quite thick, and knotted well. After several minutes of fumbling, they realized there was no loosening the knots.

"I guess we wait," Clyde murmured.

"Wait for what?" wondered Harry.

Neither man had any answer to that important question, so they fell silent and wondered what was to become of them.

OUT of the night, where the crickets were noisiest, a patch of murk attached itself to the ambulance that stood empty. Empty, that is, except for the unconscious form of Cliff Marsland locked inside.

Black-gloved hands felt about the rear door, endeavoring to open it. But the lock was some ingenious type that offered no keyhole nor any other aperture.

Flat laughter filtered through the night. The dark form made a circuit of the ambulance, seeking another ingress. The side doors possessed locks of no ordinary type. No key nor any locksmith could possibly open them.

But the queer being was not without resources. Only prepared for every eventuality.

Out of his cloak, he withdrew a blackened automatic, which he used to knock the protective glass off one of the tail-lights. This broke the bulb within.

Pulling out a dark pair of pliers, he used this to unscrew the damaged light bulb.

Another bulb was taken from the lining of his clothes, and screwed into place.

At the sound of approaching footsteps, the phantom figure withdrew.

From the concealment of brush, burning eyes watched as two men reached into their pockets on either side of the ambulance, and applied what appeared to be powerful bar magnets to the doors. Noticeable clicks came.

Evidently, the magnets actuated unlocking mechanisms, for the doors came easily open at the touch.

The men slipped inside. Slamming the doors shut, the motor came to life and the ambulance wheeled away.

As it bounced along rough road, only one tail-light showed. The bulb that had been replaced produced no visible light.

The laugh of The Shadow trailed them for a time. Then the marked hilarity ceased.

LATER, Harry Vincent and Clyde Burke heard a scratching sound through the burlap bags enveloping their heads.

"Looks like they've come for us early," whispered Burke.

Harry said nothing. The scratchings continued. The sound of a padlock clicking open followed.

The rude door fell open, and the cool of the night crept in.

Sufficient moonlight penetrated the burlap sacks. The light struck Harry's eyes, but was almost immediately intercepted by a shadowy shape.

"Who is that?" Vincent demanded.

A thin, whispering voice hissed, "Be silent while I free you."

Both men gave a startled gasp.

The burlap sacks were quickly pulled off their heads. Their blinking eyes searched about.

The tall form, about it the spectral quality of a being from another world, stood within a yard of them. A black cloak draped the figure from head to feet. From under the downturned brim of a wide, dark hat, strange burning eyes bored upon them.

A knife flashed out, severing the bindings at Harry's ankles, and lifted him to his feet. The young man was spun around, and the knife came into play again, with the result that his wrists came free of the heavy ropes dropping to the dirt.

Next, the knife blade made biting sounds as it severed Clyde Burke's bindings. Neither man spoke, for they knew who their rescuer was.

The Shadow!

The knife disappeared into the fold of the cloak, to be replaced by a flashlight whose blinding ray seared the interior of the shed.

"Follow the light!" came a low, powerful voice—one of the voices of The Shadow.

Then the flash beam traveled across the marsh. Harry and Clyde, asking no questions, followed it.

Ahead, the weird form of their unknown master glided with fantastic stealth, invisible except for the hand torch, which moved in a disembodied way, its back glow failing to illuminate the swaying drapery of the figure behind it.

Chapter XV

THE SHADOW LAUGHS

THE UNUSUAL TRIO returned to the half-sunken phaeton in the watery ditch.

It was a sad sight as The Shadow's flash beam licked over it.

"What we need," said Clyde Burke fervently, "is a wrecker."

"Where are we going to get one at this hour?" remarked Harry. "We're probably miles from the nearest town."

The Shadow spoke then, a sibilant whisper that made the flesh creep along their spines.

"It is urgent that we trail that ambulance carrying Marsland."

"But how?" asked Harry plaintively.

Instead of replying, The Shadow went to the back of the phaeton's upended trunk.

The door had sprung as a result of the accident.

Clambering onto the bumper, the master of darkness lifted it all the way, and his hands disappeared within.

When he returned, The Shadow bore heavy chain and what appeared to be a grappling hook, of the type used to dredge deep waters.

He had affixed the hook to the bumper, and the chain to the hook, which he was now paying out.

When The Shadow reached the end of the chain, he offered it to Harry and Clyde.

"I get it!" exclaimed Harry, reaching the links.

"Same here," added Burke.

"Work together," hissed The Shadow.

Both men took hold of the section of chain and began to pull hard, like sailors hauling up an anchor. They put their backs into it, and were rewarded by a lurching of the big machine.

Much as they strained their combined muscles, Harry and Clyde only managed to pull the phaeton back sufficiently far that it was resting once again on all four tires, still mired in the muck.

"It's no use," panted Burke. "We'll never get it out of there."

They looked to their dark master. A vertical blot of night so deep it seemed to be a door into interstellar space that was without stars.

Not for the first time the two agents of The Shadow stared at their master, attempting to penetrate the shadows that enfolded him so deeply.

Their eyes perceived nothing more than the sable-black cloak, and the glints of his burning eyes under the broad brim of his black hat. The darkness that seemed to surround The Shadow remained as unfathomable as the blackest pit imaginable.

Without a word, The Shadow slipped down into the ditch and they could hear him splashing about as he unhooked the chain, dropped it, then slipped behind the wheel so stealthily, it was difficult to follow his progress.

Clapping the door shut, The Shadow pressed the starter, and was immediately rewarded by the powerful engine turning over. The phaeton lurched ahead, stopped, rocking briefly, and the engine roared anew.

To the slack-jawed surprise of Harry and Clyde, the phaeton began following the ditch as if its engine had not been partially immersed. It ran well. The headlamps were working again.

They watched its tail-lights receding for a few moments. Then, snapping to attention, Harry and Clyde hurried after the black vehicle.

The Shadow ran the phaeton for possibly a quarter-mile, until he found a sloping spot where he could turn the front wheels and climb the long machine over the water.

This was not easily done, and seeing the difficulty the machine had in climbing the mud bank, Harry and Clyde leapt into the water, landed up to their knees, and clapping the trunk lid shut, put their backs into it.

Thus supported, the phaeton commenced climbing the mud bank, lurching and rocking, until it reached dry ground.

Grinning with anticipation, the two Shadow operatives rushed to the back seat, took hold of the door handles, and prepared to throw themselves in back.

At that point, a pair of very round headlights funneled out of nowhere, and transfixed the idling machine.

"Company!" husked Harry.

Clyde hesitated, his reporter's instinct causing him to shield his eyes and attempt to pierce the powerful lamps in a vain attempt to see what manner of vehicle had blundered upon them.

All that could be discerned was the shape. It was a substantial sedan, of a nondescript gray hue.

The machine ground to a halt, and the front doors were flung open. Out stepped from either side two very different silhouettes.

One was a slender, almost frail appearing man, who was not very tall. The other, who had been driving, did not appear tall, either. But his size caused Clyde to gasp.

From the front seat, a low laugh issued forth. The Shadow had recognized the driver, who was apish in build and seemed as wide as he was tall.

It was Clyde Burke who gave voice to the sign of recognition.

"That's Monk Mayfair, the industrial chemist!"

"One of Doc Savage's boys!" breathed Harry.

They froze, not knowing what they should do, and being entirely without weapons. They need not have worried, however.

For the front door of the phaeton came open wide, and out from behind the wheel flowed a patch of living darkness.

Venting a mocking laugh that pealed all the way up to the moon—or so it sounded—The Shadow produced a brace of automatics, and began firing in alternation.

The first bullet struck the sedan's door on the handle nearest the apish chemist. The second did the same for the passenger, who was Long Tom Roberts, the electrical expert.

Both men dodged wildly, and ducked off to either side of their machine.

The Shadow's automatics continued bucking and blazing, whizzing slugs this time rebounding off the windshield of the sedan, which appeared to be unharmed. And obviously bulletproof.

"Stay back!" hissed The Shadow to his men.

Harry and Clyde needed no further encouragement. They ducked back into the phaeton, wondering if their mysterious master would approve.

A moment later, they received their answer.

For the two Doc Savage assistants began returning fire with their compact supermachine pistols.

Harry, seeing pellets popping against the windscreen, splashing apart and leaving streams of oily liquid, breathed, "We're safe!"

Clyde interjected, "They must be using those 'mercy' bullets Doc Savage's men favor."

As they watched, The Shadow shifted to the left, seeking a concealing patch of darkness, firing as he ran.

A stream of mercy bullets resembling a solid red rod—thanks to interspersed tracer bullets—flicked in his direction to intercept him.

The second stream did the same.

The two Doc Savage aides were catching their target in a crossfire!

As Harry and Clyde watched, the indistinct edges of The Shadow's cloak began to lift and jump, as streams of hollow pellets found and punctured the black material. The upper part of The Shadow's black hat was sheared off as neatly as if by the swipe of a gigantic razor. Shifting, he dropped back.

But no human being could avoid that metal storm forever— not even The Shadow.

A black-gloved hand slipped into the folds of the dancing cloak and flicked upward, tossing something in the direction of one of the stuttering red rods of light.

The thrown object, a small glass ball containing two chemicals in its partitioned halves, was caught in the hose of the stream of machine gun bullets. One pellet shattered it.

There was a flash. A burst of brilliance like a photographer's flash lamp, only infinitely brighter. In the nightly murk, the glare was utterly blinding. The stuttering thunder of the machine pistols ceased abruptly. Sounds indicated that the weapons had fallen to the ground as the thwarted attackers shouted, digging at their aching eyes.

The Shadow had buried his own orbs in the black cloak before the flash. Now, the instant that the machine pistols were silent, he bounded upward, and charged for his assailants, black cloak clapping like the wings of a gigantic bird.

Flinging forward, his dark cloud of a form knocked one of the gunners out of his path, sending the other fellow end over end. This latter person was Monk Mayfair, who grunted out a bellowing "Oof!"

Monk sprang to his feet, jumped about with his fists balled but, unable to see, was reduced to jabbing futile roundhouse punches at nothing solid.

The Shadow pealed out his mocking laughter.

"Blast it!" Monk howled. "Step up and fight me like a man! You dang spook!"

Not far away, Long Tom Roberts rolled in the dirt, pale hands clamped onto his dazzled orbs.

Darting ahead, The Shadow dived into the sedan. Seizing the wheel, he sent the machine turning about, its bright head-lamps momentarily painted the raging Monk Mayfair, then swept away, leaving both men behind.

Harry and Clyde scrambled to take control of the phaeton. Harry grabbed for the wheel, while Clyde slammed into the seat beside him.

The black machine started off, following the gray sedan.

"That was a close shave!" commented Clyde, staring behind him.

"You said it!" added Harry. "Those machine pistols spit fire mighty fast."

They quickly overhauled the sedan, which pulled over to the soft shoulder of the road. A string of light stretched to the phaeton, inviting Harry and Clyde to join their master at the sedan. They hurried over.

At the wheel, The Shadow hissed rapid, succinct orders.

Then the sedan leaped ahead, showing that it possessed no common motor, for its burning tail-light dwindled like a fleeing spark.

"What about Cliff?" Burke asked Harry.

"The Shadow knows!"

Up ahead, strident laughter assaulted the night. Then all trace of the speedy sedan vanished from view.

Chapter XVI

BLACK-LIGHT TRAIL

HARRY VINCENT AND Clyde Burke let their mysterious master's instructions sink in.

"Return to the city. Await instructions," had commanded the low, sibilant voice before leaving them behind.

Vincent and Burke needed no more orders than that. They sprinted to the phaeton, piled in, started the motor. The big machine lurched about and ran for the narrow roadway, guided by Harry's expert hand.

They did not know where The Shadow was bound, nor did they concern themselves about that. They had long ago learned that The Shadow had a way of taking care of himself.

Harry drove with all the speed safety would permit. Clyde, crouched out on the front fender, kept an intent watch for more adversaries who might be lying in wait, like the lurking ambulance which had brought them so near disaster. They encountered none, and reached the highway without mishap.

The sucking and popping of the tire tread on the dew-wet pavement lifted to a howl as Harry put his weight on the footfeed. Not until the lighted windows of homes began to flick past the speeding machine, did he decrease his pace. He found the Holland Tunnel, paid the dime toll, and rolled down in.

Once back in the city, he parked the car on a side thoroughfare in the heart of midtown.

The gloom of the night swallowed Harry and Clyde, who went their separate ways.

A MOTORCYCLE cop hidden behind a billboard to catch speeders nearly fell off his cycle when the gray sedan went booming past him. He rolled his motor wheel from behind the billboard as hurriedly as he could. But by the time he had it on the highway, nothing was in sight for him to chase.

"Moses on a bicycle!" he ejaculated wonderingly. "That bird musta been doing a hundred and twenty an hour!"

Several miles further on, the sedan driven by The Shadow slowed. Leaving an acrid tang of friction-scorched rubber behind it, the machine veered onto the illuminated tarmac of a sizable private airport. It whirled up alongside a hangar and halted.

Almost instantly, the hangar doors collapsed open. Two planes stood within, a large monoplane cabin craft, and a smaller open job. Both were painted a midnight black. The engine of the open-cockpit plane—it was an autogyro—banged as its prop began spinning. The churning propeller tugged the bus out of the hangar.

The airport floodlights came on, seemingly of their own accord. In actuality, an ingenious array of sonic receptors and electrical relays explained the phenomenon. The distinctive racket of the airplane's engine automatically actuated the lights, illuminating the runway.

The plane boomed across the aerodrome, pursued by a long, boiling funnel of dust. With an eager lunge, it took the air. The gyro's fixed wing tilted as the craft banked, and the glare from the floodlights glanced yellowly from the doped fabric. Then the craft was gone in a dwindling roar, its windmill blades beating madly.

It lifted rapidly, and turned directly into the north.

Higher and higher into the wilds of upper New Jersey the autogyro arrowed. It followed a highway that wound among low hills. Vehicles traveling on this dark ribbon seemed to chase the bouncing funnels of their headlights. A shadowy form in the cockpit leaned far over the side—apparently using powerful binoculars.

The trail led to the most desolate heavily-forested portion of upstate New York.

By this time, dawn had broken, flinging its solar rays into the mountains with its disorderly ranks of sentinel standing pines.

The substitute tail-light of the ambulance was no longer visible through the ultra-violet projector mounted in the auto-gyro. It no longer mattered, for few vehicles were transiting these lonely roads and turnpikes, and the white machine stood out clearly.

The Shadow watched as the ambulance ran along the road that was straight as a ruler for many miles, then turned off onto a dirt road.

Trees swallowed it for a time, and it appeared to be penetrating toward an area that might be used by campers.

The Shadow dropped his autogyro, endeavoring to keep the white body in sight, although this was becoming more difficult by the moment. Several times, he thought he had lost the gleaming machine. Once, it disappeared entirely, as if it had stopped in some leafy shelter.

But as he circled, The Shadow picked up a gleam of white enamel paint as the rising sun touched its roof.

A softly whispered chuckle of recognition was the only emotional sign he gave.

Flying as low as he dared, The Shadow rocked his whirligig bird after the creeping ambulance, for now it was moving very slowly, along a road that was not visible from the air.

Before much longer, the long white vehicle came to an area of low hills, at the base of a range of fir-topped mountains. The place was heavily forested, then the ambulance popped into a clearing, and came to a high hurricane fence.

White-uniformed men emerged from somewhere, evidently a hunting lodge built of logs, to permit the ambulance to enter.

Other than the lodge itself, there was no sign of any other structure. All was low foothills and high mountains.

Under the beating blades, burning eyes watched in silence.

As the fence was secured behind it, the ambulance crawled along a stretch of level ground, running to the base of a low hill, and then somehow disappeared into it!

The Shadow circled, seeking an answer to the mystery.

He saw none. There was no sign in the rounded face of the low hill of any door opening into which the ambulance might have disappeared. But disappear it had.

Attempting to land, The Shadow raked the surroundings for a patch of ground where he might drop his eggbeater ship. The only such clearing stood several miles away, on the other side of towering evergreens.

Deciding against that spot, The Shadow chose to make a frontal assault.

Canting and banking his beating aircraft, he cut the engines. Immediately, a weird silence overtook the autogyro, broken only by the whistling of the wind in its wing braces.

The Shadow was going to attempt a forced landing, one made possible only by the fact that the great whirling blades, continuing to churn, acted as a brake for the plummeting black craft as it sought a safe landing.

The silence of the craft might have permitted this maneuver to succeed except that the hills and mountains forced The Shadow to hike in from the east, the same direction as the rising sun.

That solar orb had lifted sufficiently to cast early-morning shadows over the area surrounding the hunting lodge.

For once, a shadow betrayed the master of darkness.

The men on the ground were in the act of returning to the hunting lodge, when the whirling shadow crossed the structure. One noticed this aerial aberration, looked up and spied, coming out of the sun, a black bug with whirling wings like some uncanny dragonfly.

Pointing upward, his mouth fell open. He began shouting. This caught the attention of the other men, who had already passed inside. Two came running out, carrying high-powered hunting rifles equipped with telescopes.

The guards shouldered these, pointing them at the approaching aircraft.

The rifles commenced bucking against their shoulders, tiny sparks appearing at the end of the jumping and smoking muzzles.

The pair were excellent marksmen, for one of the struts supporting the wings buckled. Another whistled close by The Shadow's ear. A third actually knocked what remained of his hat off his head.

There was no point in returning fire—the range was too great for The Shadow's automatics.

Engaging the nose propeller, he booted the rudder, and got the autogyro under power once more.

The nimble dragonfly of a craft began to dance about the sky, seeking to evade the hunting rifle bullets. Unable to land or fire back, the dark avenger was forced to beat an ignominious retreat. The Shadow safely guided the fleeing autogyro behind a sheltering hill, and out of range of the riflemen.

Over the treetops floated a weird laugh. It was not a laugh filled with mockery, nor was it a peal of triumph.

It was in the nature of a promise—a sinister promise that sooner rather than later The Shadow would return to rescue his henchman.

Chapter XVII

DEMAND NOTE

DAWN HAD BROKEN over Manhattan when Monk Mayfair and Long Tom Roberts stumbled into Doc Savage headquarters, looking much the worse for wear.

The bronze man was an early riser, thus they found him seated at his ornate table that served as a reception desk.

Doc Savage was already aware of the sorry state of his two aides, thanks to a telefoto device that projected an image of the corridor outside onto a frosted plate atop the desk. His expression did not change when his flake-gold eyes fell upon them. The bronze man rarely displayed visible emotions.

Monk was the first to speak. "It didn't go so hot, Doc."

"So I see," returned the bronze man dryly.

"Let me tell it!" snapped Long Tom.

"Go ahead," said Doc.

The slender electrical wizard went into a recitation of the unfortunate events of the evening. He concluded by saying, "The Shadow came out of nowhere and rescued those two birds. But I recognized one of them. It was that nosy reporter, Burke."

Doc asked, "Clyde Burke, of the *Classic?*"

"The very same," said Monk. "He's hooked in with The Shadow somehow."

Doc Savage picked up the telephone and called the office of the *Classic*, which had a reputation as being one of the most trashy tabloids in the city.

Doc reached the assistant city editor, whose name was Rex Donney.

"This is Doc Savage calling. One of your reporters has been coming around, seeking an interview. As you know, we do not normally speak to the press."

The city editor remarked, "He must be doing it on his own hook. I gave him no such instructions."

"How long has Burke been in your employ?" pressed Doc.

"Over a year. He used to be with the *Evening Clarion*. Lost his position when the *Clarion* was taken over by the *Daily Sphere*."

"Good references?"

"He was a pretty fair crime reporter over on the *Clarion*. Then he worked for a clipping service for a while, after the depression knocked half of the newspapers in this town out of business."

"Clipping service?"

The editor warmed up. "Well now, what say we swap information?"

"I may consider an interview in the future," allowed Doc, "but first I require some answers to my questions."

The city editor ruminated over the line. "I'm not sure what to make of this, but O.K. If there's a possible interview in it for the paper. Burke had been working for this clipping service—or bureau I guess you'd call it—when he did a job of work that brought him over here."

"What was the name of the service?"

"Don't rightly recall," returned the city editor. "But the guy who ran it was a criminologist by the name of Clarendon."

"George Clarendon?"

"That's the man. He gave a good reference for Burke, so we hired him on the spot."

"Any other references?"

"Yeah, a character reference. An investment guy. Let me think of the name. Mann. That's it, Rutledge Mann. Has an office in the Badger Building."

"Thank you," said Doc, hanging up abruptly.

Turning to the others, the bronze man said, "Before joining the *Clarion*, Clyde Burke worked for George Clarendon."

Scratching his head, Monk muttered, "This is beginnin' to add up to somethin'. What, I'm not so sure."

"There is an investment broker named Rutledge Mann who Burke gave as a reference as well. Long Tom, I want you to look into this individual. See what you can dig up. Follow him if need be. He may lead you to something."

"Right," said Long Tom, hurrying out of the office.

After the puny electrical wizard had departed, Monk asked anxiously, "Any line on Ham, or that blueblood, Cranston?"

Doc Savage shook his head somberly. "None whatsoever. I have sent our private detectives out looking. This is too big a job for those of us who are presently available."

The bronze man was referring to the fact that his tiny band consisted of five men, two of whom were out of the country at the moment. Renny Renwick, the hulking civil engineer, was at present in New Zealand, working on a particularly difficult stretch of mountain railroad, a project which had defeated others in his line. Johnny Littlejohn, the archeologist and geologist in the group, was investigating a volcano in Mexico that was showing signs of uncorking.

While Monk fretted over the fate of his friend, Ham Brooks, Doc Savage picked up the telephone and called the Hotel Thermon. He got the front desk.

"Could you connect me with George Clarendon in room 216?" he requested.

"I am very sorry, terribly sorry," the clerk replied. "But Mr. Clarendon checked out yesterday, in the middle of the night. He's left no forwarding address."

"Thank you," said Doc.

Hanging up, the bronze man told Monk, "George Clarendon abruptly checked out of his hotel late last evening."

Monk grunted, "Sounds like he never returned."

"Conceivably," said Doc.

Monk asked at that point, "So what are we gonna do? We can't just sit around waitin' for word."

"We have no leads to Ham or Lamont Cranston, and now Clarendon has vanished."

"You don't suppose he was kidnapped, too?"

"Doubtful," opined Doc.

The desk telephone buzzed not many minutes afterward. Doc answered it.

"This is Dr. Lorrey," a cultured voice said.

"Go ahead," Doc told him.

"The new patient arrived safely, but there is a mystery. A black autogyro was seen buzzing the area. The guards drove it off. We don't know if there is a connection between the aircraft and the new patient."

Doc Savage's trilling piped up, sounding concerned. Low to begin with, it rose in volume until it swelled into a sound that might have suggested an anxious wind filtering through a fantastic forest of strings and wires. It trailed off in a manner that was distinctly off-key.

"In this instance," Doc related, "it is a safe conclusion to jump to. Take all necessary precautions to protect the sanitarium. Let me know if the autogyro reappears."

Doc Savage hung up, his face slightly strange.

Noticing this rare example of concern touching Doc's metallic lineaments, Monk demanded, "What's up now?"

"That was Dr. Lorrey, the individual who runs our College. Cliff Marsland arrived safely, but not long after a black autogyro appeared in the sky. Apparently the ambulance was followed."

Monk sat down abruptly. "Blazes!" he squeaked. "That means The Shadow tipped to the College, don't it?"

"It is a logical assumption to make," said Doc gravely, "and one we must take seriously. If The Shadow believes that Cliff Marsland is being held in our special place, he may attempt to free him."

"Good luck with that!" blurted Monk. "The place is practically a fortress."

"The existence of the criminal-curing College is our deepest secret," stated Doc solemnly. "We must do everything in our power to see that it remains that way."

The bronze man was thoughtful for a time. Then he asked Monk, "The other man with Clyde Burke, could you describe him to me?"

Monk made a face, and did his best. "Looked kinda like a Joe College type a few years after scorin' the winnin' touchdown for the home team."

Absorbing the details, Doc remarked, "The individual you describe would not stand out in a crowd of men, provided they were athletic in build."

"He didn't come across as the thug type," admitted Monk. "Or for that matter, neither did Burke."

"Clyde Burke would not be the first reporter who turned to crime after being down and out," suggested Doc.

"That's sure right," muttered Monk. "Say, why don't we dig up where this Burke lives and try to run him down?"

Doc Savage picked up a telephone book, consulted it briefly.

"He appears to live in Brooklyn, on Sands Street. Here is the address." Doc wrote down the address on a sheet of paper and handed it to Monk.

"If he's down there, I'll roust him and haul him back here."

"Be careful. If he is allied with The Shadow, he most certainly is dangerous."

Monk growled, "If he's connected to Ham's kidnappin', I'll

unscrew his head off before I bring him back and you can screw it back on for him."

With that, the hairy chemist charged out the door.

MONK was gone less than an hour. When he returned, his simian countenance wore a look of dejection.

"His landlord says he hasn't been seen since yesterday. It's a dead-end."

"Burke has a regular job," advised Doc. "He will have to return to it at some point. I will ask his city editor to alert me when he does."

"He's gonna wanna interview you, Doc," warned Monk. "You're pressin' your luck."

"Well, if it leads us to Burke, I may consent to such an interview."

Monk said, "I'm all for that. If that shyster Ham was gonna bust loose by himself, he woulda done it by now."

At that thought, the apish chemist cast a narrow glance at the door, as if half expecting the dapper lawyer to storm through.

When no such event transpired, Monk plopped down into a heavy leather chair and resumed his fretting.

THE MORNING MAIL brought fresh cause for concern.

Among the conventional correspondence was a letter addressed to Doc Savage which bore no return address, but in the lower corner of the envelope front was an ominous notation.

Re: Theodore Marley Brooks.

Doc opened the envelope with a letter opener and shook out the contents.

A folded letter dropped out. The typewritten text read:

> To Doc Savage:
> If you wish to see Mr. Theodore Marley Brooks, esq., alive in this world again, you will tender to me one million dollars, which I will call for once you agree to do so. Since I have

no interest in meeting you, naturally, you must convey your agreement to my terms via the newspapers. File an interview, acceding to my demands.

Otherwise, I will be forced to make Final Arrangements for Mr. Brooks.

The missive was signed: *The Funeral Director*

Monk read this and let out a bloodcurdling howl.

When he had control of himself, the irate chemist asked, "Why is he askin' a million for Ham, but only a quarter million for Cranston?"

Doc replied, "Perhaps he believes Ham is worth more than Lamont Cranston."

"Still, it's a piker amount, ain't it?"

"For Ham?"

"Naw, for Cranston. He has dough. Why stop at a quarter million?"

"That may be a clue to the identity of the Funeral Director," suggested Doc.

Monk wrinkled his beetling brow. "I don't see how. Are you gonna give that interview?"

"There is no urgency."

"No? But he's gonna kill Ham if you don't cough up some dough!"

"The Funeral Director will not harm Ham so long as the possibility exists that I will pay," Doc assured him. "This should give us at least a day to locate a trail to Ham."

"Sure hope so," said Monk fervently. His homely face brightened and a cunning gleam came into his tiny, piglike eyes. "I can't hardly wait to razz Ham about lettin' himself get snatched outside our door. Boy, that smug shyster will never live this down!"

Chapter XVIII

BURBANK ACTS

IN A CUBICLE full of shadows, a man sat at a switchboard, chewing gum methodically. His face was only half visible in the dimly-lit space and, at any rate, no one was present to see him clearly.

A light came on. He inserted a plug into the switchboard, began speaking into the telephonic headset.

"Burbank speaking."

"Report."

"No progress to report. Vincent has returned to the Metrolite and is awaiting further instructions. Burke has checked in with the *Classic*. He reports that his editor received a telephone inquiry from Doc Savage, asking about his work background and references. George Clarendon and Rutledge Mann were named."

"Instructions to Mann. Vacate investment office and continue working on backgrounds of supposed heart attack victims. Look into nameless hospital or sanitarium controlled by Clark Savage, Jr., in upstate New York. New instructions to Burke. Check into Metrolite Hotel and avoid being seen. Use room telephone to look into any suspicious activities at funeral homes in New York and New Jersey. Instructions to Vincent. Attempt to trace suspect hearse and flower car to its assigned funeral home."

There was a pause. Then The Shadow's whispering tones returned.

"Report condition of the Black Hush machine." *

"The device has been restored to working order and awaits further testing."

"Testing impractical at this time," stated The Shadow. "Load machine into van truck and report when ready."

The light clicked off and Burbank removed his headset. Rising from his chair, he moved through the open door to an adjoining room—a workshop strewn with tools of all types, ranging from welding equipment to electrical apparatus.

Under a tarpaulin in one corner stood a bulky but portable contrivance. Burbank drew the sheet from it, revealing an electrical device unique in all the world.

It sat on a thick base, which in turn rested on a cart for easy transport. From one end of the contraption emerged a flexible coil with a lens so dark it appeared to have been painted over with lampblack.

Burbank replaced the tarpaulin and began wheeling the clumsy machine out of the workshop to another space, which proved to be a garage in which a modest coupe and a motovan truck sat side by side.

Employing a removable steel ramp, he forced the wheeled machine up and into the back of the waiting van body. Securing it carefully, The Shadow's communications agent closed the back, removed the ramp and set it aside.

Returning to his switchboard, the faceless Burbank inserted a plug in preparation for reporting to his master that his task had been accomplished.

"Awaiting instructions," he reported.

Further directives came in the sinister tones familiar to radio listeners nationwide.

"Drive machine to Doc Savage headquarters and stand by short-wave radio for further instructions," said the funereal voice of The Shadow.

---

* *The Black Hush.*

Chapter XIX

WEIRD WAKE

BRIGADIER GENERAL THEODORE MARLEY **BROOKS** awoke with a start. His eyes snapped open and his nostrils flared as he took in a quick, rapid breath.

His sharp gaze shooting around the gloomy room in which he found himself reposing, the dapper lawyer experienced a moment of sheer panic.

For, other than his eyeballs, he could not move a muscle.

The last thing he remembered was being overcome in front of Doc Savage's skyscraper headquarters. After that, oblivion.

Staring up at the immaculately white ceiling, Ham took stock of what surroundings he could perceive. The close air was filled with the fragrance of many flowers. Ham recognized oleander and chrysanthemum. It was as if he had awoken in a flower garden.

His head ached from the blow to his forehead which had felled him, and there was a dull sensation of pain in one shoulder—his right.

Otherwise, the normally unflappable barrister felt as if he had been entombed alive.

Getting a grip on his nerves, Ham struggled to move a finger. He failed utterly. He became aware of someone else in the room, moving about.

A voice said, "His eyes are open."

Another voice answered, "I see it. I'd better get the Funeral Director."

"Yeah, you do that little thing."

At the words *Funeral Director*, Ham's heart sank and a queer fluttering came into the pit of his stomach.

There was a sound of rapid footfalls, then additional footsteps returning.

Strain as he might, Ham could not see any of the persons moving about the room.

A new voice asked in a cracked tone, "How is Cranston?"

Shuffling noises followed, after which one of the original speakers said,

"Still out cold, Funeral Director."

"Take no chances, Embalmer. Administer another dose of 'embalming' fluid. Then do the same for Brooks."

Ham's eyes went wide. Suddenly, he realized the significance of the odor of many flowers. He was not reposing on a hospital bed as he had first surmised, but in a casket. He was lying in state!

Furtive movements continued and then the man referred to as the Embalmer said, "It's done, Director."

"Very good," came the other voice. "Better to shut the casket lid. We shall be opening up to mourners shortly."

Then the person who had spoken first suddenly loomed above Ham Brooks' very round eyes. The man looked tough, and had a nose that was bent to one side—no doubt the result of someone's fast-traveling fist.

This man looked down dispassionately, charged the syringe, and injected Ham into a point on his shoulder that was already stinging.

Sheer fright had leapt into the attorney's dark orbs, but the dosage that was administered acted too rapidly for fear to fully roost within. Ham's eyes widened slightly, then his heavy lids closed sleepily.

Once more, he drifted off into oblivion.

Ham Brooks did not hear the sound of his own casket lid closing over him....

Chapter XX

DEEP SUSPICION

AT PRECISELY QUARTER of twelve in the forenoon, a well-dressed individual walked through the modernistic lobby of Doc Savage's skyscraper headquarters and stopped before the public elevator.

Depressing the call button, he waited briefly. After the door slid aside, he stepped in.

"Eighty-sixth floor, please," he said crisply to the operator.

"That's Doc Savage's floor," offered the operator. "You will have to report to the office on the second floor before you can be seen."

"Doc Savage is expecting me," returned the visitor unconcernedly.

So self-assured was the man's voice that the operator took him at his word, despite strict orders to the contrary.

Shrugging, the operator closed the doors and jerked the control lever upward. The elevator began ascending.

The lift reached the eighty-sixth floor with efficient speed. The visitor stepped out, walked soundlessly down the plain corridor to a solid bronze-colored door on which modest letters were inscribed:

CLARK SAVAGE, Jr.

There was an electric bell button. The visitor depressed this.

After a pause, the portal opened, and Monk Mayfair shoved

his homely physiognomy out. At sight of the well-dressed man, his small eyes narrowed.

"Speak of the devil," he grunted.

"I beg your pardon," inquired the caller.

"We were discussing you only a little while back," replied Monk, throwing the door wide. "Step right in," he invited, eyes glinting.

"Thank you," said George Clarendon, entering.

"Take a seat," said Monk. "I'll get Doc. You're here to see him, ain't you?"

"Precisely," admitted the smooth-mannered visitor.

Monk was not gone two minutes, returning with Doc Savage.

The bronze man appraised his visitor with his ever-active golden eyes and waved him to a comfortable leather chair. Clarendon carried an expensive-looking black leather valise, which he set on his lap.

"We have been searching for you," Doc stated, taking the seat behind the inlaid Oriental table that served as a desk.

Monk Mayfair stood off to one side, positioning himself to intercept the new arrival should he bolt for the door.

"Why is that?" asked Clarendon.

Doc said, "There are a number of unanswered questions pertaining to the night Sydney J. Palmer-Letts was killed."

"How may I help you?" asked the cultured criminologist.

"I discovered a handkerchief with his monogram outside your hotel room door when Commissioner Weston and I paid you a visit the other night."

A mild shock of surprise caused Clarendon's dark brows to lift. "Oh, is that so?"

Doc nodded. "Peculiar that the article should be found immediately outside your door when, according to your testimony to the authorities, you found Palmer-Letts' body before the elevator bank, several yards away."

"Perhaps the handkerchief was tracked there by a bellhop, or some other hotel employee," suggested Clarendon.

"It might also be conjectured," returned Doc, "that the man expired at your door, and was removed to the elevator to throw off the police investigation."

"Perhaps the killer did that very thing—or are you implying that I removed the body?" Clarendon countered.

Light coming through the high windows caused the reddish gem on the serious-faced criminologist's ring finger to sparkle, revealing hidden hues ranging from azure to mauve.

Doc Savage indicated it, asked, "Is that a fire opal?"

Clarendon nodded. "Yes, also known as a girasol. It is a handsome stone, is it not? It is unique in all the world. But back to the matter at hand. You called the death of the attorney, a murder. How have you arrived at that determination?"

"The discovered handkerchief was impregnated with unidentified chemicals that should not have been present. This leads to the supposition that it was chemically treated in such a way as to cause harm to the owner if he brought it close to his mouth or nose."

"An interesting theory," admitted Clarendon, nodding. "It has merit."

Doc continued, "Another possibility is that Palmer-Letts was ambushed by someone wielding a gas, which caused him to bring his handkerchief to his lips in order to fend off an offending odor, the handkerchief absorbing the vapor at that time."

"Sound reasoning. And you think that his heart failure was caused by an unknown gas?"

"It is one or the other," stated Doc. "Now, what brings you to me?"

"I have been pondering the matter of these apparent murders, and the issue of your missing man, Brooks, and the equally missing Lamont Cranston. I suggest that we join forces."

Hovering by the door, Monk Mayfair let out a rude guffaw.

Doc reprimanded him with a quick glance.

Clarendon ignored this outburst. "My thinking is this: Your

man Brooks is in peril, as is my acquaintance, Cranston. We have a common cause. Our combined expertise may ferret out the culprits."

Doc Savage remarked, "We do not ordinarily work with other parties."

George Clarendon stated smoothly, "You appear to have a great deal of influence over the police, not to mention Commissioner Weston."

"We have credentials attesting to our authority," said Doc simply.

Clarendon nodded again. "I understand that you are an honorary police inspector, Savage. But would not Commissioner Weston be upset if he learned that you had pilfered an important clue from the crime scene without sharing it?"

Monk grunted, "He's got you there, Doc."

Doc Savage said nothing. The two men continued to scrutinize one another. Tension hung in the air, which neither man acknowledged.

Clarendon broke the silence. "I wonder if you took my advice about speaking with a man named Spotter. The one who knows something of this Shadow person?"

"We have had no luck locating Spotter," stated Doc. "As for The Shadow, we do have a lead on that personage."

Clarendon looked expectant. But said nothing.

No one, in fact, said anything for a long time until Monk offered, "We were kinda suspicionin' that mebbe you might be The Shadow."

Clarendon sealed his firm lips and said nothing.

Doc Savage said, "Through our investigation, we have uncovered many items of interest. One is that you hired a former police reporter named Clyde Burke to run a clipping service during your earlier time in New York."

Clarendon nodded solemnly. "That is correct. Burke was a good man. But he found more remunerative work on the *Classic*, forcing me to abandon my clipping service, as I could find no suitable replacement."

"We have linked Burke to the individual known as The Shadow."

"How interesting," asserted Clarendon.

"We delved beyond that," continued Doc. "We have checked into your background. Although you formally resided in Manhattan, and say you have just returned from Chicago, we find no record of a George Clarendon having recently resided in the Chicago area. Nor is there a George Clarendon to be discovered prior to two years ago when you first came on the scene in this city."

"I am a man who guards his privacy well," Clarendon said sauvely.

"You are a man who appears not to have existed prior to the year 1931."

"Meaning?"

Monk interjected, "Meanin' that if anybody looks right for being The Shadow, you win the prize."

A low laugh issued forth from the masklike lips of George Clarendon. It was not precisely the laugh of The Shadow, but a similar, softer, mirth.

"Intriguing theory," he allowed. "But I am a criminologist by trade and, insofar as anyone knows, The Shadow operates outside of the law, not within its proscribed boundaries."

Doc pointed out, "So little is known about The Shadow that nothing can be stated definitely about his existence, his purpose, or his motivations."

Clarendon considered this for a time and suggested, "Since nothing is known about The Shadow, how is it possible to prove that I, or for that matter, anyone else, might be this enigmatic creature?"

"By grabbin' him by the neck and wringin' the truth out of him," growled Monk.

Doc lifted a hand, admonishing the hairy chemist to be silent.

Reaching down, Doc Savage opened a drawer in his desk, and brought out a small machine. It was the black casket that had been removed from George Clarendon's hotel room by Long Tom Roberts.

"This item is familiar to you," explained Doc. "Would you care for me to play back the recording?"

"There is no need," returned Clarendon frankly. "I have heard the entire thing. It is preposterous."

"It might interest you to know that when we replayed it, a deadly gas was produced."

One of George Clarendon's elegant eyebrows lifted slightly. "That interests me very much," he admitted. "It suggests that if the recording was played for another party, death by heart attack would result. It is fortunate for me that I took no stock in its accusations, dismissing then out of hand."

Monk snorted, "Smooth, Clarendon. Very smooth."

Silently, Doc Savage removed another, similar device, but not in the shape of a tiny casket.

"This is a recording device of my own invention," he said. "It has been in operation during this interview. Your voice has now been recorded on the magnetized steel wire. It is my intention to compare this voice with that of the radio personality who calls himself The Shadow."

A sparkle of appreciation came into the criminologist's hooded eyes.

"I see," he drawled. "Therefore you imagine that if the two voices match, then George Clarendon must be The Shadow?"

"A close correspondence would make that undisputed fact."

Raised a calming hand, Clarendon asked, "But which Shadow? The Shadow of the radio? Or one whom the police think is merely a myth?"

Monk again inserted himself into the exchange. "Last night Long Tom and I traded shots with a guy in a black opera cloak who laughed like a maniac. That guy was no myth."

"Did you record his voice as well?" challenged Clarendon.

"That opportunity has not yet presented itself," admitted Doc Savage.

"In that case, I must be going," said Clarendon, rising from his chair. "If you do not see fit to join forces with me, then I must pursue my own investigations." Clarendon smiled thinly. "Courtesy of Commissioner Weston, who is more appreciative of my skills."

"Not so fast, smart guy!" muttered Monk, blocking the door.

On his feet, George Clarendon turned his piercing gaze to Doc Savage and asked, "Am I then your prisoner?"

"Consider yourself detained for further questioning," allowed Doc.

"In that case, may I be seated?"

Doc nodded. His visitor resumed his chair and the two men locked gazes, staring at one another silently, one face inscrutable and the other calmly impassive. The black valise was again on Clarendon's lap.

"Speaking as a criminologist," prompted the bronze man, "what is your theory as to The Shadow?"

"I have none," said Clarendon frankly. "The fellow has mysterious ways. It is difficult to say on what side of the law he operates, or to what definite objectives."

There was an electric clock on the wall, and its soft grinding was the only sound for a while.

George Clarendon's eyes flicked to the clock, noticed that it was a minute shy of noon, and lifted a forearm in order to consult his expensive wristwatch.

"That clock keeps excellent time," he remarked, "for it matches almost to the second the hands displayed on my own timepiece."

The remark seemed to have no particular point, except that seconds later the minute hand lined up with the hour hand, pointing straight up. It was high noon.

At that exact moment, everything went black. Pitch black.

"*Ye-e-o-ow!*" yelled Monk. "What the heck's goin' on?"

A strange silence followed, in which the sound of the clock on the wall could no longer be heard. There were other sounds that were also absent, uncommonly so. The darkness that had clamped down on the reception room of Doc Savage was utter and absolute. No light was discernible. Not a speck.

Doc Savage reached into a drawer, and produced a flashlight, which he clicked on. No illumination sprang forth. The flashlight was of his own creation, did not run on batteries, but on a spring-generator mechanism. Doc gave the tiny crank a rapid spin, but still no light shone.

In the irredeemable blackness, the bronze man's trilling sound filtered out, sounding softly puzzled. It possessed a weirdly muted quality, as if heard through glass.

In that same darkness emerged a laugh. Strange, that laugh, sinister yet also muted. It might have been the laugh of a demon unleashed from the lower regions, but it was not any such thing. It was the laugh of The Shadow!

That wild hilarity covered the rustle of George Clarendon leaving his chair and moving in an untraceable direction.

Sensing this, both Doc and Monk lunged for the chair, and collided with it, as well as themselves.

They grappled briefly, recognized one another, and broke apart.

Monk groped about wildly, long arms sweeping. Doc employed his keen hearing and acute sense of smell.

"Block the door, Monk!" crashed the voice of Doc Savage.

The hairy chemist blundered about, found the bronze door, and put his back to it.

"He ain't gettin' past me!"

Doc Savage followed his nose, and they brought him to a window, which had been open for fresh air.

Moving toward it, he used his metallic fingers to feel about, and discovered that it had been shoved open more widely than before.

It seemed impossible, for the window opened up on a drop

to the next setback in the towering skyscraper. No man could have exited by this means and not fallen to his death hundreds of feet below.

While the bronze man felt about the window in the darkness that could not be defeated—darkness that was striking at high noon—he was forced to conclude that the man calling himself George Clarendon threw himself out the window—or by some cunning subterfuge had managed to make it appear so.

Doc moved about the reception room, sweeping about with his great arms, tripping switches, and turning on the lights, none of which produced illumination. The strange weird darkness was absolute.

As a precaution, the bronze man had mechanically locked the exit door and the other door leading to the library. There was no other exit from the room.

Yet The Shadow was nowhere to be found!

It seemed impossible! As impossible as the weird darkness that had stolen their sight.

There was a huge safe in one corner of the reception room. Doc Savage went to it and by touch tapped out a combination on the door. The warmth of his fingertips against a raised rose design actuated a cunning mechanism which unlocked the repository.

But the mechanism refused to respond to the combination.

"The Shadow is not hiding in our safe," reported Doc. "The electric lock is inoperative."

"I'll be a son of a gun!" raged Monk. "That *was* The Shadow, wasn't it?"

"It was," said Doc.

Having exhausted his search, the bronze giant found his way back to his desk, and took his seat.

Fingers exploring the table top, he found relays, pressed buttons, then picked up the telephone as readily as if he were possessed of his full vision.

No button appeared to work, and the phone was dead. Doc replaced the handset on its bronze hook.

Monk was racing around the room, pacing impatiently, cussing volubly, and stumbling over furniture.

"The electricity must be out," he muttered, sounding far away, thanks to the smothering quality of the stygian murk, which evidently suppressed sounds as well as confounding vision.

"And our auxiliary generators?" questioned Doc. The bronze man's laboratory set-up consumed so much electricity at times that he had prudently installed a pair of generators to service his needs.

Monk grumbled, "What could be causin' this? No lights, no electricity and we're blind as bats!"

Doc Savage was not slow in replying. "The Shadow," he intoned. "The Shadow caused this."

Monk grunted, "Looks like he got the last laugh. For now."

"Not yet," said the bronze man, standing up.

The bronze man went back to the window and carefully stuck his head out. He listened carefully.

Faint sounds reached his ears. They were soft, mushy. An intermittent sucking sound that repeated.

To the bronze man's sensitive nose came a faint odor of expensive hair cologne. He had scented it earlier, when George Clarendon had first appeared.

Doc told Monk, "He is attempting to escape by climbing down the building face."

"In this blasted black?!"

"Apparently." A pause. Then: "Remain here, Monk."

"Where the heck would I go? Wait a minute! Where the heck are *you* goin'?"

But the bronze giant did not reply. Suddenly, Monk realized that he was completely alone!

"Dang it!" he muttered in a frustrated voice.

Chapter XXI

ENIGMA IN BLACK

DOC SAVAGE HAD exited the office window. But he did not step out into space.

Rather, he had extracted from his inner vest of many pockets a folding grappling hook no bigger than his thumb. To this was tied a silken cord, which boasted knots and loops every few inches, serving as convenient hand holds.

Unfolding the metal prongs, the bronze giant wedged two tines between the limestone masonry and the steel windowsill and dropped the cord out.

Stepping over, he started down the handy cord, going entirely by feel.

It could be argued that this was a supremely brave thing to do in impenetrable darkness eighty-six floors above the street, but it might also be pointed out that the lack of vision made the feat less frightening than otherwise.

In any event, Doc went down the cord, which would have been a task impossible for any human lacking his Herculean strength. Cool afternoon air played with his metallic hair, disturbing it only slightly. The expression on the bronze giant's features was as if they were cast in metal.

Doc felt his way down, using his toes to brake his descent.

At one point, he stopped. Listening, the bronze man could hear the soft sucking sounds again. They were below him, off to the left.

Suspended over a Stygian abyss, Doc Savage pressed both

feet against the masonry side and bent his knees. Straightening them, he pushed away, into space.

The strength of the cord was made clear then. Doc swung to one side, landed his feet against masonry and repeated the process, dropping a few yards every time.

He was attempting to collide with his quarry in the dark.

That The Shadow was somehow aware of this subterfuge was made evident when a mocking laugh seemed to surround the bronze giant.

Doc dropped again, zeroing in on the laugh. It had an uncannily ventriloquial quality. Or perhaps it was the absolute darkness that made it seem so.

Again, a soft sucking sound could be heard. It was very close now.

Doc dropped again, and swung wide. His efforts were rewarded when he collided with something solid!

The side of a skyscraper is no place for a battle. Especially when the two combatants were hanging in precarious positions over yawning space, certain doom waiting them below.

Yet the two grappled.

With a free hand, Doc reached out, seized a lean forearm. It felt like banded steel. His opponent struggled to break away, almost succeeded.

Briefly, Doc's trilling issued forth, indicating that he was surprised by the wiry strength of the other.

"Surrender!" Doc demanded.

The sardonic laugh of The Shadow was the only response.

Doc Savage was holding on by one metallic hand, the toes of his feet scaling the masonry wall, as his unseen foe struggled to break his grip.

The Shadow's uncanny laugh changed quality, becoming less confident as the bronze vise of a hand refused to relinquish its obdurate hold.

"Stalemate," whispered a sinister voice.

"Surrender!" Doc repeated.

But The Shadow had other plans.

A foot suddenly hooked Doc's right ankle, and caused him to falter. In that instant, the bronze giant's grip loosened.

The Shadow pulled free, and there followed a flurry of motion in the oppressive noonday midnight.

Suddenly, the bronze man became aware of a weight pressing against the cord from which he hung like a muscular spider. A sawing sound came. A knife!

The Shadow was attempting to cut his supporting cord!

Moving with blinding speed, the Man of Bronze did the only thing reasonable. He attempted to scamper up the line, above the point where the blade was biting into his life line. But as fast as he moved, the blade bit more rapidly.

The cord parted. Abruptly, Doc's toes were scraping downward. Then he was tumbling without support, or any method of arresting his fall.

As he fell, the sinister laugh of The Shadow seemed to follow him down....

Chapter XXII

THE ELUSIVE SHADOW

IN THE RECEPTION room office many floors above, Monk Mayfair heard a muffled yet sickening thud.

Flinging his hairy bulk to the window, he craned his blunt head out and bellowed down: "Doc!"

The laugh of The Shadow mocked his frantic outcry.

Monk's tiny eyes bugged out ludicrously, but failed to penetrate the uncanny darkness that had struck. "Doc! Doc! Where'd you get to?"

The anthropoid chemist reached into his coat and yanked out his superfiring machine pistol holstered there. He pointed its muzzle downward and was about to spray lead in all directions when a faint sound reached his small ears, growing in volume.

It was Doc Savage's eerie trilling. Faint at first, it seemed to gather strength.

"Doc?"

"Here." His resonate voice carried over the distance distinctly.

"What happened?"

"The Shadow cut my cord. Fortunately, we had descended to only a few feet above the eighty-first setback, on which I appear to have landed."

Monk called down frantically, "Whatever you do, don't move. No tellin' how close to the edge you are!"

"I am going to crawl to a window."

"Where's that chucklin' hobgoblin?"

"He does not appear to be at hand," replied the bronze man.

"Where did he get to?" Monk demanded in frustration.

Doc did not respond. The bronze man was too occupied in inching his way to the safety of a window. He reached one in due course. It proved locked, however.

From his vest, Doc took a glass cutter, diamond-tipped, and scored the glass. The diamond point traced out a screechy circle.

With an elbow, he knocked in the circular cutout in the pane. It shattered on the floor. But the opening was wide enough for him to reach in and unlatch the lock, which enabled the bronze giant to open the pane normally.

He was on the verge of heaving up the sash when all light returned.

It was not a particularly sunny day, being overcast, but the sudden influx of solar light hitting the bronze man's optic nerves caused Doc to throw an arm over his eyes to shield them. He gave himself time and blinked until he felt it safe to look at the world without flinching.

Surveying his surroundings, Doc discovered a strange object clinging to the side of the skyscraper. It was a round disk of rubber. The bronze man stood tall enough to reach up and pull it free. It took some doing. He had to twist it hard before the powerful suction grip would release.

For that was what the rubber disk was—a suction cup.

Carrying it, the bronze giant walked around the setback until he discovered an open window in the east-facing side of the building. Obviously, it was the window into which The Shadow had made his silent escape.

Doc entered, and found himself in an office. It was empty. The business depression had landed while the skyscraper was being completed and, as a result, a great many of these office suites were untenanted—a fact the average citizen did not realize.

Doc passed through and reached the corridor. There was no

indication of where The Shadow had gone. Kneeling, Doc attempted to locate sign. There had been a residue of Autumn dew on the setback ledge, and a trace had adhered to the shoe soles of the supposed George Clarendon. Doc was able to follow this for a time, but the dew ran out and he lost the moist trail.

Doc then located an elevator and reached the eighty-sixth floor, where he found Monk waiting in the corridor door.

"Monk, get one of our special lanterns."

"Right."

Doc Savage went to his desk, called down to the lobby, and told the guard on duty there, "A well-dressed man named George Clarendon may be attempting to leave the building." Doc gave a concise description of the supposed criminologist. "Watch for him."

Down in the lobby, a frantic voice was saying: "All hell has broken loose down here. The lights went out. It's broad daylight and the lights went out! What on earth is happening?"

"Remain on duty," instructed Doc. "We will be down directly."

That proved to be more optimistic than otherwise.

Accepting the unusual lantern from Monk, Doc told him, "We will take the elevator to the lobby."

"If we can find it," grunted the hairy chemist whose tiny eyes were still squinting in the restored light.

They found it all right, and when they reached the bank, depressing the call-bell button summoned the cage.

They were whisked downward. That was when Monk noticed the large rubber suction cup in one of Doc's hands.

He grunted in understanding. "He pulled a human fly bit, didn't he?"

Doc nodded. "The Shadow must have carried four of these nested in his valise, which he used to scale the wall."

"Smart cookie. But how did he black out the building?"

"It is evident that The Shadow is in possession of an ultra-scientific device which has the reach to quell all electrical activity and prevent ordinary sight."

"That makes him dang dangerous." Monk suddenly snapped his fingers. "Wait a second! Wasn't there something in the papers a few months back about a gang of crooks who were knockin' over joints with a black ray of some new type?"[*]

Doc nodded. "We were out of the country when those robberies took place, but the gang was destroyed. The device was never recovered."

"Do you suppose The Shadow was back of them robberies?"

"It is distinctly possible," admitted Doc.

"That brands him kind of a supercrook, don't it?"

"The Shadow," advised Doc Savage, "is a master mind of a very high order."

THE CAGE reached the lobby floor and stopped with a jar. They piled out and found Gus, the lobby guard.

"No sign of him, Mr. Savage. But the lights are back on."

Doc nodded. Snapping a switch of his lantern, he began pointing the dark lens all about the marble floor. The device produced ultra-violet rays. Invisible to the unaided eye, the emanations brought out certain substances otherwise unseeable.

At first, his golden eyes found little, but soon luminous blue footprints sprang into life.

Monk howled, "He got away!"

Gus objected, "No one by that description went out of the building."

Doc asked, "Did a man of any description leave by this door?"

"Yeah. But he was a skinny duck with red hair and thick glasses. Nothing like the fellow you described, Mr. Savage."

"He was in disguise!" howled Monk, barreling out the door. Doc Savage was right behind him.

Reaching the street, they followed the spectral footprints,

* *The Black Hush.*

which were brought into visibility by the ultra-violet lantern's invisible light.

"Good thing we had that special floor mat installed in our reception room, huh?"

"Yes, Monk. Any visitor stepping into the office would pick up the impregnated grains of powder which fluoresce under the application of so-called 'black' light." Flake-gold eyes tracked the sidewalk. "Looks as though he went around the corner."

The luminous trail, which was distinct at first, faded as the clinging powder was worn off shoe soles, just as the dew had earlier diminished as a trail.

The prints, now very irregular—mere patches and not outlines of soles—led to a drugstore belonging to a national chain.

They went in and followed the tracks to the back and a bank of wooden telephone booths.

Inside one, a man was making a call.

Monk charged up and flung open the booth door.

Within, a man who looked like a hobo dropped his jaw almost to the linoleum floor at sight of the gorilla-like apparition.

"What gives?" he complained.

Reaching in, Monk grabbed the man by his shirtfront and hauled him off the wooden bench.

The man came as readily as a rag doll.

Standing him on his feet, Monk looked the hobo up and down.

"Those shoes don't exactly go with that outfit," he groused.

"What's it to you, buddy?"

"Official business!" snapped Monk. "Furthermore, if you give me any more lip, I'll run you in so fast your pants will catch fire."

Doc Savage inserted, "How did you come by those shoes?"

"Mind your business, bo."

Doc said, "It is obvious those are not your shoes." Doc showed his official police identification. "Now who gave them to you?"

"A guy," the worthy said. "Said they hurt his dogs. Handed me a ten spot to seal the deal. I know good kicks when I see them. So I swapped brogans. Now turn me loose before I get sore."

"The Shadow buffaloed us again!" yelled Monk, releasing the panhandler.

Back on the sidewalk, they looked up and down the street, but to no avail. They no longer had any discernible trail to follow.

But Doc Savage was not yet discouraged. They made a circuit of the block, looking at vehicles parked along the street, one of the busiest in New York.

"Whatcha lookin' for now?" demanded Monk.

"It stands to reason that the device that produced the uncanny darkness was parked in the immediate vicinity. Probably concealed in a truck or similar large vehicle. I am looking for a truck that is out of place."

"Good thinkin'," muttered Monk, who began scrutinizing any machine that might be suspicious. "Suppose it might be a hearse?"

"Doubtful," said Doc.

It being midday, the area was choked with commercial vehicles of all sorts. Delivery trucks were common. None stood out. They snorted and rumbled along, intent upon their business.

Employing his police credentials, Doc requested of certain drivers that their machines be opened up for inspection. Cooperation was given. Results were not to be had.

Finally, Doc and Monk were forced to give it up as hopeless. The suspect vehicle—if any—had fled the vicinity.

Returning to the eighty-sixth floor, they took stock of the situation.

"We are no further along in our investigation than before," remarked Doc.

"Whatcha mean, Doc?"

"We know that George Clarendon is The Shadow, but, since

Clarendon is a fictitious personality, we still do not know the actual identity of The Shadow."

"Won't Commissioner Weston be flabbergasted when he finds out his old pal is The Shadow!"

"We will not tell him just yet."

Monk blinked. "Why not?"

"Because Weston rejects all possibility of an actual Shadow," declared Doc. "That will be our line of investigation."

Monk made a face. "Well, one thing is for sure. The Shadow is a crook. He tried to kill you down there."

Doc Savage looked thoughtful.

"Well, didn't he?" pressed Monk.

"The Shadow may have realized that we hung suspended mere feet over the setback, and that I would land safely on its ledge."

"I still say he's a bad one."

But the bronze man did not offer any further opinion on the subject. Instead, he went to his desk. On it reposed an envelope that had not been noticed before.

It bore no address, and the flap was sealed.

"Do you suppose The Shadow left that?" blurted Monk.

"He might have scaled it toward the desk before exiting the window in the dark," admitted Doc.

"The nerve of that tricky devil!"

Taking the envelope, Doc passed through the huge library and into the laboratory, where he subjected the envelope to several tests before daring to open it.

"No tellin' if he rigged it to bite you," muttered Monk approvingly.

When the envelope showed no trace of poison, or other lethal artifice, Doc Savage opened it. Monk read it alongside him.

On the folded white sheet of paper, the following was written in vivid blue ink:

Doc Savage

Marsland belongs to me. Return him.

Monk yelled loudly, "That cinches it! He's crooked through and through!"

As they watched, the blue letters faded until the sheet was devoid of all writing.

"Disappearin' ink!" scoffed Monk. "What a cheap stunt."

But then something happened that stifled the hairy chemist's skeptical mirth.

A silhouette appeared on the blank sheet. It showed the outline of a man in profile, a large black hat upon his head, his prominent profile dominated by a sharp, eagle-like nose. It seemed to come into existence like a signature without words.

"Blazes!" squawled Monk. "Lookit that!"

They could almost hear the laugh of The Shadow mocking them from afar.

Chapter XXIII

INTERVIEW BAIT

IN THE BLACK-WALLED room where the sun never penetrated, The Shadow sat patiently.

No light was displayed anywhere; there was only a strange clock whose concentric circles marked the relentless passing of time. If the absence of light bothered the solitary occupant, he gave no sign of this. He merely waited. With apparently infinite patience.

Presently, a tiny light beyond the desk went on.

A voice spoke. "Burbank."

"Report!"

"Have returned to station," said the voice of Burbank. "Black-ray device turned on Doc Savage headquarters at noon sharp, as per short-wave instructions. Operated successfully for twenty minutes. Ray proved to be most effective when aimed at Doc Savage office from skyscraper of comparable height. Machine shut down and spirited away without challenge, or discovery."

Soft laughter, almost a chuckle, told that The Shadow already knew this.

"Instructions to Burke. Await visitor at Metrolite Hotel. Interview visitor upon his arrival and file story with assistant city editor."

A pause.

"Instructions to Vincent. Continue canvassing funeral homes for suspect hearse and flower car. Expand search to include

New Jersey and Long Island. Do not risk discovery. Only report findings."

"Instructions received," replied the methodical Burbank.

The light went out. Darkness returned to the unlit room, and there came a swish of an unseen cloak as The Shadow stood up and made his careful exit.

NOT twenty minutes later, George Clarendon entered the lobby of the Metrolite Hotel, and strode briskly up to the desk clerk.

The clerk looked up, blinked owlishly. "How may I help you, sir?"

"I am here to pay a call on Mr. Clyde Burke."

"Very good, sir. Whom shall I say is calling?"

"George Clarendon. Burke is expecting me."

"One moment." The desk clerk lifted the phone and spoke, saying, "A Mr. George Clarendon here to see you, Mr. Burke. He says that he is expected."

"Send him right up!" replied an eager voice.

The clerk hung up the phone and said, "Room 317, Mr. Clarendon."

"Thank you." The visitor walked around the corner to the elevators, and found one car waiting.

The operator ran him up to the correct floor, and he was soon knocking at the door.

Clyde Burke opened the panel and a pleasant smile wreathed his thin features.

"Mr. Clarendon! It's been a long time."

"Yes, it has," agreed the criminologist. "May I come in?"

"I was told to expect you," said Burke. He eyed his visitor curiously, for he understood that his former employer was the mystery man known as The Shadow, had known it since he had first gone to work for the self-declared affluent criminologist.

He did not know if Clarendon was the actual true name of The Shadow. In fact, he rather doubted it.

As they took comfortable seats, Clarendon began speaking. His manner was very self-assured.

"I have just returned to the city from Chicago. I was drawn here because of the recent wave of inexplicable heart seizures."

Burke nodded. "They are beginning to add up."

"Quite so. In addition, I suspect this may be the work of the blackguard who only yesterday kidnapped my fellow clubman, Lamont Cranston, as well as the prominent attorney, Theodore Marley Brooks."

Interest flickered across Burke's lean features. "Do you connect that brazen abduction with the mysterious death of the other lawyer, Palmer-Letts?"

"There is no doubt but that Sydney J. Palmer-Letts, who happened to be Lamont Cranston's personal attorney, met his end when paying me a visit—or attempting to do so."

Burke leaned forward eagerly, his pencil inscribing shorthand into his reporter's notebook. "What is the connection?"

"Upon my arrival in the city," said Clarendon smoothly, "I rang up Palmer-Letts, and invited him to pay me a call. My intention was to alert him to the cluster of heart seizures, for my analysis of the pattern of these deaths suggested they were not accidental. Moreover, that other victims were yet to be struck down."

"Go on," prompted Burke.

"As a man of means, and one whose acquaintanceship I have enjoyed during my days when I was a member in good standing at the Cobalt Club, I reasoned that sooner or later Lamont Cranston was likely to succumb to a similar fate. I further reasoned that these deaths must be motivated by extortion. I wished merely to convey my suspicions to Mr. Cranston via his attorney."

The reporter's profile furrowed. "Why then didn't you go to Cranston directly?"

"We had been out of touch so long, I thought it indiscreet to bring the matter to Cranston's attention directly. Moreover, I wished to study his attorney when I conveyed my suspicions to him. I happen to be a keen student of human nature and I reasoned that, if Cranston were under any threat, he would have shared this with his lawyer, Palmer-Letts, and I would be able to read this fact in Palmer-Letts' reactions."

"But you never had the opportunity?"

"Sadly, no. I learned of Cranston's abduction immediately after the murder of Palmer-Letts."

Burke finished scribbling, then looked up. "Do you have a theory as to the master mind behind these secret killings?"

"I do," returned Clarendon. "By some means a gas was introduced into the rooms in which the men were found dead. This vapor, while unfamiliar to me, produces in a victim a close semblance to an ordinary and perfectly natural heart attack. They would have been styled perfect murders, had the perpetrator ceased with only one, or possibly two, victims. The number of dead piling up suggests to me two certainties. One, that there are unknown others who have paid the ransom, and whose lives were spared. Two, the perpetrator is an older individual, possibly elderly."

Burke looked very interested at this point. "How did you to conclude this?"

"In the one public instance, that of Lamont Cranston, he demanded a ransom of one quarter million dollars. Why a quarter million and not a full million? The answer is elementary. This is a man to whom two hundred and fifty thousand dollars is a considerable sum of money, whereas today it remains a handsome figure, but not the staggering amount of a generation or two ago. Hence, we are speaking of a criminal in his twilight years, attempting a final seizure of wealth."

"That narrows it down," admitted Burke. "Do you have any specific suspect in mind?"

"I do," supplied Clarendon. "In fact, I believe I have deduced the exact identity of this secret criminal. As a rule, men of advanced years do not suddenly turn to crime. He has operated in a criminal way before this, but has eluded the law every time. I do not wish to reveal his identity publicly, lest I draw a defamation lawsuit. But I am prepared to share my theories with the police and let them concentrate their forces on the apprehension of the perpetrator."

Burke finished transcribing, and inquired, "Anything else, Mr. Clarendon?"

"That sums up my conclusions," concluded Clarendon.

Burke exulted, "In that case, I want to call this in to my city editor. What a scoop! This will blow the story wide open!"

George Clarendon arose, saying, "I am pleased that you see it this way, Burke. Very glad to see you once again. For the record, I am staying at the Hotel Spartan."

"The Spartan," repeated Burke. "I'll bet the police will want to contact you there."

"I am quite certain they will," the criminologist answered, turning to go.

While Clyde Burke talked excitedly to his city editor, George Clarendon let himself out, closing the door softly behind him.

As he walked along the corridor to the elevator shaft, the soft laugh of The Shadow caressed the floral wallpaper.

Chapter XXIV

GUN FRAY

THE NEW YORK *CLASSIC* was a tabloid of the most disreputable sort. A survivor of the yellow journalism era, and a holdover of the recent collapse of the New York newspaper market, it had managed to hold circulation through bad times.

Many read the sheet, for its sensationalistic slant appealed to a certain class of reader, but many more turned their noses up at it.

So it developed that neither Doc Savage nor any of his men read Clyde Burke's interview with the criminologist calling himself George Clarendon.

Criminals of the lower-class, however, devoured the *Classic*, since it specialized in covering the criminal element.

So, too, did Detective Joe Cardona. He brought the paper into the office of Commissioner Weston, and announced, "Your friend Clarendon has turned up again. Staying at the Spartan."

Weston frowned heavily. "The Spartan? That doesn't sound like the George Clarendon I know. It rates as rather a down-at-the-heels establishment."

Weston accepted the paper, and ran a quizzical eye down the columns.

Then he looked up. "Odd that Clarendon did not bring this to my personal attention."

"It says here that he's leery of lawsuits."

Weston winced. "If his theory has any merit, Clarendon need

not fear any such repercussions. We will take his suspected killer into custody and get to the bottom of it." Weston banged his desktop for emphasis.

Cardona asked, "Want me to run over to the Spartan and talk to him?"

Weston nodded. "Go ahead. But be discreet."

"What if there's trouble?"

Weston looked pained. "What do you mean?"

"Just this," returned Cardona. "Anyone could read this interview. Including the kidnapper Clarendon claims he can finger."

This possibility had obviously not occurred to the police official. "I will order Inspector Klein to send a detachment of picked men to the Spartan. They will take a room on the same floor as Clarendon. In the event of trouble, they will be on hand. Take your time arriving, Cardona. We do not wish to seem too obvious."

"I get you," said Cardona, exiting.

Weston returned to his own reading, his lined face a florid frown.

THE HOUSE DETECTIVE at the Hotel Spartan registered worry on his smooth-shaven features.

The cause of his concern had been quietly filtering into the East Side hotel over the last hour. Now they were arrayed about his lobby, lounging in smoking chairs and pretending to read newspapers. Over a dozen of them.

Unfamiliar cars had parked along the street, depositing these strangers. The cars remained. At times, the loungers went out to confer with their waiting drivers. All this transpired beneath the iron shadows of the elevated, whose intermittent thunder every time a train rattled by drowned out low-toned exchanges and made the dingy brick façade of the old hotel tremble as if in fear.

The house dick worried that these unfamiliar faces were gamblers intending to stage a game in one of the rooms. The

Spartan didn't permit that. Past police raids had made management stiffen its rules for guests.

The detective conferred with the desk clerk. They spoke in low whispers.

"Looks like trouble brewin'," the dick reported.

"Could be a mob rubout," suggested the paling clerk.

"Too obvious, but you never can tell about these things," the detective allowed, shifting away.

The clerk quietly summoned a bellboy. "Follow those men and find out what room they visit," he directed. "They certainly are not guests. And they don't look good."

But as the bellhop turned away, a man sidled into the lobby. He was small of stature and beady of eye. A cloth cap pulled low concealed his sharp features.

Habitues of the underworld would have recognized him. For this was the shifty little trailer called Spotter.

Spying two of the loiterers, Spotter joined them. The conference they held was not audible to the house detective, much as he strained to eavesdrop.

Had he been able to overhear the exchange, the house man would have been privy to the following:

"Better shuffle off," Spotter whined.

"What's doin', Spotter?"

"A bunch of flatfoots are parked up on the sixteenth floor. I spotted them comin' over in ones and twos. Overheard one latecomer say to the other to go up to Room 616. Somethin's up. And it don't look right."

"The goods?"

Spotter nodded. "The goods."

The tough man gave a wise grin. "I knew hirin' you to act as a lookout would pay off, Spotter. Thanks. Let's all ankle back to our cars. Maybe we can stall long enough to figure something out."

Word was passed from man to man. The group of rowdies

tried to be casual about it, but it was obvious that they were vacating their listening post, for all filed out rather quickly.

The clerk blew a long breath of relief. "That's a load off my mind," he smiled. Then to the bellboy: "Go back to your bench."

One man remained. He had overheard everything, for he had been seated in a remote corner, his upper body shielded from view by an open newspaper held high in both hands.

This nondescript individual strolled over to a house telephone, and picked up the receiver. He asked to be connected with Room 616, speaking so low that the desk man never guessed that the caller was standing just a few feet away in the now-deserted lobby.

Up in Room 616, Detective Sergeant Markham answered the ringing telephone. His voice was recognized, for the caller skipped all preliminaries and gave swift instructions.

"Change in orders. Return to Headquarters. Make it snappy."

Into the instrument, Markham said: "We just got here. But if you say so, boss. We'll be right in. Don't take any wooden nickels before we get there."

IN THE nearly-empty Spartan lobby, the man speaking into a house telephone concluded his call: "Sure—O. K. on the wooden nickels." His voice was almost a perfect invitation of chief of detectives, Inspector Timothy Klein.

The man left the telephone, his tall, slender, immaculately-clad form moving with a surprising springiness. His face, however, was pale and somewhat like a solemn mask. Despite the fact that he wore glasses with very dark, smoked lenses, his eyes were unnaturally bright. Rather like living coals.

The desk clerk watched the man approach and call for a good brand of cigar. As the clerk made change for a dollar bill, he recalled that this man had been seated in a dark corner of the lobby for fully half an hour. The fellow had been there when the baker's dozen of rough-looking men came in, then left so hurriedly.

"I was waiting for a friend," the stranger said easily. "It seems he is not keeping the appointment, so I will be on my way."

He lit his cigar, and then slowly crossed the empty lobby and passed through to the front door.

The strange eyes of the man affected the clerk. He rubbed his jaw and muttered: "We sure are having some funny customers tonight."

He glanced through the plate-glass windows, to see which direction the man with the strange gaze took. The clerk saw nothing but a shadow which seemed to fade into other, spidery shadows across the street, cast by the elevated trestle. He did not dream that was the same fellow who had failed to meet his friend.

"He sure got out of sight quick!" the clerk commented.

SLIDING into an alley, the stranger removed his dark glasses and made other alterations in his appearance.

Then he returned to cross the street, and reentered the lobby of the Hotel Spartan, looking entirely different from before.

The unfamiliar men who had previously caught the attention of the hotel detective and desk clerk were distributed among parked automobiles up and down the block and around the corner. They were engaged in various occupations, such as reading newspapers and smoking cigarettes.

In reality, they were watching for a certain man to exit the hotel.

One of them caught sight of the new arrival—who was not in fact new to the scene. It was the ratty underworld spy, Spotter.

"That's him!" he vouchsafed to a companion seated beside him. "That's Clarendon. He wasn't inside after all!"

Someone whistled. Another whistle answered. Furtive signals, these.

Crossing the street, George Clarendon did not appear to notice these unusual sounds of the city.

Around the corner shot a black machine. It was a flower car, but boasted no bouquets.

It hurdled fast, screeched to a halt and then men lunged from either door. Two others lifted up from the bed of the flower receptacle. They cradled submachine guns, pointed them.

"Hands up, guy!" one shouted.

George Clarendon reacted like chained lightning. Hunching low, he made a dash for a parked coupe, which absorbed the shock of bullets from the chattering Tommy-gun.

As auto glass crashed and jangled in steel frames, Clarendon ducked into a side street. The darkness absorbed him.

The curbside loiterers came charging in the direction of the alley mouth, brandishing an assortment of revolvers, flat automatics, with a few waving blackjacks.

Converging, they began to collide with each other, shouldering one another in a mad effort to be the first to open fire.

One man managed to break free of the pack. Stumbling forward, he pointed a long-barreled automatic at the gloomy murk.

Spying a tall dark shape, he growled, "We were gonna take you for a ride, but maybe this way is quicker."

Then he hesitated. It was something strange about the appearance of his intended victim.

The gunman got a good look at the strange eyes for the first time. It was hardly a flicker. But rather a fierce smoldering in those weird, glowing eyes.

A queer admixture of emotions heaved up in the fellow's vile breast. He let out a yell.

"Hell's bells!" he bawled. "That ain't Clarendon—it's The Shadow!"

The pale fists of the apparition thrust into view. They held two pistols, from the muzzles of which protruded plumes of powder flame. The exploding weapons filled the murky alley with thunderous clapping, the first shot from each gun sounding as one.

The frightened gunman took a bullet in the shoulder, which spun him around madly. He reeled off, leaking crimson.

The others were sweeping forward, trampling their reeling comrade.

The Shadow continued to fire. But now he pointed his smoking gun barrels up and over the dodging heads of his enemies. Triggering them in alternation, he drove lead and thunder. And every electric street-light bulb in sight exploded in a shower of glass and short-circuited wires which spurted hot green-white sparks amid fizzing noises like mad cats.

For an instant, silence lay in the street. Electric tension, as of a spring bent back and about to snap.

Then the spring *did* snap!

Somebody made a strangled sound.

From every part of the alley, guns bawled terrific noise. The man who had made the sound—he was not The Shadow, as the red powder lightning showed—screeched and flailed his arms, then fell dying.

The gunmen were shooting blindly, wildly, and in the darkness, The Shadow laughed uproariously. It was a defiant laugh, a laugh that told the crooks that their shadowy foeman was unafraid of death.

Suddenly, the peals of laughter ceased. Guns had fallen silent.

Amid the swirling powder smoke, the surviving killers squinted.

The hanging smoke had formed a dense fog, which smarted the eyes, making vision difficult.

"He's gone—vanished!" one thug screeched.

The eager gunmen raced down the alley. The one who had proclaimed that The Shadow had evaporated was making a guess. It was wrong. The Shadow had not fled. Where another man would have charged away wildly—and fallen blindly into possible traps—The Shadow had faded back to see what his opponents would do.

"My sweet foot!" one barked. "He's probably hidin' in them ash cans."

Nervously, the survivors advanced purposefully, kicking at the cans strewn to either side. Some searchers were understandably reluctant to disturb the barrels, whose lids might well conceal the violent figure in black.

One man was muttering, "If we get him, the Funeral Director will make us wealthy."

That emboldened some of the others.

The muttering voice guided The Shadow as nicely as though a spotlight had been turned on the fellow. Steely white fingers captured his scrawny throat. A fist collided with the point of a jaw, making a snap of a sound. The fellow crashed down onto the concrete.

A flowing black cloak smothered the operation, and the noise was lost in the banging and rattling of ash cans.

No one saw the lurking figure, for he had kept close to the grimy brick wall, where night shadows clotted darkest. In the darkness, under the cover of his concealing cloak, he drew on his black gloves.

Back across the alley, he whipped, cloak swirling to reveal flashes of lining resembling rich velvet dipped in blood. Down the street he surged like an angry thunder cloud.

Shattered street lights had plunged the entire block into darkness.

So little time had elapsed that the gunman had not yet reached the end of the alley. The murder gang was moving cautiously, for they numbered only three, and they knew the unbelievable fighting qualities of their quarry.

They did not hear The Shadow approach—from the rear—and knew nothing of his presence until a pair of black-gloved hands seized two of them, banging their heads together like billiard balls. The pair collapsed, as slack as cloth dummies, when released.

There was one survivor. "What the hell?" he exploded, eyes corkscrewing about.

Invisible black hands probed the murk. But the survivor had ducked, expecting something of the sort.

"Hey, you lugs—what's wrong?"

Missing him, The Shadow kicked. His foot connected squarely with the other's legs.

The fellow shot into the air and down the alley as if dynamite had exploded under him. Crashing against a brick wall, he bounced back to the pavement, out cold.

A thin flash beam leveled; The Shadow followed it to the terminus of the alley.

He was briefly revealed, attired in a flowing cloak and large black hat.

That was when the two laggard Tommy-gunners spotted him.

The Shadow aimed a single automatic, and picked off one. The zimming slug turned the man around twice. His Tommy-gun began stuttering, stitching holes here and there and everywhere, breaking brick and caroming hot lead off into space.

Rat-tat-tat-tat-tat!

A second submachine gun joined in the leaden torrent. It rattled slugs against the sides of buildings.

Reaching into his cloak, The Shadow took out a steel tool resembling a shortened crowbar.

Cloak flowing behind him, he leapt for a manhole cover, covered it.

With a mighty wrench, he pried up the manhole cover, flung it aside as if it were a mere tin trashcan lid, and disappeared down the well.

A searing stream of bullets ripped across the space where he had just been. No human being could pass through that metal cyclone above the manhole opening. Not even The Shadow.

One of the attackers shrieked, "Keep 'im from comin' back up. We'll jump down onto that hole and nail 'im good this time!"

IT WAS a tense and perilous situation. Clutching their smoking pistols, a pack of human wolves crept up on the dark well into which The Shadow had oozed.

One killer, peering down below, saw the strange dark form and shot at it with a revolver.

The bullet, hitting steel pipes and glancing off, left a smear of shiny lead like a dirty chalk mark.

Another killer appeared beside him.

The Shadow went into a cross passage, reached another conduit, and went up the ladder. Behind, men clamored in bloodthirsty pursuit.

Suddenly, one of the men fired a pistol into the tunnel. A slug ripped completely through a pipe. The black, strange figure of The Shadow lurched and sank a little.

Turning, features obscured by the brim of his downturned hat, The Shadow pointed a blackened automatic in their direction. The weapon began vomiting fire, throwing the men about. Some had been clipped, others readily broke before the storm of lead. They scattered like tenpins struck by a remorseless black bowling ball.

Instantly, The Shadow whipped up a ladder, put his shoulder to the underside of another steel manhole cover. It gave before his great strength. His weird, shadowy form flowed upward.

A lone gunman had remained on the street, staring down the manhole cover into which The Shadow had vanished, pursued by his fellows.

Unexpectedly, up the street another manhole cover clanked aside. A smoky sepia shape lifted into the air with a tremendous leap, clearing the other manhole.

The fantastic form took the surviving assassin somewhat by surprise. His gun turned loose thunderously while the storm cloud of blackness came flying up the street.

The Shadow moved like an arrow shot from a bow and dived behind the wheel of the flower car, which crouched close by.

Clapping the door shut, engaging the engine, he sent the

vehicle roaring away. Desultory shots followed him, but the surviving gunmen had little will left with which to fight.

Above the fray, the laugh of The Shadow could be heard, signaling that he had turned the tide against overwhelming odds!

The thwarted killers were picking themselves up, gathering up the wounded and the dead, thinking that they had successfully driven off their superfoe, even if they had failed to slay him as intended.

The sound of the retreating motor dwindled in the distance, then curiously, it stopped.

The ears of the assassins were ringing—a direct result of so many firearms discharging at close quarters. At first, they believed that they were hearing things. Or not hearing them, rather.

"We gotta beat it!" one barked to the others. "The cops won't be slow about bustin' in."

Then came another sound—that of an engine approaching at high speed. The threatening roar grew in intensity.

One assassin growled low, "That sounds like that damn flower car, comin' back for more!"

"The Shadow ain't that crazy," gulped another. "Is he?"

In another moment, they had their answer.

For the short black machine charged up a connecting street, and above the motor moan rose a strident laugh. The wild defy of The Shadow!

It pealed out in rolling, taunting waves, like a demonic surf hitting a beach.

One black fist on the steering wheel, the other pointing out the driver's window and ahead, The Shadow triggered his automatic in a blistering challenge to his enemies. The muzzle bucked with every blast. Flame spewed.

Scattering, mobsters returned fire blindly. Powder-driven slugs cut down the slowest of the murderous crew. Men grunted in pain, cursing heavily.

Seeming to ride a wave of high hilarity, The Shadow careened through the intersection unfazed. Bullets pocked the flower car's shining skin, gashed at its glistening chrome and glass windows.

Then, abruptly, something unexpected happened. Veering, the seemingly unstoppable machine seemed to stub its rubber toe. The flower car's front tires cut sharply, the vehicle lurched, and then it rode up on the sidewalk.

The maneuver appeared to be unplanned. Nevertheless, a shadowy monster shape suddenly emerged from behind the wheel, to blaze away with twin automatics.

Would-be assassins, rushing forward to polish off their attacker, suddenly reversed into full rout.

The Shadow dispensed bullet justice and mocking laughter in equal measure, driving their hasty retreat.

Falling back, the cowed killers found the safety of sheltering automobiles. Reloading, they jabbed back sizzling lead with matching determination.

Twisting and whirling, The Shadow managed to evade every organ-seeking slug.

Then, in the distance, police sirens set up a low wailing.

With a final laugh of defiance, the dark avenger circled around the lopsided flower car and flitted into an alley. The spiteful bark of his avenging guns and taunting laughter was heard no more. There was only the keening of sirens.

"Everybody scatter!" a man called out. "We'll come back for that damn car if the cops don't nab it."

The police, arriving in force a moment later, concentrated their efforts on the Spartan and its immediate surroundings. There was a lot to do. The dead and wounded lay about in gory profusion. As they knelt to question the latter, these croaking killers, too, expired—until there were no survivors to interrogate.

Thus was the flower car was left unmolested, its engine still running until it ran out of gas and quietly died, unnoticed.

Chapter XXV

RADIO RUSE

THE SHADOW NEGOTIATED the grimy back alleys and side streets that made this section of lower Manhattan so unsavory after the sun went down.

Finally, the moving blot of a form emerged on an avenue far from the scene of the recent gun battle.

Hailing a cab, the shadowy one gave an address in Queens. Huddling in a corner of the vehicle, the silent passenger did not make a perceptible movement en route.

When he was dropped off, The Shadow did not speak. Nor did he enter the modest home he had designated. Instead, his flitting form picked its way from dark alleyways to pools of shadow created by the absence of light.

Two blocks distant, a miniature golf course had grown up in weeds. The business depression had forced the closing of several such spots. This one stood near a residential section called Jackson Heights, and the thickness of the weeds told that no one had teed off there in easily a year.

He turned into that, crossed it, reaching the rear wall of a shabby, second-rate hotel. A fire escape zigzagged a spidery frame of steel down the side of the structure. The bottom of the fire escape was a full dozen feet above the ground.

The patch of murk that was The Shadow spread as it settled in under the fire escape. Suddenly, it sprang upward, soaring as though it had taken wings. Black-gloved hands clasped the metal bars of the landing.

Finally, The Shadow ascended the fire escape to the third floor. The sash of the window slid up, and he disappeared inside.

A flashlight penciled the beam across the room to a rickety dresser. A sheet of paper appeared in the light as if by magic, then a fountain pen gripped in a long, slender hand. On the third finger of one hand the fire-opal flung stabbing shafts of light, like a fractured rainbow.

The pen scratched, trailing words which stood out on the paper in script as blue as a proverbial blueblood's life fluid. Inscribed thoughts from the mind of The Shadow!

> The Funeral Director's minions were successfully lured to their doom by George Clarendon, although their destruction was at the hands of The Shadow.
>
> The trap was a warning to the master kidnapper not to harm Lamont Cranston.
>
> The flower car was abandoned, and its license tag number learned. It may be traced to an owner, even if the name of the owner is fictitious. If not, the ultra-violet light bulb traded for the original tail-light might provide a telltale future clue.
>
> The Funeral Director now knows that The Shadow is hard on his trail. He will search for George Clarendon, but to no avail. That personality has served its purpose and must vanish forever.
>
> How can Lamont Cranston be rescued, so that his property does not fall into the hands of heirs, and The Shadow lose the cover identity he has carefully crafted?

The pen left off its scratching. Slowly, as if blotted out by some magic solution, the written words faded from sight, until all that remained was a dry sheet of blank stationary.

The nib of the pen then inscribed three words:

The Shadow knows!

A soft laugh, not quite a chuckle, was heard. It lasted only long enough for the final inscription to evaporate. Then the flash ray collapsed, restoring dimness to the room.

The wan, sickly glow from the single bulb hanging over the desk did not reach as far as the door. It was quite dark there. This gloom seemed to absorb the black-cloaked figure of The Shadow. It was as though the murk was swallowing something that belonged to it.

The door did not open immediately. There was a faint stir of movement just inside it. A moving blot intercepted the light, the door opened a crack, and something like a black ghost eased out, and made its furtive way to the rear exit door.

Little could be discerned of the sable-hued apparition. Which hardly mattered since there were no witnesses to its spectrally soundless departure.

TWO blocks south of where the hotel and miniature golf course stood was a street which carried considerable traffic. A newsboy walked along that street, his arms laden with the first editions of an evening paper. Raucously, he shouted the headlines, pausing occasionally in hopes that a customer would call to him from one of the homes lining the thoroughfare.

"Paper!" he yelled. "Evenin' paper!"

He was finding few patrons that night. There was little news of interest, other than the Palmer-Letts death, and that was not of a sufficiently flaming nature to sell many papers. The newsboy paused beside some shrubs which grew close to the walk and felt to make sure his few pennies had not found a hole in his ragged trousers pocket.

He sensed a tug at his bundle of papers and looked down. One newspaper was gone. In its place lay a dollar bill. Startled, the urchin peered about, but could see no one.

"I ain't got the change for that, mister," he offered uncertainly, feeling someone must be near.

There was no answer. The newsboy stood there a long time, wondering, the dollar bill clutched in his grimy fingers. He called again that he did not have the change. Then, receiving no reply, he swaggered off. The urchin hoped more strange things like that would happen to him.

"Been many a night since I made a whole dollar," he grinned.

A FEW moments later, some blocks distant, a taxi driver was surprised to hear the door of his machine open and close. He had seen no one. A deep, pleasant voice gave an address.

"The Excelsior Garage."

The driver turned his head, but his passenger was only a dark blot in the rear. Fares were scarce and the man did not care to chance losing this one by seeming too curious, so he drove toward the address he had been given.

He did not see his passenger turn a thin string of a flashlight beam on the paper the newsboy had sold so mysteriously.

The headline was stark:

POLICE HUNT CRANSTON KIDNAPPERS

Reading over the front page, the passenger learned little that was new. The missing multimillionaire clubman and world traveler remained unfound. Headquarters suggested that tips were being followed up, but details were scant. No one had gotten the tag numbers of the kidnap cars. Nor had any funeral parlor reported a stolen hearse or flower car.

There was mention of a niece, who was related to Lamont Cranston. She had refused all interviews, but one enterprising scribe had managed to gull her into commenting. This resulted in a feature about the grief displayed by the young woman. She had been pallid and hollow-eyed, the account ran. She had been able to discuss her uncle only in monosyllables, so greatly was she grieved. It was strictly sob sister stuff.

Most of the news about the Palmer-Letts death was a rehash of that printed earlier.

ATTORNEY'S SUDDEN DEATH
SIXTH PROMINENT HEART SEIZURE

It is the personal opinion of this writer that these deaths are a sad consequence of the present depressed business conditions resulting from the recent stock market crash. Police officials are inclined to lean to this same theory.

No other connection has been learned between the deceased individuals other than the obvious, that each was a man of financial consequence. It will be recalled that it was exactly this class of businessman who suffered most in the aftermath of Black Friday, 1929.

The flash went out and the cab window rolled down silently. The paper was tossed out of the moving vehicle. After that, there was no movement in the rear seat. At intervals, when the machine came under street lights, the interior seemed filled with nothing more tangible than dark shadows.

The spot where the cab stopped was half a block from the Excelsior Garage, a dead-storage vault for unused automobiles near the Garment District, which kept open all night. A bill floated through the window and landed on the front seat beside the driver. Puzzled, determined to get a look at his unusual passenger, the man twisted around.

"I'll be damned!" he swore softly, explosively. The rear seat was empty! The passenger was gone, although the driver had not heard the door open.

Wonder held him for a moment, then he drove on, trying to forget the startling incident.

THE GARMENT DISTRICT was riddled with narrow alleys. A black shadow attached to no living form eased into one, merged with its unwelcoming darkness, and busied itself for a time, removing items from a black leather valise it had carried in.

When this was finished, a sprightly, broad-shouldered, rather burly looking fellow stepped out into the glow of street lamps. He wore a taxi driver's uniform, the cap of which was a little large and rested low over his eyes.

Walking briskly, he entered the Excelsior Garage. The garage attendant knew him and they exchanged casual greetings. Then the hackman surrendered a claim ticket and waited patiently as a car elevator resembling a monster Ferris wheel was wrenched into motion.

Vehicles were carried around this ingenious mechanism until a battered-looking black-and-white taxicab came into view and was driven off the moving platform by an attendant.

"There she is," he announced jauntily, stepping out. "Looks like you haven't taken her out in a dog's age."

"Just blew back into town," rejoined the chipper hackman. "Watch me make the mazuma now!"

The cabby placed the black valise containing compass and chart in the front of the ancient flivver. He got in, started the motor and drove off whistling cheerily.

The engine of the two-tone cab ran very smoothly for such a dilapidated-looking machine. After it had gone some blocks, a drunk in evening dress stumbled into the street. Because he was directly in the path, the taxi was forced to stop. But when the drunk staggered around to open the door, the machine was gone, leaving the fellow standing there foolishly.

The taxi halted before an all-night drugstore, one of a nationwide chain. Getting out, the wiry looking driver went inside.

Stepping into a telephone booth, he dialed a private number.

"Burbank."

"Report."

"Mann has discovered no record of a hospital or sanitarium owned or operated by Clark Savage, Jr., but is handicapped by the forced closing of his office. Vincent continues to canvass for missing hearse. No leads developed."

"Instructions to Burbank. A flower car has been abandoned six blocks north of Hotel Spartan. Attach radio direction device to chassis and replenish gasoline tank."

"Instructions received."

The Shadow hung up.

Returning to his cab, he got behind the wheel. Driving to a secluded spot, he parked in the shelter of several forlornly leafless oak trees.

There, he sat silently for an hour while Burbank accomplished his assignment—or did not. Sufficient minutes ticked by according to the dashboard clock to fill out the full hour. Only then did the sepia figure break his strange immobility.

With motions amazingly speedy, the mysterious driver set up his portable radio receiver and aligned the directional loop aerial. Compass and map came into use.

One and then another quick line was drawn across the chart. The finger with the fire-opal ring on it rested on the spot where the two lines intersected. The spot was—no doubt of it—on Long Island. The flower car had been moved. The fact that it stood parked on Long Island could only mean that the police had not impounded it, owing no doubt to The Shadow's foresight in letting the engine run until all gasoline had been consumed, then refilled by Burbank. Therefore, it had been reclaimed by one of its scattered drivers.

"The Funeral Director is there!" whispered the taxi driver.

Then a low, terrible, unearthly laugh came from his lips, a sound which a stranger would have sworn could have been uttered by no earthly being.

The Shadow had located the Funeral Director! Located him by taking directional radio bearings on the tiny, but powerful transmitter contained in the black metal box which Burbank had affixed to the chassis of the flower car. The transmitter sent out a continuous series of dashes on the wavelength designated by the telephonic instructions to Burbank.

It was only a few seconds later when the dilapidated-looking black-and-white taxi flung away from the spot, traveling at terrific speed.

Hunkered behind the wheel, The Shadow was grimly silent.

Chapter XXVI

THE STRANGE DEATHS

DURING THE DAY, Doc Savage had been busy.

The bronze man had remained in his headquarters for much of it—a circumstance that caused Monk Mayfair to fret endlessly.

"Ain't we ever gonna get anyplace?" he complained to the bronze man.

"Progress is being made," Doc told him calmly.

Monk wrinkled his homely features. "Yeah? Well, where is it?"

"You might," Doc suggested, "examine the afternoon papers."

"Gotcha," said Monk, who promptly ambled out to fetch the latest editions.

The homely chemist was not alone. When he reached the lobby, he discovered that the lobby newsstand was doing a rushing business.

Barging in, Monk accosted the proprietor, asking, "How's tricks?"

"Lively, Mr. Mayfair. What will you have?"

"One of every late edition."

"Help yourself."

"Don't mind if I do," grinned Monk. He began to gather up copies.

No money changed hands. Doc Savage owned the stand, had set its proprietor up in business. The newsy had once been a nationally infamous gunman, well up on the list of public enemies. The man would have been greatly shocked to know this bit of his past history—he was a graduate of Doc Savage's unique criminal-curing "College" and retained no memory of his past.

He was a mild-looking man who did not fit the reputation he'd once had, and so had gone unnoticed in the big city, his headline-causing depredations having all occurred in the Middle West.

"Regards to Mr. Savage," he called after the departing chemist.

Monk lugged his bundle of the latest editions to the elevator and carried them up to the eighty-sixth floor, perusing the front pages as the cage whisked him upward.

POLICE LINK MYSTERY DEATHS

That was one startling headline.

Another read:

SILENT KILLER STALKING RICH MEN
EPIDEMIC OF HEART FAILURE?

Screamed another scarehead, adorning one of the tabloids addicted to sensationalism.

When he returned, Doc Savage was consulting with a man Monk had never before seen. He was a red-headed individual who had almost but not quite outgrown his childhood freckles. The bronze man introduced them.

"Monk, this is Mike Durwell."

The redhead nodded in a friendly manner. "Pleased to meet you, Mr. Mayfair."

"Likewise," returned Monk. His tiny eyes narrowed.

Doc Savage explained, "Mike Durwell runs the Inter-Continental Detective Agency."

"Ran, you mean," said Durwell, cracking a lopsided grin.

Monk squinted. "Whatcha mean? Doc don't use private snoops."

"Mr. Savage bought my outfit yesterday and saved us from going under."

"Is that right?" said Monk dubiously.

"Business has been bad with the depression," explained Durwell. "It didn't help that we took an expensive suite down on the second floor when this rockpile first went up."

"Durwell was just briefing me on his latest discoveries," said Doc.

"I'm all ears," said Monk, grinning.

Durwell launched into his recitation. "I've been looking into the background of the men who have succumbed in the recent spate of heart attacks. It isn't a pretty picture. A lot of them were crooked."

"Crooks!" blurted Monk. "They were a bunch of swells, accordin' to the papers."

"My operatives have uncovered otherwise," said Durwell.

That reminded Monk of his burden of late editions, so he tossed them on Doc's desk saying, "The papers have got wind that most of these heart attacks are connected, but I ain't read how yet."

Doc imparted, "I informed Commissioner Weston of my suspicions, and he released an official statement under the understanding that we were not to be quoted directly."

Monk whistled. "What do ya expect to flush out of the woods, Doc?" demanded the hairy chemist.

"That remains to be seen," replied Doc. To Durwell, the bronze man said, "Continue with your report."

Mike Durwell cleared his throat and resumed speaking.

"Many of these men had built up good fronts, but they didn't stand up to some conscientious digging. Let's start with Bedford K. Guerry, the paper manufacturer. Turns out he had been embezzling from his own company to feather his own nest. And he's just the first on the list of welchers. Take Clarence Kissman, the banker. There's money missing from his vault. The bank examiners are on it."

"Blazes!" squeaked Monk. "What does that mean?"

"It means," suggested Doc, "that the individual calling himself the Funeral Director has been targeting men he knew to be unscrupulous, but who also had secret funds with which to pay extortion demands."

Monk grunted, "Sounds like the Funeral Director might have a Robin Hood complex."

"That is doubtful, but it might be significant." The bronze giant eyed the head of the detective agency, and commented, "Lamont Cranston has enjoyed an impeccable reputation."

"So I far as we know, it still stands. But Cranston goes out of town a lot. Tibet to Timbuktu. Safaris in Africa. Cruises down the Amazon. The depression doesn't seem to have nicked him any."

"Inherited wealth?"

Durwell nodded. "That's what we understand. By the way, one of his relatives just landed at the Cranston mansion to take charge of his affairs. A dame named Weltha Cranston. Seems she's a niece. Brought along her fiancé, a chap named Donald Hume. Maybe they figure if Cranston doesn't come back alive, they'll inherit the place."

"Nothing suspicious in that," said Doc.

"No," admitted Durwell, "but the way this is going, anything could pop out of the woodwork and say Boo!"

Monk had his nose buried in the newspapers, digesting the details that Doc Savage had leaked to the police commissioner. They were scant. There was nothing about a lethal gas being used, nor was the Funeral Director mentioned by name. Only a suspicion that the dead men were felled by the same inexplicable agency.

The kidnapping of Lamont Cranston and Ham Brooks was not mentioned. That story ran beneath the other and, while the matter was given significant column inches, it was largely recap, followed by a comment by Commissioner Weston that his detectives were doing everything in their power to find the missing notables, but so far no substantial clues had been uncovered.

The involvement of Doc Savage was being kept out of that matter as well.

"Is there anything else?" Doc asked Mike Durwell.

"We got a line on that shifty bird called Spotter. One of my best men is on it now. Should have him in hand by nightfall."

"Do not bring him here," ordered Doc. "We will question Spotter in your offices."

"Whatever you say, Mr. Savage."

AFTER the agency head had left, Monk looked up from his papers and asked, "What made you decide to buy his outfit?"

"With Renny and Johnny out of the country, we are short handed. There is a lot of leg work associated with this case, and we do not want to cooperate too closely with the police."

"Why not?"

"Detective Cardona has shown a certain sympathy for The Shadow, whether warranted or not."

"You don't suppose The Shadow's the one blackmailin' these swells?"

"Perhaps Spotter can shed some light on the question," suggested Doc.

Monk nodded. "Where's Long Tom, by the way?"

"At this moment, Long Tom is endeavoring to obtain electrical work at radio Station WNX."

"The frequency The Shadow broadcasts over! What good will that do?"

"Tomorrow is Thursday," reminded Doc. "The Shadow broadcasts every Thursday night."

Monk's tiny eyes narrowed. "You think that maybe you can snag The Shadow when he shows up to do his program? Then you think he's the same bird passin' himself off as George Clarendon?"

"With Ham's life hanging in the balance," said Doc grimly, "no bets should be overlooked."

The bronze man picked up the desk telephone and called the Commissioner of Police.

Ralph Weston answered in his usual brusque fashion, which softened when he heard Doc Savage's distinctive voice.

"We are getting nowhere in our inquiries," Weston snapped peevishly. "It is confounded frustrating."

"My operatives have come up with a link connecting most of the men who have perished from premature heart failures."

"Of course there is a link! They were all men of wealth."

"They were also, according to a private investigator in my employ, men of shady dealings," stated Doc. "I will have a messenger bring you his report."

"Please do that. I will have Cardona look into it once he returns from the Hotel Spartan."

"What is going on at the Spartan?" asked Doc.

"George Clarendon gave an interview to the *Classic* in which he claims to have deduced the identity of the killer of rich men who also kidnapped Cranston and Brooks. He has taken up residence in the Spartan. The manager called in a complaint that a tough crowd has been congregating there. I sent a squad of my best plainclothes detectives there to keep an eye on things in case an attempt is made on Clarendon's life. Cardona is on his way to join them."

Doc Savage did not divulge his belief—it was more than that now—that George Clarendon was a front for The Shadow. Instead, he said, "Monk and I will drop over there. I am interested in Clarendon's theories."

"I will look for your report," said Weston, hanging up.

Turning to Monk, Doc stated, "George Clarendon has surfaced at the Hotel Spartan. He has given a newspaper interview claiming to know the identity of the Funeral Director, which he has not divulged."

"The crust of that fake!" howled Monk.

They rushed to the super-speed elevator, dropped to the secret sub-basement garage where the bronze man kept a small fleet of automobiles, ranging from sedans to delivery trucks, and climbed into a low, front-drive roadster.

A ramp carried them up to the street. Monk drove, Doc Savage rode the running board, a habit of his when riding into danger. This way he could see trouble before it found him.

On the way, they heard a newsboy hawking his wares.

"Wuxtra! Criminologist claims to know identity of kidnapper! Wuxtra!"

As they approached the corner where the urchin was giving forth, the light turned red. Doc purchased a paper while he waited for it to change.

Monk took the sheet and spread it out over the steering wheel. Doc grasped the latter and steered while the homely chemist perused the article in question.

"Blast me!" he howled. "Pipe the name of the reporter who wrote it up."

Doc took his alert golden eyes off the way ahead long enough to spy the byline.

"Clyde Burke," he said.

"Could be a trap," muttered Monk.

"Yes," agreed Doc. "But for whom?"

The homely chemist grabbed the wheel in both hairy hands and, bringing his big foot down on the accelerator, mustered up a grimace that would have frightened King Kong.

"I aim to find out," he growled, taking a corner on two wheels, forcing Doc Savage to cling to the windscreen posts more tightly.

Traffic parted for them with alacrity.

Chapter XXVII

MASSACRE

THE RIDE FROM Doc Savage's headquarters to the Hotel Spartan was not very far when measured in miles, but in the early evening traffic with workers still filing out of their office buildings and congesting the crosswalks and intersections, it took some doing to reach their destination.

So it was that when Doc and Monk pulled up, the police had already cordoned off the block which the hostelry occupied.

The air was filled with the stink of burnt cordite, and brass buttons glinted on numerous blue tunics like blank eyes. It was also very dark, for they noticed that a number of street lamps had been shot out.

Braking, Doc and Monk piled out, shouldering through the crowd.

"What went on here?" demanded Monk of no one in particular. "A young war?"

"Mob rubout," volunteered one citizen.

"Yeah," added another. "Racket boys put someone on the spot, all right."

"Any idea who?" asked Doc.

"No," said a third person, "but there are a lot of bodies—a damn lot of them."

Another offered wide-eyed, "They say The Shadow done it."

By this time, Doc spied the well-worn dome of Detective Cardona's derby hat amid the sea of police uniform caps. The bronze man arrowed toward the ace sleuth.

Seeing Doc approaching, Cardona strode over, swarthy features grim, his habitual stubby cigar switching from one side of his mouth to the other.

"It was a regular gang war," he began. "We're still sorting it out. It looks like the murder crew staked out the hotel, and were laying for George Clarendon. They're all dead in the street, every one of them. No sign of Clarendon, though."

"George Clarendon is The Shadow," said Doc Savage firmly.

Detective Cardona took a step backward, and tilted up his derby. He looked as taken aback as if one of his cigars had turned into a cold hot dog.

"You don't say?" he murmured, eyes narrowing.

"It might be more correct to state," clarified Doc, "that The Shadow was pretending to be Clarendon, who is a fictitious personality."

"The Commissioner isn't going to like hearing this," said Cardona darkly. "Weston and Clarendon were pretty tight. The Commissioner has hopes of being let into the Cobalt Club. He thought Clarendon would get him in, but he left town. Now his second sponsor, Cranston, is being held for ransom."

"It might not be wise to mention this to Weston," advised Doc. "Inasmuch he does not believe in the existence of the being calling himself The Shadow."

"You have a point there," admitted Cardona.

They were moving through the darkened streets. Owing to the absence of reliable light, Cardona had a flashlight in hand and was employing it liberally.

"I recognize a bunch of these mobbies," he told Doc, bathing stiff faces in the glow. "Freelancers, everyone of them. Hired guns. Torpedoes. Up-and-comers. But they're all bound for the morgue now."

Doc Savage moved among the dead, studying their faces. The bronze giant also recognized a number of them.

"According to witnesses," supplied Cardona, "a bunch of them were picketed outside, and jumped a man crossing the street.

From the description, it was Clarendon. He ducked into an alley and the gunmen followed him in. That's when the shooting started. Clarendon kind of melted away in the crossfire. No one saw clearly what happened after that, but the people who heard it said it was the gun battle to end all gun battles. And the wild laughter made their blood freeze."

Monk blurted out, "The Shadow gunned all these guys down?"

Cardona declared, "That's about the size of it. Don't tell me how. But I've seen it happen before. The Shadow can handle those two smokewagons of his the way another man can shoot with one. And he never misses."

Monk looked impressed. "The Shadow's a pretty fair hand with a pistol, eh?"

"A dead shot—in every sense," Cardona concurred.

Doc asked, "Why were your men not on top of this? This massacre could have been prevented."

"Detective Sergeant Markham sent a contingent to the Spartan, and they were holed up in a room waiting for something to pop. Then they got a call from Inspector Klein, saying to break it up and return to Headquarters. After they withdrew, the shooting started. Someone called it in, and I came racing over. On my way here, I ran into the squad and made them turn around."

Cardona paused, chewed his cigar briefly.

"When I checked in," he continued, "Klein told me he never made that call. But Markham said it sounded exactly like him."

"Is The Shadow known to be a voice mimic?" asked Doc Savage.

Cardona examined the unlit end of his cigar, commenting, "If he wasn't known for that trick before, I'm giving him the credit tonight."

They talked to every available witness, including the desk clerk who had seen most of the action, although not all of it. They came away with a fair picture of the night's proceedings, but no explanation for the battle.

Doc Savage offered this: "It is obvious that George Clarendon gave that newspaper interview for the express purpose of luring the minions of the master kidnapper to the Hotel Spartan. But what was his intent?"

Cardona grimaced. "If it was to stage a massacre and thin out the Funeral Director's mob, he certainly succeeded."

Monk offered, "But what did he get out of it?"

Doc Savage looked around. "Perhaps The Shadow stirred up a trail to the Funeral Director."

Monk scratched the back of his nubbinlike skull while Detective Cardona rubbed his jaw.

"How do you figure that?" wondered the sleuth.

"If there were any survivors," the bronze man pointed out, "they would have retreated in their own automobiles."

Cardona looked around at the dead being loaded into morgue wagons.

"If," he grunted.

"Right now," added Doc, "The Shadow may be following any survivors back to their master mind."

"Which leaves us exactly nowhere," gruffed Cardona unhappily. "We don't know what automobile that might be, nor what face The Shadow is wearing tonight."

Doc Savage had his spring-generator flashlight out and was using it to examine the street. He gave every indication of looking for something specific.

Faces interested, Monk and Detective Cardona followed the bronze man as he made his silent and purposeful way around the block.

Finally, in the latticelike shadow of the El, the bronze giant discovered something that interested him, and began following some trail that the others could not see.

Monk could not contain his curiosity.

"Whatcha, find, Doc?" he asked.

"Tire tracks," replied Doc, coming to a halt and directing his flash ray this way and that without dwelling on a definite spot.

At the earlier abduction of Ham Brooks and Lamont Cranston, Doc Savage had studied the tracks left by the black hearse and its companion flower car, and committed them to memory. He recognized the distinctive treads of the latter here.

"Cardona," said Doc. "Based on the tread marks and wheelbase width, it appears that the mysterious flower car has been in the vicinity. It is probably the vehicle The Shadow is following, if my surmise is correct."

"I'll put out a dragnet," said Cardona violently. "If that damn snatch car is anywhere in the city, we'll run it down."

"Monk and I will make our own reconnoiter. We will be in touch."

Chapter XXVIII

TOMBSTONE TROUBLE

THE TREAD MARKS of the flower car had led them due east when they petered out.

In a city of cross streets such as New York, this was meaningless, of course. The fleeing car could have taken a turn in any direction in order to defeat pursuit. No doubt the driver also knew that the police were watching for the mystery hearse and its attending flower car.

Thus it was that Doc Savage assumed that it might now be creeping along anywhere in the city, or had slithered into one of the other boroughs of New York, if not New Jersey.

Instead of driving aimlessly and trusting to luck, the bronze man headed west to his combination boathouse-hangar warehouse, rolled inside, and climbed aboard a cabin gyroplane of his own devising.

Under power, the gyroplane rolled out onto a concrete apron, slid down this slipway and took to the water like an ungainly duck. It was soon wallowing on its floats on the choppy Hudson.

Unlike the aeronautical marvel that is the modern autogyro, this true gyro had the ability to rise straight into the air, as well as fly horizontally like a plane.

Doc revved up the nose propeller, which coaxed the tiny ship into taxiing, then brought the overhead rotors into play. This was necessary to break any suction that might keep the floats from lifting free of the river chop.

Once airborne, Doc set the gyroplane rising like an elevator, then commenced crisscrossing the canyons of lower Manhattan.

Both Doc and Monk were wearing special goggles that worked in concert with an infra-red projector located in the trim ship's bawling nose.

Together, these devices allowed them to see the ground below in stark relief. Colors were unobservable, only deepest shadows, interspersed with the grayest grays. It was a grim prospect, like an old silent film, but it served.

Monk muttered, "This will be like tryin' to find the old needle in the farmer's haystack. Except that's a lot of concrete haystacks down there."

"Keep your eyes sharp," reminded Doc.

Doc Savage flew as low as safety permitted. A black flower car would not be easily discerned, even under the powerful infra-red beam, for it was fully night. Moreover, the Manhattan streets were choked with traffic, as might be expected on a weekday night.

Still, the bronze man seemed determined to make the effort. The fact that the odds were against him seemed to matter little. It was the only lead they had.

Passing over lower Manhattan several times availed them nothing.

Monk was growing discouraged, and fell to muttering complaints to himself. It had now been two nights since Ham Brooks had been abducted, and the lack of progress was wearing on the simian chemist's normally robust nerves.

Then Doc Savage's golden eyes suddenly veered east in the direction of Sunnyside in Queens, Long Island.

Seated behind him, Monk noticed this, and looked over. He gave out an explosive grunt of astonishment.

For buzzing the air was a black autogyro, its braced wings outflung like a ruler.

"I'll be a monkey's uncle," burst out Monk. "You don't suppose that's—?"

Doc Savage noted, "The police have an autogyro at their disposal, but it is marked. That ship is not marked."

"Could be the bus that buzzed our upstate institution."

"If that is the case," rejoined Doc, "then it is likely that The Shadow is piloting that autogyro."

The windmill plane was flying slowly, an indication that it was either searching for something, or following a vehicle on the ground.

Monk rummaged around for a portable infra-red projector, and aimed it out the window in the direction of the cruising autogyro.

This allowed both men to see it more clearly through their goggles.

"Can't make out a blamed thing," complained Monk. "All I see in the cockpit is a blasted blackness."

It was an open cockpit, but Monk's bitter observation was correct. Try as he might, Doc's scrutiny of the autogyro failed to discern anything about the unseen pilot.

"I don't see 'im wearin' any hat," grunted Monk.

"A hat would be blown off by slipstream," said Doc. "No doubt he is wearing a flying helmet and goggles."

"What say we mosey on over and take a closer look?" suggested Monk.

Doc Savage shook his head. "If that autogyro belongs to The Shadow, following it will be the same as following the flower car."

Monk guffawed, "If this is a wild-goose chase, it's sure an interestin' one."

Doc Savage drove the gyroplane due east, cutting in a silencer that suppressed the engine noise. He fell in behind the autogyro, whose braced wings stretched out on either side, in stark contrast to the bronze man's wingless streamlined craft.

Seen up close, it was a modern ship, and very expensive. Doc

Savage recognized the make and model, but observed no registration numbers on tail or fuselage.

"Suspicious," muttered Monk.

"Very," agreed Doc.

Stealthily, they followed the ebony autogyro, always keeping behind it, but at a distance that made it less likely that they would be spotted by the pilot, who appeared preoccupied with his search.

The night air was cool and clear. The skies were overcast, as if the parading clouds were promising rain. The lack of moonlight helped with their aerial trailing.

Doc Savage sent the gyroplane scooting upward, and began jockeying his ship around, in order to see if the autogyro was, in actuality, following an automobile of any type.

From the studied way the autogyro twisted and turned, that seemed highly likely. So far there was no sign of the vehicle being sought, however.

Then Monk spotted something. On a hunch, he dug out a different pair of mechanical scanning goggles and clapped them over his tiny orbs. These resembled condensed milk cans and were sensitive to black-light rays.

"I see a light bouncing down there."

The homely chemist leveled a hairy beam of an arm.

Doc saw nothing through the infra-red lenses, Monk passed over his set, which Doc quickly donned. The bronze man leaned the gyroplane to get a better look. He saw it, too, visible through Monk's goggles.

"The Shadow has somehow attached an ultra-violet light to the machine he is shadowing," Doc decided.

"Slick."

The aerial pursuit continued for another dozen minutes or so, when the autogyro commenced to cavort—turning, circling, dropping lower.

This series of maneuvers unavoidably brought the eggbeater

craft pointing in the direction of Doc Savage's supersilenced gyroplane.

"He spotted us!" barked Monk.

Doc Savage said nothing. Flake-gold eyes tracked the gyro.

For a moment, it seemed as if the pilot was uncertain how to react to discovery of pursuit. He continued circling, losing altitude.

A hand snapped out of the open cockpit. They could see that it was gloved in black. It pointed downward, stabbing with a long, commanding forefinger.

Then, banking, the pilot abruptly chopped power, and the autogyro began to plummet, its prop still.

"Is he makin' an emergency landing?" howled Monk.

Doc Savage corrected, "Not an emergency, but a stealth landing. He is preparing to pounce upon his quarry."

"Oh, yeah? Well, let's pounce on him! Heck, let's pounce on everybody!"

Wordlessly, Doc Savage jockeyed his gyroplane for the ground.

Both aircraft were about to alight upon the same patch of ground, and the stage was set for a confrontation. Reaching into his coat, Monk yanked out his superfiring machine pistol and thumbed off the safety latch.

"Make sure you use mercy bullets only," cautioned the bronze man.

"If the shootin' starts," Monk flung back, "that black bird is going to be throwin' a lot of lead."

"Try not to get in the way of any of it," cautioned Doc.

And then the entire ship reverberated with a jar, for the gyroplane's floats touched down on solid ground.

THE TWO whirlygig planes now alighted, in all places, among the cracked and leaning headstones of an ancient burial ground, dating from before the Civil War.

Doc Savage and Monk hastily flung themselves out of the

gyroplane's enclosed cabin. They ducked under the great wind-mill rotors, which were still winding down.

A few dozen yards away, the other gyro had settled safely.

They were again wearing their infra-red goggles, and Monk carried the lantern which projected the infra-rays. This illuminated the autogyro with stark intensity.

Its rotors, too, were slowly turning. But unlike the gyroplane's windmill, these broad blades were not powered. When the mystery pilot had cut juice to the power plant, the free-spinning rotors continue to twirl, acting as a parachute brake as the black ship dropped from the sky. This permitted the autogyro to land safely, rolling only a few feet.

Rushing toward the machine, Monk found the cockpit empty.

"Blazes!" he squeaked. "Vanished already!"

Doc reached the black ship, peered into the open cockpit, dropped back in disappointment, and began studying the terrain all around.

The grass grew so luxuriously it was not difficult to pick up the trail. Green blades were mashed down, exuding juice, while others were straightening up, showing that a man had gone in a specific direction.

Doc signaled silently for Monk to follow. The hairy chemist pointed the sharp muzzle of his machine pistol before him.

They trampled grass as they moved, goggled eyes searching for their quarry.

But even in the strangely illuminated darkness, there was no sign of The Shadow. Assuming that the pilot was he.

Suddenly, Monk noticed something.

He bit down on his tongue to keep from exclaiming, and tapped Doc Savage on the arm. Pointing, he indicated a lean, shadowy form high in the nearby oak tree, like a great roosting bat with close-folded wings.

Doc Savage spotted the apparition. It consisted of a hat, of the shapeless slouch type, below which draped a long black cloak fluttering in the cool night breeze.

It appeared that the one they sought had slipped up into the heavy interlacing branches of a sprawling oak, and was poised there either to snipe, or to fall upon them when they got close enough to strike.

"I can nail him with one shot," whispered Monk.

Doc shook his head. "If he falls from that height, he could break his neck."

"That's his lookout," grunted Monk.

"Pretend you do not see him," suggested Doc.

Shifting about, the bronze man drifted away from the oak tree, and they both pretended to be searching elsewhere.

They moved in a cautious circle, away from the towering tree, then shifted back, pretending to have lost the trail.

The weird, shapeless thing in the branches rippled in the breeze. That was the only evidence of its macabre presence.

Monk exclaimed loudly, "Where the heck did he get to?" to give a note of convincingness to the charade.

By this artifice, they wound their way back to the vicinity of the oak tree, and took shelter beneath its spreading branches.

"This is spooky!" Monk complained. "Where did he go?"

"It is difficult to say," said Doc Savage, assisting the imposture.

Above their heads, the dark folds of the cloak stirred. A sudden gust of night air set them to chattering madly. The figure seemed poised to act.

Abruptly, the bronze man lifted his mighty arms and grasped a low-hanging branch.

During the youth in which he had lived in many parts of the world, Doc Savage had acquired many unusual skills. Among these was the ability to climb trees and move along jungle lanes with the agility of a monkey or tree squirrel.

The skill was not normally of use in the city, but here the bronze giant showed that it could be.

In a flash, Doc had lifted himself onto the branch. With an acrobatic skill that would have impressed a circus performer, he sprang upward into the higher branches, metallic hands reaching for the fluttering cloak.

Muscular arms surrounded the black scarecrow, capturing it.

Since it was imperative to take the lurker by surprise, lest the foe open up with his twin automatics, the bronze man put everything he had into that final lunge.

He miscalculated in only one degree.

Doc expected to slam into a resisting body, after which he intended to grasp a tree limb he had already picked out, and swing from it to another, thence to the ground, with his enemy in hand.

To his utter surprise, the bronze man encountered only empty air, along with a black cloak and hat that had been suspended in the branches to make it look as if the makeshift scarecrow were the silhouette of a human being.

Reacting with astonishing reflexes, Doc missed the branch he was aiming for, but caught another and managed to break his fall sufficiently so that when he landed in the grass, no lasting harm was done.

Monk charged up, supermachine pistol ready to spit fury.

Doc jumped to his feet, clutching the long black cloak in one hand and the hat in the other. The expression on his moon-burnished features was unreadable, but the wild trilling issuing forth from his parted lips bespoke of his frustration.

"He made a dummy for us!" exploded Monk. "Heck, he made monkeys of us, too."

"The Shadow is very clever," agreed Doc, looking about in the night.

From somewhere that might have been very near, or considerably far, a spectral laugh floated through the branches of the great oak tree. It wafted around the sagging headstones that resembled blunt, chipped monster teeth, sounding somehow sinister as well.

The sound might have had a ventriloquial quality. Perhaps it was because the author had so completely secreted himself in the evening darkness, they could locate no direction from which the demonic laughter was coming.

"Remind me," gritted Monk with fierce frustration, "to get the last laugh on this dang spook!"

Chapter XXIX

THE MAN IN THE COFFIN

THE LAST LAUGH was destined not to belong to Monk Mayfair. At least, not yet.

As the strident laughter trailed off, Doc Savage began moving through the grass, scanning the surroundings.

"The ultra-violet lantern, Monk," he requested.

The homely chemist surrendered the device, which emitted no visible rays.

The bronze man accepted it and, lifting it high, began moving to the faded grass, attempting to pick up fresh footprints. He had some difficulty doing so, which seemed to puzzle him a bit. His trilling piped up, faint and pensive. The golden flakes of his eyes whirled more animatedly than normal.

Try as he might, the bronze man could not locate a trail. No sign showed itself. Not even in the sickly grass which grew about in such wild profusion.

"Maybe he's some kinda ghost," observed Monk.

"No ghost, but a very clever individual," admitted Doc.

They came at last to the fence that had sealed off the old cemetery from vandals. Working along, they came to a gate, which was padlocked, its chains going to rust.

No time to fuss with the lock, so Doc Savage removed a container from his gadget-carrying vest, which when opened revealed a kind of putty. He applied this substance to the padlock and using an igniter, set it to sizzling ferociously.

This was thermite, a volatile welding compound which made

short work of the padlock, reducing it to incandescent molten steel. The rust-caked chain fell away, and Doc pushed the gate open.

They found themselves on a residential street, and looked both ways.

There was no sign of The Shadow or, for that matter, anyone else. The area seemed sleepy, for no one had stepped out to scrutinize the gyros, one of which had landed with a clatter of beating blades.

Since they had arrived in relative silence, it is possible that no one noticed them.

Doc Savage seemed to sniff the air, and his trilling issued for a time. This time it sounded intrigued.

"This way," he told Mark.

The hairy chemist followed him, looking faintly baffled.

That bafflement lasted until they had moved up the street a few blocks and then turned right, whereupon they found themselves confronting a sprawling white building that was immaculately groomed. Shrubbery appeared as if it were sculpted. It barely shook in the fitful night breeze.

There was a sign in front. It read:

SUNNYSIDE FUNERAL HOME

"Man alive!" squeaked Monk. "That flower car musta come here!"

Doc nodded. "It stands to reason that the hearse and the flower car were attached to a funeral home but, with so many such establishments in the greater New York to New Jersey area, narrowing it down was proving very difficult."

Monk grunted, "That blasted Shadow figured it out for us!"

"His intelligence has already been demonstrated," reminded Doc.

Treading quietly, they advanced upon the funeral home.

There were a few pale yellow lights in some of the windows, but the place did not appear busy. No cars were parked in the lot set aside for mourners. Nor was there any sign of any outside activity.

Exercising extreme caution, Doc Savage and Monk Mayfair crept up, knelt in the concealment of the well-manicured shrubbery, and studied the establishment.

There was nothing unusual about it. It seemed to be a typical suburban funeral parlor. If not prosperous, it was certainly in good repair, showing every sign that it did a steady business catering to the bereaved.

Monk breathed, "This is the kind of joint the Funeral Director would hang out in, ain't it?"

Doc nodded silently. "While the name this arch-kidnapper used might have been a bit of theatrical artifice, the hearse and the flower car strongly suggested such a headquarters."

Monk's eyes narrowed. "Do we bust in?"

The bronze man shook his head. "Stealth is preferable."

Suiting action to words, Doc carefully crept closer. He walked with no excess movements, pausing here and there, showing that he had once learned the art of stalking from a Cherokee brave. This particular red man could sneak up on a dozing bear, pluck a tuft of fur, and retreat before the bruin awoke.

In this instance, any lurking bear was likely to have been armed to the teeth. Doc moved with all the stealth with which he was capable, for despite wearing a bulletproof vest, he was not immune to bullets where he wore no protection, such as his head.

There was a portico, where mourners were received. This was in front of the circular driveway, large enough to receive limousines and hearses as well as ordinary automobiles.

The bronze man was making for this, with the intent of testing the doors to see if they were open.

He never got close enough to discover if they were.

Guns started detonating, bright muzzle flashes illuminating darkened windows. Glass shattered, men screamed, and more guns blasted apart the formerly quiet night.

Someone had a Tommy-gun, and it began chattering.

Without any further warning, lead began to fly in their direction.

Doc and Monk were forced to drop flat, and clap their hands over their heads in an effort to protect their brains.

To the first frightful burst, Monk began returning fire with his supermachine pistol. The weapon discharged shells with a long, hooting moan.

If this had any effect, it was not noticeable amid the cacophony of gunfire.

In that mêlée, the sound of The Shadow's laughter rose into a crescendo that made the skin want to prickle and crawl. After-chuckles seemed to chase one another like frisky imps.

"He's inside!" Monk yelled, his words drowned out by sub-gun thunder.

Doc was rolling toward shelter in one direction, while Monk crawled in the other. They had fought in the war together and understood that the closer one kept to the turf, the greater the chances flying lead would whistle harmlessly over their crawling forms.

Another ghoulish stitching of Tommy-gun fire split the night. There was no telling whence it was coming, or where the bullets were flying, either. They remained low on the ground, waiting for a lull.

When the awaited interval came, it was not a lull. It was an explosion. A grenade had gone off. No mistaking it. Shrapnel punched faintly smoking holes into the sides of the building.

A few bits fell, and actually started small fires in the dry grass.

That was when the first lull came. It was brief. The sound of a powerful motor starting came, followed by another.

They never quite got clear about from what shelter the hearse and the flower car came, but the black machines careened and blundered from in back, charging through ornamental bushes, destroying them in their mad dash to escape.

Monk sent a hot burst of mercy bullets after them, but they

did no good, merely splashing against the black auto bodies and safety glass.

Doc Savage leapt to his feet, charged for the hearse, and attempted to jump on its running board.

He almost made it. But someone in the back seat, where the coffin normally rests, shot out the glass and drove two slugs into Doc's chest.

The bronze giant was violently spun around, slammed to the ground in part by the force of the lead, but also because he wished to preserve his life.

The ebony machines slammed down the road, tires squealing, engines whining madly. The lull that followed was a true lull. It persisted.

Still, it was five minutes before Doc and Monk felt that it was safe to climb to their feet and approach the damaged building.

"Sounds kinda like they had themselves a young war in there," Monk muttered.

"They were not shooting at us," agreed Doc Savage.

But the normally talkative Monk said nothing as they located a door and forced it in, smashing it off its hinges with their shoulders.

They found a dead man almost immediately.

Doc applied the light of his small flashlight to the dead man's gore-besplattered face and said, " 'Bats' Belfry."

Monk grunted. "I recognize that yegg. He's a terrible hophead. Well, that's another one for the morgue wagon. Or maybe they can just dump 'im into one of these coffins around here."

They moved from room to room, finding no one and nothing, but in one chamber they came to a bier where two caskets lay in state, surrounded by wilting bouquets of floral arrangements.

One coffin had been flung open and muslin liner was in disarray as if the person or body that had reposed within had been hastily and forcibly removed.

The other casket was sealed.

Doc Savage approached this, lifted the heavy lid.

Inside, a man lay in repose, eyes closed, seemingly not breathing.

Monk eased up and asked, "I'm afraid to look. Is that Ham?"

"No," replied Doc Savage solemnly. "This appears to be Lamont Cranston."

"Alive or dead?" asked Monk.

Doc Savage took hold of the man's wrist, felt for a pulse, found a strong, sturdy one and pronounced, "Alive."

Looking around, Monk grunted, "So where's Ham?"

"We will search for him."

GOING to every room on both floors, they found no one and nothing. No clue as to the whereabouts of the missing lawyer.

Finally, they returned to the state room, where Lamont Cranston lay in an open coffin, apparently undisturbed by all the recent commotion.

Doc Savage studied the man, noting his strong masklike features, the supple hands with their lean, capable fingers.

Monk said, "If we shake him awake, he might give us a clue to where Ham went."

Reaching into his vest, Doc Savage removed a small leather case, which he popped open. Reposed within was a hypodermic syringe and a small bottle of solution.

The bronze man carefully charged the syringe, and prepared to administer a stimulant in the hope of reviving the missing millionaire.

Before Doc could do so, Cranston gave a jerk, shook his head. His eyes came open, looking at first dazed, then increasingly clear. The calm-faced man seemed to recover with remarkable speed, suggesting a strong constitution.

"Where am I?" he asked groggily, immediately sitting up.

"In a danged funeral casket," supplied Monk without sympathy.

Slowly, Lamont Cranston sat up and stared about him. He took in the banks of funeral bouquets, and said, "I remember now. I was kidnapped and taken here. With a man named Brooks."

Chilly blue eyes fell upon the tall figure of Doc Savage and said, "Brooks was taking me to see you."

"Where is Ham now?" demanded Monk.

Cranston felt of his head, and showed all outward signs of a man experiencing a severe headache.

"I do not know. He and I were placed in adjacent coffins, and injected periodically to keep us from moving. Dreadful, frightening experience."

Monk yelled, "They musta hauled him off in that hearse!"

"No doubt," stated Doc. To the millionaire, he asked, "Cranston, are you up to a ride in a gyroplane?"

"Gyroplane?"

"It is important to get you out of here before the authorities arrive."

"Why is that?"

"You may be our only lead to the missing Ham Brooks. Additionally, I am interested in learning why you consulted with our associate."

"I should be happy to satisfy your curiosity, if you will give me a hand."

Cranston stepped out of the coffin, but he was very unsteady on his feet. Doc was compelled to lift the man up and bear him out of the destroyed funeral home.

Fortunately, the sound of sirens did not begin to stir the night air until they reached the burial ground and their waiting gyroplane.

"Remarkable looking craft," remarked Cranston, eyeing the resting machine.

As they started to pile into the cabin, Cranston noticed a similar aircraft silhouetted nearby and wanted to know, "Who owns that autogyro?"

"The Shadow," said Doc Savage.

"The Shadow!" whispered Cranston. He sounded very strange when he mouthed the words.

"Yeah," said Monk. "Know anythin' of 'im?"

"I have heard his terrible laugh over the radio," admitted Lamont Cranston. But after that admission, he grew very silent and would say no more.

Chapter XXX

THE EVASIVE MR. CRANSTON

THE GYROPLANE PILOTED by Doc Savage dropped onto the Hudson River like a dragonfly alighting onto a lily pad.

By advancing the throttle, the bronze man sent the tiny craft scooting toward the great apron of concrete, steering by means of small rudders fitted into the back of the ship's twin floats. The overhead rotor, no longer under power, turned lazily.

The prop howled as it hauled the gyro up the sloping spillway, and through a great door that rolled upward in response to a radio signal from the cabin.

Great interior lights came on as well, throwing the normally gloomy vault of a warehouse into relief, disclosing the small armada of aircraft ranging from a single-seat racing plane to a great tri-motor that was more advanced than anything constructed in Europe.

Snapping switches, Doc braked the plane and the motor fell silent, prop blades freezing.

Monk helped Lamont Cranston out of the cabin first. He walked stiffly, as if from long confinement. His well-molded features were very pale.

The millionaire globetrotter had recovered some measure of his composure, for he stood looking about the place with the knowledgeable eye of a world traveler.

"You have assembled quite a fleet in the short time you have been in operation," Cranston commented.

"Thank you," said Doc. "I have read of your travels. You have explored many out of the way spots far from civilization."

"Club life bores me," Cranston frankly admitted. "One can only suffer the company of Commissioner Weston at intervals. My mansion, although it provides me with every comfort, often grows cloying and stifling, for I live alone except for my staff. Travel invigorates my zest for life."

"Speaking of the Cobalt Club," inserted Doc, "we understand you were acquainted with a man named George Clarendon, who is also a member."

Cranston nodded seriously. "Yes, Clarendon. A criminologist, after a fashion. I know little of him. He is an acquaintance, which is putting it precisely."

"We have good reason to believe that George Clarendon is The Shadow," disclosed Doc.

Lamont Cranston's face grew pensive, and his lips sealed.

"I would know nothing of that," he bit out.

There was something in the millionaire's eyes that seemed evasive.

Doc Savage changed the subject slightly. "It has come to light that in recent weeks you have been receiving letters of extortion."

Cranston looked vaguely peeved. "Who told you this?"

"The police investigation into your abduction brought certain letters to light," explained the bronze man.

"I see," mused Cranston, who was looking about, studying the rafters and noticing a peculiar looking submersible that sat in a dry dock at one end of the great vault of the warehouse.

"Your household staff indicated that you had taken to listening to the radio personality who calls himself The Shadow during his Thursday night broadcasts."

Cranston tore his eyes off a staging platform that stood before a steel cargo door high up along one wall, and remarked dryly, "I imagine that there are many who tune in to that rather popular program."

"Have you any reason to suspect that your extorter is the same person as The Shadow?"

"Now that you mention it," allowed Cranston, "I had been inclining in the direction of that exact thinking. But have since reconsidered."

Doc scrutinized the man steadily.

"What caused you to change your mind?"

"I would rather not say at this time," replied Cranston.

"Have you any clue as to the nature of this extortionist?" pressed Doc.

"None whatsoever. Except that he called himself the Funeral Director. And it would seem that you have rescued me from a funeral parlor, so I imagine that the name this nefarious person has assumed is not some ghoulish conceit, but a mark of his actual trade."

Monk Mayfair was walking around the place, checking various alarms, looking for signs of entry, as well as waterfront rats, which sometimes found their way within the warehouse structure.

When he returned, the hairy chemist wondered, "What can you tell us about our friend Ham?"

"Attorney Brooks, insofar as I know, was being held captive in a casket similar to mine. From time to time I awoke, as if from a dream, to hear voices speaking, and twice the lid of my coffin was lifted and I was administered an injection calculated to keep me passive."

The millionaire allowed a slight shudder to course through his lean body.

Evidently, the memories of his recent captivity had seared themselves upon his brain.

Doc Savage asked, "Why did you seek out the advice of Ham Brooks?"

"It was purely by happenstance," confessed Cranston. "I did not wish to bring certain concerns to the attention of my own attorney, and made a dinner appointment with Commissioner

Weston to lay the matter before him. But Weston was not available, and I remembered that Attorney Brooks was connected to your group of adventurers. Purely upon impulse, I paid him a call. We were on our way to visit you. The rest you no doubt know."

"What was this matter?" asked Doc.

Cranston hesitated. "I do not think it wise to lay the particulars before you now, after all that has transpired."

Doc pressed, "Why did you not bring this to your own attorney's attention?"

"I felt it was beyond his abilities to manage, given that he handles my financial affairs only."

"You mean *handled,* don't you?" inserted Monk.

Lamont Cranston looked momentarily blank. His sharp blue eyes shifted from the homely chemist to the bronze man, as if searching for an answer.

Doc advised him, "I regret to inform you that Sydney J. Palmer-Letts perished the other night while paying a call on George Clarendon at his hotel."

"Perished?"

Doc nodded. "Palmer-Letts succumbed to a heart attack of the type that has been striking down wealthy men over the last month. We have reason to believe that he was targeted for death, although the motivation remains unknown to us."

Lamont Cranston fell silent. "Poor beggar," he said finally. "He was my father's attorney before me."

Eyes suddenly snapping into focus, the millionaire asked Doc Savage, "What is your theory as to the agent of death?"

Doc told him, "Either a gas, or else a chemical surreptitiously introduced into his handkerchief, caused Palmer-Letts to inhale the lethal fumes which struck him down."

"How diabolical!" murmured Cranston. "But what was the motivation?"

"None comes to mind," Doc informed him. "Either Clarendon lured him to his doom, or someone wished to prevent Palmer-Letts from reaching the criminologist."

"You mean The Shadow, do you not?" prompted Cranston.

Doc Savage said, "The Shadow is an enigma of many layers. A frank explanation of his interest in you would be appreciated."

Cranston's deep-set eyes stared back. And met the bronze man's golden gaze frankly.

"What makes you believe The Shadow was interested in me?" he challenged.

"Because your behavior suggests that you are interested in him," retorted the bronze man.

Again, the millionaire fell silent. "Whatever I have to say," he admitted finally, "I will divulge only to Commissioner Weston, with whom I have had a long and trusted acquaintance."

"Very well," stated Doc. "We will take you to Commissioner Weston's office."

"I thank you, but I need to muster my reserves before I meet Weston. I would prefer to return to my mansion in Westfield, for I imagine my household staff has been frantic in my absence."

"It might be better if you spoke to Weston immediately, since you may have information that will clarify the problem of the missing Ham Brooks."

"I take your point," allowed Cranston in a reluctant tone. "Very well, then, let us visit Weston."

Doc Savage selected a subdued sedan from three automobiles that stood parked in one corner of the great warehouse.

Monk opened the rear door for the millionaire, saying, "I guess you're used to sittin' in back, with someone else driving."

"Thank you," said Cranston, sliding in and taking a seat.

Monk slammed the door, and hurried over to take the wheel.

As is his habit, Doc Savage stood on the running board, balancing himself with his sure feet, capable metallic hands gripping the door posts.

Monk set the machine into motion, and an inner door rolled up in response to a dashboard radio signal. The sedan eased out into the night, paused in the blaze of its own headlights, then Monk turned north, and picked up speed.

It was black night now, and traffic was thinning, the theater hour having passed.

They were rolling west. Doc Savage by keeping his eyes alert, watched the road ahead, glancing now and again at things that caught his attention. A cruising prowl car. A down-and-out man folding up his corner apple stand. Another selling pencils two for three cents at another corner. These sights were becoming more common as the depression grew deeper.

At the wheel, Monk Mayfair was saying, "That stuffed shirt Weston is gonna get an earful tonight."

Doc said nothing to that. In back, Lamont Cranston appeared to be lost in his pensive thoughts. The strain of the last few days seemed to have taken a toll and he sank deep into the cushions in back, his chin resting on the white front of his shirt.

From time to time, Monk flashed tiny eyes back at him through the rear-vision mirror, and noticed that the multimillionaire appeared to be nodding off, evidently exhausted from his difficult ordeal.

Soon enough, the apish chemist stopped looking. Traffic became difficult, so Monk wheeled the nimble machine out of his intended path, jockeying the steering wheel in an effort to skirt other vehicles.

Once a taxicab came scooting around the corner at a higher rate of speed than was wise, and Monk wrenched the wheel hard in order to avoid it.

The sedan ended up swapping ends and, climbing onto the sidewalk curb, upset a mailbox with one steel fender. The trunk sprang open, but almost immediately clapped shut again, gravity and the weight of the spare-tire carrier apparently dropping the steel hatch back into place.

"Dang drivers in this town get worse every day!" Monk mumbled.

"You O.K. back there?" The hairy chemist asked after he got the machine going again.

There was no reply, and Doc Savage rapped out, "Monk, pull over!"

The apish chemist swung the wheel over hard, bumping the curb, and flounced around in his seat. The back of the sedan was clouded with shadowy darkness and it was difficult to penetrate it.

While Monk was straining his eyes, Doc Savage stepped off the running board and threw open the rear door.

This let in some wan streetlight, disclosing an unbelievable fact: the back seat was entirely empty!

"What gives?" Monk yelled.

"Cranston evidently slipped away during our collision," Doc explained tightly.

The two men started a general search of the vicinity, making their way backward to the point at which they had collided with the battered mailbox.

The blocks in this sector were crisscrossed with dark alleys and festooned with ironwork fire escapes.

Monk Mayfair searched all of these with his small eyes, covering a great deal of frontage but with no useful results.

"Got clean away!" complained Monk. "But how?"

Doc seemed on the point of offering a theory, when the soft sound of a high-powered motor came to their ears. It was receding into the night.

Monk's blocky jaw dropped. "That sounds like our bus!"

They ran, but of course it was too late. The crimson tail-light of the sedan was dwindling along the avenue, and as if to answer the question, in the night floated a stridently mocking laughter.

"The Shadow!" yelled Monk. "That's The Shadow! Where did *he* come from?"

Doc Savage did not answer. Instead, he cut down an alley in an attempt to overhaul the machine by guessing at its probable course.

The bronze man proved prescient. For no sooner had he popped out at the opposite end than the sedan came sweeping by.

Doc Savage reacted with the chain-lightning speed for which he was becoming famed. He stepped off the curb, moving fast, and leaped for the running board of his escaping machine.

It was a feat as fanciful as those performed by Hollywood cowboys changing horses at full gallop. The bronze man managed to succeed.

Strong bronze fingers took hold of the side-window pillars and his feet found the jouncing and vibrating running board.

Behind the wheel, the driver threw the vehicle hard to the left, and lined up with the curve.

Doc Savage was endeavoring to slip his hand into the narrow crack of the partly open window, when some instinct impelled him to look ahead.

The sedan was charging toward a lamp post, the driver plainly intending to scrape against it, in order to dislodge the unwanted passenger.

Doc made a last ditch effort to shatter the window with his fist, but it was safety glass. It cracked under his pounding fist, but did not give in.

With the cast-iron standard looming ahead, the bronze giant had no choice but to throw himself clear.

He landed on an arrangement of milk cartons and newspapers from which a street corner vendor was crying the evening newspaper headlines.

The flimsy crates shattered under his hurling bulk, and Doc Savage was forced to roll until he came to a stop against a gritty brick wall.

Climbing to his feet, he saw the sedan careening around the

corner. The taunting laugh of The Shadow hurled back at him as if to challenge the bronze man to try again.

But it was no use. Doc Savage knew that.

He handed the newsy a twenty-dollar bill to cover the damages, and raced to a police call box in an effort to alert Headquarters that the missing millionaire who might or might not be The Shadow was racing through the city in his stolen sedan to an unknown destination.

After that, the bronze man called Mike Durwell and requested he put his operatives to work scouring the city for the fleeing sedan.

Doc then rejoined Monk Mayfair, who was boisterously jumping up-and-down in thwarted wrath.

The hairy chemist stopped long enough to growl, "How many guys is this blasted Shadow, anyway?"

Doc told him, "The Shadow merely impersonated Lamont Cranston. You will recall that we followed The Shadow to the funeral home, only to discover Cranston in the coffin. No one else."

Monk scratched his bristled head. "What the heck does *that* mean?"

"The Shadow may have simply transformed himself into a semblance of the missing millionaire in order to avoid capture."

Monk blinked. "So we *did* capture him, didn't we?"

Doc Savage shook his head slowly. "We rescued Lamont Cranston from his abductors—or so we thought. We captured no one."

"So is Cranston still missin', or not?"

"That," said Doc Savage, "remains to be seen."

Chapter XXXI

SPOTTER'S STORY

THE EIGHTY-SIXTH FLOOR of Doc Savage's headquarters was busy with visitors by the time the bronze man and Monk stepped off the super-speed elevator and entered the reception room.

They had taken a taxi to the building, after a futile hour of ranging about the city. The stolen sedan had evidently vanished.

Long Tom Roberts was waiting for them.

"Any news on hand?" he asked Doc.

Monk answered that, saying, "We had a line on him, but hit a dead end. We thought we rescued Lamont Cranston, but it turned out it was The Shadow in disguise." Monk sounded frustrated.

Long Tom looked at Doc Savage, "How did he manage to pull that off?"

Monk muttered darkly, "Cranston, or The Shadow?"

To which Long Tom replied, "Either. I'm not sure who is which."

"Join the dang club," complained Monk. He settled into a chair and stared bleakly into his broad palms. Their inability to make any progress in locating the missing Ham Brooks was getting the homely chemist down.

Doc Savage reminded, "The Shadow is a master of impersonation, the likes of which we have never before encountered."

Which was saying a great deal, since it was widely believed

among the bronze man's circle of friends that Doc Savage was the best impersonator of personalities outside of Hollywood.

Doc went on to say, "Cranston reminded me of George Clarendon in certain ways, but I confess that while I harbored my suspicions, I failed to penetrate to the truth."

Long Tom spoke up. "Well, you can add this to the pile of mysteries: I followed that Rutledge Mann around town, and he went to an old building on Twenty-Third Street and dropped some mail into an dingy-looking office that looked deserted."

"Whose office?" asked Doc.

"The name on the door was B. Jonas," Long Tom revealed. "Asking around the building, nobody knows him. And no one could remember seeing anyone coming and going from that office. It looks like the owner up and died, taking the key with him."

"We will look into that office," said Doc. "You might set up a hidden television eye on the place first."

"That was my thought," said Long Tom.

At that point, the telephone rang. It was Detective Joe Cardona.

"No soap," he said. "No trace of your missing sedan anywhere in the city."

"I did not think you would be successful," returned Doc.

The detective ace wanted to know, "So who stole it?"

"All evidence points to The Shadow."

Cardona's whistled low and slow. "Well, we had better keep this to ourselves."

"That is an excellent idea. Thank you, Detective," said Doc, hanging up.

Monk regarded the bronze man. "You didn't tell him about Cranston?"

"Until events are clarified, it would be better not to point fingers unnecessarily."

"Meanin' that Cranston might be in the clear?"

"It is also uncertain what The Shadow's business is in this investigation."

Monk looked puzzled in a simian way, but said nothing.

Doc Savage turned to Long Tom Roberts and said, "Go ahead and install a television scanner at the B. Jonas office. Also, do not forget our plan to eavesdrop on the sound booth from which The Shadow broadcasts."

"I already set that up," supplied the electrical genius. "I finagled a job there."

"That's tomorrow night, ain't it?" grunted Monk.

Doc eyed the wall clock, which was tolling again. The hands showed that it was after one a.m.

"Tonight," corrected the bronze man.

"Then I'd better get cracking," said Long Tom. "See you later."

No sooner had the slender electrical wizard departed than the phone rang again. This time it was Mike Durwell. He sounded pleased with himself.

"We nabbed Spotter. Want to come down?"

"We will be there directly," promised Doc.

They took the regular elevator to the fifteenth floor, and Durwell let them in.

THE UNDERWORLD spy who called himself Spotter was a wizened little man with shifty eyes and clothes that looked as though they had not been washed since the previous Sunday.

"I got nuthin' to say to any of youse," he was whining when Doc walked in.

At sight of the bronze man, Spotter looked up with widening eyes and croaked, "Mother of mine! That's Doc Savage! You're bigger than the papers said you were."

Monk got over to one side of the shriveled-looking crook and placed a hairy paw on his thin shoulder, growling, "We wanna ask you some questions, and we better get some quick answers on account of we're kinda in a powerful hurry."

The pressure of Monk's apish fingers was grueling. Spotter scrunched up his ratty face and grimaced. Monk applied more pressure. The prisoner winced and squeezed shut his eyes.

Opening them again, he saw that the apish chemist was still there and the bronze giant continued looming over him. They were not figments of his guilty imagination.

"He's kinda tough, Doc," clucked Monk.

"Is this the third degree you're givin' me?" demanded Spotter truculently. "On account of if it is, I've stood up to them before. You won't break me."

"Our methods are distinctly different," responded Doc Savage.

From a pocket the bronze man took out a flat case, extracted a syringe and began filling it from a vial.

"What's that?" wondered Spotter. "Dope?"

"Truth serum," replied Doc matter-of-factly.

Sweat began to bead up on the shifty crook's upper lip and his eyes narrowed to a rat-like thinness.

"Maybe you better ask your questions first before dosing me with that junk," he mumbled. "Might save us all some time."

Doc appraised him silently and placed the syringe on the table.

"It is said that you know something about an underworld figure who calls himself The Shadow," he prompted.

Features paling, Spotter practically jumped out of his seat. Monk pressed him down back into it.

Spotter was as white as a sheet when he began blabbering. "The Shadow! He's a bad one, he is. No one knows who he is, but crooks who run afoul of him don't come out so good."

"Is The Shadow a criminal?" demanded Doc.

Spotter shrugged. "I don't know if The Shadow is even human! Don't act like it. That crazy laugh of his, the way he slips in and out of joints unseen, he might even be a damn ghost for all I know."

Monk allowed, "This bird may not be all that far off."

Spotter nodded firmly. "You gents know what I'm talkin' about?"

Monk offered, "We had a kinda run-in or two with him ourselves."

The little crook shuddered on his seat. "I still get the goose-flesh thinkin' about that laugh."

Doc Savage advised, "Tell us everything you know about The Shadow. Leave nothing out. We may not need to use the needle on you, after all."

Spotter let out a wheezy sigh of surrender. "For a long time, The Shadow was a rumor you heard down in the badlands," he volunteered. "Mobbies would run across him, and check out fast—on account of The Shadow put the permanent kibosh on them. Get me?"

Doc nodded somberly.

"I wasn't sure what to make of this talk, crazy tales and all," resumed Spotter. "But one day I saw him. It was over at the Pink Rat. There were these two crooks, and The Shadow came out of nowhere and piled into them. He was like a moving ball of blackness, bigger than a man should be, and he took those two gorillas apart like he was the wrath of Old Nick himself. All the time, he was laughin' that creepy laugh of his."

"Did you get a good look at him, Spotter?" interposed Durwell.

The little crook shook his head, and said, "Not a good look, no. But I saw something. Under that hat brim of his, I caught a flash of white, on the lower part of his face. It looked kind of like a bandage. It reminds me of someone I once heard about."

Spotter shuddered momentarily.

"Who?" prompted Doc.

"Long ago, there was a guy. I never knew his name. But there was a lot of talk swirlin' around him, too. The whole underworld was afraid of him. Scuttlebutt says he had been a spy during the Great War. Got himself wounded. Wounded bad, too. Smack in the face. So bad he had to keep the lower part of his phiz covered up. I put two and two together. I think The Shadow is that guy everyone used to be afraid of."

Monk said to Doc, "Didn't Marsland say that he knew The Shadow under another name during the war?"

"He did," confirmed the bronze man. Addressing Spotter, Doc asked, "What else can you tell us about The Shadow?"

"They say that guys who go up against him, either die or disappear. No one knows who he is, and if anybody's ever got the better of him, they ain't talkin' about it, see? That goes for me, too. That's all I got to say. I don't want The Shadow gunnin' for me. He's poison. Do you understand what I'm sayin'? *Lead* poison."

That seemed to be the end of that.

But Doc Savage took a chair and, moving it in front of the stool pigeon, dropped into it. His flake-gold eyes bored into the criminal's shifty orbs.

"You are leaving out something important, Spotter."

The wizened crook tried to look away, but there was something hypnotic about the bronze giant's compelling golden gaze. They whirled relentlessly and Spotter's will to resist broke.

"One time," he wheezed, "some wise guys got it into their heads that they could put The Shadow on the spot down at the radio station where he gives his Thursday night talks. So they got a guy inside—one who knew radio. He worked there for a month and kept his peepers open. But he never spotted The Shadow. All he learned was that The Shadow would arrive at the broadcasting booth by a twistin' passage and no one ever saw him come or go. The booth was hung with black velvet curtains, see? The Shadow would just appear, speak his piece, then vanish back down that crazy corridor. No one knew nothin'."

"Go on," encouraged Doc.

"That's when they asked me to help out. I hung around the front of the building day and night, lookin' for any bird who might be The Shadow. I saw a thousand ones come and go, but if any of 'em was this Shadow, I never tipped to it." Spotter folded his thin arms. "That's it. That's all I got to tell."

No one spoke for the longest time; Spotter shifted in his chair uneasily.

"I spoke my piece, now how about lettin' me go?"

Mike Durwell looked to Doc Savage, who nodded in acquiescence.

Durwell said, "You're free to go, Spotter, but keep your nose clean. Before you know it, you'll be a jailbird."

"I've been in jail before," sneered Spotter. "I don't plan to go back, but it don't scare me none if I do."

The little underworld spy stood up and started to sidle out of the office.

Pausing at the door, he flung back one last morsel. "Don't let The Shadow know I was gabbin' about him. He'd plug me in an instant. He's plugged a lot of others who got in his way."

The door shut with a clap, and Doc Savage said to Mike Durwell, "That was helpful."

"My pleasure. I don't see that this takes you any much further than you already are, but I'm pleased to help."

A frown touched Durwell's forehead.

Noticing this, Doc Savage looked to him questioningly.

"I was just thinking," Durwell fretted. "Spotter has quite the reputation in the underworld as a spy and a trailer. Doesn't mix in with the serious crooked stuff. He's never been known to stick anyone up or knock over a bank. But he helps out those who do. Lives on the fringes of the underworld."

Monk demanded, "What's your point?"

"As I said, Spotter is a trailer. Another word for a trailer is a shadower. He shadows people, and is said to be the best in his line."

Monk frowned suspiciously. He jumped up abruptly. "You ain't sayin' maybe that little runt is The Shadow?"

Mike Durwell looked abashed. "The thought just crossed my mind, which is why I bring it up."

Monk made a lunge for the door, but Doc Savage stopped him with a few words.

"Never mind, Monk. Spotter is not The Shadow."

Monk demanded, "Are you sure?"

"Quite sure. Spotter has too small a frame to possibly be the man who impersonated George Clarendon, never mind Lamont Cranston."

Monk subsided. "Too bad. Because if he was The Shadow, I woulda torn him limb from limb until he spilled everything he knows."

"Still," inserted Mike Durwell, "you have to admit that it's funny that the only person who knows anything about The Shadow is a crook who shadows people for a living."

On that peculiar note, Doc and Monk adjourned to their suite of offices on the eighty-sixth floor.

Stepping off the private elevator, they discovered an unfamiliar man attempting to leave a package outside of Doc's bronze portal.

Chapter XXXII
ANOTHER CASKET OPENS

THE UNKNOWN INDIVIDUAL was stooping as he laid the package against the portal. His manner was noticeably furtive, surreptitious.

Doc Savage motioned for Monk to remain silent. The hairy chemist made ready fists.

Equally silent, the bronze man stole up on the man, unawares. He reached down and took the fellow's scrawny neck in his corded hands.

The intruder emitted a yelp of surprise and tried to struggle. This proved futile. Doc Savage might have possessed steel vises instead of hands. His grip could not be broken.

Reaching into his coat, the skulker yanked out a stubby revolver, attempted to bring it to bear.

Doc saw the weapon coming out, glinting of nickel. One bronze hand flashed out and shucked the pistol from the man's helpless fingers. The bronze giant thumbed the cylinder out of the revolver frame, shook it vigorously. Unfired shells fell clattering to the floor.

Tossing the harmless weapon to Monk, Doc gathered up the flailing fellow into his massive arms and carried him into the reception room as if he were but a small child.

Following Doc, Monk scooped up the package. His arms were so long he barely needed to stoop.

It was a long box swathed in coarse brown butcher paper and tied with twine.

Monk frowned at it. "Want I should check this out with the fluoroscope?"

Doc nodded. He placed the captive in a leather chair and worked on neck nerves some more.

The fellow found that he could not move from his seated position, no matter how hard he tried. His brow became a smear of sweat.

Struggling mightily, he found speech.

"What—what did you do to me?"

"What is your name, fellow?" Doc demanded.

"Ain't sayin'."

"What was in that package you were leaving?"

"Why don't you open it and see for yourself?"

"Sometimes enemies of mine try to leave bombs at my doorstep," suggested Doc.

"It ain't a bomb."

"Then why were you leaving it at such a late hour?"

"I was told to."

"By whom?"

"You'll see when you open it," the man said stubbornly.

Doc studied the man. He possessed a crude kind of nerve, of the type petty criminals sometimes evince. Spotter was another such.

After a few minutes, Monk Mayfair returned and said, "It's no bomb. Looks like another of them casket gimmicks."

"Give it here," requested Doc.

The bronze man took the package. The twine had already been undone, and the object lay revealed in a nest of butcher paper. He set the small black casket on the massive ebony table.

Opening it, Doc received a surprise. No trace of it appeared in his impassive features, but something flared in his flake-gold eyes.

For, once the lid lifted, up popped a mechanical doll dressed in evening clothes.

The tiny figure sat up at the waist. The wide-eyed head screwed about in alarm.

A tinny voice cried, "Help me! They will kill me if you do not pay the ransom."

Monk yelled, "That sounds like Ham! Looks like him, too!"

Turning, he seized the intruder by the throat and demanded, "Give, brother. Everything you got, or I'll wind your head around like that doll's before I drop you out a window."

The immobile man released a flood of perspiration that immediately soaked his hair. "I—I had orders to leave that."

"By the Funeral Director?" asked Doc.

"Yeah."

"Who is he?"

"And where can we find his digs?" inserted Monk, squeezing anew.

"I can't say! I mean, I don't know. I've never been there. I only joined the gang a while back, and most of the men are dead now—since The Shadow gunned them down."

It sounded like the truth. The man was really frightened. Between his inexplicable paralysis and Monk's hairy hand, he feared for his immediate future.

Doc asked, "Your name?"

The man hesitated. Monk squeezed his neck forcibly, producing a squawking response.

"Creece! Lee Creece."

"The cook who has gone missing from the Cranston household?" asked the bronze man.

Creece did not respond, other than to hang his head guiltily.

Doc prompted, "You were installed in the household staff to pave the way for the attempt to extort Lamont Cranston."

"G-guilty. They—they did away with the previous cook to open the door for me. It worked. That part, that is. But Cranston was tougher than we thought. He wouldn't cough up any dough. So it was decided to kidnap him."

"Where is Cranston now?"

"The Director had been holding him and that lawyer, Brooks, at a funeral home he operates. But The Shadow busted that up, too. He's been holy murder on the Funeral Director's organization. And the old boy's hopping mad about it, too."

Doc Savage had carried the unused truth serum from Mike Durwell's office and now proceeded to use it on Lee Creece.

"Don't!" he squawled at sight of the needle. "You can't do that to me."

Monk peered at him. "So you know what we're gonna do, eh? You musta been hearin' things."

The man's eyes grew sick. He looked to the bronze man, swallowing hard. "I had a pal, and you got 'im. I met him later, and he didn't know me. He didn't remember nothin'."

Monk hid a grin. The fellow must have been talking about a graduate from Doc's criminal-curing "College."

"Sometimes we cut their nerve systems in two," the homely chemist growled convincingly, "and they forget how to put one foot in front of the other. I saw a grown man we caught once going around on all fours like a orangutan. Guess he kinda forgot how to walk."

Lee Creece's horrified gaze shifted back to Monk Mayfair, and Doc Savage took the opportunity to lay hands on the terrified crook's upper arm.

The needle went in, and a few minutes passed in which the man's faint struggles diminished, after which his head lolled onto his chest as if inebriated.

"He's not so tough," remarked Monk.

After a while, Doc began asking Creece questions. They were the same questions as before, but the answers this time came slowly and were slurred. The man had no resistance left. It quickly developed that he had been telling the truth. His story was substantially the same.

The only new fact which came to light was that the man had been a cook in the house of a rich stockbroker who had lost his shirt in the stock market plunge. Out of work and unable to secure gainful employment, Lee Creece had fallen in with bad companions and been lured into a blind fling at crime.

"There is nothing more to his account, Monk," decided Doc.

"Dang! I thought we had a line on this Funeral Director for sure."

"Prepare him for delivery to our place upstate," directed Doc.

"The ambulance boys are probably sleepin'. Wanna wait 'til morning? This mug ain't goin' nowhere."

"See that he is comfortable," requested Doc.

The bronze man repaired to his laboratory, where a short-wave radio set crackled quietly. But no instructions from the Funeral Director to his underlings could be heard.

A telephone—one of many scattered about the spacious laboratory—began buzzing insistently. It was a number known only to his aides.

Doc glided to the nearest instrument and picked up the handset. "This is Doc Savage."

Without preamble, a sepulchral voice began speaking:

"Out of blackness I come, into the dark I go, no one knows where or how. Wherever crime is, there come I to act as police and judge and jury. Wherever strange things happen, there come I to make strangeness clear. No one knows who I am, or what I am, but every one knows what I do. Every one who does wrong fears me, for… I am The Shadow!"

A weirdly ghoulish chuckle followed. The line went dead.

Pronging the switch hook, Doc called the building switchboard and requested that the call be traced.

The chief operator was quick to report, "I am very sorry, Mr. Savage, but the call cannot be traced at this time."

"Thank you," said Doc, who was not surprised. He had not thought that it could.

The telephone set reposed on a low table and Doc opened a drawer, revealing a wire-recording instrument. It had automatically recorded the call when the bronze man had touched a decorative carving.

Switching off the device, Doc carried it into the reception room, where he set up a similar recorder with which he had earlier recorded the voice of George Clarendon.

Replaying each recording in alternation, the bronze man detected subtle similarities in the very different tonal qualities of the individual speakers, but quickly became satisfied that the two speakers were one and the same individual.

Then he played a recording he had previously made of the radio broadcast personality identifying himself as The Shadow. Doc had only to review it once to satisfying himself that all three speakers were the same man.

The message was clear. The mystery man was warning Doc Savage that The Shadow was law unto himself, and would act accordingly.

Chapter XXXIII

INSTRUCTIONS

THE GRAY SEDAN belonging to Doc Savage ended up parked in the vicinity of the Garment District.

The driver—who no longer resembled Lamont Cranston—exited quietly and traced his way through the grubby streets.

Pausing at an alley, he disappeared within its grimy length. The sound of his footsteps was soft, but soon vanished from hearing.

In the sable-hung room minutes later, a blue light clicked on.

Pale hands came into view. Where before they were bare, now one long digit was adorned by a gold ring set with an ever-changing fire-opal stone.

Headphones came off a hook and a tiny white light went on. "Report!"

"Nothing to report," said Burbank. "All agents active without result. Doc Savage investigation has hampered normal operations."

"Instructions to Burke. Continue telephonic canvassing of funeral homes for sign of kidnap hearse and flower car. Instructions to Vincent. Go to Badger Building and retrieve from Mann's secretary sealed envelope waiting there. Do not open. Proceed to Jonas office and deliver to mail slot."

"Instructions received."

"Instructions to Burbank. Crate the black-ray device. It will be recovered for permanent storage."

"Instruction received."

The light went out, and the headphones were returned to their wall hook.

In the darkness, The Shadow sat in grim silence. He did not laugh, for his efforts had been for naught, foiled in part by the adventurer calling himself Doc Savage.

Chapter XXXIV

THE WHITE CRUST

IN THE MORNING, Monk Mayfair ambled into Doc Savage's great laboratory. He found Doc standing before an imposing all-wave radio set in one corner of the room.

The bronze man was listening to a sputtery carrier-wave hiss emerging from the loudspeaker grille.

Monk screwed up his homely features, and wondered, "What have you got on, Doc? The police short-wave?"

The bronze giant shook his head. "No, this is the frequency used by the cook, Creece, when he communicated to the Funeral Director through Lamont Cranston's short-wave radio."

"I get it. You're listenin' for instructions to his men—whatever's left of them."

"Those men The Shadow gunned down last night may not comprise all of the mob," suggested Doc. "Many might have been hired for the express purpose of silencing George Clarendon."

Monk grunted, "Yeah, the badlands are full of birds who ain't hardly anythin' more than hired guns."

Hearing nothing of interest, Doc left the set on, and strode through the impressive workshop, into the library, and on through to his reception room.

Monk trailed him on bandy legs. "Want I should ring the ambulance boys?"

"Go ahead, but use this phone." The bronze man tapped one of several telephones that reposed upon his ornate desk.

Monk looked at it. His beetling brow furrowed.

"Ain't that connected to the line that was tapped?"

"It is."

"Did you fix it?"

Doc Savage shook his head firmly.

Monk grinned. "So you want The Shadow to know that we're sendin' another candidate up to the College?"

"He knows about the place, but may not suspect its true purpose."

"I get it. You're layin' a trap. Slick."

"Request the driver to pick up Creece at the warehouse this evening."

"What time?"

"Eight. It will be dark by then. And The Shadow will have concluded his evening broadcast."

Rubbing his hands together, Monk beamed like a friendly gorilla. "I'm suddenly lookin' forward to tonight's shindig."

"Employ an excess of caution, Monk. The Shadow is a killer."

Nodding, Monk picked up the telephone and made the call.

While he was speaking, another telephone rang. Doc answered the instrument. It was Mike Durwell.

"One of my men found your missing sedan, Mr. Savage. It was found near the Garment District. Abandoned. What do you want to do about it?"

"Let it be. Thank you."

Doc hung up and told Monk of the find.

THE HAIRY CHEMIST scratched his bullet skull at its bristly apex. "Reckon he'll come back for it?"

"It is a possibility. But not likely." Doc began putting on an overcoat. "We will retrieve the sedan and see what clues we can discover."

As they started for the door, one telephone rang again. Monk scooped up the handset.

"Yeah?" The apish chemist listened intently. Hanging up, he told Doc, "That was Long Tom. He discovered—"

"I heard every word," said Doc. "You fetch the sedan. I will look into the other matter."

Doc took the super-speed elevator to the sub-basement garage while Monk rode the other to the lobby, where he hailed a cab to Times Square.

A moment later, Doc Savage emerged from the secret garage driving a nondescript coupe. He drove with expert skill to Twenty-Third Street and a rundown building that might have been built prior to the turn of the century.

Long Tom had reported a man had been seen going to the office marked B. Jonas. On the theory that anyone showing interest in the disused space might be The Shadow, or perhaps one of his underlings, the bronze man had hied over there.

Long Tom met him outside.

"He's still up there."

"Description?" prompted Doc.

"It was one of the two we clashed with the other night, over in the Jersey meadows. I didn't get a good look at him then, but there's no question it's the same guy." Long Tom described a well-built young man with regular features, concluding, "He didn't look like a crook—not that you can always tell."

As they conversed, someone came down the granite steps and the electrical wizard inclined his chin in the man's direction.

"That's him."

"Follow him," directed Doc. "I will see to the office."

Although they stood in a corner of the lobby and spoke in low tones, the young man noticed them. Spotting the towering figure of the bronze giant, he ducked back, went pounding up the stairs.

Doc Savage flashed after him, reached the stairs and mounted them three at a time.

The sound of the man's scuffling shoes told that he had reached the second floor.

The bronze man gained the landing and, Long Tom at his heels, looked both ways.

A pistol shot rang out and Doc ducked back, shielding Long Tom from a leaden unpleasantry.

A second slug came whistling along and Doc was forced to hang back, broad back pressed against a sheltering corner wall.

From his gadget vest, he extracted a small glass globe. It was filled with a milky substance that sloshed about.

Flinging this down the corridor, the bronze man again retreated, this time to avoid a chemical cloud which erupted when the globe shattered on the corridor floor.

Fumes burst and rolled in all directions, like a gaseous octopus spreading out blind tentacles.

"Tear gas?" questioned Long Tom.

Doc shook his head, said, "No," and waited.

By the time it seemed safe to peer out, the hallway was a pale haze.

Doc ventured into it, not bothering to don a gas mask or goggles, which told Long Tom that it was safe to follow.

The undersized electrical wizard batted at the billowing stuff with his hat, but cleared away little of it.

He watched his bronze chief, thinking that the stuff was meant to show footprints, or perform some other chemical miracle. But Doc did not seem to be watching the well-worn marble flooring.

Instead, he checked office doors, found them locked and seemed for a moment a vaguely baffled figure in the indoor fog.

Throwing up a window at the far end helped disperse the cloudy stuff. It did not smell very bad, being vaguely remindful of diluted ammonia, but which caused a rasping of the throat and made the tongue feel dry. Long Tom was soon obliged to breathe through his nose.

As much as they searched, they found no trace of the young man who had eluded them so expertly.

"He's good," remarked Long Tom.

"No doubt an escape route was already in place," commented Doc.

They went up to an upper floor and then to the door marked B. JONAS.

It looked as if it had not been opened in many years. There was a rime of dust on the frosted glass door and cobwebs festooned the panel.

Doc Savage touched one of the latter, and it stretched without breaking.

"Rubber cement," he pointed out.

Long Tom breathed, "A blind. I have a television camera mounted in the transom across the hall, and have been watching from an office I rented. He came up the stairs and dropped a letter in the mail slot. Didn't use the elevator."

Doc Savage picked the lock and they went in cautiously.

The interior was as dusty as expected. There was not much furniture. A desk, rather old. A swivel chair. Some writing utensils. No telephone.

Nothing else of consequence caught their eye as Doc and Long Tom flashed glances around.

Doc had picked up the letter that had fallen to the floor when the visitor had dropped it through.

It was sealed. Doc considered a bit before opening it, and instead walked over to a grimy window and pulled up the shade. This let in welcome light.

Holding the envelope up to the morning sunlight, Doc attempted to read the paper within.

He discerned a blue-inked message. Long Tom could see traces, too.

"From The Shadow?"

"Or to him," suggested Doc.

"That means if we open it, we'll just have time to read it before it vanishes."

"That is a chance we will have to take," said Doc.

There was a letter opener on the spare desk, lying atop a faded green ink blotter. Long Tom grabbed it and offered the instrument to Doc. But the bronze man declined the thing.

Instead, he removed a small tool from his vest. This was a tiny knife. The bronze man used it to slit the end so carefully it did not rip the front or back.

Sliding the missive out, he unfolded it.

The message was brief, and in a code. Doc had just time to scan it before the bright blue ink faded. After which the sheet was blank.

"Damn," muttered Long Tom. "All for nothing."

"No," said Doc. "For I have memorized it."

"Think you can solve it from memory?"

"We will see." Pocketing the envelope, Doc went in search of the building superintendent.

The fellow had not much to offer. "B. Jonas," he mused, rubbing a pointed jaw. "That office was there before I took this job. Never saw the man who works there, but he mostly comes in at night. Rent is paid promptly the first of every month, so we don't bother the gent."

"Can you describe the man?"

The super shook his head. "No, can't say that I can." He frowned at a sudden thought. "Come to think of it, I never laid eyes on him."

"Thank you," said Doc, exiting the building.

The bronze man went in search of a police call box and asked Headquarters to be on the lookout for a man whose clothes and exposed skin were a ghostly white.

"It will look as if he had been encrusted in salt."

After Doc hung up, Long Tom said, "That chemical deposited something on the guy who got away, didn't it?"

"Yes."

"Shouldn't we be crusting up, too?"

"Look at your clothes."

Long Tom peered downward, winced. His suit had turned as white as if he had rolled about in a salt pan.

He looked back at Doc Savage, who was unaffected.

"Your duds seem fine."

"Treated with a chemical that prevents the white fog from precipitating."

A few minutes later, Monk Mayfair pulled up in Doc's sedan and they piled in.

Doc apprised Monk of developments.

The simian chemist asked dubiously, "Does that mean we're gettin' somewhere?"

"That depends," said Doc.

"On what?"

"On whether the police can trace the man who fled."

THEY found him, all right. Not an hour later. He had walked several blocks, and was seen slipping into the Metrolite Hotel.

They drove over there, and were met by a Detective Sergeant Markham.

"Cardona told me to expect you, Mr. Savage," said Markham.

"Where is he?"

"Room 334. Lives here. Has for a couple of years now. Name's Harry Vincent, or at least that's what he calls himself."

Doc went to the desk clerk.

"What can you tell us about Harry Vincent?"

The man did not have to think very hard. "Not much. Quiet fella. Comes and goes. Doesn't say a lot. Think he's a drummer, or some kind of salesman. Never talks about his work. Friendly sort, though."

Markham grunted. "No visible means of support. We can run him in on that alone."

They took the elevator to Vincent's floor and knocked. There was no answer.

Markham stepped up and hit the door with his truncheon. The panel groaned.

"Police! Open up, Vincent. We know you're in there!"

Still no response.

Doc Savage drew back and seemed to be about to turn away. Then he reversed course and hit the door with one foot, smashing the lock.

The panel burst inward, its latch destroyed. The force of the bronze man's aimed kick literally ripped loose the upper hinge so that the door ended up hanging askew.

Markham rushed in, Police Positive drawn.

They searched the room, but found only one trace of the missing man. His coat and trousers, hat and shoes. All encrusted with a salty residue.

Dresser drawers were thrown open and some articles of clothing had spilled out. Ties and handkerchiefs mostly. They were not gaudy, as might be worn by a typical hood, but reserved and tasteful.

"Packed in a hurry," decided Markham.

"Means he skedaddled," said Long Tom.

"But where to?" grunted Monk.

A check of the lobby produced the information that Harry Vincent had not been seen exiting the Metrolite.

"Might have run out the back way," suggested the hotel detective.

"I'll have the dragnet spread," vowed Markham. "We'll get him."

But they failed utterly to discover any trace of the fellow.

Back in the lobby, Doc Savage led his men back to their sedan, saying, "Long Tom, best to get over to the radio station before it gets too late. Monk and I will return to headquarters."

AS the sedan rolled away, watchful eyes stared down from behind the parted window blinds of a high hotel room.

Withdrawing, Clyde Burke turned to Harry Vincent, who had emerged from the shower and was toweling what he could of the white crust that had stained his exposed skin and hair.

"Good thing I rented this extra room in case of trouble," he remarked.

Harry nodded. "Things ought to pop when Doc Savage figures out that message I left."

"Think he'll crack it?"

"He is said to be a genius at most disciplines."

Clyde grunted, "Doc Savage is all metal and as bright as a penny, I'll give him that."

The telephone rang and Clyde answered it. It was the familiar voice of Burbank, The Shadow's night contact man.

"Instructions."

"Go ahead," Clyde prompted.

"Slip out back way at earliest opportunity. Register at reserve hotel. Engage separate rooms. Await contact. Our man incommunicado for foreseeable future."

Burbank hung up and Clyde turned to Harry Vincent.

"Guess we pack all over again. According to Burbank, Rutledge Mann is out of commission."

Worry overtook Harry's handsome face. "Between the Funeral Director and Doc Savage, The Shadow's organization is taking a real beating."

"If I know The Shadow," Clyde declared, "he will turn the tables on the both of them."

Hastily, they began throwing their guns and dwindling supply of clothes into traveling bags.

Chapter XXXV

SURPRISE VISITOR

A T DOC SAVAGE'S headquarters, the bronze man handed Monk the now-blank sheet of paper and requested, "See if you can bring out the lost writing with chemicals."

"Gotcha." Monk ran the note into the big laboratory and began mixing solutions.

Meanwhile, Doc Savage sat down at his desk table, drew a pad of paper and applied sharp pencil lead to it.

Working entirely from memory, he transcribed the enigmatic message exactly as it stood before it had faded into oblivion.

The rendering was perfect. Doc had mimicked the handwriting, too, in case it would prove significant. His memory was phenomenal.

Then, working silently, he attempted to crack the code. It was not simple, nor was it terribly hard. It was a variation on a known substitution code, which permitted a knowledgeable reader to translate it rapidly, but was designed to defeat unfriendly eyes by virtue of the fact that the writing vanished within a minute of perusal.

Translated, it read:

> Doc Savage
> If you are reading this, you richly deserve your reputation.
> Although you rebuffed George Clarendon's overtures, we have common cause. As a gesture of my goodwill toward you, I share the following.

The Funeral Director is known to me. There is a clue to his identity in his chosen profession.

Beware of visitors bearing unexpected tidings.

I await Marsland's safe return. Permit no harm to come to him while in your custody.

The missive was unsigned.

Doc's startled trilling brought Monk Mayfair running.

"What's up, Doc?"

The bronze man handed him the translated message.

Monk whistled, whether in admiration of the bronze man's mental feat, or from the contents of the translated message, was uncertain.

"What's he tryin' to tell us?"

"That The Shadow is one step ahead of us."

"Slippery cuss."

"The Shadow is an exceedingly cunning individual," admitted Doc. "He will be difficult to run to earth."

"I didn't get far with the piece of paper," Monk reported. "That vanishin' ink is special stuff; the usual reagents won't bring it out again."

"No matter."

THE PHONE rang. It was Mike Durwell.

"A visitor to see you. Says he's related to an old friend of yours, a gent named Coffern."

Doc brightened uncharacteristically. "His full name?"

"Ernest Coffern, brother to Jerome."

"Send him up," directed Doc. "But look into his background and report what you discover."

"Already did. A man by that name is listed in the telephone directory. Lives out on Long Island. City Directory says he's retired."

"Thank you," said Doc, hanging up.

"Since when is Durwell screenin' our visitors?" wondered Monk.

"It is part of his job," supplied Doc. "He has established a screening office to intercept unwanted visitors."

"Yeah, we're gettin' quite a rep at that. Say, wasn't Jerome Coffern that chemistry tutor you had, the one that got killed a while back?"*

"Yes, but I was not aware that he had a brother."

"You think he's a phony?"

Doc Savage said, "Let us see what he has to say, before jumping to hasty conclusions."

WHILE they waited for the visitor to ascend in the elevator, Doc Savage got busy at the great table which served as his desk. Moving an ink blotter aside, he revealed a square of frosted glass—an ingenious television receiver. It was wired to a hidden camera built into the corridor outside.

Doc snapped a switch, and the frosted glass pane became illuminated. It showed the plain, modernistic corridor and the elevator doors.

"Workin' just dandy," marveled Monk.

Doc said nothing. The device was one that he and Long Tom had perfected and was easily ten years ahead of anything in commercial development at present.

Clearly visible thanks to the transmitter's advanced iconoscope, the elevator door indicator arrow showed that the car was nearing the eighty-sixth floor. It stopped. The door rolled aside.

Out stepped a man who even in the black-and-white image looked as if he had seen many years. His walk was spry, but his hair had a faded quality that suggested it was either gray or white. His clean-shaven features were by contrast as smooth as a much younger man's.

Monk offered, "I'll let him in."

---

* *The Land of Terror.*

Going to the door, the simian chemist threw it open without waiting for a knock.

The visitor, who had been on the verge of applying his knuckles, started. For suddenly the plain bronze door framed a vision that might have stepped out of an African jungle.

The man looked as if he wanted to take flight. His eyes grew round.

Monk reached out a long arm, and took the new arrival by one thin forearm, piloting the oldster into the reception room.

"Here he is, Doc," presented Monk.

The man had his hat in his hands, and was all but crushing the felt crown in bony fingers. That he was advanced in years was obvious from the way he carried his old bones, but his face was unnaturally smooth, entirely devoid of wrinkles.

"Mr. Savage? Very pleased to meet you. My name is Ernest Coffern. My brother was—"

Doc spoke up. "Jerome, who was one of my teachers."

The nervousness fled the visitor's smooth-shaven features and he managed a crooked smile.

"Jerome spoke of you often. In unusually high terms, I might add. My late brother was a leader in his field, but he said that you had overmastered him in a very short time."

"Please be seated," said Doc, ignoring the flattery.

The old man availed himself of a comfortable leather chair. Monk took up a position beside the windows, and folded his hairy arms, his skepticism melting somewhat.

Doc stated, "Jerome Coffern never mentioned having a brother."

"He was rather private, as you know. But it is no surprise to me. When we set out upon our paths in life, he remained in this area, while I lived for a time in Philadelphia. Jerome pursued the sciences, in which I also dabbled as a youth, while I went into business."

"What business?" queried Doc.

Coffern smiled. "Many businesses. I am somewhat of a gadfly. Building up and selling enterprises as my interests shift. I am presently at liberty. Which is to say, I have retired. When my brother passed away in such a horrible fashion, I naturally came up for his funeral. Looking about, I decided I would relocate to Long Island."

Doc nodded. "What brings you to see me today?"

"As you might imagine of someone with my background, I have amassed a respectable pile of wealth. Much like my brother, I have lived a substantially private life. But I am not unknown. I fear that, because of my substantial holdings in life, this strange person who appears to be felling men of means may target me next. Knowing of your deep affection for my late brother, I thought to come to you for assistance."

"Have you been threatened?" asked Doc.

The old man hesitated. He ran nervous fingers through his hair, which was the gray of old cotton.

"This came by post, yesterday."

Tendering an envelope, the visitor resumed his seat.

The letter contained within was short and to the point:

> Ernest Coffern:
> You have been selected to contribute to your future Final Expenses. You will therefore withdraw the sum of one quarter million dollars from your bank account, and leave a green light in your attic window. Thereby will I know that you have acceded to my thoughtful request.
> If this green light has been lit, I will write you again and tell you where to deposit your Final Expenses.

The letter was signed, *The Shadow.*

By this time Monk Mayfair had sidled over to the desk, and read along over Doc's shoulder.

"Blast me," he muttered. "According to this, The Shadow is another name for the Funeral Director."

Ernest Coffern looked up, one eyebrow quirking, and asked, "I beg your pardon?"

Doc explained, "Other men have been put in your position. But their letters were signed by a person calling himself the Funeral Director."

Coffern considered that a moment, rubbed his smooth chin and offered this, "The letter did say something about final expenses. Is that not normally the term associated with the cost of interring a deceased person?"

"It is," admitted Doc. "But the threat letters previously discovered have never been signed by The Shadow."

The bronze man glanced back at the note, remarked, "The ink used here is black."

Again, Coffern quirked a grayish eyebrow.

Doc supplied, "It has come to our attention that whenever The Shadow writes messages, he does so in a vivid blue ink which disappears shortly after being exposed to the air."

"This does not seem to be the case in this instance," allowed Coffern. "Otherwise, I do not know what to make of any of it."

Doc suggested, "Perhaps The Shadow is another name for the Funeral Director, after all. It may be that he did not care to take a chance that the ink would fade before you could read it."

"Logical," admitted Coffern. "That intriguing datum aside, I throw myself upon your mercy, Mr. Savage. Whatever should I do about this wretched threat?"

"You have the money demanded of you?" asked the bronze man.

"I do. But I am naturally loathe to part with it. For it represents the greatest portion of my material holdings."

"According to this letter," Doc stated, "it appears that someone will be watching your attic window for a green light. Perhaps we might accommodate them."

"Would that not commit me to making the required bank withdrawal?"

Doc shook his head slowly. "Not if we catch whoever is awaiting the signal. Where do you live?"

"Holmwood. Do you propose that we go there now?"

"There is no point in waiting, especially if the author who wrote this note is watching your home."

Ernest Coffern stood up, offered a polite bow and said sincerely, "Mr. Savage. I am in your debt."

Doc returned sincerely, "Your brother holds a special place in my memory."

Nothing more was said. They took the express elevator to the sub-basement and Doc Savage selected the sedan which had earlier been appropriated by The Shadow.

His face puckering in concern, Ernest Coffern volunteered, "My own machine is parked in a garage not far from here. I prefer that we travel separately, if you do not mind."

"We will pick it up on our way," said Doc.

THEY stopped before the nearby Empire State Garage, and waited for Coffern to come out. He piloted a rather sporty cabriolet car and they followed it over the Fifty-Ninth Street Bridge, through the borough of Queens and on into Long Island.

They had learned from Coffern his address, but Doc allowed the old man to lead the way.

As Doc drove, Monk wondered, "He sounded like a right guy to me."

"Our visitor showed knowledge of my association with Jerome Coffern not in the public record," admitted the bronze man.

"So he's no phony?"

Doc did not reply to Monk's question directly. Instead, he remarked, "I detect no familial resemblance to Jerome Coffern."

"Old age wrinkled up Jerome pretty good. This brother don't even look his age. That might explain it."

"It might," allowed Doc inscrutably. "But recall The Shadow's warning about visitors bearing unexpected tidings."

Monk made a face. "He might be tryin' to throw a monkey wrench into our investigation," he offered.

"That is another possibility," Doc allowed.

Monk scratched his rusty bullet skull. The apish chemist did not know what to think.

Once out of Queens, they ran through a number of homey suburbs, then passed into an area that was more rural. Early Fall leaves were a riot of colors.

Along the way, they encountered a water truck that was sprinkling a single-lane dirt road to keep down the dust.

The wide truck rumbled along, preventing their passing it. Every time Coffern attempted to slip around, the truck blundered over into his path. The driver appeared oblivious to the polite tootling of the horn. The old man seemed incapable of coping with the slow-moving obstruction.

Monk muttered, "Wouldn't you know it?"

After a bit, Ernest Coffern pulled onto the soft shoulder of the road, braked his machine, and got out.

Doc eased alongside him and rolled down his window.

"There is a turn-off up ahead," Coffern revealed. "It will take a little longer, but it is an efficient detour under the circumstances."

"Lead the way," said Doc.

Coffern returned to his vehicle, resuming his course.

Doc Savage once again trailed behind him and, after a few minutes, Coffern turned off into a wooded area.

This road twisted and turned, and it wasn't long before they lost sight of the car up ahead, which became obscured by leaves that were turning brown and gold.

"Hope we don't lose sight of him," remarked Monk. "We'd have a heckuva time findin' his house in this blasted forest."

Sure enough, they seemed to have lost the lead machine after a particularly convoluted series of turns. The autumn leaves with their spectacular display did not help visibility. The cabriolet was a canary yellow.

Doc was forced to brake and leave his vehicle. He studied the dirt intently for a time, and his trilling piped up briefly.

Monk grunted, "Did we lose him?"

"There are no tire tracks to be seen."

"This road is pretty dusty; there should be tread marks."

Instead of answering, the bronze man lifted the trunk of his machine, and began extracting an apparatus contained in the space within.

Placing this on the ground, Doc threw it open. When the interior was disclosed, Monk's homely features gathered together.

"Is that rig what I think it is?" he wondered.

"It is," replied Doc.

Kneeling, the bronze giant began throwing switches, warming up the device.

UP AHEAD, Ernest Coffern eased his vehicle to a careful stop, after turning into a thickly wooded area.

He brought forth a pair of binoculars, and was watching the road along which the Doc Savage machine should shortly appear.

It was not long before his watchfulness was rewarded. The sedan rolled slowly along the dirt track, as if the driver was creeping along cautiously, uncertain of his course.

The car advanced carefully and methodically, until it hit a section of road that had been strewn with pine needles.

When the tires began crushing the bed of needles, there was an unusual reaction.

The creeping machine literally jumped into the air, almost straight up, driven upward by a blast of heat and fire which tore the machine asunder.

It slammed back to earth on all four tires, which were now shredded and began burning merrily.

The sedan, its canvas top, and the rubber of the tires all began to twist and melt as evil black smoke arose from the twisted wreck.

Ernest Coffern, watching from a distance, managed a tight smile, and returned to his vehicle. Giving the starter a spin, he got the motor going and began coasting down a slight hill, to another road, onto which he turned and drove west.

Behind, evil black smoke coiled and spread up from the funeral pyre for a machine and its occupants.

Chapter XXXVI

TRICKERY TRAP

THE EXPLOSION HAD not been entirely unexpected. Doc Savage had set up his contraption in the shelter of a number of copper beech trees and, since the trunk sat on the ground, he and Monk were crouching over it when the force of the explosion blew yellowing leaves off the trees and sent complaining crows scattering.

"*Ye-e-o-ow!*" Monk yelled as he clapped his hands over his modest ears.

Doc Savage merely turned away, closing his eyes to avoid flying grit.

The hot blast warmed their faces briefly. But that was all the damage done when their sedan exploded. Which was to say, none.

When they stood up, the stink of burning gasoline and scorched rubber had rolled in from the direction where Doc and Monk had abandoned the sedan.

"It's a cinch nobody stuck a bomb in our machine," he mumbled to Doc. "Dashboard indicator lights would have tipped us off."

Doc Savage nodded. "No doubt a land mine was buried along this road, with the intention of detonating when the weight of an automobile depressed its trigger mechanism."

Monk made a homely fist of his face. "That sneaky bird calling himself Ernest Coffern musta set it up!"

"There is no other conclusion to be drawn," agreed the bronze man, searching the trees with his golden eyes. He stood up, Monk following suit.

They listened. Above the raucous cawing of the crows, sounds of a car motor starting and receding came clearly.

"He's gettin' away!" howled Monk.

But that was premature. Like a flash of lightning, Doc Savage pitched into the woods, racing after the fleeing machine.

The bronze giant was fast. He jumped into the trees, and leapt from sturdy branch to heavy bough, covering a great distance in short order.

Before Monk could get himself organized, the bronze man had leapt to the dirt of a narrow forest lane. He was soon charging after the town car, a metallic Mercury.

The machine perforce could not travel very fast on the rutted road, with its crazy twists and turns. It was necessary to slow down often to negotiate these turns, lest the machine overturn.

The first inkling the driver had of trouble was when a bronze blur reached in the open window and seized the steering wheel. His head swiveled about.

Running alongside was Doc Savage, one hand holding the steering wheel fast, the other taking hold of the window post.

Doc had mounted the running board, and reached in to grasp the hand brake. He gave it a jerk.

The machine wrenched to an abrupt halt, rocking on its springs.

The driver—the one calling himself Ernest Coffern—had been struggling to turn the wheel but the obdurate bronze fingers had kept it fixed in place.

The old man was breathing hard, and seemed not to know what to do or say.

DOC SAVAGE opened the driver's door, and took him by an arm. The driver was entirely unresisting. As a matter of fact, Doc had to hold him on his feet, for he swayed as if on the verge of fainting.

Finally, Coffern gasped, "What—what is happening?"

"There was an accident," advised the bronze man matter-of-factly.

"Accident! It sounded as if a bomb went off."

"I judge it to have been a mine, concealed in the roadway to destroy an unwary vehicle."

The man calling himself Ernest Coffern seemed at a loss for comment.

Doc studied him carefully, asked, "Why were you running away?"

"I was not running away!" insisted the other. "I was endeavoring to reach my home, and call the authorities. That blast sounded awful, and I knew I could be of no help at my advanced age. This was the only thing I could think to do."

Doc admitted, "That is sound judgment."

The old man seemed to react and asked, "Where is Mr. Mayfair? Did he—?"

"Monk also survived," stated the bronze man. "He should be along directly."

A few minutes later, the hairy chemist put in an appearance, looking as ferocious as an enraged gorilla.

Confronting the old man, Monk demanded, "What's the idea of leadin' us into a trap?"

Coffern grew indignant at that accusation. "I did no such thing! We were taking a shortcut because of that water truck. It was unplanned. You cannot accuse me of being the author of this outrage."

Monk's small eyes looked as if they were turning red with rage.

Doc Savage gently reminded, "Mr. Coffern has a point. We took this detour to avoid being delayed."

"Anybody could'a bribed that driver to block our way," growled Monk. "And who the heck would stick a mine way out here in the woods?"

The old man shrugged his bony shoulders in answer. "I confess that I have no idea. It seems a preposterous, if not outrageous, thing to do."

All agreed to that assessment.

Curiosity overtook the oldster's smooth face.

"If your auto ran over a land mine, how on earth did you survive the explosion?"

Doc explained casually, "We became suspicious of the path, and sent the car on ahead of us."

Coffern blinked rapidly. "On ahead? I fail to understand—"

"The machine was outfitted to be operated by radio remote control. After we exited the sedan, we piloted the car by radio, observing carefully from a distance to see what happened. This precaution proved to be very worthwhile."

Coffin emitted a short, nervous laugh, remindful of a horse neighing.

"Worthwhile, you say? That precaution undoubtedly preserved both of your lives."

Monk commented, "Doc is full of precautions. That's why he's still alive, even with all the enemies he's earned."

"I daresay I have a greater appreciation of his skills than I had before," allowed Ernest Coffern.

Doc Savage said, "Let us be on our way then."

Visibly relieved, although looking understandably nervous still, Ernest Coffern began to slide behind the wheel, but Doc Savage arrested him.

"Better let me drive," he suggested. "You appear to be under some strain."

Nodding briskly, the man said, "Yes, yes, of course. Be my guest."

Doc took the wheel and clapped the door shut, Monk sliding into the back.

The supposed Ernest Coffern seemed momentarily reluctant

to join them, but finally he climbed into the passenger seat beside Doc Savage.

Engine restarting, the cabriolet rolled forward, negotiating the woodsy path carefully.

Colorful Fall leaves rustled in the trees and made crunching sounds as the rubber tires rolled over the fallen ones.

In the back, Coffern asked, "What if we happen upon another mine?"

"Highly doubtful," said Doc Savage.

To this, Coffern offered no remark.

At last, they came out into a macadam highway, and Coffern said, "Turn left."

Doc complied. The machine rolled onto smooth blacktop and they entered an area of houses that were substantial and spaced well apart.

They listened for the sound of police sirens, but heard nothing of the sort.

Monk remarked, "Funny, I don't hear cops...."

"This is a rather secluded area of Holmwood," suggested Coffern.

They drove on in silence until Ernest Coffern lifted a thin finger and pointed out a brick home of the Tudor style.

"Some dump," said Monk slangily.

There was a sweeping driveway and a two-car garage that had once been a horse barn. Doc drove onto the grounds, and stopped before the barn doors.

"It is better that you park elsewhere," said Coffern hastily. "My other machines are inside, and I do not want them blocked."

Doc backed away from the barn, and all three men exited the vehicle.

From the noisy cacophony of the innumerable crows in the nearby trees, the area had once been a great wood from which exclusive residential tracts had been carved out.

They walked to the front door, and Doc Savage noted the nameplate on the doorbell.

It read:

Ernest Coffern

This, unmistakable proof that this was the home of an individual bearing such a name. Nevertheless, Monk began worrying one cauliflower ear.

As Coffern inserted a key to the front door, the hairy chemist undertoned to Doc, "Maybe he's on the level. That's his name, all right."

Doc said nothing.

Coffern entered, and moved briskly into a foyer that was well appointed. The interior was somewhat gloomy, although it was broad daylight outside. When the man failed to snap the light switches on, it did not seem significant.

Raising his voice, Coffern announced, "We have visitors!"

Turning, the oldster smiled weakly and explained, "Just alerting my staff. They are very protective of me, since I live all alone, except for them."

Doc stepped inside, Monk shuffling rather flat-footed behind him.

He looked around approvingly, noticing tasteful wall paintings, and remarked, "Swell digs."

"Please come into my study," invited their host.

So deftly that it seemed natural, Ernest Coffern slid around a corner, out of sight.

Came a soft hiss, like a startled snake. Something chewed at wood, for splinters flew unexpectedly.

"Silenced gun!" warned Doc.

They took shelter behind assorted furniture of the overstuffed horsehair variety.

"Someone stationed on the upper floor," Doc cautioned. "The

bullet angled down the staircase, and struck a banister, deflecting it."

Monk unlimbered his supermachine pistol, and was searching for a target with his eyes.

Doc waited. He carried no gun. He did not use ordinary methods. Sometimes it was decidedly inconvenient.

Ears alert, they heard the shifty whetting of feet in the back rooms and above their heads, indicating numerous enemies jockeying about for position to take potshots at them. They saw no one.

No lights showed anywhere. The entire dwelling was ill-lit. Window blinds were drawn, contributing to the general air of gloom. Dusk was falling, adding to the encroaching darkness of the house interior.

In anticipation of war, Monk reached into his coat silently and withdrew an extra ammunition drum for his super-firing pistol. He did not share Doc's strict notions about going unarmed.

Doc listened. The raucous cawing uproar of the crows outside was sufficient to blanket whatever sounds the others were making.

Suddenly, Monk sighted someone, lay the gunsight against the shadowy form and let out a short burst of mercy bullets.

The indistinct figure shifted abruptly.

"Missed!" Monk complained.

Rustling noises indicated furtive activity deeper into the dwelling. Enemies organizing.

Doc lifted his voice, "Coffern! Are you safe?"

The cracked voice returned, "They have me! Oh, save me!"

Monk turned to Doc Savage and mouthed a single word, "Bluff?"

"Conceivably," responded Doc, using his fingers to make sign language.

From a pocket, the bronze man palmed a small flashlight, set it on a table, and turned on the light.

Predictably, it drew a bullet. The flash gave a jump, and fell clattering to the floor.

Savage removed from an inner pocket a small case containing rows of liquid-filled marbles in a padded bed of cotton. Picking two, he pegged them in different directions.

They burst on the floor, releasing a gas that volatilized instantly.

Doc and Monk held their breaths, knowing that the contents were a chemical solution that brought instant unconsciousness once breathed into the lungs.

The volatile stuff was potent only for about a minute. After that minute passed, they stood up and advanced.

They were not shot at. But the house was very busy with footsteps and other shuffling sounds. A crash indicated that someone had knocked over a floor lamp with disastrous results.

They entered a room which brought them up short.

It was full of stuffed animals of all types, ranging from foxes to squirrels to mounted bats, their ribbed wings spread to expose brownish membranes. The expected moose, elk and deer heads stared glassily out of wooden trophy plaques.

"Looks like a taxidermist's idea of heaven," muttered Monk.

There was no furniture in the room. Other than the trophy heads on the walls, the space was quite bare.

Behind them, the heavy door slammed shut, and there was a distinct click of mechanism.

Grimacing, Monk hit the door with his burly shoulder. But the hinges refused to budge. The door only groaned. So Monk hit it with a rusty-knuckled fist.

An inset panel split lengthwise, but the door continued to hold fast. Two of Monk's furry knuckles split, too.

By that time, Doc Savage was moving toward the solitary

window. So intent was he upon escape that the bronze man failed to realize that something was happening within the walls.

Overhead, the wallpaper split open. Liquid spilled down. It was highly pungent stuff.

Both Doc and Monk were chemists, so they needed only one whiff to realize their predicament.

"Stuff'll knock you out cold!" roared Monk, and spun for the door.

Doc had his coat off, and wrapped the garment around one metallic fist, which he used to smash the obstructing pane apart. For the window had been sealed in some fashion.

The pungent liquid deluged their shoulders. It fell upon Monk, racing across the room, soaking his skull, making his coat sodden. Both he and Doc Savage kept both hands clamped over their eyes to keep out the reeking stuff.

Eeling through the window, onto the landscaped lawn, the pair ran away from the house, leaving their ruined coats behind.

"Don't breathe!" Doc warned, using as little of the air remaining in his lungs as he dared.

They did not get very far, however. Exertion made breathing imperative. Strained lungs needed to be filled. Sobbing intakes of air carried the noxious stuff that soaked them deep into their lungs. They reeled, went down.

Doc Savage and Monk lay upon the grassy sward, with the rude crows calling loudly in the background as if in mockery. Their fingers moved feebly. But that was all.

Chapter XXXVII

THE TRAP IN A TRAP

TWO OR THREE minutes later, the man calling himself Ernest Coffern, flanked by two others, approached gingerly.

Doc Savage and Monk Mayfair were not able to move to any significant degree. They could, however, understand what was being said.

An unfamiliar voice said roughly, "Look at them two! A bronze-plated sucker and his stupid stooge!"

"Do not underestimate either of them," cautioned the voice of Ernest Coffern.

"Well, they fell smack into it, didn't they?"

"They did," agreed Coffern. "But remember that the buried mine failed to finish them."

"Either way, they're prize chumps. They thought you were interested in saving your own life. Hell! You were only trying to lure them into your house, into the trap."

"What's the dope that spilled on 'em?" asked the second man, who had been silent up to this point.

"A mixture of ether and chloroform, and some other potions."

"You sure know how to brew 'em," said the second man approvingly. "What are you going to do with these two? Savage never coughed up the dough for that lawyer pal of his."

The second man suggested, "Maybe someone will pay a ransom for these two!"

The man they knew as Coffern shook his head vigorously.

"The only reason Doc Savage became interested in us, is because we abducted attorney Brooks. We have far more to fear from The Shadow, who is an old enemy of mine."

"The Shadow!" breathed the first man, awe coming into his jocular tone. "The way he gunned down those torpedoes you hired still gives me the shivers. They say it was a turkey shoot."

Coffern said querulously, "Get the others. Load these men into the hearse. We will take them to the mortuary."

"For disposal, you mean?"

"Yes. The crematorium has been fired up. We will throw them into the flames."

"Want us to shoot them both in the head first?" asked one man uneasily.

"They have been nothing but trouble," croaked Coffern. "We will fling them into the flames alive. Now bring the hearse around and place them in the back."

One man went to get the hearse while someone got the others. A half-dozen men were crowded about, looking down at Doc Savage and Monk Mayfair lying helpless in the grass. Their faces winced despite themselves.

Between the two, Doc and the gorilla-like chemist weighed a quarter of a ton, approximately. Moreover, even in repose they presented formidable figures, despite having torn off their coats and shirts and anything else that had been soaked by the awful potion that had overcome them.

Two men stooped to lift up Doc Savage and the bronze man's hands suddenly reached out and clutched an ankle of each man. So unexpected was this that the astonished pair gave out yelps and tried to jump back. One succeeded in hopping free of his shoes, but that was all.

By kicking furiously, they managed to pull free of the metallic fingers, which was a testimony to how weakened the bronze giant had become.

Cursing volubly, the two men stepped back, and one complained, "My ankle kind of stings."

The second grumbled, "Mine, too."

Then both men rolled up their eyes and keeled over, falling to the grass without further comment.

This caused all the others to draw back and pull assorted revolvers from concealment.

"I thought he was down for the count!" demanded one man.

"Evidently there is more reserve strength in him—and more tricks," grumbled Ernest Coffern.

A hasty conference was held and Coffern abruptly announced: "As your Funeral Director, I have made an important decision. If we kill Doc Savage in cold blood, we will bring the wrath of the authorities down upon our heads as never before. Understand that they have only dire suspicions that these heart attack deaths are contrived. But no concrete proof. Savage is searching for his lawyer friend. Let us take Cranston away. His family may yet pay the ransom. Abandon all others; perhaps they will leave us alone."

"Are you sure that's smart, Funeral Director?" asked a man.

"It is my decision, Undertaker. Now get about your business. We will relocate to an alternate headquarters."

The men did not need to be told twice. The hearse soon arrived, and they began filling it with the necessities.

Last to go inside was a long ebony casket, then the back door was snapped shut with a hasty finality.

The hearse tore down the sweeping driveway, followed in short order by the black flower car. Both disappeared into gathering dust.

The raucous calling of crows seemed to give them encouragement.

SOME time later, Doc Savage shrugged off the effects of the noxious brew, and managed to sit up.

From his equipment vest, he removed a stoppered vial of chemical stimulant and a hypodermic needle. With the latter, he injected himself in his thigh, and gave Monk Mayfair the remainder of the dosage.

Soon, the simian chemist was sitting up, smacking his lips, blinking his small eyes and asking, "What the heck hit me?"

"Were you awake for any of it?"

Monk shook his head stupidly. "I was cuttin' in and out." He smacked his lips thickly. "So what happened?"

"The man calling himself Ernest Coffern is, in actuality, the Funeral Director. This is—or was—his headquarters. They have departed with Lamont Cranston."

"Got away again!"

"They spoke of leaving Ham Brooks behind to appease our wrath."

Monk leaped to his feet, bandy legs wobbling slightly. "Well, my wrath is gonna need a lot more appeasin' than that!" he ground out.

They found their feet, walked up the drive and entered the house, whose front portal yawned open.

Inside they made a careful search of the house. The place appeared to have been used sparsely, for a great deal of the furniture in the rear rooms lay under dust covers.

It was as if the occupants of the house had been away, and had returned but lately.

Doc's flashlight, he found, was intact on the floor. Recovering it, the bronze man went through the house rooms, upstairs and down, finding nothing of interest.

Finally, they located a door leading to the basement and crept down groaning wooden steps.

There they discovered Ham Brooks. He was lying in an open coffin, his eyes wide open, jerking back and forth in their sockets. As they approached, they called to him.

"Ham?" said Doc.

But the wide-eyed barrister did not respond.

Shoving forward, Monk thrust his head over Ham's head, gripping the sides of the casket.

"Hiyah, shyster," he greeted. "Looks like you finally met your maker."

Ham glared intense hatred.

Monk continued, "You look pretty natural lyin' there. Can you move at all?"

Frantic jerking of his eyeballs was all the dapper lawyer offered, so Monk took Ham's nose in between thumb and forefinger and gave it a twist.

"That's for telling that babe that I had a wife and thirteen and a half brats. I still owed you for that."

The helpless attorney's murderous glare became rawer.

"And I'll have you know," Monk continued amiably, "that even though Doc was prepared to pay your ransom, I talked him out of it."

Ham closed his dark eyes in frustration.

"That is enough, Monk," admonished Doc.

The bronze man stepped in, and gave the recumbent attorney a quick examination.

"From the sallow color of your skin and the look in your eyes, it appears that you have been injected with a muscle relaxant."

"Sure," added Monk. "I was just kiddin' you. The stuff won't hurt you none. It just makes your muscles kind of useless. A big dose would lay you out, though. I guess you got that dose."

The dapper lawyer tried to speak, and managed to move his wide, mobile mouth, but his words were unintelligible; the drug also affected the control of his tongue, very much as would a powerful anesthetic, locally administered.

Reaching down, Doc Savage extracted Ham from the white muslin bed of the coffin, and carried him upstairs to the first floor.

They laid him out on an upholstered sofa, after removing the dust covers.

"Can you do anything for him, Doc?" whispered Monk in an aside. He didn't want the dapper lawyer to think he was actually concerned about him.

Doc shook his head somberly. "The dosage will have to wear off. It is too dangerous to try to revive him otherwise. Monk, try to find a house with a telephone. This place does not have a working line. Summon the local authorities."

While the hairy chemist rushed off to do so, Doc continued his search of the place.

He discovered very few personal effects. What he did unearth indicated that the owner of the house was, in fact, named Ernest Coffern. A photo album included pictures of Jerome Coffern, whom Doc had known very well in past years.

His eerie trilling lifted, filling the gloomy house.

This was proof of two things: the existence of a brother to Jerome Coffern and the undeniable fact that the man calling himself Ernest Coffern was, in truth, not that brother. For no likeness of the man claiming to be him was present among the pictures.

Having established this to his satisfaction Doc returned to the basement, and continued his search.

During his initial foray, the bronze man had detected certain chemical odors, even though his nostrils were somewhat impaired by the noxious attack in the taxidermy room.

In a walled-off section of the basement near the coal cellar, Doc found a small laboratory which appeared to be given over to experiments of a gaseous nature.

His roving flashlight also disclosed a patch of flooring that had been recently disturbed. The cracked floor was concrete at one end, close-packed dirt at another.

The bronze giant located a spade and began digging. The toil he engaged in was grimly silent.

DOC SAVAGE was still digging when Monk Mayfair came lumbering down, trailing a phalanx of bluecoats whose brass buttons shone in the weak cellar light.

"Whatcha doin', Doc?" greeted Monk. Then his small eyes got very strange.

A police sergeant bustled up and looked down, commenting, "I see you found a body."

Doc nodded.

"Any notions as to whose it is?" asked the bluecoat.

"If my surmise is correct, these are the remains of the owner of this property, a man named Ernest Coffern."

The sergeant looked at the grisly remains and said. "I know him. Heard he went south to Florida last winter. Never did hear that he came back."

It was impossible to tell whose corpse this was, for the face had fallen into ruin. The man had been dead a good many months.

"I better call for the Medical Examiner," gruffed out the sergeant, pounding back up the stairs. "Looks like it's going to be a mighty long night to me."

Detectives arrived not long after. Doc Savage conferred with them for a while. The bronze man was forthcoming in all that had happened, but left out certain details.

"It is important for my associates and myself to get back to New York and continue our investigation," he concluded.

"Well, I'm not stopping you," said the Chief of Detectives. "Do you need a ride?"

"I would prefer the loan of the radio car, if that is not too much trouble."

The official did not hesitate. Such was the sterling reputation of Doc Savage. "Go ahead and take mine. I'll send someone into the city to fetch it later."

"Thank you," said Doc.

By this time, Ham discovered he could move after a fashion, but still needed help to leave the gloomy brick house.

They placed him in the back seat of the police sedan, and Doc took the wheel.

Once they were underway, Monk looked at his watch and remarked. "Look at the time. The Shadow oughta be goin' on the air any minute now. I wonder what Long Tom is doin'?"

Doc turned on the dashboard radio, and dialed to station WNX. Static sizzled. Chimes signaled the hour of seven.

Soon, a sneering voice came over the loudspeaker, laughing in a way that made the flesh creep unpleasantly.

"That sure sounds like him," said Monk.

"Sounds like whom?" wondered Ham from the back seat, his tongue loosening.

"The Shadow, that's who."

Ham's smooth brow furrowed. "Why are we listening to that frivolous program?"

"Because," Monk told him, "that's who we're fighting this time. The Shadow."

"Rot!" sneered Ham. "There is no such person as The Shadow. He is a creation of some radio writer."

"That's his laugh floatin' out of the airwaves!" retorted Monk.

Ham Brooks evidently was still regaining his senses, for a memory slowly intruded upon his awakening brain. "Who was it who mentioned The Shadow to me the other day?" he murmured to himself.

Doc Savage suddenly asked for silence. The voice of The Shadow was speaking.

"What is behind the rash of men falling victim to premature heart attacks? Who is the Funeral Director? What is his true aim? If you are wise in the ways of crime and criminals, it may be possible to deduce his identity."

Monk snorted. "Bunk! He's bluffin'."

The voice of The Shadow returned. It was mocking now.

"One clue is his choice of residence. Why would the Funeral Direc-
tor pretend to be a man named Ernest Coffern? The clue lies in his
last name."

"Blazes!" yelled Monk. "Is that dang spook psychic? How did
he know that?"

The chilling answer was a flat mocking laughter followed by
the intoned words: *"The Shadow knows!"*

Chapter XXXVIII

INSIDE THE CURTAINED BOOTH

LONG TOM ROBERTS did not look very much like himself as he entered the midtown broadcast studios of Station WNX, which were located in a modern office building.

His pallid features were ruddy, and he had pinned both jug ears close to his skull with dabs of gum arabic. He wore a peaked cloth cap and carried a steel box of electrical tools.

"You're early," grunted the station manager.

"I like being early," groused Long Tom, who was calling himself Jeff Thomas. "Sometimes I get to go home early if I finish up fast."

"See what's ailing our auxiliary transmitter," the station manager gruffed.

"Sure thing," said Long Tom, chewing gum furiously. It was another part of his disguise. By keeping his jaw working, there was less chance that his lean face might be remembered clearly.

Finding the engineering room, Long Tom hovered about the device, unscrewing and removing inspection ports, swapping out vacuum tubes and tinkering with wiring.

There was really nothing wrong with the innards. He had slipped into the station after hours and replaced a sound wire lead with a bad one, then called the next morning, looking for work. He was hired that afternoon. The staff engineer had been unable to figure out the problem.

This was his first day on the job.

Long Tom consulted his watch. It was ten minutes to seven,

the hour in which *The Shadow* program went out over the airwaves.

Long Tom exited the engineering room, and wandered out to seek the water cooler.

Pretending to be unfamiliar with the layout, he managed to come within eyeshot of the black-velvet curtained isolation booth set off in the west corner of the building.

"What's going on in there?" he asked someone.

"Did you just blow into town?"

"Nope. What's it to you?"

"The Shadow broadcasts from that special booth."

Long Tom allowed his features to reflect interest. "The Shadow, eh? I heard of that bird. Laughs like a know-it-all, while he lectures the tykes about avoiding crime. Who is he?"

"No one knows. Talk from the higher-ups is never to disturb The Shadow when he's broadcasting. It's part of the publicity, you see. Some small-fry crooks and others think The Shadow is real. Get me?"

"Well, ain't he?"

The fellow lowered his voice confidentially. "Not in the way they think. He's a voice actor. Although no one knows his real name, never mind his face. He comes and goes through a secret door in back."

"What's the point?"

"I told you—it's all about publicity. The Shadow is a bigger deal on radio than anyone else you can name. But once it gets out who he really is, the jig is up. As in down."

"Guess I get it," Long Tom said vaguely. "Any harm in my peeking?"

"It's strictly against the rules," he was told. "And it's a firing offense."

"In that case," said Long Tom, "I'll get back to my tinkering."

"That's a cute word for it!"

"Ain't it, though?" said Long Tom in a tough tone.

Long Tom breezed back to the engineering room, but thought fast. All of the station's electrical circuitry came through here. Long Tom opened the junction box, examined the fuses, noted the labels, and selected two.

He shut down two junction boxes by throwing a lever. That action threw a portion of the offices into darkness. It was absolute.

DONNING special goggles and using an infra-ray flashlight, he slipped out into the maze of corridors and artfully avoided colliding with rushing forms.

"Lights! Let's have some lights!" someone called frantically.

"Workin' on it," Long Tom yelled. "Stay in place. You'll get hurt runnin' into one another."

That brought a semblance of calm to the place.

In this fashion, Long Tom worked his way to the area of the blacked-out broadcast booth.

The program had already gone on the air. Long Tom could hear the intonations of The Shadow's sepulchral voice coming from a loudspeaker piping the program into the offices.

"I am… The Shadow.…"

The laugh of The Shadow pealed out next, making his skin crawl weirdly.

There had been a door on the side of the isolation booth. Long Tom tried it. Locked.

Taking out a lock-picking set, he inserted two steel probes into the aperture and worked furiously while The Shadow spoke.

"My hand reaches out above the underworld, to pluck men of evil from their lairs and hurl them to their doom."

The weird laughter sounded again.

"Criminals tremble at sight of my spectral figure. They fall before the thunder of my mighty weapons."

Another laugh, harsh and mocking, sneered out.

"He's got that laughing bit down pat," Long Tom muttered.

Finally, the lock surrendered. Pointing his flash ray ahead of him, the electrical expert sprang inside.

There stood a low table, black as night. On it stood a mixer board and a carbon microphone on a table stand, the call letters WNX cut into the metal rim.

But no one was seated there!

Beyond the empty chair stood a door. Long Tom raced to it, flung it wide and pounded down a twisting corridor.

He did not get very far. Behind him, the chilling laugh of The Shadow pealed out anew.

"Let men of crime heed my warning. I bring death to those who deal in evil. I am The Shadow!"

"Blast it!" Long Tom exclaimed. "He's still broadcasting."

Returning to the booth, the slender radio wizard examined the vacant desk. He saw the wire then. It was a telephonic line, leading into the mixer board. Then he understood.

The Shadow was broadcasting remotely, employing a wired-wireless set-up. His voice was coming in via a telephone line from some possibly distant place.

Long Tom wore overalls whose pockets were stuffed with the tools of his trade. He extracted one of these now. One was a device designed to register the presence of current-carrying wire. The indicator needle quivered when he brought it into proximity of the telephone wire.

First, he began tracing the line backward. It led to the gloomy twisting corridor that resembled a carnival fun house. It looked as if it were hung with black crepe.

Tracing the electrical readings, Long Tom found that the telephone wire led to the rear of the building, and disappeared into the thick walls.

Long Tom found an exit door. It was not locked on the inside. He flung it open, and exited into a dim-lit corner of the building, where stood the freight elevator.

Lifting the gate, Long Tom entered and pulled on the heavy rope, which sent the blocky cage rumbling downward to the basement. From there, he climbed a staircase which gave out on a side street.

Standing on the sidewalk, the puzzled electrical genius stared skyward.

The wire in question emerged from the brick façade and stretched to a telephone pole.

Shinnying up the pole, Long Tom swiftly tapped it.

The voice of The Shadow was still speaking.

"Who knows what evil lurks in the hearts of men? The Shadow knows! Men of crime, hear me. Beware! I am your doom!"

Muttering, "This could take all night," the puny electrical wizard climbed down and decided to go back for his satchel of tools. Time was of the essence, but good tools cost money. "Besides," he told himself, "I'm going to need my rig to track down that nasty-voiced Shadow."

The truth was, Long Tom was as stingy as Ebenezer Scrooge. He would rather part with a lesser finger than a hard-earned penny.

He recovered his tools, restored the lights and told the station manager, "Transmitter's fixed up. I'm going home early."

The man exploded, "Early? You just got here!"

"Like I said before, I work fast. Job's done. So I'm finished for the night."

"You're more than done. You're fired!"

"Don't forget to mail my check," called Long Tom as he hurried out of the building.

Chapter XXXIX

STRANGE SANCTUM

THE SHADOW'S WEEKLY broadcast had long since concluded when Doc Savage entered Manhattan's concrete canyons. It was now twilight. Lights were coming on all over the metropolis.

Conversation had been sparse in the intervening hour.

Doc and Monk were anxious to learn the reason why millionaire Lamont Cranston had sought Doc's counsel. Ham Brooks had fallen asleep in the back seat, his brutal ordeal having sapped his endurance.

When they reached the sub-basement garage of Doc Savage's midtown skyscraper headquarters, the bronze giant took the elevator up, carrying Ham in his great arms as if he were a small child.

"Once he wakes up," Monk observed, "he's going to be comin' at me with that pig sticker of his."

"You certainly baited him severely," commented Doc.

Monk chuckled to himself. "I might never have a chance like that again."

Doc said nothing. He tended to overlook the personal foibles of his associates—men who were in their professions rated as geniuses, but insofar as personalities went, were decidedly eccentric.

Monk and Ham had been friendly antagonists going back to their original association in the Great War, where their feud originated over a matter of stolen hams. It was a long, complicated story and did not bear repeating. Suffice it to say that neither man had covered himself with glory. But the going rarely got so tough that they forgot their perpetual quarrel.

Reaching the eighty-sixth floor, Doc Savage laid Ham out upon a comfortable divan in the great library and retreated to the reception room to check his telephone calls, which were routinely recorded by an ingenious phonographic robot which both answered in his own voice and preserved any messages a caller left. Feeling brave, Monk draped the sleeping lawyer in a white sheet meant to suggest a shroud.

He walked away, chuckling. "Wish I had a lily to stick in his folded hands."

When the apish chemist sauntered back into the reception room, Doc Savage reminded, "The ambulance will be at the warehouse to pick up Lee Creece in a half hour."

"I better mosey on over there in case The Shadow shows up."

"I will go with you," said Doc.

But then the telephone rang, changing their plans.

Doc scooped up the receiver, and listened.

"Doc, it's Long Tom. I've cased the radio station. The Shadow broadcasts remotely, through the telephone wires. I've traced the line to a building near the Garment District."

"The Garment District is where our sedan was abandoned by The Shadow."

"That's right! The trails seem to be converging."

"What is the address?"

Long Tom gave it.

"Await me there," directed Doc.

"Right." Long Tom disconnected.

Hanging up his receiver, Doc told Monk, "Long Tom has a line on The Shadow's secret headquarters."

"You mean lair, don't you?"

Doc directed, "Go to the warehouse. I am meeting Long Tom. We cannot be certain that The Shadow overheard the tapped conversation about Lee Creece. He might not show his face."

Monk grinned his broadest.

"With luck," he said enthusiastically, "one of us is bound to run into that spooky scarecrow before the night is over. Heck, maybe by the time Ham wakes up, we'll have this whole case wrapped up!"

With that, they made for the elevator, claimed waiting machines in the sub-basement and went their separate ways into Manhattan traffic.

DOC SAVAGE was the first to arrive at his destination.

It was tucked into the commercial section of Manhattan, which extended southward to the end of the isle. Theatrical and residential districts were to the north. Hence, the night traffic did not penetrate down here.

The street was virtually deserted.

He found Long Tom, billed cap yanked down over ruddy features, hawking newspapers on a windy street corner.

Doc rolled down the window.

Long Tom explained, "Paid the proprietor to let me run his stand while he took a dinner break." He winced, thinking of his depleted wallet. "It's that building over there."

The bronze man eyed the indicated structure without exiting. He spied the suspicious telephone line immediately.

"That wire could connect with any number of offices within," he noted.

"I have everything we need to run it down," Long Tom said flatly. He toed his satchel of tools lying under a tent of wind-torn papers.

"Keep watch," said Doc, stepping out and picking up the satchel.

Long Tom looked disappointed, but he understood the wisdom of the bronze giant's command. If The Shadow or any of his henchmen were to return, it would be Long Tom's job to prevent them from taking Doc Savage unawares.

As a precaution, Doc Savage took a turn around the building before entering. His flake-gold eyes were very active.

Nothing seemed unusual about the structure, except its age. It belonged to a bygone time. Skyscrapers erected since had dwarfed it in size and significance. No doubt only fly-by-night businesses operated from within its doubtless austere confines.

Doc noted a section of sidewalk that suggested a special elevator for deliveries to the basement. This was not unusual, but a rather modern touch.

On the north side of the building, Doc noticed something odd. He stopped. It was a side door, its exposed hinges encrusted with ancient rust. High in one corner of the door frame, a cobweb wavered in the night breeze.

The bronze man tested it. The steel panel refused to budge. Additionally, there were other things about the door which appeared out of place.

First, the hinges had been installed on the outside, hence their rusty appearance. The other oddity was the quality of the old cobweb. It possessed a faint shine in the weak street illumination.

Touching it carefully, bronze fingers discovered the truth.

The "web" was artificial, a concoction of rubber cement. It was the same artifice that had made the B. Jonas office door appear to be disused.

Picking the rusty lock might or might not accomplish anything. The steel panel appeared not to have been disturbed in a decade, and the inner lock mechanism might be inoperative.

The bronze man began to scrutinize the door frame. His metallic fingers looked as though they could be used for cold chisels, but they possessed uncanny sensitivity. He brought them into play.

Feeling around the edges of the frame, Doc found something that felt like a fat quarter. This was serrated, and inset so that it could not be detected by casual inspection, but rather discovered by touch alone.

The serrations suggested a movable wheel, so the bronze man thumbed the edge. It turned. There came a faint click.

To his mild surprise, the door opened. Contrary to its hinge arrangement, it opened inward, not outward as might be expected. The outer hinges were false, as false as the cobwebs of rubber cement.

Cautiously, Doc held the door open, slipped inside and shut it behind him. He found himself in a blind corridor. There was no light, so he flicked on his flash ray. This disclosed the fact that the corridor had no ceiling fixtures, nor doors of any kind.

Regardless, the bronze giant advanced. He moved carefully, making almost no sound, flash ray sweeping, golden eyes searching.

At one end of the strange corridor, an iron heat register was set in the dusty floor.

This was larger than the normal apparatus, and was fitted with a serrated wheel which turned the louver blades of the vent. It appeared very old, possibly a relic of the days before steam heat predominated.

Kneeling, Doc turned the wheel, opening the vents. Down sprayed his flash beam, questing.

The light appeared to land on a rug that was the color of sable. Rugs are not a common office building basement furnishing, so he widened the beam of his hand torch and shifted his position. The light appeared to gleam off a wall that was as black as polished onyx. Undoubtedly enameled.

This appeared to pique the bronze man's curiosity, and he set down the flashlight, leaving the beam on, and plucked from his vest a small screwdriver.

This Doc used to remove the screws that held the register in place on the floor. Removing them all, he inserted bronze digits into the open spaces framing the vent and, exerting himself, carefully lifted the entire mechanism.

This he set aside, and used his flash ray again. The light, now fully wide, exposed what appeared to be a black-walled laboratory of some sort. Glass beakers and retorts gleamed when the beam touched them.

Pocketing the flash, Doc sat on the edge of the aperture so that his feet were dangling below, then dropped free, grasping the hardwood edge with strong fingers.

Dangling for a moment, he let go.

The bronze man landed lightly on the black rug, and paused, listening.

He detected no sound of breathing nor any other indications of occupation.

Flashlight out again, Doc drove the beam around.

There was no question that this was a laboratory, but of a type that might be found in a police criminal investigation department. A glass-topped work table stood in the center, and in one corner squatted a deep sink molded of coal-colored porcelain. There were tools used in ballistics tests such as a helixometer, which was employed to measure the rifling of gun barrels, as well as various compound microscopes. There was also a chemical section, suitable for testing for poison or to reveal invisible inks in secret messages.

All four walls were faced with shiny black enamel, but one was pierced by a sable curtain.

Moving toward this, Doc found that it parted in the middle, and so passed into another room.

The walls of this space were also black, but not shiny like those of the laboratory. The sable rug absorbed the sound of his careful footsteps.

There was not much furniture in the main room. An ebony desk, over which hung a droplight. Beside it was a coffer of similar hue. There was also a filing cabinet.

Roving his light around, Doc turned on the droplight. To his surprise, it emitted a cool blue spray that painted the surrounding darkness with an eerie and spectral illumination.

There was no doubting the nature of the place. This was the secret hideaway of The Shadow!

It was as weird a chamber as might be imagined. It was not spacious, but the combination of black walls, floor and furniture—even the ceiling was black—made it seem much larger. The effect was as if one stood in the infinite blackness of interstellar space, unanchored to any physical reality.

Looking downward gave the bronze man the unsettling sensation of floating above an impossibly deep abyss. He shook off the feeling.

Doc took the chair and began taking inventory of the desk items. There was a strange clock, which consisted of three concentric circles, each marked with numbers. The clock was electrical in nature. The revolving of the concentric circles lined up the calibrated digits denoting hour, minute and seconds in such a way as to display the time.

There was an ink well, and a fountain pen. Doc examined both and made a mark on the tip of one finger with the pen. The ink was very blue and almost immediately faded from sight. More proof that this was the abode of the mysterious Shadow.

Standing up, Doc went to the coffer next. He had to use his flash to examine the exterior, for even under the weird azure light its ebony surfaces were difficult to discern.

It appeared to be a repository for something, but there was no lock. That in itself was suspicious. Doc felt around carefully, and brought out a steel probe. The probe brought to light a small red wire, which suggested a booby trap or alarm.

The bronze giant had carried in Long Tom's satchel of electrical tools and used several items to disarm the booby trap. One was a pair of pliers, the gripping snouts of which were extremely long and thin.

Doc did this successfully. Once that was safely accomplished, he managed to open the coffer.

Within were a number of heavy tomes, bound in black leather. They resembled ledgers. He opened one.

Inside the massive volume, he discovered carefully inscribed writing. Doc perused the first few pages, grew absorbed by what he discovered, and carried the massive tome over to the ebon desk and laid it open.

Doc Savage began reading. As he skimmed along, his eerie trilling emerged from his parted lips, rising and falling tunelessly, exhibiting its uncanny ventriloquial qualities, seeming to sound in the blue atmosphere like the product of a creature from another sphere.

Chapter XL

THE SHADOW LEARNS

A BLACK-AND-WHITE TAXICAB eased along the waterfront district on the Manhattan side of the Hudson River.

There, piers, covered wharfs and brick warehouses bulked somberly in the night. The taxi moved toward a great covered wharf jutting out onto the river. Small waves whacked the stout pilings.

The two-tone machine slowed as brakes were applied, then it ground to a silent halt. A shapeless black blot detached itself from the front door, which closed noiselessly. It seemed to lengthen itself, and was taken into the gloom cast by the warehouse structure.

Flitting like an inky fragment of night, it made a silent reconnoiter of the place. It paused at a side door, testing the lock, but moved on, evidently dissuaded from attempting to enter by that means.

Finally, it reached the river end, where it came to the massive doors beneath the faded sign reading:

HIDALGO TRADING COMPANY

The place was devoid of windows, but there must have been loopholes or some other artifice such an an electric eye for, no sooner had The Shadow slipped onto the wide, sloping apron of concrete that served as a ramp for amphibious aircraft, than floodlights of tremendous power came on. Not only did they bathe the structure in a glare like sunlight, but also the water for hundreds of yards in every direction was illuminated like a night baseball field.

This eye-searing glow painted his dark-draped form.

With a weird twist, The Shadow faded out of the scalding glare.

The darkness had hardly swallowed him, however, when the phantom form poised on the riverbank for an instant, then slipped into the cold, turbulent water.

The great black hat vanished as The Shadow began swimming. The form which shot through the water, driven by powerful strokes, was black as the liquid given off by an octopus. Indeed, the figure itself was remindful of the devil-fish in its shapelessness, although instead of one eye, it had two. Both glowed like burning coals.

The Shadow reached the boat landing stage beside the warehouse on its far side, but did not clamber upon it. Hovering close to the edge, he studied every detail of the platform, which floated on sealed oil drums.

The platform was wired with an alarm! The slightest weight placed upon it would actuate an indicator inside the warehouse. The contacts and wires of the alarm apparatus were cleverly concealed. But The Shadow had seen them.

The dark smear that was The Shadow floated along the platform edge, skillful fingers ferreting out the secrets of the wiring.

A guard suddenly appeared on the floating platform, plainly visible in the floodlights. He looked out across the water, toward the sound of a passing speedboat. A moment later, he turned his eyes downward. He saw nothing but a ragged spot of shadow, which seemed to be drifting silently along the concrete facing of the warehouse. The man, curious, watched it until it disappeared, seeming to slowly sink beneath the surface.

The Shadow reappeared on the opposite side of the warehouse. He had dived under some pilings. Like a bucketful of black ink dumped into the heaving, uneasy waters, he haunted this side of the structure.

The warehouse was quite a large one. Evidently, it had been a steamship pier at one time, although hardly one that serviced the giant greyhounds of the ocean-going class, before being converted to this modern use as a seaplane hangar.

There was a door high up on the structure's side, a solitary steel panel that ran along a rusty track bolted to the outside of the old edifice. Above it jutted a wooden framework for a block-and-tackle arrangement. Doubtless, this was a relic of the days when cargo was conveyed by deck crane between the former steamship pier and a docked vessel.

No stairs of any kind led up to the blank panel. It no doubt opened onto the upper rafters of the warehouse.

Beneath this portal, The Shadow paused, treading water. The door was closed. Black-gloved hands drew from beneath a sable cloak several sections of hollow steel tubing and screwed them together into a long, thin pipe. To this was screwed an iron hook.

Removing a short crowbar from his cloak, The Shadow fitted the round end into the muzzle of one automatic. Then he took the weapon into his teeth.

Quickly, he stripped off his dark gloves, revealing long-fingered hands possessed of undeniable sinewy strength and a flashing fire-opal ring. Gloves vanished into concealed pockets.

The Shadow's robed arms shot upward, hoisting the complicated contrivance.

A moment later, the hook engaged the wooden crosspiece framework of the block and tackle. The Shadow tugged, testing, then lifted free from the chop. Like a fantastic black spider running up a thread of his web, he climbed the tubing, going hand over hand. River water ran down his cloak hem in long strings.

Reaching the door, he tested it. Locked, naturally.

The Shadow hung before the door, released one hand, and

used it to grasp his automatic, while holding onto the pain-fully thin pipe with the other. It was a feat of confident strength that would have impressed Houdini.

Employing the gun handle, The Shadow inserted the tapered end of the crowbar attachment into the edge of the door.

What next followed smacked of the impossible.

Perched precariously, The Shadow employed his fantastic strength to force the heavy door to roll along its track. Concrete facing cracked. There came a snap, as of metal breaking.

The door rumbled along its track, disclosing a somber interior.

The dark figure of the night slipped inside, like a bat returning to its belfry. The tubing was lifted in, unjointed and stowed under the sable cloak in separate pockets to prevent clinking.

The Shadow found himself among the rafters of the place. The smell of engine oil and Diesel fuel reached his flaring nostrils. Hooded orbs perceived great modern aircraft resting on the floor below, ranging from a streamlined tri-motor to a spidery gyroplane.

Taking out a hand torch, he wrapped one bare fist around the lens, then clicked it on. His long-fingered hand glowed like a warm coal through which shadowy finger bones and knuckles showed as if in an X-ray film.

The light produced was dull and red, but it was sufficient to show that The Shadow stood on a wooden platform. On either side, the platform extended in both directions in the form of an iron catwalk, much like a fire escape.

A soft whispered laugh told that The Shadow found this to be suspicious.

Moving his burning fist around, he discovered half-concealed wires.

Clicking off the flash, The Shadow extracted one of the hollow joints of tubing from inside his cloak and tossed it on the iron catwalk. The tubing struck, rolled slightly.

For a moment, nothing happened. Then the tubing turned

white-hot and melted. A powerful electric current had been turned into the catwalk!

The sizzle of the melting metal was not loud, but created a flash of light. This, in turn, appeared to trigger a silent alarm, for hurried footsteps came running.

Below, a searching man directed a powerful flash beam upward. It chased around among the heavy rafters.

Pressing close to the pitched inner roof, The Shadow lowered his head so that his hat brim concealed his features. He stood motionless as the beam traveled along; the questing ray failed to disclose him.

Undaunted, the man commenced climbing a ladder, by which he reached the catwalk in question. Pointing the torch ray ahead of him, he negotiated the iron trestle, which vibrated with every cautious step. A revolver was clutched in the other hand.

"Is anyone up here?" he challenged.

In reply, a weird laugh rippled out.

"Who's that? Speak up!"

Out of the clotted murk stepped a towering apparition. It was turned, blocking the way, resolute and unmoving, resembling the personification of Death itself.

A pale fist peeped out of the tower of living midnight. On one finger glowed a fiery gem, which seemed to burn with the same intensity as that of the coal-red eyes above it.

In that rock-steady fist was a monster automatic that looked as if it had been blackened by shoe polish. The muzzle pointed at the approaching guard, who froze.

Again, taunting laughter resounded among the rafters.

"I know you," blurted the unsteady guard. "You—you're The Shadow!"

The Shadow eyed the man intently.

"And I know you," he intoned.

The man blinked. "You—you do?" he stammered.

"Our trails crossed three years ago. You are One-Ear Shawn, the bootlegger!"

"You got me wrong, Shadow. My name is Chuck Hatch. Honest!"

Smoldering orbs searched the man's quivering features like a hawk studying a cornered field mouse.

"The Shadow knows your face, Shawn. Do not deny it."

"Never heard of the guy. What are you doing here?"

"How long have you been in the employ of Doc Savage?" hissed The Shadow.

The man gulped before answering. "Less than a year. W-why?"

"And before that time, what did you do?"

The one who said his name was Chuck Hatch looked momentarily flustered.

"I—I was…." His eyes blinked in rapid confusion.

"Speak!"

"I—I don't remember, Shadow."

"What do you remember?"

"I remember being in this place upstate, where they educated me."

"Educated you in what way?" pressed the phantom figure.

"To hate crime, for starters. Then they taught me a trade, but that didn't go so hot, so Doc Savage himself took me on. I watch over his boathouse."

"This warehouse is more than a boathouse," intoned The Shadow.

"Savage don't like us to talk about this place. It's supposed to be a secret."

"Tell me more about the 'college' upstate, Shawn."

The man winced. "I'm not supposed to talk about that, either. And I tell you that ain't my name."

"The Shadow never forgets a face. You are One-Ear Shawn, who lost his left ear to a knife wielded by a rival distiller." A cold gun muzzle reached out and pressed the quaking man's jaw, tilting his head, bringing his left ear into the light.

"You're wrong, I tell you! My ear got ripped off in the train derailment. And I never touch the hard stuff. I'm against drinking."

"What train derailment?"

"The one I was in—the wreck that cost me my memory. I woke up in Savage's private hospital upstate and they put me back together. Fixed my ear."

"With plastic surgery…" whispered The Shadow.

"Yeah, yeah! Savage did that himself. He used a new technique. Said it had never been tried before. But lamp my ear. Looks almost natural, don't it?"

"Yes, very natural, Chuck Hatch."

Relief washed over the man's agitated features. "You got it now. I'm Chuck Hatch. You got me confused with that other guy, the crook with the missing ear. I'm no crook. Hell, I hate all criminals. Ask Doc Savage. Do you think he would trust me to guard his place if I was crooked?"

"No," hissed the voice of The Shadow. "Doc Savage would not trust a criminal such as One-Ear Shawn…."

Just then, the throaty mutter of an approaching engine told of a vehicle sliding onto the property.

To the keen ears of The Shadow, the rattle of its pistons was a familiar one. This was the ambulance which had transported Cliff Marsland upstate, and now was presumably conveying the henchman known as Lee Creece to this place.

The heavy bang of a door came next. The sound seemed to snap the nervous guard out of his trance, for a finger tightened on the trigger of his revolver.

A searing slug plucked at The Shadow's concealing robes, but he stood his ground as if unstruck.

A return blast from the automatic made the revolver jump out of the guard's fist. It hit the catwalk, making sparks. Only then was it clear that the man wore vulcanized rubber shoes over his regulation footgear, protecting him from the electrical current.

With a flash of crimson cloak lining, The Shadow abruptly

merged into the gloom, leaving Chuck Hatch wiping perspiration off his brow. It was cold. Cold sweat produced by piercing eyes in the sinister half-hidden countenance of The Shadow....

LEAPING from the open cargo door, The Shadow entered the water feet first. His black-clad form sank like a steel bolt. Down, down, he went. Then a powerful stroke of his hands brought his figure horizontal. He swam underwater, away from the warehouse, using only his feet, their frog-like kicks propelling him through the water with amazing speed.

His hands took from inside his garments the same steel tubes he had joined together to enter the warehouse window. He screwed these together, but did not add the steel hook. They made a light steel tube about ten feet in length.

The Shadow swam underwater a distance that would have been impossible for an ordinary man. Then he stroked upward until his eyes discerned the glare of the floodlights on the surface of the river.

Up went the metal tube. The Shadow placed the end to his lips. Gently, he blew out the water. After that, he breathed deeply through it.

On the concrete apron of the warehouse, one of Doc Savage's men was scrutinizing the river with night glasses, through which night appeared as bright as twilight. His simian shape told that this was Monk Mayfair. But the apish chemist did not detect the tube, since it was hardly larger than a fat fountain pen.

From high in the warehouse, Chuck Hatch called down, "It was The Shadow, Mr. Mayfair! I ran him off. Winged him, maybe!"

Rushing to the river bank, Monk began spraying mercy bullets with his shuttling superfiring pistol. The tiny missiles perforated the choppy waters, but produced no other result discernible through the night glasses.

Hopping up and down, Monk vented some choice words. They did not appear to help the situation, either.

When The Shadow had renewed the air in his tremendous lungs, he swam again. Later, he repeated the breathing process. Not once did he appear near enough the surface of the river to be discovered.

Finally, long after the floodlights had ceased to cast a milky glow on the water, he came to the surface. The tube was unscrewed and stowed away. Floating, The Shadow carefully placed an adhesive over the slight wound in his side, where the guard's bullet had nicked him.

Treading water, he gazed toward the distant shore for several seconds, as if debating his own great strength and deciding just how fast he could swim without exhausting his energy unnecessarily. Then he struck out.

To an onlooker, it would certainly not have looked as though The Shadow was swimming to conserve his strength. The strokes were enormously powerful. A long line of swirling water and bubbles lengthened behind his cleaving form.

However, he was not forced to swim the entire distance to shore.

A speedboat putting out to sea came puttering along, and The Shadow hastily affixed his steel hook to his breathing tube.

This he used to snag a cleat on the speedboat's superstructure. In the dark, this daring operation was not noticed.

Thus was The Shadow towed in the wake of the power boat, until it neared a dock, and the engine was cut.

Disengaging his hook, The Shadow found the mucky river bottom with his feet and made his way to dry ground.

Had there been any witnesses to his arrival on land, they might have been excused for believing that a drowned sailor from some forgotten river wreck was making his way home.

Striding out of the water the apparition broke down his ingenious hook-and-tube arrangement, stowed the segments away and, from the folds of his trailing cloak, pulled forth his shapeless hat, clamping it back on his head.

The inky cloak, spreading, covered his form like turbulent

smoke. The garment was evidently woven of a light, waterproof fabric, for it had not hampered his swim and showed no sogginess from its recent immersion.

Crepuscular shadows still lay close to the waterfront buildings. The Shadow's flitting figure merged with one of these. His long, supple fingers worked briefly with his face.

When he stepped out of the murky patch, he had once more become the sprightly, rather burly looking taxi driver. So perfect was that disguise that no resemblance to The Shadow remained. He strode whistling down the shabby street.

Into a nondescript drugstore he turned, and entered a telephone booth in the rear. He dropped in a nickel and called a number. Listening, he heard only a loud buzzing on the wire.

The operator told him: "The telephone you called does not appear to be working. It may have been disconnected by the subscriber."

"Thank you."

Satisfied that Rutledge Mann had vacated his office per instructions, he inserted another nickel.

The Shadow was soon connected to a gruff, harried voice, which identified itself as "Donney, Classic. Speak your piece!"

The voice that emerged from The Shadow's lips was not his own. But it was instantly recognized by the assistant city editor of the Classic.

"This is Burke."

"Burke! Where the hell have you been?"

"Busy running down facts on the Funeral Director," shot back the familiar voice of the crime reporter. "Listen, my Wise Owl column is due tonight, and I haven't time to come in. But I got a hot tip. Remember One-Ear Shawn?"

"You mean the late One-Ear Shawn, don't you?"

"No, he's alive and kicking. Now hand the phone to someone free to take my copy, will you?"

"Hold the line, Burke. The late edition is about to go on the press. We can just get it under the wire."

APPROXIMATELY twenty minutes later, a man walked into the lobby of the Olympic Hotel in downtown New York. He was a brisk, thick-featured individual with slightly stooped shoulders and a face which was as absent of emotion as a mask. He wore a conservative business suit and attracted no attention in the lobby, which was filled with patrons thus attired.

In his billfold, he carried a driver's license that identified him as Henry Arnaud, a businessman hailing from Cleveland, Ohio. Beyond his prominent nose and strong features, he bore no resemblance to George Clarendon, or for that matter to the absent Lamont Cranston. But in recent days, he had been both of them!

The prosperous-looking individual went directly to the writing room, which happened to be empty at the moment. Seating himself and producing a fountain pen and paper from an inner pocket, he wrote two messages.

The first one read:

> You will proceed at once to the Lamont Cranston residence.
> Endeavor to learn of any arrangements being made to pay ransom to the Funeral Director.
> Weltha Cranston is in danger. You will protect her.

The supposed Henry Arnaud did not sign the communication. He sealed it in an envelope. Using the hotel pen and ink instead of his own fountain pen, he inscribed on the face of the envelope:

TO HARRY VINCENT

The second message read:

> You will assist Vincent. But remain in the background. Do not make yourself known to the Cranston household unless you think it advisable. If not practical, identify yourself as a reporter.

This missive the man also placed in an envelope, on which he wrote with the hotel ink:

TO CLYDE BURKE

Pocketing both messages, the man left the writing room and entered an elevator. At the seventh floor, he got out and walked down the corridor, glancing at the room numbers.

The envelope addressed to Harry Vincent, he slid under a door numbered 711. He waited there an instant—and someone in the room picked up the message.

Moving along the corridor to room 713, Arnaud deposited the missive addressed to Clyde Burke in the same manner. That also was received by someone on the other side of the panel.

Neither recipient made the slightest effort to see who had delivered them.

The man rode downstairs in the elevator and walked rapidly from the hotel. He turned to the left.

A uniformed policeman, strolling along swinging his club, glanced at the man from force of habit. He had a fleeting, but striking glimpse of deep piercing eyes which played with a hot light, as though they were living coals. The officer walked on a couple of paces. Then the memory of those unusual eyes impelled him to look back.

The cop started violently and rubbed his own eyes.

The stranger had disappeared!

However, about where the man should have been, an irregular patch of shadow lay close to a building. The blot of darkness seemed to flow, to possess crepuscular life.

The officer stared at the nearest street lamp to see if it was casting the weird shadow. It was not.

When he looked back, The Shadow was gone!

Chapter XLI

CONFRONTATION

DOC SAVAGE WAS deeply engrossed in his perusal of the thick black tomes which he had extracted from the ebony coffer in The Shadow's hidden headquarters when a faint series of sounds impinged upon his sensitive hearing.

The first was a grinding noise, as if hard bricks were grating against one another. This was followed by the soft fall of footsteps above. The footfalls were approaching steadily, like a revenant creeping along an empty hallway.

The footfalls were not coming from the laboratory through which Doc had literally dropped in for a visit, but from another direction entirely. The bronze man understood that this section of the basement stood in the north corner of the old office building. The approaching personage appeared to have entered from the rear.

Doc moved swiftly, first extinguishing the blue light. Then he replaced the thick volume he had been consulting, and closed the coffer with care and speed.

The footsteps were overhead now. They paused.

The bronze giant retreated to the adjoining laboratory. In its weird darkness, he waited, holding his breath lest the sound of his respiration betray his presence.

Beyond the curtain, a blue light sprang into life. This was not the overhead lamp, but a mellow indirect glow, and appeared to have been activated by the sliding back of a section of soot-colored ceiling.

The next sound was peculiar. It was the noise of a man descending a short flight of stairs. But no such steps existed within the dark lair of The Shadow!

Hovering by the curtain, Doc produced a slim black tube, a monocular of his own invention. He examined the other room surreptitiously.

There, he spied an elongated figure descending a makeshift flight of steps. These were the four open drawers of the filing cabinet, which had mechanically opened at varying degrees, so they formed a short set of inclined steps.

Once the cloaked arrival reached the rug, the filing cabinet doors reclosed as silently as they had opened, and the weird being of darkness stood in the cool blue glow for a moment, apparently surveying his surroundings.

A rippling stirred the black patch that was The Shadow. The sepia cloak spread and gathered height. A soft laugh, almost a chuckle, issued forth from unseen lips, hidden behind the high red collar of the sable garment.

With a rustling of heavy fabric, The Shadow took his seat.

No sooner had he sat down than the soft laugh came again, only this time it possessed a sinister undertone.

As if divining the meaning of that laugh by telepathic means, Doc Savage grasped its significance. The Shadow was aware of his presence. This was not the result of some cabalistic art, but was more simply explained.

The warmth of the chair the bronze man had vacated gave away his recent occupation.

With a swish and swirl of sable fabric, The Shadow stood up, and took a turn around the room. He went first to the black coffer, hovered over it for a half minute, then straightened.

A sepulchral voice intoned, "I know that you are present in the sanctum of The Shadow!"

With that, black-gloved hands slid into the cloak and reappeared with a brace of heavy automatics.

Carefully, making no noise, Doc faded back, still holding his breath in precaution.

Reaching into his vest, he sought one of his anesthetic-filled glass balls which could swiftly overcome any foe. Unfortunately, the delicate nature of the thin-walled spheres proved problematic. For it was necessary to carry them in flat protective cases.

The bronze man had time enough to find the case with questing fingers, but no more.

For, with a mighty surge, The Shadow flung forward, parting the curtain with his upraised automatics.

Possibly Doc had an opportunity to evade the imminent lead. The various black work tables and counters would have afforded him temporary shelter from flying lead. And his trained reflexes verged on the superhuman. But he did no such thing.

Instead, the bronze giant planted his feet wide apart, made metal blocks of his fists and stood as resolute as a graven statue.

The big bores of the matched automatics pointed at him, and lean fingers began squeezing triggers.

All this took place in fractions of moments. To all appearances, the twin muzzles were about to explode in his direction.

Doc Savage wore as part of his many-pocketed undervest a lining of chain mail that would turn any pistol slug. But his head and limbs were left unprotected. He was not immune from serious injury, or sudden death.

Suddenly, The Shadow lifted one automatic, pointing it at the dark ceiling. The other, perhaps with a trigger that was more sensitive, discharged.

A bullet zimmed across the room and scored Doc Savage's left bicep, ripping his coat fabric and leaving a gouge which began leaking scarlet. He did not flinch.

It was no blemish against The Shadow's marksmanship. For at the last possible instant, the dark avenger had jogged his gun hand to one side, thereby avoiding the infliction of a more serious wound. He had recognized his foe.

Both muzzles came back in line, holding the bronze man under threat of imminent doom. A thin curl of gunsmoke drifted from one bore.

From the concealed mouth of The Shadow came another laugh, this time of high hilarity, an uproarious outburst that told that the master of darkness was both impressed and amused by the audacity of this Herculean interloper who had penetrated his deepest dwelling place.

Doc Savage folded his mighty arms, as if daring The Shadow to fire again.

But the cloaked master did not. His burning eyes, over a jutting, hawk-like nose, drilled into the bronze giant's flake-gold orbs.

"We appear to have a stalemate," suggested Doc Savage.

The Shadow said nothing. His eyes continued to burn like coals. His gun muzzles were unwavering. The uncanny laughter died off, trailing away to inaudibility.

Suddenly, Doc Savage lunged. He moved from a standing position, but so fast did he fly that he became a bronze blur.

The Shadow appeared to sense the move, for he threw his smoking automatics aside and rushed in to meet his attacker.

Doc Savage was considered one of the strongest men ever to live, and few in the Twentieth Century were his equal. But as the two antagonists collided, the metallic giant discovered that the trailing cloak and ebony clothes concealed muscles of spring steel.

Inexorable fingers caught his wrists, pinioned them briefly, before Doc shook one off, and twisted.

The Shadow lifted off his feet and went flying, thanks to a swift foot colliding with an ankle. The cloaked form careened headlong, but somehow through muscular contortion, got control of his flight, and managed to avoid crashing into a rack of test tubes.

Alighting like a mammoth bat, he pivoted, long cloak swirling, revealing the crimson lining in a flash like luminous blood.

This time, it was The Shadow who leaped forward.

Doc sidestepped. Metallic hands, reaching for the man beneath the cloak, clutched only the empty fabric. The cloak tore free, leaving only the high red ruff of a collar, which was anchored in some fashion that resisted tearing.

The Shadow's hat was now askew.

Picking up a test tube, Doc pegged it, knocking off the headgear and exposing the dark hair. Without the enshadowing brim, the upper face of The Shadow was revealed—hooded eyes, burning blue, and prominent nose framed by high cheek-bones that seemed to hollow into a drawn lower face that could not be seen.

The Shadow laughed anew, this time in mockery. But the mouth that produced that strident sound remained covered.

Doc Savage attempted to close upon his foe. He was fast as greased lightning, but his smoky foe was equally swift, evading him again. Once more, taunting laughter pealed out.

Recognizing that he was wasting time, Doc Savage reached into his vest for the case of thin-walled anesthetic balls.

The Shadow also dipped a hand into a coat pocket and performed some rapid manipulation.

The bronze man noticed this, and hesitated, not knowing what to expect next.

Out came a long-fingered white hand. On one finger gleamed the fire-opal ring worn by George Clarendon, for the glove had been discarded.

Doc's eyes captured the tips of two fingers. They appeared to be smeared with a paste-like substance.

"You are not George Clarendon," stated Doc.

"No," intoned the man in black. "I am The Shadow!"

Lifting his thumb and forefinger, The Shadow snapped his digits once.

The report produced was loud, but the accompanying flash was greater still. Even prepared as he was, Doc Savage could not avoid the sting of the eye-hurting flare.

For The Shadow had surreptitiously smeared two chemicals upon his fingers, which, when snapped, produced the unexpected phenomenon.

Momentarily blinded, the Man of Bronze staggered back.

In the unnerving darkness created by damaged optic nerves, The Shadow laughed again. This time the laugh was triumphant, otherworldly.

The malignant mockery approached the blinded bronze man. It sounded like the laugh of doom. Doc backed away, trying to avoid bumping into glassware and chemicals.

When he felt something hard-edged digging into the backs of his legs, he was forced to halt.

Doc had slipped one hand into a coat pocket also, but briefly.

The Shadow noticed this gesture with a quick, birdlike gaze, but the fingers coming into light appeared metallic and smooth.

Blinking furiously, the bronze giant waved his hand before him as if to fend off his approaching attacker. The gesture was weak, aimless, non-threatening.

Unexpectedly, a metallic forefinger drifted out to scratch The Shadow's gaunt cheek with deceptive speed.

A sudden intake of breath told that The Shadow had been taken by surprise. He faded back, fingers going to the injured cheek, but feeling only a scratch. For that was all it was—a scratch.

The black one milled around, then began staggering.

By the time he fell to the carpeted floor, The Shadow was unconscious, the victim of a powerful chemical anesthetic.

It was not the simple magic that it seemed, but a species of sleight-of-hand. For Doc had merely to reach out a hand gently. The fingertip was cunningly capped by a bronze thimble tipped by a tiny hypodermic needle no larger than a bee's stinger, and the impact as it struck the other discharged the needle's contents.

Doc Savage stood in the morbid silence and waited for his eyes to commence working again.

When they did, he went to the fallen form, and rolled him over, revealing the lean, hawk-like features.

Pulling down the red ruff, he exposed the lower countenance, which in the weird light showed a cadaverous gauntness, a hollowness remindful of a fleshless skull.

In the strange atmosphere, Doc Savage's trilling came to life, as astonished as a ghost who had been trapped in a spider-web, winding and winding about like an ectoplasmic imp escaped from the nether regions.

The bronze giant studied the face of The Shadow, a visage that was both distinct and unrecognizable.

Then he did a queer thing. He stood up and, setting a wooden stool beneath the ceiling panel down which he had dropped, Doc levered himself back up into the blind passage, and restored the iron grate.

He left the building, closing the trick door behind him and rejoined Long Tom Roberts, who was still industriously hawking newspapers.

"You were in there a long time," Long Tom observed.

Doc nodded grimly.

"Any luck?"

"The secrets of The Shadow are known to me," he said.

Long Tom looked pleased. "That means we can catch him that much easier."

But Doc Savage did not reply to that. Instead, he led Long Tom away from the sanctum of The Shadow, not revealing anything of what he had discovered within.

When Doc Savage reclaimed his machine, he drove it in the direction of the Hidalgo Trading Company warehouse, where Monk Mayfair had gone in hope of encountering The Shadow.

Chapter XLII

COMPLICATIONS

WHEN DOC SAVAGE pulled up to the shore end of the Hidalgo Trading Company warehouse, Monk Mayfair had long since settled down.

This did not mean that the homely chemist's simian fury had abated. Far from it. He looked like he wanted to chew nails with his great apish teeth.

Monk came charging out of the warehouse side door, saying, "The Shadow beat me to the punch."

"Meaning?" asked Doc.

"He got here ahead of schedule and busted into the place. The guard had a run-in with the blasted spook."

"Hurt?"

"Naw, but The Shadow recognized him. Called 'im by his right name—One-Ear Shawn."

Doc Savage's trilling piped up, low and concerned.

"This was an eventuality I had not foreseen," he said grimly.

"Well, tell me about it!" snorted Monk. "The guard is one of our graduates, and after you fixed him up, nobody thought his own mother would recognize 'im."

Doc Savage entered, Long Tom trailing behind him.

They found the guard who thought he was a man named Chuck Hatch sitting in a chair, looking somewhat confused. At sight of the approaching bronze giant, the guard stood up abruptly, and said plaintively, "I think I winged him, Mr. Savage. I think I winged The Shadow."

Doc asked the guard to recount the entire encounter.

This the man did eagerly, climaxing with, "I know I put a bullet into his cloak, but I don't know if I struck meat, bone—or none."

Doc turned to Monk Mayfair, saying, "Did you discover anything on the water?"

"Not a dang thing," grumbled the hairy chemist. "I took a boat out and looked for blood. Nothin'." He shrugged sloping shoulders. "Maybe The Shadow drowned."

"How long ago?" queried the bronze man.

"Three hours back."

Chuck Hatch inserted, "It was quarter to ten, Mr. Savage."

Doc said without explanation, "The Shadow did not drown. He is very much alive."

Monk's jaw dropped, then clicked shut. The gorilla-like chemist was accustomed to the bronze man pulling deductions out of thin air, but this was fast work, even for Doc Savage.

Long Tom was looking at the still-open cargo door high in the inner wall and wrinkled his bulging forehead. This was difficult to do. The flesh lay very tight against his skullbone.

"How the heck did he get up there?"

Chuck Hatch replied, "He had some kind of a gimmick where he screwed some pipes together and put a hook on the top. He shinnied up that thing like a monkey." Glancing at Monk, he added, "No offense, Mr. Mayfair."

"None taken," returned Monk blandly.

"What of Lee Creece?" Doc asked Monk.

"I left 'im back at headquarters. I figgered he'd only get in the way or worse—get himself shot up if I tangled with that Shadow. Also, I got to thinkin' and decided it might be bad if The Shadow captured him."

Tiny eyes lanced in the direction of Chuck Hatch.

The guard said, "There's another thing, Mr. Savage. The

Shadow called me by a funny name. One-Ear Shawn. Claimed he recognized me."

Doc Savage said steadily, "Did you recognize The Shadow in turn?"

"No, I didn't. He was all bundled up. I could only see his eyes and that big beak of a nose of his."

"Then it is highly unlikely that The Shadow did recognize you, in the gloom of the rafters," suggested the bronze man.

"It was pretty dark up there, but he knew I had a missing ear." Chuck Hatch looked perplexed. "How did he know that?"

Doc Savage had no immediate response to that, for it was a difficult question. Long Tom Roberts may have saved the day when he quipped, "Only The Shadow knows."

This brought a bit of a chuckle from the guard who had formerly been a bootlegger named One-Ear Shawn. "That's a good one, Mr. Roberts," he said. And that seemed to close the subject.

Doc Savage went to the radio room in one corner of the commodious warehouse. He set the dial to the little-used frequency that the Funeral Director had employed to communicate with his henchmen.

Static issued forth from the loudspeaker grill. But nothing else. Doc left the radio on for a time, as he considered circumstances.

"There is still the matter of the missing Lamont Cranston," he vouchsafed.

Going to a telephone on a cubical desk, he put in a call to Commissioner Weston and asked after the latest developments. The police official had gone home for the evening, the hour being late, so Doc requested Detective Cardona instead.

"Well, nothing has broken on the case," Cardona reported sourly. "Anything on your end?"

Doc told him, "We are still pursuing various leads and clues. But in the course of events, we have recovered Ham Brooks. We are keeping this quiet for the moment."

Cardona whistled. "Any word on Cranston?"

"Not as yet. We will keep you up-to-date."

Terminating the telephone call, Doc Savage turned to his men and said, "We will repair to headquarters and plan our next stratagem."

They left Chuck Hatch, formerly One-Ear Shawn, to guard the warehouse.

Retrieving his machine, Doc Savage noticed something at the back of the ambulance. The glass cover of one tail-light had been shattered.

Bending, Doc examined this, and noticed the state of the light bulb within. It was whole and unbroken.

Long Tom and Monk joined in the examination.

It was the electrical wizard who commented, "That does not look like an ordinary tail-light bulb to me."

"That is because it is not," said Doc. Standing up, he directed Monk to get behind the wheel and start the engine.

The hairy chemist complied, depressed the brakes, yet the tail-light did not illuminate.

Going to the trunk of his car, Doc Savage took out one of his special ultra-violet lanterns and a complicated pair of mechanical goggles. He switched on the lantern, which expectedly produced no visible illumination. The goggles he held before his golden eyes.

In the darkness, the tail-light showed bright white through the goggle lenses. Without them, it appeared dark.

Handing the goggles to Long Tom, Doc remarked, "Ultra-violet bulb."

Long Tom nodded. "I'll bet anything that The Shadow switched bulbs on us over in the Hackensack Meadows when we ran into him that first time."

Doc nodded gravely. "He did the same with the flower car that fled the scene of last night's shooting affray. This explains how he was able to trail the ambulance containing Cliff Marsland to our institution upstate so easily from the air."

By this time, Monk was out of the ambulance and contributing to the conversation.

"That Shadow pulls more doggone rabbits out of his big black hat than you do, Doc."

Doc Savage said nothing. He got behind the wheel of his machine, and a few minutes later both vehicles were heading back to the skyscraper headquarters just a handful of blocks away.

THEY found Ham Brooks waiting for them when they arrived.

The lawyer had evidently gone to his Midas Club residence, for he was freshly attired, and had replenished his sword cane from his stock of spares.

At sight of Monk Mayfair, he separated the cane from the dark barrel, and announced, "I woke up under a sheet, with my face covered. I thought I was dead. I nearly had heart failure."

Monk repressed a grin and commented, "A lot of that goin' around these days."

Ham eyed the homely chemist suspiciously. "What do you mean, you evolutionary atavism?"

"Heart failure is the leading cause of death among the lawyer class, on account of they rarely have any. Heart, that is."

"Did you just insult my profession?"

"Maybe. But I was aimin' directly at a certain Fancy Dan who got into Harvard because his father snuck him in the back door when no one was lookin'."

Ham Brooks could take an insult. Had absorbed many from the apish Monk over their long association. He was used to it. But to poke fun at his alma mater? That was too much.

Screaming rage, the dapper lawyer lunged at the hairy chemist, leading with the point of his glittering blade.

Monk lost his half-grin, and bounced out of the way.

Ham chased him, swept around, and severed the back of Monk's belt. Owing to his narrow hips and bandy legs, the apish chemist needed the belt to keep his trousers up. Severing of the leather strap caused his pants to drop, tangling up his hairy legs, and revealing a pair of fire-engine red shorts, which the homely chemist favored during the cooler months.

The unexpected sight so convulsed Ham that he left off his attack, and began doubling over with laughter.

Long Tom, normally not much of a jokester, joined in the mirth.

A twinkle came into Doc Savage's eyes, but he said nothing.

Scrambling to reassemble his pants, Monk found his feet, and was uncharacteristically red-faced.

But, wonder of wonders, this seemed to sober Ham severely. He abandoned his attack, saying waspishly, "Let that teach you a lesson, you hairy mishap of evolution."

"Do that again and I'm liable to mop up a lot of floor with you, you chaser of ambulances!" Monk snarled, baring his teeth.

Doc interposed, "Ham, you have much to tell us, I assume."

Sheathing his sword cane, the elegant attorney got control of his hilarity, and said with as much dignity as he could muster, "Lamont Cranston told a peculiar tale."

They gathered around the attorney to hear it.

Ham related, "For the last three years, the person calling himself The Shadow has taken over the Cranston mansion, and this Shadow person has been impersonating the globe-trotter."

Doc asked, "Where was Cranston all this time?"

Ham said, "That is the peculiar thing about it. Cranston is permitted to come and go on occasions, during which time The Shadow withdraws from the estate. When the real Cranston goes on a trip, The Shadow steals back into the picture so seamlessly that his household staff have never suspected that they served two masters. Cranston has put up with this only because this Shadow fellow has proven that he is capable of denouncing the real Cranston as an impostor."

Doc suggested, "Cranston came to you for help in resolving the situation? Is that it?"

Ham shook his head. "Not exactly. Cranston was going to the police commissioner, who was unavoidably detained. He came to me instead, in the hope that I would take him to see you. Cranston was rather desperate. You see, an unknown extortionist was demanding one quarter million dollars from him. When Cranston failed to comply, a death threat was received. He suspected The Shadow as being the author of these threats."

Doc nodded. "The rest we know."

"What are we going to do about it?" demanded Ham. "It is an outrage how Lamont Cranston has been treated."

Doc Savage explained, "We have a great many problems to solve. The man who abducted you worked for a master kidnapper calling himself the Funeral Director. He has been extorting men of wealth and standing. When they refused to bargain, he has been assassinating them with a gas that feigns natural heart attacks. Cranston's personal attorney, Sydney J. Palmer-Letts, was a late victim, but the reason for his being targeted remains unclear. There are others."

Ham frowned. "I seem to recall Cranston revealing that Palmer-Letts had a meeting with a man named Clarendon."

"George Clarendon is another name for The Shadow," advised Doc, "but not his true one."

"That reminds me," declared Monk, who was holding up his trousers with both furry hands, "we oughta check the late papers to see what's been doin'."

"Do that," suggested Doc.

The homely chemist ran down to the lobby newsstand for that purpose.

Doc Savage continued telling Ham, "We have yet to find any trace of the missing Cranston, although it appears that the Funeral Director operates out of a number of funeral homes in the greater New York area."

Ham nodded grimly, "That would explain the black hearse and the other macabre tools he employs."

Monk burst in not long after, waving several newspapers. "Lookit this!"

They expected the simian chemist to display headlines covering the Funeral Director's latest depredations. Instead, Monk unfolded a copy of the *Classic,* and pointed a stubby finger at an inside column bylined Clyde Burke.

Doc accepted this, read it swiftly.

The Wise Owl column began with a question:

> Whatever became of One-Ear Shawn?
>
> Wise guys in the badlands are asking that question tonight. Two years ago, Horace "One-Ear" Shawn, so-called because of a missing ear, vanished from his usual haunts. He has not been seen since. A mob rubout? Did rivals take him for a ride? Was he put on the spot? Or is something even more secretive and sinister lurking behind his disappearance?
>
> The rumor mill has it that One-Ear got his bum ear fixed and went into a new line of work. A few of his former rum-runners swear they have seen him, but far from his old haunts. Could it be that he's gone straight? Is One-Ear now legit?
>
> Maybe The Shadow knows. No one else has the straight dope. Unless it's that miracle man, Doc Savage. He seems to have a bronze finger in everything from aeronautics to zoology. They say his supreme specialty is surgery. Has Doc Savage opened up a clinic for crooks who want to be straightened out?

Doc handed the paper around, but it was Monk who exploded, "Blazes! Burke is tauntin' us!"

"No," corrected Doc Savage. "The Shadow is taunting us through the column written by his man."

The hairy chemist grimaced and shook a rusty fist ceilingward.

"When we catch this floppy-hatted hobgoblin," he grated, "remind me to cave in his blasted beak!"

Long Tom flung to the telephone, called the *Classic.* He spoke rapidly, listened hard, then slammed down the receiver without saying goodbye.

"His editor says he hasn't seen Burke in over a day. He's getting pretty irate about it, too. That column was called in by telephone just a few hours ago."

Ham remarked, "It appears that The Shadow is hinting that he can blackmail us."

Doc Savage said nothing. He was looking at the headlines now. They screamed about a wave of heart failures troubling the city.

Papers were distributed. One of the leading sheets seemed to have the story most succinctly:

MORE MYSTERY HEART STOPPAGES

Since 6 o'clock last night, the following suspicious deaths have occurred:

Jules "Sugar" Marion, Park Avenue playboy, died in his expensive apartment. The coroner pronounced it heart failure.

Harold "Stinky" Finster, police informant and former bootlegger, dropped dead as he was being arrested on lower Fifth Avenue. Heart attack was the established cause.

Arthur Flack, prominent investor, was found dead in his study. Police suspect a heart seizure.

Monk exploded, "Hey! Look at them last three deaths! We didn't know anything about them!"

Doc said grimly, "Most of the previous deaths were those of men of bad character. Here are two men, a stockbroker and a Park Avenue notable, who are not criminals."

"Unless they're crooked, too," Monk mumbled.

Long Tom ran slim fingers through his pale hair and murmured, "This is all becoming more baffling every minute." He looked at Doc Savage. "Do you think these last three deaths have any connection to the Funeral Director?"

"It is impossible to say without investigating further," stated

Doc. "Ordinary people succumb to heart attacks every day. The press may be falling victim to a growing hysteria."

"We must find this fiend without delay," declared Ham. "But where do we start?"

"I wonder," the bronze man said slowly, instead of answering him, "what has become of Harry Vincent and Clyde Burke?"

"For that matter," frowned Ham, "where is The Shadow?"

Doc Savage did not comment on that point. Normally reticent, the bronze man seemed more tight-lipped than usual.

In that silence, Ham mused, "If The Shadow is so involved with the affairs of Lamont Cranston, it stands to reason that he might be haunting the Cranston mansion for his own purposes—whatever they are."

Doc Savage looked to his aides. "There is still the matter of conveying Lee Creece to our institution upstate. We cannot hold him here much longer."

Turning his aureate gaze in the direction of Long Tom Roberts, he stated, "Long Tom, I have a special task for you."

"I'm all ears," said the puny electrical wizard, who seemed oblivious to the fact that his aural appendages would have impressed a baby elephant.

Chapter XLIII

THE LURKER IN THE LIBRARY

AGAINST THE SEDATE walls of the palatial estate of Lamont Cranston, an irregular blot of darkness suddenly appeared. It swept around a corner and seemed to fade into a side door. The door was locked.

There followed the faintest of scratchings as some instrument worked on the lock. Then the panel swiveled inward. It shut again an instant afterward.

One wing of the residence was brilliantly lighted. Two persons were ensconced in the solarium, talking a little, but for the most part silent in a worried way.

Weltha Cranston paced the library. She was a fair-skinned young woman of perhaps twenty-five. A crown of black tresses framed an oval face decorated by cornflower blue eyes. The frequency with which her picture appeared in the Sunday newspaper Roto sections was probably a more accurate gauge of her extraordinary beauty than anything else. She was watching a man curiously absorbed by the signs of strain his features showed.

Donald Hume, Miss Cranston's fiancé, sprawled in a nearby chair, pretending to read a book, but actually admiring the ravishing picture that dark-haired Weltha Cranston made. His chief distinguishing feature was a lantern jaw that looked as if it belonged on the prow of an old-time sailing ship.

Neither of the pair noticed an object like a large black blanket which had noiselessly appeared and was hovering just beyond the open door. Nor did they see the queer, piercing eyes which ran over them, identifying each by items which the newspapers had carried in connection with the Lamont Cranston disappearance.

Those strange eyes seemed to convey a feeling of uneasiness to those upon whom they rested. Or possibly Weltha Cranston had been considering a question and selected that precise moment to ask it.

"This waiting for word of Uncle Lamont is becoming maddening!" she declared. "Why don't the kidnappers communicate more directly?"

Hume lifted his smooth-shaven face to her, hesitated visibly, then gave a nervous reply which did not directly answer her question.

"According to your uncle's servants, the police believe the original demand letters had arrived at this residence without benefit of stamp or postman," he muttered.

"It gives me the shivers," she returned. "It makes one imagine someone stealing into the home, to leave their sinister demands. What if they return?"

An instant after Weltha Cranston mentioned her concern, the fantastic, blanket-like patch of gloom had swayed out of the lighted doorway.

The apparition flitted about, going from room to room, choosing chambers which were unlit. Finally, it found its way into the spacious baronial library, whose walls were lined with bookshelves, many devoted to foreign lands and their people and customs. It was the library of a world traveler.

There, the shadowy one worked in the darkness, entirely unseen.

When the darksome shape concluded its toil, it emitted a chuckling laugh that grew in volume. The sound carried, crawling along the walls.

In the solarium, Weltha Cranston wrenched bolt upright.

"What—what was that?" she asked uncertainly. "It—it seemed like a laugh, a horrid laugh!"

Hume brushed a nervous hand over his high forehead.

"It—it didn't sound human to me," he declared.

They searched the residence. But nothing did they find. Doors and windows, all were securely locked.

Not quite satisfied, they returned to the solarium, where Hume murmured, "That queer laugh reminded me of something."

"What?"

"There is a chap on the radio who calls himself The Shadow. Makes strange pronouncements on the nature of crime and criminals. Speaks as if he is judge and jury over all. His laugh is very much like the sound we thought we heard."

Weltha said sternly, "If we both heard the laugh, then it was *not* our imagination!"

"Quite so," the lantern-jawed man admitted. "Perhaps we should go over every room in the house."

"I will rouse the servants, and we will conduct a thorough search."

No sooner had the young woman spoke those words, than the laughter returned. It seemed to make the very walls quiver in resonance.

They swapped startled looks.

Weltha Cranston blurted, "That sounds like—"

"The library!" Hume said tightly. "You remain here, dear. I will investigate. Do not follow me."

As the determined Hume rushed from the solarium, the unsettling laugh pealed out again, this time much more fearsome in its volume and proximity.

Weltha Cranston retreated to the vestibule, the better to trace to the source of the shivery sound—or flee the manse, if it came to that. On her attractive features roosted concern, but not fear. She appeared to possess the strain of bravery that had made her globe-trotting uncle a resolute and fearless plunger into wild countries around the world.

Chapter XLIV

THE RESCUER

THE LIBRARY OF Lamont Cranston's palatial home was in an uproar.

The weird laughter of the unknown intruder in black had drawn Donald Hume, fiancé to Weltha Cranston, in the direction of the tastefully paneled room.

Hume plunged into the library, fumbled for the light switch, but failed to find it, owing to his unfamiliarity with the dwelling.

Fate seemed to step in. Through one high window blazed the beam of a flashlight, cast by some unknown person outside. It produced a hot calcium illumination that stabbed the eyes of the mysterious personage within, painting him in the act of replacing a volume on a shelf.

Hume had no time to wonder who had wielded the helpful light. He was momentarily transfixed by the sight of the raider.

The apparition was robed in black, in the fashion of a monk from medieval times. A sable cowl concealed his shrouded features in deep shadow.

A gloved hand lifted. It held a dagger by the hilt. The robed arm snaked backward.

Realizing that the intruder had been on the point of hurling the weapon at him, Hume charged his foe.

The cowled apparition flung his blade, which shot past the lantern-jawed defender, and embedded itself behind him with a dull *thunk!* Then he tried to draw his revolver, but saw that he could not get it out before Hume reached him. The latter was extremely powerful in build, and was plainly capable of making short shrift of the murderous assailant.

Seeing this, the attacker wheeled and ran. He made for the door, tore it open, wide-sleeved arms flapping. Pretty raven-haired Weltha Cranston still stood in the vestibule, where she had darted upon hearing the diabolical laughter.

Weltha Cranston showed herself to be a remarkably brave young woman. She leaped at the robed invader, tried to hold him. He struck her savagely with his fist, knocking her away. He pitched for the front door.

Looking over his shoulder, the robed one saw Hume charging close behind him. The front door was an elaborate, expensive panel of stained glass which had been created by some master in medieval times. The black apparition had no time to open it. He simply held his black-robed arms in front of his hooded head and jumped headlong through the panel.

Seeing the jaggedly colorful fangs of broken glass looming ahead, Hume hesitated, wrenched the door open and plunged on.

Displaying great presence of mind, he clicked on the switch controlling the lights on the front veranda. The sudden electrical blaze outlined the fleeing monk, and unexpectedly disclosed a man who came leaping from the portion of the landscaping which the library window fronted.

The new arrival was a young fellow of powerful build, with a handsome face. He brandished an automatic as he ran. In his other hand was gripped a common flashlight.

The attacker clutched at the revolver in his robe pocket. It was tangled in the folds of cloth. All of his attention centered on the recalcitrant weapon, so he forgot to watch his feet. He stumbled over a low bush, fell down. The mishap caused him to tear the pocket completely out of his robes, thus freeing the revolver.

Grabbing it up, he began triggering it with mad abandon.

Gun flame illuminated his half-hooded face, throwing his twisted features into what Hollywood movie wizards call "horror" lighting.

The powerful young man fired back, then veered for the shelter of an ornate fountain. Hardly was he behind it when a bullet hit the rough stones and ricocheted with a loud wail. Another struck a stone and splattered like a raindrop.

The young man crawled to the other side of the fountain. He was just in time to see the robed attacker vanish from the zone of light cast by the veranda fixtures. He leapt erect, fired again.

The fleeing apparition twisted and yanked the trigger of his gun. The bullet came close enough to the young man to persuade him to duck for shelter.

He got up again instantly, however. The flapping fugitive was crashing away through the shrubbery like some sable ghost of old.

It took nerve to follow the fleeing man. But the young man did it, keeping low and dodging around carefully trimmed trees. He sent another bullet snapping at his quarry, but did not draw an answering shot.

He knew then that he had lost the trail. He prowled around, cautiously, for he half expected each moment to be the target of a bullet. But none came.

An automobile engine burst into roaring life a short distance to his left. He sprinted headlong in that direction, only to arrive in time to see a red tail-light sweep around a curve in the drive and vanish through the open gate. The car howled away.

The young man pocketed his weapon disgustedly, deciding the would-be killer must have had the machine concealed close by for just such an emergency as this.

He was turning away when a cautious voice came out of the darkened shrubbery.

"Are you O.K.?"

The powerful young man breathed: "You bet. I was wondering if a stray bullet had struck you, Burke."

"No," Clyde Burke replied disgustedly. "I tried to beat that fellow to his car, but he ran like a cat tearing out of a dog kennel."

Harry Vincent laughed softly. "Did you get the license tag number?"

"No, it was smeared with mud. An old trick, but it worked."

Vincent wondered, "Did you hear that laugh a while ago?"

"Yes, it sounded like The Shadow, but it wasn't him. That cowled monk probably, trying to pass himself off as The Shadow."

"Did you get a good enough look at that automobile to pick up its trail?"

"I'll need a lot of luck with the head start it got," reminded the reporter.

"Do your best," directed Vincent, "and stick to its trail. I'm going back and talk to Miss Cranston. This excitement should simplify my job of guarding her."

"O.K.," agreed Burke, withdrawing into the shrubbery.

A moment later, the sound of the coupe in which they had arrived could be heard above the steady chirping of night crickets.

Harry Vincent walked back to the house.

WELTHA CRANSTON and her fiancé were waiting near the front of the huge residence. They eyed him in frank wonder and curiosity.

Vincent introduced himself in a pleasant voice. "My name is Harry Vincent."

"I am Donald Hume," Hume said solicitously. "This is my fiancée, Miss Weltha Cranston."

"Was it you who shone the flashlight through the library window, Mr. Vincent?" asked Miss Cranston. "Hume told me of it."

Harry smiled and nodded. "I was coming up the walk and noticed a commotion through the library window, but did not realize that robed man intended to throw his knife until it was almost too late. Fixing him in my torch ray was the only way I could warn you quickly."

Hume offered his hand. "I don't know how you happen to be here, Vincent, but I don't give a damn. You saved our lives. I want to thank you."

"And that goes double," Weltha Cranston said. She smiled engagingly, then added: "You certainly have a lot of courage to follow that would-be killer as you did."

Harry returned her handclasp, discovering with the touch of her fingers that a delicious sort of warmth suffused his arm. That surprised him. It pleased him, and it displeased him, too. Young women, even extremely beautiful ones such as Weltha Cranston, usually left him cold. A long time ago, he had made one venture into the unfathomable wilderness of feminine hearts, which had nearly turned out disastrously. After that, he had vowed never again.

"Mind telling me how you happened to be around?" Hume asked curiously.

Harry hesitated a moment, then offered: "I came here under orders to watch the house. I spotted a strange figure in black slip into a side door from a distance."

"You are a detective?"

Harry shook his head. "Well, not exactly."

"Who gave you your orders?" queried Hume suspiciously.

With an apologetic smile, Harry shook his head. "I am very sorry, Mr. Hume, but I cannot tell you that."

Instead of showing disappointment, Weltha Cranston seemed rather to like the manner in which Harry Vincent showed clearly he intended to keep good faith with whomever his employer was.

"Did George Clarendon send you here?" Hume demanded.

At mention of that name, Vincent started, his eyes widened slightly and his lips parted in surprise.

"You know George Clarendon?" he asked.

"I am not acquainted with the man personally," Hume explained. "As a matter of fact, I never heard of the fellow until tonight, when he called me on the telephone. He told me that he was sending a capable man to guard the estate."

Harry looked very interested when Hume paused, but did not ask for a further explanation. Nevertheless, the man gave it voluntarily.

"Would you like to hear all about this, Vincent?" he asked.

"I certainly would," Harry declared.

Weltha Cranston had become wide-eyed with surprised interest as she listened. Obviously, she knew nothing of George Clarendon.

Hume placed a protective arm around her shapely shoulders. "I have not told Miss Cranston, here, a thing about it. I will have to do that now. I like you, Vincent, and you saved our lives. So I see no harm in telling you, also. You are naturally curious and entitled to an explanation. After all, it is no secret."

They entered the mansion, and found their way into the living room, where a grandfather clock ticked remorselessly. As a matter of precaution, Hume drew the shades before they began speaking.

Hume said: "As I am sure you have read in the newspapers, Miss Cranston's uncle, Lamont Cranston, has been kidnapped. We have been anxiously awaiting his return, when we received a threatening phone call, demanding that Miss Cranston pay for her uncle's safe return."

Hume paused to offer Harry Vincent a cigar.

"Tonight," he continued, "George Clarendon called me. In some mysterious way, he had learned from the police that Weltha had been threatened. Clarendon said he wanted to talk to us. I was not exactly convinced of the man's trustworthiness, so I phoned the police commissioner in New York on Miss Cranston's behalf, and was told by his office that Clarendon was a recognized criminologist of sound reputation, and furthermore a member in good standing of the Cobalt Club. This jibed with Clarendon's representations that he knows Lamont Cranston."

"You told me nothing of this, Hume!" gasped Weltha Cranston wonderingly.

"I did not want to worry you, dear," returned Hume solicitously.

The lantern-jawed man lit a cigarette with a hand that shook slightly, betraying an excited state of mind which had not affected his voice.

"This George Clarendon made a puzzling statement over the telephone," he said. "He declared that he desired my information for somebody—or something—he called… The Shadow!"

Harry Vincent leaned back, closed his eyes and blew out smoke drawn from his cigar.

So George Clarendon desired Hume's information for The Shadow, did he? This made Harry smile secretly within. For he had a pretty fair idea George Clarendon was The Shadow. Or, more properly, The Shadow was, at times, George Clarendon.

Who The Shadow truly might be was a subject Vincent did not trouble himself to ponder very often. He was very loyal to his dark master, and trusted him implicitly. If The Shadow was really a criminologist named Clarendon, it was no business of his.

All this was incredible, but it was no more incredible than the things he knew The Shadow did, however.

Harry jerked his thoughts back to the business at hand. He opened his eyes and said: "The Shadow… I seem to have heard of such an individual. His voice is broadcast over the radio. Miraculous things are attributed to him."

Hume eyed Harry levelly. "Are you in league with The Shadow?"

Harry smiled and replied: "I am very sorry, Mr. Hume, but I cannot answer any questions concerning my employer."

Hume, unoffended, nodded. "I understand. And I respect a man who can keep a confidence, Vincent."

"Thank you," Harry said sincerely. Turning to the attractive woman, he asked, "Have you heard from the criminal who has your uncle, Miss Cranston?"

The girl showed a little spirit. "I am Lamont Cranston's only close relative. When I heard of his abduction, I immediately came to Westfield to take charge of his affairs. The master mind—whoever is behind all this—telephoned. He informed me that Uncle Lamont would be killed if I did not do exactly as I was told. I was scared. I agreed to do what he wanted. His first order was to take out the demanded sum of money—exactly a quarter of a million dollars—and to light a green light in the tower once this was accomplished. But when I set about to do that very thing, I learned Uncle Lamont's lawyer had passed away suddenly, leaving me with no way to accomplish the demands made of me. Since then, I have been dreading another telephone call."

"Evidently," Hume inserted, "the absence of a green signal light caused tonight's incursion."

"That explains it, all right," said Harry firmly.

Hume looked at his watch. "It is frightfully late, but I suppose we should call the police."

"My employer prefers that you do not," advised Harry.

Hume looked slightly skeptical, but then Weltha Cranston laid a quelling hand on his arm, saying, "I think we can trust this man, Hume."

The warmth that came into both her voice and her eyes made the blocky-jawed Hume momentarily uncomfortable.

"Very well, if you say so," he said thinly.

"I say so." Turning to Harry, she stated, "Mr. Vincent, you seem to be a capable person. Where do you suggest we start?"

"With the knife that was thrown."

A hasty search discovered that it had split a wall panel in the library, so great was the force with which it had been hurled.

Harry discovered it, and without touching the formidable blade, studied the weapon intently.

It was some sort of dagger, lightweight and slim of blade. The handle appeared to be fashioned of ivory. And into the ivory, so that it discolored and cracked the material, was burned two words:

Final Warning!

Weltha Cranston gasped.

"Do they mean to do away with Uncle Lamont?" she blurted.

Grimly, Harry Vincent replied, "Unquestionably. If you are to recover him, you will have to pay the ransom that is demanded."

Weltha wrung pretty hands anxiously. "But I do not have sufficient funds. The sum this ghoul demands only Uncle Lamont can muster together. And, even as his niece and sole heir, I cannot access his wealth in order to ransom his life. It's sheerly impossible!"

Harry said quietly, "We will find a way. My employer never fails."

As they considered the situation, a French telephone sitting on a stand rang shrilly.

"Cranston residence," Weltha said into the instrument.

A mordant voice inquired, "Have you ever read Edgar Allan Poe's 'Premature Burial?' You really should, you know."

The call disconnected abruptly.

"Whatever did he mean?" breathed Weltha, replacing the delicate receiver on its cradle.

The man's voice had come over the line so distinctly that Harry Vincent and Donald Hume had both heard every word. Hume was slow to pick up on the significance of the charnel suggestion. Not so Harry Vincent.

"We had better check the library again," he said, suiting action to words.

Harry went to the exact spot where the abbot in black had been lurking when his timely flash beam had transfixed him. Scrutinizing the spines on the shelves, he recognized an antiquarian edition of Poe's *Collected Works*. In contrast with the surrounding volumes, it stood on the shelf slightly ajar.

Harry took it down, only to discover that the book was not a book at all, but a miniature black casket tricked out to resemble a book when seen from the side.

"What is it?" wondered Weltha, eyeing the macabre thing.

Holding it flat, Harry lifted the casket lid.

Up popped a mechanical doll, which bore a striking resemblance to the missing Lamont Cranston. It wore a tiny tuxedo and its head was covered by a top hat.

No sooner had the simulacrum sat up, than its tiny jaw began waggling. It seemed to speak:

"Help me! Save me. They are going to bury me alive if you do not pay the ransom. Alive, do you hear? Oh, woe is me! Woe!"

Weltha Cranston turned her beauteous face from the horrid sight, clapping hands over her ears to keep out the tinny mechanical puppet voice.

"How revolting!" she murmured.

"The devils!" gritted Hume, clenching his fists.

Vincent slammed the lid shut, saying, "The reason for the intruder in the library is now clear. He planted this, intending later to make that call, hoping you would be terrified and mystified as to how it got there."

"He was half correct," Hume husked, eyeing Weltha Cranston.

Together, they withdrew from the library, leaving the terrible presentiment of macabre doom behind.

WHILE Weltha Cranston struggled to compose herself, Donald Hume regarded Harry Vincent sheepishly.

"I guess I was mistaken about you," he admitted grudgingly.

Harry did not care greatly what the man thought, but he was polite enough not to say so.

They were again considering whether to call the police when the telephone rang again. Hesitantly, Weltha answered it.

"For you!" she said, turning to Harry Vincent.

Harry leaped forward, took the instrument, said: "Yes!"

Clyde Burke's voice came hurriedly from the receiver. "I followed him. He went into a mortuary. I'm talking from a drugstore nearby."

"What's the address?" asked Harry.

"At the foot of Wildwood Street."

"Wait there!" Harry directed. "I'll be right down. If he leaves, follow him. Give the soda fountain clerk a message for me."

Hanging up, he wheeled on Weltha Cranston and her nervous fiancé. He told them the drift of Clyde Burke's call.

"Burke is a reporter I sometimes work with," concluded Harry.

"What about calling the police?" Hume demanded.

"There are times," Harry said grimly, "when the police only rush in and complicate matters. I'll decide about that when I look the ground over."

Hume looked doubtful.

"The police have already proven helpless against the Funeral Director," Weltha Cranston pointed out. "Frankly—I have more confidence in Mr. Vincent than I have in them. He appears to be a very capable young man. So we will wait to hear from him before we call the authorities."

Donald Hume scowled. "If you say so, dear," he allowed. But he sounded less than enthusiastic. "If you ask me, you're making a mistake."

"I'm sure we're not!" Weltha retorted heatedly.

Had their position been less serious, Harry would have smiled. The jealousy of Donald Hume rather amused him.

Vincent turned to go.

"You must—you must be careful!" Weltha Cranston implored huskily.

Harry looked at her, deeply moved by the concern in her tone. Then he leveled an arm at Hume.

"You guard her," he suggested. "If anything else happens that forces you to call the police, tell them I went out to search for the burglar, but don't mention where."

Donald Hume nodded in sullen agreement.

Weltha asked, "Have you sufficient bullets for your gun?"

Harry shook his head.

"My uncle has amassed a sizable collection of hunting rifles and pistols," she informed him. "Uncle Lamont is a big-game hunter, you know. You are welcome to some of the weapons."

"An excellent idea," agreed Harry.

The black-haired young woman led the way downstairs to a combination trophy room and gymnasium in the basement. Weapons of every variety from ancient swords and daggers, and suits of chain mail and armor to modern super-power elephant rifles decorated the walls.

Harry selected an automatic pistol of foreign manufacture, a gun which was very reliable and had nearly the range and killing power of a rifle. This he pocketed, together with a supply of the long cartridges the weapon used.

Weltha Cranston saw him to the door and gave his arm a squeeze.

"Good luck," she said fervently.

Harry borrowed her trim little sport coupe and was soon skimming along the macadam highway.

Chapter XLV

THE MORTUARY

HARRY VINCENT JOINED Clyde Burke at the drug-store soda fountain, not three blocks away from the mortuary to which the reporter had trailed the fleeing machine. The vehicle which had been driven by the robed interloper who had infiltrated the estate of Lamont Cranston was not in sight.

They conversed briefly. Harry related all that had transpired at the Cranston mansion.

"Miss Cranston is in a spot," he finished. "She can't lift a finger to ransom her uncle. Doesn't have the money herself."

"Sounds like a fix, all right." Clyde Burke eyed Vincent. "Kinda like the girl, don't you?"

Harry scowled at Burke good-naturedly. "Don't be silly! She's a sweet, spunky kid. That's all!"

Clyde said, "Oh, I see!" chidingly. Then the reporter glanced in the direction of the solitary pay telephone in the back. A crease of worry troubled his brow.

"I called Burbank as soon as I hit this joint," he explained. "Thought he would call back with instructions from The Shadow by now...."

Harry nodded soberly. "Doc Savage has put a crimp into The Shadow's operation, all right. Cliff has disappeared. Mann, too."

"Maybe The Shadow is hunting down Cliff."

"Which means that we are on our own," concluded Harry glumly.

Clyde slid off his stool. "Then let's get cracking. If we're lucky,

Lamont Cranston is being held in that mortuary. Our job is to spring him."

They exited into the cool of the night.

The two young men used a great deal of caution as they neared the mortuary. The place was dark. It was after normal business hours.

They descried a lookout loitering on the grounds when the shadowy individual struck a match in order to light a cigarette. The burning tip of the cigarette betrayed his presence.

A block away from the funeral home, they hovered. Both Shadow agents were armed, but they could hardly shoot their way in without good cause. Therefore, they would have to use strategy.

Back along a high hedge wall, they moved, exploring their way through the landscaping. It was profuse, but kept in good trim.

"There's a back door!" Clyde exclaimed softly. "It would make too much noise to force it, though."

They slipped up to the back portico, around which dry Autumn leaves skittered and swirled in a playful breeze.

Harry felt of the door, calculating the amount of noise forcible removal would make. Too much to chance. There was a small glass window. If removed, it seemed possible to reach and grasp the inner door handle.

"You wait here!" he told Clyde. "I've got an idea."

Creating as little noise as possible, Vincent moved away from the funeral establishment. A block distant, he found the red metal box of a fire alarm. It took him only an instant to turn in an alarm.

Back to Clyde's side, he hurried. They hunkered down in the darkness and waited expectantly while dead leaves chased around them like dried imps.

Soon the wail of fire truck sirens filled the damp air. The clanging of bells made a jangling syncopation. The uproar came nearer.

When the din was at its loudest, Harry and Clyde worked feverishly with the door. Employing a glass cutter Clyde habitually carried, they etched around its circumference, wincing at the screechy sound produced, got the pane loose at the bottom, and tilted it back sufficiently to permit its removal.

Gingerly, both men placed the fragile glass onto the portico without breaking it.

Into the mortuary, they slipped.

All was dark within. They crept from room to room, pistols pointed ahead of them. The place was a web of gloom. They evaded furniture by feel. Most of the low furnishings consisted of coffins resting on wheeled catafalques. The pungent reek of formaldehyde and other embalming fluids filled their nostrils, made them want to pinch their noses shut.

They swiftly realized that these cadavers were awaiting disposal in a crematorium, where they would be incinerated to fine ash.

By placing their ears to the coffin lids, they were able to tell that the bodies housed within were deceased, for the soft sounds of breathing would be evident otherwise.

The clamor of the fire engines had successfully blanketed the noise they had made in gaining entrance. Outside, they could hear the firemen demanding angrily where the fire was.

Two men suddenly appeared inside the funeral home, stepping out of one of the side rooms which seemed to be offices. One ran to the door, where a fireman was questioning the lookout guard.

Harry gripped Clyde's arm. Together, they crept for the back door.

Burke breathed: "They must have taken Cranston away!"

Harry started a whispered reply—held it back.

"Someone's coming!" he hissed.

Two men were moving in the dimness.

"Who the devil could've turned in that fire alarm?" one asked uneasily. "Wonder if something is wrong?"

"How do I know?" snapped the other. "We persuaded them the fire wasn't here, anyhow."

"I wonder—"

The first man did not finish. He halted, listening.

Harry and Clyde had by this time retreated to a safe spot behind funeral drapery. They clutched the fine black cloth, in hope of stilling its disturbed quivers.

As they listened, stealthy footfalls sounded. The rustling of a man moving with care drew near. Harry and Clyde held their breaths. Had they been spotted?

Suddenly, a swishing sound followed by an unpleasant impact was heard.

This was punctuated by the thud of a sprawled body.

Harry winced. Clyde had been struck down!

As he prepared to step out, gun in hand, Vincent was startled by a voice very near to his hiding place.

A man spoke: "I gave your friend a skull-tap with the barrel of my gun. If you don't step out smart-like, you'll get the contents. Get me, shiny shoes?"

Only then did Vincent realize that his highly-polished shoes peeping out from under the drapery had betrayed them!

Harry knew that if he came out blazing, he must start shooting blind. In the crossfire, Clyde would be a helpless bystander. Probably the first to die.

"I surrender," he said prudently.

Stepping out, he handed over his gun to a thin-faced man with beady eyes.

The gunman who took it studied Vincent's handsome features.

"I know you!" he snarled. "You were the bozo I collided with at Cranston's place. What's your game, nosy-nosy?"

Harry decided to make a clean breast of it—but not entirely clean.

"Private dick. I was hired to find Lamont Cranston. I trailed you here."

"Too bad for you," sneered the other gunman. "And too bad for Cranston. His time is just about up. That snooty niece shoulda paid that ransom."

Harry spoke up. "She couldn't. Cranston has his money locked up so tight she couldn't get at it. She would, if it were possible."

"Is that right?" demanded the first gunman.

"Sounds like a story," scoffed the other. "I say we blast this meddler down."

The beady-eyed one rubbed his jaw thoughtfully. "Hold on. Better let me talk to the Director first. This is a new wrinkle, one we hadn't figured on."

Harry was prodded at gunpoint into a spare office where there was a radio sending and receiving set, which operated telegraph-style, with a sending key.

In the better light, Vincent could see that the two gunmen were hard-featured types with the chilly eyes of casual killers.

He was made to sit down. A gun was placed at the back of his upper spine, where the coldness of the steel muzzle made hackles rise on the nape of his neck.

The set was warmed up. Tubes glowed. A hiss emerged from the thing. This was shut off when the first man inserted the leads of earphones into a jack.

The thin-faced radio operator began tapping his key. He listened, hands pressed to the receivers over his ears.

"You gettin' orders?" asked the one who had Harry covered.

The radioman took off the receivers.

"Yeah!" he growled. "I already got 'em. Watch me carry 'em out!"

The radioman drew a heavy automatic from his pocket and bent over Harry Vincent. Lifting the weapon, he brought it down with terrific force on Harry's head.

"That's that," he chuckled evilly. "Get the other one. We're clearin' out of here."

As the other man hastened to obey orders, the radioman went

to a wall picture. This opened outward on concealed hinges, revealing a recessed safe door and combination dial.

Rapidly, the man worked the dial. Instead of opening the safe door, he snapped the portrait back into place, then exited the office as rapidly as possible.

Moments later, the limp forms of the two Shadow agents were lugged out of the back of the darkened mortuary, and unceremoniously thrown into the back of an idling hearse. The rear door was slammed shut and the funereal black machine eased out of the grounds and into the night, motor muttering.

"Take a last look," the driver told his companion. "I set the timer on the hidden fuse in the safe. Funeral Director's orders. He figures if these two snoops trailed their way here, the word is out."

Looking out the back window, the passenger grunted, "Gonna blow sky high. That cellar is packed with T.N.T."

The remark was no exaggeration. For, not ten minutes later, there came a ripping report behind them, and the night sky flared up, throwing buildings into stark silhouette and denuding several tall trees of their remaining leaves.

A sound like low, rolling thunder seemed to follow them.

"That settles that," snapped the driver.

"We're sure runnin' out of hideouts fast," the other complained.

"Don't you sweat that. The Funeral Director has plenty of jack. And more comin' in every day. He'll keep us in grand style."

The hearse traveled on for a time, the beady-eyed man at the wheel and his hard-faced companion grimly silent, until at last it came to the locked gates of a cemetery.

The driver got out, unlocked a padlock that kept the two wrought-iron doors sealed, and walked them apart.

Reclaiming the wheel, he guided the hearse onto a graveled path that wound through tombstones and elaborate statuary commemorating the dead. Moonlight made the marble and granite relics stand out in stark relief.

As they made their way along, they approached a brick crematorium, its fires banked, tall smoke stack quiescent.

"We gonna toss 'em in the furnace?" asked the second gunman.

"Nope. The Funeral Director had a better brainstorm. He thinks these two might be workin' for The Shadow. So they get the works in the worst way."

The other looked puzzled. "What's worse than being tossed into the crematorium to burn?"

The driver managed a particularly ghoulish bark of laughter. It might have been authored by The Shadow himself. But it was too cruel.

"Wishin' you had been!" he chortled.

THE NEIGHBORHOOD of the mortuary was in a pandemonium. The terrific explosion which had annihilated the place had rocked houses for blocks around. Excited citizens poured from their homes and rushed to the scene of the blast.

Two complete sets of fire apparatus had arrived with the earliest of them. But one man, a near neighbor, had been the first on the scene. And that man had been witness to a curious incident.

He had stood to one side, staring at the hungry flames which consumed the shattered pile which had been the mortuary. Chancing to peer at the ground beside him, he had seen a shadow. It was long and unusually dark. Such a strange shadow, indeed, that he had looked around to see what made it.

A man was standing beside a scorched oak tree nearby, a tall figure clad from head to foot in somber black. The face of the man was invisible, obscured by the collar of his coat and the low brim of the large black hat. Only a pair of glowing, piercing eyes shone beneath that hat brim.

Presuming the strange man to be an earlier arrival on the scene, the neighbor had asked a question.

"Ain't this a kick in the head? What do you think made it blow?"

He received no answer—in words. Instead, the fellow thought he heard a spectral whisper. An eerie sort of a sound that seemed beyond reality. A strange, incredible laugh!

The neighbor glanced at the fire, then back—and the weird inky form was gone. This, despite the fact that it seemed incredible that the man could have walked from view so quickly!

The neighbor puzzled over the incident, wondering about the man he had seen. The neighbor had never heard of The Shadow— did not dream that was the figure he had encountered.

For The Shadow, arriving belatedly after receiving word from Burbank, had witnessed all!

Seeing the polished black hearse depart, he deduced its likely destination.

Chapter XLVI

TOMB OF DOOM

PERHAPS HALF AN hour after the terrific explosion, a small and somewhat dilapidated black-and-white taxicab pulled onto a darkened street near the cemetery to which Harry Vincent and Clyde Burke had been conveyed by hearse. A person experienced with motors would have listened to the running engine under the hood and known that it was one of extreme power. But outwardly the car was very ordinary.

The driver guided the machine to the cemetery gate, and stopped. The door of the machine opened. Apparently, no one got out. But an instant later, the darkness nearby seemed to stir as if it possessed life.

The closed but unlocked gate of the burying ground opened and shut without producing any complaint. Previously, it had creaked rustily. Then The Shadow appeared, soundless as a silhouette.

A sweeping, all-inclusive glance of those hot, strange eyes took in the moonlit prospect before him—ranks of headstones, elegant memorial statuary, here and there the hard outlines of a family crypt.

Bulking large on a low promontory stood a solitary structure that was neither crypt nor vault. It was a crematorium, apparently not currently in operation. The Shadow swept in that direction, resembling a black revenant abroad in the night.

For he spied the severe outlines of the funeral hearse parked adjacent to the forbidding brick structure.

Slipping up to it, The Shadow discovered the machine to be empty of occupants. The driver's compartment was deserted.

In the back of the hearse lay a long black coffin. All doors were locked. They would not budge.

The fact that there was only one casket meant that it was unlikely to contain either of his captured agents.

Crouching at the hearse's rear, The Shadow went to work on one of the tail-lights, removing the cover and swapping out the tiny bulb with one of the special ultra-violet ones which he carried in a padded pouch within his cloak for such eventualities.

He no sooner finished his toil when the door of the crematorium rattled as it opened.

Noiseless as a fog, The Shadow faded from view.

His unuttered plan was to follow the hearse, should it depart the cemetery.

But as two men exited to reclaim their ominous machine, they spoke, and the words of their exchange prompted a change in plan.

"How long do you think those two will last?"

"A day, maybe two. No one will hear them, either. The granite is too thick for that."

"Horrible way to die."

"In the days before they invented embalming, a lot more people than you think went out that way."

"Gives me the shivers just thinkin' about it."

The hearse engine spun over; the grim-looking machine wheeled around, onto the road.

Neither occupant was aware of the fact that the vehicle's tail-light was dark.

HARRY VINCENT was the first to awaken. All was dark.

He sat up. Feeling about with his hands, he discovered himself to be sprawled in a litter of debris. He clutched at something, immediately threw it away, for it squeaked and squirmed. A rat!

"Burke!" he breathed.

At first there was no response. Harry blinked, attempting to see in the irredeemable blackness. But his eyes refused to function, or so it seemed.

Listening, he heard the soft pulse of regular respiration. Someone nearby.

Having no other recourse, Vincent sniffed the air. It made him want to gag. Beneath the dank, musty smell, there were other disagreeable odors. A fetid miasma.

Climbing to his feet, Harry swept his groping fingers about. His head ached from the unexpected blow it had received.

Harry's hands, seining the black abyss that was the unknown space, encountered an obstruction. It felt like a wall. Thick, of heavy stone. Cool to the touch.

Following it with exploring digits, he found a corner, and another wall at right angles to the first. This led to another, and then a fourth at which point Harry decided he had reached the spot where he had started his exploration.

There was a door. Cold, metallic. It seemed heavy. There was no handle, however, which struck Harry as very strange. Just cobwebs. Something skittered along his knuckles. A disturbed spider. He shook it off.

Having no other option, Vincent moved inward, where he discovered a low stone block of some size. It seemed to reach only as high as his belt buckle.

Atop the flat surface he discovered a warm body.

A man groaned. Harry stepped back in alarm.

"Who is it?" he hissed.

Another groan sounded. Then a disturbed shuffling.

"Harry?"

"Clyde?"

"Where are we?"

"I do not know, but we appear to be trapped in a stone chamber. There is a door, but I could do nothing with it."

Clyde climbed off his perch and the two found one another.

"Lead me to the door," Burke requested.

Harry took Clyde's outstretched hand and led the way.

There, Clyde felt of the door.

"I think I know what this might be," he breathed.

"What?" asked Harry, eagerly.

"It might be my imagination—I half hope that it is—but we just came from a mortuary and we are fighting a fiend calling himself the Funeral Director."

"Go on," said Harry eagerly.

The reporter's next words made the moist interior of Harry Vincent's mouth dry up.

"Could this be a—burial crypt?"

Harry's imagination needed no further prodding. That would explain everything from the fetid odor of decay to the dankly close confines.

Harry croaked, "Have we been—"

"Entombed?"

"I was going to say buried alive."

As the horrible realization sank into the brains of the two Shadow agents, they began banging on the iron door, shouting at the tops of their lungs.

"Help!" Clyde shouted. "We are trapped in this tomb!"

Harry added, "Can anyone hear us?"

But no one, evidently, did.

For no sounds reached their eager ears, nor did the ponderous portal budge.

Twenty minutes of this exhausting effort caused the dejected pair to sink to the gritty floor while they considered their situation.

"Our only hope is that Burbank got word to The Shadow," mused Clyde.

"Yes," agreed Harry. "But The Shadow would go directly to the mortuary. Not here."

"True," admitted Burke. "But he will not rest until he has tracked us down."

Harry thought about that. It gave him a sinking feeling. Finally, he offered, "If The Shadow trailed us here, he would find a cemetery. It will be crammed with crypts and burial vaults. How would he know which one to open—if any?"

"You have a point there," allowed Clyde Burke.

The two men sat in sullen silence as they considered their likely fate. Service to The Shadow had offered peril and excitement aplenty. Both men knew that the Grim Reaper might claim them at any turn along the danger trails they daily traveled.

But never in their wildest imaginings did they envision coming to such a grisly end. The thought of what lay before—aching thirst and certain starvation—depressed their spirits.

Burke laid an ear against the stone wall, but heard nothing.

"For all we know, it might be day *or* night," he said miserably.

Harry broke the crystal of his wristwatch against stone and carefully felt of the hands.

"It's three o'clock. But whether a.m. or p.m. is just anyone's guess."

"I vote that we've been out only a few hours," decided Clyde. "We should grab some shuteye. Raise a ruckus when we think it's day, and a caretaker might hear us."

But sleep proved hard to come by. Their nerves were keyed up, and their position became suffocating. Harry's skin felt hot and dry, despite the mucid moistness of their surroundings. How could they escape from a place as impregnable as this?

There was one ray of hope. The Shadow! That strange master of the midnight dark had more than once rescued his aides from predicaments nearly as forbidding as this.

But could even The Shadow find a spot so well-hidden? Harry and Clyde's spirits settled into deep gloom. They had left word as to their mortuary destination, but that was all. There was presumably not even a clue to tell The Shadow that they had fallen into a trap contrived by the Funeral Director.

Finally, exhausted, both men fell asleep, hoping that dawn might introduce some small ray of sunlight through a chink in the great granite crypt that was almost certain to be their tomb.

THEY knew not how long they slept.

When Harry and Clyde roused to wakefulness, it was because the door against which they were leaning abruptly and ponderously squeaked open. Both men were precipitated onto their backs.

Blinking, they found themselves staring upward at a terrifying apparition.

A tower of absolute darkness loomed over them. It was shapeless, yet possessed definite form. It was a wide cone of a thing, topped by an imposing black hat. Beneath a brim so wide it seemed exaggerated, smoldering orbs made their pounding hearts leap with a mixture of fear and relief.

Then low sounds came from the sepia figure, soft words with an eerie whispering quality.

"Step out," intoned The Shadow.

Then he moved backward, the gloom of the night seeming to swallow him.

Clambering to their feet, Harry and Clyde followed eagerly.

"Thank goodness," breathed Harry.

"But how—?" gasped Clyde.

Pausing, The Shadow turned in his measured pacing, cloak swishing. A sable hand pointed an accusing finger beyond them.

Their heads swiveled about. Chill moonlight illuminated the face of the crypt. A single word was carved in relief upon the lintel over the iron door:

CRANSTON

"Is—is that how you figured out where we would be?"

The Shadow nodded, causing his enshadowing hat brim to dip in acknowledgement.

"It was there that Lamont Cranston was being held prisoner," he whispered. "But he was removed when you were placed within—consigned to dwindle out your days until natural doom took you. You were conveyed here by a black hearse. It was the same machine in which Lamont Cranston was kidnapped. But the license tag is different. The hearse bearing Cranston departed before I could stop it."

"Is Cranston alive?" asked Burke.

"Yes. But he has been removed for reasons that are unclear. It is my task to locate him."

The Shadow moved on, black cloak swaying.

"Return to the Cranston residence to resume your duty," he continued in his sibilant style. "Protect Weltha Cranston. Leave the tracking of the hearse to me. Take the black-and-white taxi you will find parked by the gate. Search the house for concealed dictographs or microphones. The ears of the Funeral Director appear to be everywhere."

Then The Shadow vanished.

After he had departed, Harry and Clyde looked to one another. Had it been their imaginations? They looked back at the granite mausoleum, whose heavy door had been closed. It might have been all a dream—or nightmare.

No, it was neither, they quickly realized. For the unpleasantly fetid charnel odor still clung to their clothes and clogged their nostrils, reminding them of the unpleasant reality of it all.

Silently, they turned and picked their way out of the cemetery that had almost proven to be their final resting place, until they were redeemed from the tomb—by The Shadow!

Chapter XLVII

GAS!

HARRY VINCENT AND Clyde Burke remained concealed in the brush until they were certain that the Funeral Director's henchmen had long departed. Their grisly experience had been nerve-shattering. Now that it was over, and they had time to think about the ghastly narrowness of their escape, both became shaky and perspiring.

"Whew!" gasped Clyde. "I'll bet my hair has turned gray as rabbit fur."

They made their way to the cemetery entrance. Abruptly aware of a bulge in his pocket, Harry felt and discovered a small, flat flashlight. The Shadow had placed it there, of course. Again, Harry breathed a blessing on that marvelous master of the darkness who was their benefactor.

"Well, he prepares for everything!" Vincent remarked shakily.

Using the flash, they progressed along the winding road at a run. The spectral wrought-iron gate appeared ahead. Searching near it, they discovered the black-and-white taxicab. The machine had been run into the concealment of bushes which furred a bit of solid ground beside the entrance.

They drove the machine to the highway and wheeled toward the city. Neither young man said much. The recent horrible experience bulked too large in their thoughts to permit of easy conversation.

"We're to return to guard Weltha Cranston," Harry Vincent stated at last. He made himself laugh, but there was no mirth in the sound. "I'm beginning to think we're not even able to take care of ourselves."

A flashy front-drive roadster was parked in front of the Cranston estate, Donald Hume's machine. Harry and Clyde left the two-tone taxi near it and hurried up the walk.

It was a relief to have Weltha Cranston open the door for them. Donald Hume stood at her shoulder. When he saw the disheveled, mud-caked figures of Harry and Clyde, a faintly amused smile twisted his lips.

"You have met with—er, further reverses?" he inquired with a trace of sarcasm.

Harry and Clyde were in no mood to be ridiculed. Vincent managed to keep his temper. Clyde, however, glared at the other so violently that the overly unctuous fellow hastily wiped the smug sneer off his countenance and became very solicitous.

In Lamont Cranston's private study, with a few cryptic sentences, Harry told of the ghastly charnel experience, revealing for the first time that he and Burke had been rescued by the enigmatic personage they believed to be The Shadow.

"How gruesome!" Weltha Cranston gasped. "And what a remarkable person The Shadow is!"

Hume nodded as he listened to the recital of what Harry and Clyde had undergone, his amused face had become sober. For the first time he seemed to comprehend the unbounded evil of the Funeral Director. He shifted his feet nervously.

"You must have a change of clothing," he suggested. "My own garments will fit Mr. Vincent." He studied Clyde Burke's thin frame. "I am afraid, however, that they will not fit you, Mr. Burke."

"Uncle Lamont had a cook—before Creece—who was about your build," Weltha Cranston told Clyde. "We still have his clothes. You can put them on—if you wish."

Clyde wrinkled his nose at the terrible odor of decay which his disheveled garments exuded. "I'll be glad to."

The two young men bathed and changed clothing in an upstairs bathroom.

"Given that the premises have been recently burgled," Harry reminded, "we had better start looking for anything suspicious."

Both Harry and Clyde received considerable training as detectives in the service of The Shadow. Their search was thorough.

It was Harry who discovered a dead light bulb in a table lamp on the study room desk. He unscrewed this. There was a grayish quality to the bulb that seemed suspicious.

Breaking the bulb in the wastepaper basket, he discovered why it did not work. For exposed within was a tiny microphone in place of the carbon filament.

Working together, he and Clyde took apart the ceramic lamp stand, fathomed the purpose of a complicated apparatus they discovered within. An amplifier-converter contrivance by which sound impulses from the microphone were changed into wired-wireless waves and put on the city lighting circuit!

"Clyde!" he gasped. "We told our story in this very room! What dunces we were! The Funeral Director probably overheard the whole thing! He may have learned we were saved by The Shadow!"

Clyde Burke nodded soberly and said: "That's another bad break for us. Man alive, I wish we'd have some decent luck for once!"

"That microphone must explain how the Funeral Director knew so much about our doings?" Weltha Cranston murmured when she was shown the disassembled lamp. She was pale of face, and trembling a little.

Clyde Burke glanced about. "Where's Hume?"

The lantern-jawed man was not with them.

"Hume!" Harry called out loudly.

"Here!" came Hume's shout. "Come! I found something! Darned if I know what it can be!"

The fiancé of Weltha Cranston was in the room of Stanley,

the driver, who had been consigned to the guest house along with the valet, Richards.

On the nightstand sat a small box resembling an old music box, but in the shape of a casket, faithfully detailed down to the silver fittings for the pallbearers.

Hume's lantern jaw was sagging, as if he lost control of it. Color had washed out of his stunned features.

"I cannot imagine how anyone could have slipped in to leave such a grisly relic behind," he said hollowly.

"What do you say we give the thing a try?" Clyde suggested. "I'd like to see how it works."

Harry hesitated. He shook his head emphatically.

"We will leave it alone," he said. "After all, we're not positive the Funeral Director knows we are alive. If it should be booby-trapped, we'd only be falling into another trap."

"What if it contains another message?" Clyde countered.

"Any message would include instructions. Better not to know them, and maybe buy time while we figure out how to locate Lamont Cranston. For if we respond, it might be falling into the snare of a deadline imposed by the Funeral Director. In this instance, preserving silence gives up time to work."

Seeing the logic of that, Clyde agreed. He replaced the casket, handling the thing as gingerly as though it were a rotten egg.

"I suggest we search the rest of the house," Hume offered seriously.

"Not a bad idea," Harry allowed. "But our first duty is to guard Miss Cranston."

"To be sure!" Hume exclaimed. "The two of us had best remain with her, while the other searches." He glanced about the valet's quarters. "This room is as good as any to keep guard in."

"Who will hunt?" Clyde wanted to know.

They decided that by matching coins. It fell to Hume to search.

"That's just as well," he said promptly. "I am more familiar with the house."

Hume left them, a bit nervously, it seemed to Harry Vincent. They heard him moving furniture and tapping the walls downstairs for secret recesses. He was doing a good job, for the sounds were almost continuous.

"He is a bit—a bit impossible at times," Weltha Cranston offered. "But I think his motives are the highest."

Harry nodded. He had decided the same thing. Hume might be nerve-grating at times, but it was more the effect of the fellow's flippant personality than anything else.

The girl shuddered and sank weakly into a chair.

"This cruel Funeral Director!" she murmured brokenly. "What a monster. To think that—!"

She did not finish.

From downstairs came a high-pitched howl of terror. Hume's voice!

HARRY VINCENT and Clyde Burke pitched for the door. But the same thought halted them both. Weltha Cranston! They couldn't leave her here, alone and unprotected.

Harry drove a gaze around the room. The one closet gaped empty. He eyed the window. The shade was down. No one could look in from the outer night.

"Get in the closet!" he breathed to the girl. "Scream if you hear the slightest alarming sound."

Vincent hurried Weltha Cranston into the little cubicle and closed the door. He and Clyde leaped out of the room and pelted down the stairs.

Noise of conflict came from the rear of the residence. But as their feet clattered loudly on the staircase, the tumult subsided.

Cautiously, Harry and Clyde crept through a great formal dining room, a smaller family dining room, and pushed back a swinging door which gave into the big kitchen.

Donald Hume sprawled on his back on the floor. His arms were outflung, his eyes closed. Irregular rivulets of crimson were creeping out of his hair and spreading across the floor. There was a fresh greenish bruise on his lantern-shaped chin.

No one else was in the kitchen. The rear door was open, however.

Clyde Burke gulped: *"Listen!"*

Faint scuffle noises reached their ears from upstairs.

Harry Vincent spun, gun in hand.

"Come on!" he yelled. "They jumped Hume to draw us away from the girl!"

Back through the house they sprinted, crashing chairs out of their path. Clyde, leading, slipped and fell on the polished hardwood floor at the foot of the stairs. Harry passed him, and mounted the steps with great leaps. Clyde, on his feet again, pounded after him.

They reached the door of the valet's room. Their shoulders battered it. The panel was locked!

They rammed the door again. The solid hardwood belted them back.

Aiming his long-snouted automatic at the lock, Harry tugged the trigger three times. The lock flew completely out of the door, leaving a jagged hole. They knocked the panel ajar, and lunged through.

Hardly were they inside when both clutched wildly at their eyes. The room was impregnated with tear gas!

They staggered about, completely blinded.

Chapter XLVIII

CLYDE BURKE TRAPPED

THE BITING FUMES of the tear gas affected their eyes like showers of needles. The shocking agony held Harry Vincent speechless an instant.

"Clear out of the room!" he managed to shout. "We're helpless!"

They retreated, fumbling sightlessly for the door. As they located it and stumbled through, Harry thought he heard a sound from outside the window. He was not sure.

Catching Clyde's arm, Harry guided him into a bathroom. Finding the cold-water knob of a shower, he gave it a spin. They held their heads under the beating, icy spray. It did not seem to help their eyes much.

The minutes which followed were endless ages.

"I can see a little!" Clyde groaned at last. He mopped his face on his sleeve. "Let's go."

Harry, holding his quivering eyeballs apart with two fingers, discovered he also could see somewhat.

Back into the upstairs corridor, they went. The valet's room showed unmistakable signs of a struggle. The door of the closet where they had left Weltha Cranston was ajar. Too, the window shade was now up, the sash open.

Moving to the window, Harry Vincent squinted painfully. A ladder slanting downward showed how Weltha Cranston had been carried away.

"They went this way!" he growled.

Harry scrambled through the window and down the ladder. Clyde Burke trod Harry's fingers in his haste to follow. Anxiety making them wildly reckless of a possible ambush, they ran searching through the shrubbery.

But they found no trace of the young woman. The only thing that might have been a clue was the abrupt moan of a speeding automobile engine sounding in the distance—the machine might have driven from the Cranston mansion slowly and silently, then, safely clear, accelerated into high speed.

"Not a chance of following it!" gritted Harry. "We can't even tell from the sound what street it is on."

Faces drawn and grim, the disgusted pair went back into the Cranston domicile. They made their way to the kitchen.

Donald Hume, consciousness partially regained, was sitting on the floor. He gazed at them in a befuddled way.

"The Funeral Director's thugs got Miss Cranston!" Harry told him bluntly.

Hume gave every indication of nearly fainting at the words. His pale face now the color of freshly kneaded putty, contorted in horror. His lips twitched.

"It was—it was my fault!" he wailed. "Oh—it was my fault!"

"What happened to you?" Burke asked him.

"Ruffians leaped upon me," Hume moaned. "Several of them. I had pocketed my revolver while I searched. They seized me before I could draw it. We struggled—then I must have been hit over the head. I remember nothing more."

The lantern-jawed man got shakily to his feet, both hands pressed to his scalp.

"What are we to do now?" he whimpered. "Oh, this is ghastly! Those brutes attacked me to decoy you downstairs. Because I allowed myself to be taken off guard, it is directly my fault they captured Miss Cranston." His shoulders shook convulsively. "And to think I was fool enough to sneer at your own misfortunes earlier in the evening. I am deeply sorry for the way I acted."

"That's all right," Clyde told him, moved by the shaken man's remorse. "Any ordinary fellow seems to be helpless against the Funeral Director. Our only hope is—The Shadow!"

They moved together to a downstairs bathroom to get bandages from a medicine cabinet and dress Hume's gashed head.

THEY were in the bathroom when the telephone rang. Animated by sudden hope, they rushed to the instrument. Clyde, who happened to be nearest, reached it first.

Lifting the receiver, he said eagerly: "Yes?"

"This is the agent of the Prince *Clyde* steamship lines," said a slightly shrill voice. "The liner on which you wish to *go to* South America will dock at our East River *wharf* two weeks from today. The name of the *vessel* is the *Doranic*. I am sorry to trouble you at this hour, but you wanted the information as soon as I received it. Is this arrangement satisfactory?"

"It is!" breathed Clyde.

The receiver clicked at the other end of the line. Burke hung up.

"The Shadow!" he gasped. "His emphasized words were 'Clyde go to wharf vessel *Doranic!*' It must mean that The Shadow is waiting for me on the *Doranic*."

"You are sure?" Harry Vincent demanded.

"Of course. The emphasized words prove it!"

"That means you are to go alone," Harry muttered in disappointment. "All right. Good luck to you, Burke!"

Clyde Burke, running for the door, threw over his shoulder: "Thanks! It's time we all had some good luck. What we've had so far has all been bad!"

"And be careful!" Harry shouted after him.

The final warning stuck in Burke's head as he sprinted down the walk and scrambled into the black-and-white taxicab. It had the effect of making him unreasonably cautious from the instant he left the Cranston manse.

Clyde did his best to keep one eye on the road and the other on the rear-view mirror mounted on the jet-hued left fender. At each street intersection, he stabbed an alert gaze right and left.

He passed a few rattling milk carts and white-clad milkmen delivering bottles in metal carrying racks. The automobile of an occasional early worker rolled along the streets. Dawn was not far off.

Clyde noticed nothing to alarm him. The taxicab engine suddenly backfired; its flow of power faltered. Eyeing the gauge, Burke saw that he was out of gasoline.

He searched anxiously for a filling station. Finally, he found one. The cab engine died completely a few yards from the pump, but the machine had enough momentum to coast the remainder of the distance.

Clyde looked for the attendant. No one was in sight, although the station was brilliantly lighted. Clyde would have driven on, except that he was entirely out of fuel. Fuming at the delay, he left the cabin and went in search of the attendant.

He found the fellow in a nearby hamburger stand, consuming eggs and coffee.

"I want my tank filled—quick," urged Clyde.

The attendant scowled. He was a loutish looking man with a disagreeable air of truculence. "I'm eatin' now, see!" he said as he continued to dine with aggravating slowness.

Clyde colored angrily. Fellows of this character were trying on the nerves under any condition, but doubly so now. He carefully masked an impulse to take a poke at the oaf. Drawing a five-dollar bill from his pocket, he let the man see it.

"I'm in a hurry," he stated tightly.

The mannerless attendant scrutinized the bill. "That's different, brother!" he declared. He left the lunch stand and filled the two-tone taxicab with gasoline.

Clyde paid him and sent the hack out of the station with the whistle of spinning tires. He had wasted several minutes.

To complicate matters further, Clyde proceeded to get lost

en route to his assigned destination. He knew this portion of New Jersey in a general way, but some of the details had become confused in his memory. He expended ten minutes finding himself.

But at last he swung onto the waterfront street near the wharf. Wheeling into the side road where they had parked before, he put a foot on the brake and slowed up.

Just as a matter of precaution, he looked around. It was lucky he did!

Behind him, two big sedans were hurtling into the street! A smaller coupe trailed them.

The police reporter knew trouble when he saw it. He slapped the gear lever into mesh and bore heavily on the accelerator, simultaneously working the clutch.

THE ENGINE in the black-and-white hack was no ordinary stock-car variety. Clyde got a kick out of the way the taxi seemed to squat and leap down the darkened street. At the next corner, he gave the wheel a twist, apprehension over upsetting the vehicle violently tightening his throat muscles.

But the way the machine took the sharp curve was a revelation. The cab rode as though it were fully loaded. Bars of pig iron must have been bolted to the underpart of the body to give it weight.

Clank! Clank! Clank! The sounds were extremely loud, like sledgehammers hitting the cab. Clyde took a chance, and looked back. Bullets were hitting the rear window glass—and splattering like drops of muddy water! The glass was bulletproof! The cab body must be of armor plate, too!

Vastly relieved, Clyde gave all his attention to driving. Around more corners, he whipped. A glance at the rear-view mirror showed the three pairs of headlights still rocking in pursuit.

He clenched his teeth and took another corner. The cab was thundering along a boulevard now. Down it, the howling chase volleyed.

With nothing to do but hold the wheel rigid and keep the foot-feed jammed to the floorboards, Clyde had a moment to think. The cars behind must be the Funeral Director's men. But how had they gotten upon his trail?

His eyes rested momentarily on the speedometer. It registered a bit past ninety miles an hour! Some bus, this! It was fortunate no traffic haunted the boulevard at this hour before dawn.

The headlights reflected in the rear-view mirror were dwindling in size. He was outdistancing the Funeral Director's men! Clyde decided to keep to the straightaway. That seemed his best chance.

Some minutes later, he peered at the rear-vision mirror again. The pursuing headlights were mere pinpoints now. Clyde made a tightlipped smile. A bit more lead, and he would turn into a side road and let them pass.

Then Clyde frowned slightly. A new sound appeared to have joined the moan of the great engine beneath the cab hood. A puzzling sound, hardly loud enough to be real!

Clyde furrowed his brow more deeply—and the concrete roadway ahead suddenly became a great, blazing sheet of flame!

There was no time to slow the car. Nowhere to turn it. Straight into the billowing clouds of citrine vapor which had come from the explosion, it hurtled.

Feet braced, teeth sunk in his lips, Clyde Burke fully expected death. He thought a bomb had destroyed the roadway.

But the roaring car whipped through the yellowish vapor with nary a jar. The pavement was intact!

Clyde drew a great breath of relief into his lungs. Then his eyes protruded. He gagged, choked violently. A cloying odor penetrated his nostrils. His head swam.

Gas! A different sort than that which had earlier overcome Harry and himself! Clyde failed to recognize the new smell. Fear of chemical agents such as mustard gas surged up within him. They meant a horrible, suffocating death!

Clyde trod heavily on the brakes. If he could just stop the

cab and stagger far enough to hide himself in the countryside before he collapsed!

The swimming of his head became a dizzying spin. The road seemed to turn into a writhing gray snake before his eyes. The rod-like beams of the headlights acquired fantastic, crooked shapes.

Clyde gave the wheel a wrench to keep the taxi on what he thought was the roadway. The car, traveling much more slowly now, careened. Suddenly, it upended, rocked, and went tumbling off the roadway shoulder.

The armor-plated machine rolled downhill. Like a pebble in a tin can, Clyde Burke was thrown about. He tried to cling to the wheel, but lost his grip.

His head hit something—he never knew what it was. His spinning brain became darkly blank.

Chapter XLIX

HARRY VINCENT
TO THE RESCUE

STANDING IN THE door of the Cranston home, Harry Vincent watched Clyde Burke vanish down the darkened path toward the road. Harry's right hand was clenched tightly on the doorknob. He felt vaguely uneasy.

The telephone call to Burke had left him with a queer feeling of doubt. In the back of his head uneasiness lurked. Suppose that call had been a trick to decoy Clyde into the hands of the Funeral Director?

It was this grisly possibility, unfounded as it was, that prompted Harry to call his last warning: "And be careful!"

Harry closed the door after Clyde was gone. He stood a moment eyeing the jagged bits of colored glass which clung to the panel. It was the same door through which the black-robed villain who pretended to be The Shadow had leaped earlier in the night.

"That happened tonight!" Harry muttered. "It seems like an age ago." He glanced at a clock. "Less than an hour until dawn!"

Behind him, Donald Hume was wiping sticky crimson off his abashed face.

"I shall dress my wound," he said, and went back toward the bathroom from which the ringing telephone had called them.

Harry remained just inside the front door. He felt strangely uncomfortable, as if something were wrong. The feeling was persistent, although he assured himself it was only his nerves.

Urged by a hunch, Vincent went to the telephone, lifted it, and put the receiver to his ear.

The line was dead! The wires had been cut somewhere, because no current hum pulsed the receiver diaphragm.

Harry hastily dropped the instrument, drew his pistol—another of the thin-snouted, high-powered foreign automatics from the Cranston collection—and backed to a spot where he was out of range of the windows.

His brain raced. Had the wires been severed before or after Clyde Burke's conversation? If before, it meant a portable instrument had been attached near the residence.

Harry combed his hair with his fingers. The discovery had greatly increased his perturbation. More overpowering than ever was the feeling that something was wrong.

Suddenly, Vincent made a decision. He would follow Clyde Burke! That would not be disobeying The Shadow's orders, since the command had evidently emanated from their cloaked master. With Weltha Cranston abducted, there was nothing for Harry to do here except await any ransom demand.

Harry lifted his voice in a call to Donald Hume.

"I'm going to trail Burke! Do you want to go along?"

He waited for an answer—but none came!

With an uneasy ejaculation, Harry sprang toward the bathroom.

Crash! The brittle sound was unmistakably the bathroom window breaking. Fragments of glass rang like bells in the bathtub.

"Help, Vincent! The Funeral Dir—"

That was Hume's voice—terror stricken!

Loud smacking sounds and grunts came from inside the bathroom. They subsided abruptly. A voice, hoarse and unlike Hume's, gave an order that Vincent could not understand.

Harry reached the bathroom door. Finding it locked did not surprise him. Standing to one side, he gave it a kick. Two bullets burst through at him. The slugs missed Vincent, thanks to his caution in standing to one side.

Harry did not fire back. Pivoting, he ran into the kitchen and across it to the rear door. He did not plunge recklessly outside, however. Instead, he seized the high stool from before the enameled mixing table, plucked a gauzy curtain from the window, wrapped it around the stool, and tossed the makeshift man-dummy through the door into the night. It did not draw a bullet.

The stool had hardly hit the ground when Harry leaped outside. He was not shot at or attacked. Around the house he spun. Electric light streamed from the shattered bathroom window.

No sign of Hume or his assailants was to be heard or seen. Harry strained his ears. Only silence!

Moreover, Hume's flashy roadster was nowhere to be seen.

He did not go nearer the window, but crept back into the house. Bracing himself before the bathroom door, he gave it a sudden kick. The panel caved inward.

"Empty!" Harry grunted.

Donald Hume had disappeared. Yet it was incredible that the Funeral Director's men could have made off with the lantern-jawed man so swiftly and silently. But the fact that he was gone was evidence that they had.

Harry made a furtive search through the house and grounds. No trace of Hume did he find.

Crouched in the gloom beneath a flowering bush, Vincent decided to follow Burke, as he had intended. There was nothing he could see of the vanished Hume. Moving furtively, he made his way to the Cranston garage and entered. Two machines were there, a big town car and a smaller business coupe.

Harry entered the coupe and guided it out of the grounds, momentarily expecting an attack. But none came.

He drove swiftly toward the city, where steamship piers jutted out from the Hudson River banks.

AS THE COUPE rolled into the neighborhood of the steam-ship office, Harry Vincent was astounded to discover the black-and-white taxicab in which he knew Clyde Burke must be riding. It was ahead of him a couple of blocks.

"Now I wonder what delayed Clyde?" murmured Harry, genuinely puzzled.

As a matter of fact, Clyde had been delayed by running low on gas and becoming lost. Hence it was that both young men reached the foot of the street at the same time.

Harry hardly discovered the black-and-white hack before he saw something else. Two big sedans! They had been parked at the curb, but now were in motion.

Clyde turned into the side street to park. The two sedans rolled after him.

"A trap!" Harry bit out. "That call was a phony, sure enough."

He twisted the small coupe after the big machines. Not many yards separated him from the sedans when they wheeled into the side street.

Harry reached for the horn to blow a warning. But Burke didn't need it! He had taken alarm. His two-tone machine shot ahead like a dog sighting a tomcat.

"Quick work, that!" Harry breathed.

The two sedans sped in pursuit. Harry brought up the rear. Around corners the procession thundered, tires squawling on asphalt. The machines bucked over irregularities in the pavement. Soon, they were volleying down the wide boulevard.

Harry did not need to slacken his pace to stay a bit in the rear. It was all he could do to keep the two sedans and Clyde Burke in sight. Indeed, Clyde was speedily outdistancing them all.

Whether the Funeral Director's villains knew that he was following, Harry could not tell. But they were ignoring him, concentrating on catching the reporter. Scant luck were they having!

Harry glanced uneasily at the speedometer. A trifle over

seventy-five miles an hour, it registered. Burke must be doing better than ninety, judging by the way he was gaining.

Structures along the road became blurred, then almost nonexistent. Minutes passed, made unpleasantly long by the terrific pace of the chase.

"Good grief!" Harry exploded. He suddenly stiffened. Points of light had appeared in the sky above Burke's distant cab. An airplane!

Unexpectedly, there was a vivid red flash in front of Clyde's machine. The plane had dropped a bomb! Vincent could see it sprout a great mushroom of yellowish vapor that looked like smoke. Into this Burke's two-tone taxi dived.

The sight wrenched a moan from Harry's lungs. "The devils!" he grated.

Vincent slammed on the coupe's brakes. The car rocked and careened from side to side, threatening to turn turtle. But Harry got it stopped without mishap.

He thrust his head outside. The plane had banked about, its lights clearly indicated. It was making for his coupe!

Vincent saw he could never escape the speedy aircraft in the coupe. He sprang out with the idea of concealing himself in the roadside brush. But with a bawling howl, the plane swooped low.

A bomb smacked the pavement nearby, flinging up a great gush of red flame. Yellowish vapor billowed toward Vincent.

Harry sprinted. He succeeded in evading all but the very edge of the spreading cloud.

"Gas!" he growled.

Its cloying odor pervaded his lungs, made his head swim. His legs seemed to grow numb and useless. He stumbled, fell headlong.

Every move a tremendous effort, Vincent crawled toward the fading Autumn growth which walled the roadway.

HARRY VINCENT managed to drag himself only a few yards when one of the sedans, backing down the road, came to a stop nearby.

"Grab him!" a voice barked. Men got out and seized Vincent.

Although benumbed, he was not unconscious. Harry was dizzily aware of what went on around him. Dragging him to the sedan, the attackers bundled him inside.

A large box of an apparatus occupied part of the rear seat. A beady-eyed man sat before this, wearing a headset of receivers. A portable radio transmitter! That explained how the plane had been summoned.

The plane banked low over the sedan. One of the Funeral Director's henchmen tilted a spotlight upon it, and Harry saw that it was a cabin monoplane, equipped with bomb racks!

The radio operator leered at Harry. "We didn't expect to get you, too," he sneered. "This is just about all of you."

Grinning evilly, the man placed a foot on Harry's face and rubbed it about with a grinding motion.

Vincent tried to make an angry retort, but his tongue was entirely out of his control. He could hardly understand the sounds of his own making.

Men were dragging an inanimate figure from the black-and-white taxi. Clyde Burke! Vincent moaned. Clyde appeared horribly battered, possibly dead!

The unmoving reporter was deposited in the second sedan. Not a word was spoken. The other auto twisted away from the curb, entered a boulevard, and rolled away with alacrity.

Then the first sedan began running along the pavement in its wake.

"You two have been a lot of trouble to our outfit," snarled the radioman.

Vincent said nothing. He could only glower under the threat of gun muzzles. Although he knew perfectly well he could not speak intelligibly, Harry made another meaningless babbling noise. The radioman's grinding foot had been very painful, and he hoped, by making them think that he was willing to talk, to avoid further mistreatments.

The ruse failed.

"Guess he can't talk on account of the gas," the radioman remarked. "It'll wear off in about an hour. I'd better tie and gag him."

He proceeded to suit action to words, lashing Vincent until the hemp bit deeply into his flesh. Strangely enough, the effects of the stupefying vapor made Harry unable to feel the ropes which were corded tightly about his ankles and wrists. The stuff seemed to work on his muscles like an anesthetic.

His brain was only mildly affected, however. The gas, although it rendered the young man nearly incapable of movement, did not induce unconsciousness. In a vague, dreamy way, Harry could see and hear what went on around him.

It soon turned out that it would have been better had he not possessed his awake senses.

"What are we gonna do with them this time?" asked the man driving.

"Entombing them didn't do the job. So it's the other thing."

The questioner paled. "I guess we got no choice in the matter," he muttered.

"Yeah. Ashes to ashes, like they say."

"And dust to dust," intoned the other.

The two machines rolled along. Harry noticed as dawn crept along that his ambushers were wearing matching black suits and ties. They resembled a gathering of morticians.

The realization made the hair at the nape of his head rise up and gooseflesh creep along his arms.

Once out in sparsely-settled country, the driver pulled over and they seized Harry roughly and stuffed him into the rumble seat of their machine. The lid slammed down, locking him in tight.

"That way he can't attract attention," the radioman sneered as the sedan rumbled along once more.

The claustrophobic combination of being squeezed in, combined with the lightless space of the trunk, made Harry think of the dank tomb from which The Shadow had plucked him only hours before.

Vincent shuddered in spite of himself. He had no delusions about what he was headed for.

If his hunch was correct, Harry reflected that he would rather be consigned to the cold and bleak confines of a moldering crypt than the terrible fate to which the men of the Funeral Director were now conveying him.

Chapter XL

THE SHADOW'S TRAIL

THE MORNING SUN was bathing the shrubbery with roseate light when the burly taxi driver walked through it to the Cranston mansion, striding along the curving driveway. A few yards from the building, however, he turned aside and was quickly swallowed by the few shadows still remaining. He made no sound circling the house. The most alert of observers could hardly have seen him.

The Cranston estate had a moribund air of desertion. Servants were no doubt asleep in their beds.

The taxi driver slipped into the house. He had a key.

Sepulchral quiet impregnated the interior. No noise broke it—but a tall, fantastic shadow suddenly loomed in the un-lighted entranceway. It hung there a full minute. Two eyes appeared in the upper portion of the dark figure, inspecting the way ahead. Weird, piercing orbs, they radiated a hot, queer light that made them smolder like living coals.

In the doorway, the strange splotch settled near the floor as smoke settles to the earth when a storm threatens. The gloomy smear flowed for the vestibule. There it stretched up, gathering startling height.

Once inside, a flashlight popped into life in the curtained semi-gloom, drove out a thread-like beam.

A spot of luminance came to rest on a man sleeping in an upholstered sofa chair. It was Stanley, the Cranston chauffeur. He had changed from his uniform and was keeping vigil, as befitted a faithful servant. No doubt he had lost considerable sleep in previous days, what with the house being overrun by insistent reporters and unfamiliar occupants, and was dozing, slumped down in his chair, eyes closed.

Moving from room to room, The Shadow's glowing orbs picked up clues with unerring precision. And back of those optics, a marvelous brain fitted the clues into a story-pattern.

The eyes of a police detective would have noticed nothing of consequence.

But the penetrating gaze of The Shadow seemed to be all-seeing. It was such a phenomenon as only a mind of tremendous power could produce, a brain of intense driving force and uncanny discernment.

A bit of colorful leather scraped from a shoe on the sill of the window in the chauffeur's room came under the scrutiny of a magnifying glass. The Shadow knew instantly that a young woman had been dragged from that window! For the bit had come from one of Weltha Cranston's fashionable shoes.

Vague traces of the tear gas still remained in the room and explained why Harry Vincent and Clyde Burke had not been able to prevent her capture. It also explained why Stanley was sleeping elsewhere in the habitation.

The questing ray soon fell on a nightstand, revealing a polished black coffin in miniature. Lifting this, The Shadow opened the grisly relic.

Inside was a folded note resting in black velvet. Opening it, he read:

> MISS CRANSTON
> THE FUNERAL DIRECTOR UNDERSTANDS YOUR FINANCIAL PREDICAMENT. OTHER AR-RANGEMENTS ARE BEING MADE. AWAIT AC-TION.

A knowing laugh, sinister and sibilant, issued forth. The light clicked out. Moving toward the door, this eerie figure again became a dark smear of prowling shadow. This smoky apparition flowed out of the room and was lost in the deep murk beyond.

Here and there, the flashlight came to life again. Blood was a sticky stain on the kitchen floor. Inside the downstairs bathroom, on the edge of the broken window, was a crimson fingerprint. The flash probed it, driving a brilliant string of light against it from many angles.

The Shadow knew the prints of Harry Vincent and Clyde Burke. This one belonged to neither of them. He studied the print, then went to Donald Hume's room and studied others there. The beam of The Shadow's flashlight, so thin that it seemed nothing more than a gossamer thread of pale cobweb, wove about the chamber. He knew then that Hume had been in the bathroom.

The smashed-in door meant that either Harry or Clyde had tried to rescue him.

The thin flashlight beam seemed to collapse in midair as it was extinguished. A clock somewhere in the great, palatial mansion ticked off sufficient seconds to make a minute. The murky form of The Shadow did not move.

Then a murmuration came from the sepia shade—soft mirth with a whispering quality.

Abruptly, The Shadow abandoned the piecing together of clues. He floated up the winding staircase, past the closed bedroom doors and out of hearing of the sleeping servant, to the attic tower room, whose locked door surrendered to his key.

Warming up the short-wave set, he discovered that it had been tuned to an unfamiliar frequency.

The Shadow heard the commands which directed the release of Lamont Cranston, passing mention of the attention-drawing attack on Donald Hume at the Cranston mansion and the use of the tear gas to discourage pursuit of Weltha Cranston's abductors. Reference was made to the orders to lure Clyde Burke away from Harry Vincent by the use of emphasized words embedded in a false telephone call.

A chuckle of appreciation for the cleverness of his antagonist, the Funeral Director, emerged from The Shadow's immobile lips at that. For his superfoe had divined from listening to the broadcasts over WNX that the man of darkness often employed that subtle subterfuge to communicate with his agents.

More striking still, the dark avenger recognized the querulous tones of the Funeral Director. It, too, confirmed his previous deductions. Beyond any doubt, he knew the identity of his enemy.

Manipulating the dial, The Shadow tuned to another frequency, spoke a single commanding word: "Report!"

The methodical enunciation of Burbank came over the ether. *"Nothing to report."*

"Vincent has deserted his post."

"No word from Vincent since last report."

"Report received," acknowledged The Shadow.

Shutting off the set and closing the radio room door, the cloaked figure floated back to the ground floor, where a gloved hand lifted a telephone receiver to confirm that the line was dead.

Stanley still dozed in his chair, his rangy form completely relaxed. If any thoughts were haunting the subconscious of his sleep they must have been grim ones because his pallid lips were twisted into a worried grimace.

The eerie figure made no sound in passing. Burning eyes shifted and bore on the sleeping Stanley. It was then that the chauffeur stirred. Something must have penetrated his subconscious, warning him. Perhaps it was an instinct handed down from some prehistoric ancestor who had acquired another sense to protect himself from ravenous beasts of prey while he slept.

Stanley opened his eyes. But the man's lids had hardly started to flicker when the patch of shadow shrank and widened and became an inky puddle on the floor. It oozed for the door.

For a split second as it floated through the opening, the weird blot of murk was visible to Stanley. The chauffeur jerked up rigid in his chair. The short hairs on the back of his neck lifted like hackle feathers on a scared rooster.

The stolid Stanley was not superstitious. He had never believed there was such a thing as a ghost or a shadow of the night. But now he was having his doubts. His eyes, glassily protuberant, yanked toward the vestibule. Breath coming out of the chauffeur's lungs was a procession of jerks.

Abruptly, Stanley gathered himself together and sprang from the chair to the front door. He saw nothing—although it seemed to his startled gaze that the portal was just closing soundlessly. He pitched forward and wrenched it open.

The chauffeur's darting eyes discerned no sign of life. Convinced suddenly that the whole thing was the ending of a bad dream, Stanley started a relieved chuckle.

The mirth died a shocked croak.

For the laugh of another being was jarring the air about his ears! Strange, sinister, it echoed in disturbing peals, like astral bells resounding from another sphere, echoing and reechoing in an uncanny chorus.

Drained of all courage, Stanley retreated to the familiar safety of his master's mansion, blocking his ears to keep out the fast-fading laughter.

CALMLY appropriating the big town car in the Cranston garage, The Shadow drove away from the estate.

The large machine rolled swiftly, carefully keeping within the speed limit whenever it came under the scrutiny of a traffic cop.

The Shadow could not return to his sanctum because the secret lair was no longer a secret, thanks to the detective skills of Doc Savage. Nor was the estate of Lamont Cranston available to him. He could not very well turn up there as Cranston with the real millionaire still among the missing.

He eventually pulled up before the shabby, second-rate hotel near the abandoned miniature golf course in Jackson Heights. Getting out, the driver entered the establishment.

A blowsy, middle-aged clerk was sitting sleepy-eyed behind the desk.

"Have a good night, bud?" he asked.

"Bum!" grinned the taxi driver.

"Uh-huh," mumbled the clerk. "Business slow for everybody, seems like."

The taxi driver strode to his room, unlocked the door, and went in.

It was the same room from which The Shadow had entered furtively via the fire escape earlier in the night—the room from which he had taken the radio direction-finding apparatus.

The personality of the taxi driver seemed to disappear just inside the door. A trailing black cloak rapidly enveloped the figure of The Shadow, causing him to become almost invisible in the room. He drew the shades, which made his surroundings gloomy.

The large brown suitcase still stood at the head of the bed, where it had been left.

Over the suitcase hovered the darksome figure of The Shadow. Although light could have been had by lifting the window shades, the flash beam came into play. The hand, the strange girasol casting ruby reflections from the third finger, appeared and opened the suitcase, disclosing the compact short-wave set.

Querulous orders given by the Funeral Director continued to emerge from the speaker. To them, The Shadow listened intently.

Patiently, The Shadow continued monitoring the short-wave frequency. Crackling hiss punctuated by an occasional *whooshing* sound was all he heard for a time.

Then an excited voice said, *"We nabbed that nosy reporter, as planned. The other one was taggin' along behind him, so we dropped a bomb on him."*

"Excellent!" wheezed the voice of the Funeral Director. *"Holding them hostage in the event that The Shadow should close in on our*

operation has proven to be terribly risky. We will dispose of these meddlers in the usual manner."

"But the—place won't be operatin' until the morning. You know it shuts down every night at seven."

"No matter!" snapped the Funeral Director. *"That is a mere trifle. You know where to take them. Now sign off and be on your way."*

The transmission ended.

The Shadow clicked off the short-wave set. Harry and Clyde were once again in the toils of the Funeral Director. This time, they were slated for certain destruction. It was only a matter of hours. Having no knowledge of where they had been ambushed, he could not pick up their trail to the place of doom.

And for once, The Shadow did *not* know!

THE SOILED window blind of the hotel room rolled upward. The window sash lifted. Something exceedingly black seemed to trickle out.

A stenographer walking to work chanced to glance at the side of the hotel. She rubbed her eyes suddenly, for she had seen a thick black shadow appear in the bright morning sunlight. A shadow where there was nothing to cast one!

"Holy smokes!" she gasped. "What is that thing?"

Open-mouthed, she watched the patch of gloom descend the fire escape, moving with incredible speed. It dropped from the landing and vanished in the rubbish which littered the abandoned pocket-edition golf course.

The stenographer kneaded her eyes again. When she walked on, her face was somewhat pale. She could not understand the fantastic thing she had seen.

"I must be going crazy!" she laughed nervously. "I'm sure seeing queer things."

Her feelings were pretty much the same as those felt by a taxi driver in the next block a moment later. He was unaware he had acquired a passenger until a voice spoke over his shoulder, giving orders.

"Cripes, you gimme a start!"

Pivoting, the driver saw only a dark-clad man whose features were completely hidden by the downturned brim of the large black hat.

"Airport," instructed the shadowy passenger.

"I'm going to get my eyes examined," the cabby muttered, and bore down on the gas. The machine ran out of town, and turned east into a less settled patch of Long Island.

Some large buildings, airplane hangars, came into view ahead. This was a private airport, one of several around New York City in which The Shadow had secreted his personal ships for emergencies.

The passenger ordered the cab to halt, got out and dismissed the machine with a crisp twenty-dollar bill. He walked to the collection of hangars. The big structures appeared deserted. The hour was too early for much to be doing about the place.

The Shadow made for a certain hangar. He entered through a side door of the corrugated structure. He possessed a key.

Within reposed a black monoplane, a single-seater. The Shadow donned a black leather flying helmet and goggles from a locker, then climbed into the open cockpit of the trim craft.

The exhaust stacks commenced spitting popping noises and brownish smoke. The engine warmed a bit, then increased its speed. Under the pull of the propeller, the monoplane rolled clear and onto the tarmac.

The motor began hammering hard, and the black craft went scooting along the runway, lifted its tail and took to the air after a very short run. The pilot was obviously skilled.

The sleek ship boomed northward, heading in the direction of upstate New York. On and on it flew, attracting no more attention than any other ship in this air-minded age. The fact that the monoplane bore no identification numbers could not be discerned from the ground.

The black aircraft made outstanding time. Its sleek shadow was soon falling over a mountainous region. The pilot banked his dark bird, circling until it spied a solitary hunting lodge nestled at the foot of a mountain peak.

The black ship instantly pointed its baying nose to the sky. Higher and higher it mounted. Then it leveled. A darkish lump of a figure swelled up on the cockpit rim, hung there an instant, then dropped off the craft into space.

The monoplane, controls locked in neutral position, sped away through the sky. It would crash somewhere—but probably not until it was over the Saranac Lakes.

As for the dark figure which had dropped—a black, billowing mass like smoke squirted out above it. With a low boom of a sound, it became a parachute. A black parachute.

Silently, it lowered The Shadow into the forest. Black-gloved hands tugged at the shroud lines on one side of the chute, causing it to slide sidewise, heading for a certain spot.

Below, nothing seemed to move in the morning sunlight.

When the shaggy fir forest was a score of feet below, The Shadow gave a quick twist and came free of the parachute harness. His landing in the forest created no more furor than a fluttering blackbird.

Darting away, he evacuated the spot while the parachute bell settled to earth like a collapsing monster of sepia silk.

The Shadow did not venture along the winding forest paths, but flitted through the primeval tangle of fallen branches and thorny brush, displaying an eerie woodcraft that reduced the piney labyrinth of growth to something as easily negotiated as a landscaped city park. By this means, he avoided any snares that might lie along the better trammelled routes.

The location he sought loomed ahead. Beyond it, reared a hurricane fence, some sixteen feet high and evidently electrified. Behind it, men garbed in plain blue uniforms were approaching the gate, some toting rifles.

The Shadow had been seen! The man of midnight had anticipated this but, with his two main agents in criminal hands, he was gambling that he could free Cliff Marsland for the battle ahead.

That hope proved premature.

Working his way around, The Shadow found a spot where a springy-limbed maple tree grew close to the fence, which was topped with snarls of vicious barbed wire as an added discouragement.

As the guards worked open the gate, The Shadow slithered up this tree and into the leafy shelter of its crown. Its leaves were already turning shades of brown, and red and gold, and this property more than anything proved to be The Shadow's undoing. For his midnight-black garments failed to offer ready concealment amid that riot of Autumn hues. A patchwork of sable betrayed his lurking presence.

"There he is!" rang out an excited shout.

"Nab 'im!" yelled another voice. "He can't get down and run."

The Shadow could have shot several of the guards. But he made no effort to do so, realizing it would be a futile gesture. They would fire back, and a single bullet could easily dislodge him.

Instead, he dropped onto a heavy branch, and raced along its twisting length. With a tremendous leap, he cleared the fence, great cloak spreading like raven wings lined in scarlet.

Rolling, The Shadow landed safely, springing to his feet.

So swift had been his maneuver that the guards had no opportunity to squeeze off rifle shots. Not many yards away stood the log hunting lodge, the only structure in view. Its massive door stood ajar. Within was a welcoming gloom.

The Shadow raced for that, cloak trailing.

Rifles cracked behind him. Bullets knocked up clumps of grass, clods of sod. Slugs snapped at his heels, but failed to down him.

Reaching the cabin door, The Shadow hurled himself in, wheeled, and slammed the log door shut, dropping the bar.

The small windows were heavily curtained, so darkness seized the space.

In that sheltering gloom, The Shadow laughed. Soft, yet sinister, that mirth issued forth with a flavor of satisfaction.

It had not yet trailed away when a curious sound materialized but feet away, behind him.

Low, melodious, yet without tune. It might have been a breeze sifting through the towering pines, seeking musical expression. Up and down the scale, it ranged.

The Shadow pivoted, hooded eyes seeking the source, his matched automatics leaping into his fists.

"Speak!" hissed The Shadow.

In the deep gloom, strange golden orbs regarded him, and a firm voice said, "You will not shoot."

The beginnings of a laugh started.

Then a bronze hand lifted into view. A stray strand of sunlight slipping through a chink in the logs spotlighted it, thumb and forefinger touching.

The digits snapped—and a flash of light erupted, mixing with a loud report.

Too late, The Shadow moved to shield his eyes. The nascent laugh was choked off as, suddenly, other hitherto hidden forms surrounded him. He could not see them for his piercing eyes had been stunned by the unexpected flare.

"Got you at last—damn you!" Long Tom Roberts gritted. He seized The Shadow, barking at the others: "C'mon! Give me plenty of help here!"

Blackened automatics were wrenched from The Shadow's iron-fingered grip by hairy fingers. Metallic hands took his hard shoulders, bore him to the floor. It took some doing.

"Blazes!" squeaked Monk Mayfair. "He's stronger than he looks!"

Up stepped Ham Brooks, who inserted the tip of his sword cane into the thrashing cloaked form, pressing hard. The Shadow subsided, overcome by an anesthetic compound which coated the upper blade.

"That does for you!" sneered Ham.

Handcuffs were produced, snapped tight over The Shadow's wiry wrists. He was lifted bodily and carried out into the sunlight his blinded orbs could not perceive, and away from the lodge, toward the low hill which concealed Doc Savage's secret institution for the reclamation of habitual criminals.

"This little war of ours is about over!" Monk exulted.

Chapter LI

THE EVIL FIEND

LAMONT CRANSTON COULD not guess where he was.

The millionaire only knew that he had been lifted out of his coffin, and carried into a dark room. The room was hung with funeral crepe. Lurid red-bulbed table lamps reposed on a tasteful pair of pedestals on either side of an ebony armchair, creating a harsh atmosphere. The chair into which Lamont Cranston had been placed was plain. This appeared to be a sitting room, such as can be found in most funeral parlors. Sickly pale lilies stood about in ceramic vases, adding to that somber impression.

Behind the black armchair, the crepe parted and out stepped a ghoulish figure.

The man wore robes such as a medieval monk might wear, and the large cloth hood threw his face into deep shadow. The glare of the scarlet lamps seemed to distort his half-hidden features into unrecognizability.

The weird figure announced: "I am—The Shadow!"

Cranston said stiffly, "If you are The Shadow, then I am the Mayor. For I have met The Shadow, and you are not he."

The monkish figure sat silent for a time. Hidden eyes stared at him. It was clear that he had no immediate retort, his false assertion having been successfully challenged by his captive.

The voice quavered, "No matter. For you are being released."

Cranston frowned. "Has the ransom been paid?"

"No, but it will be." A macabre cackle emerged from the hood. "For you will be the one paying it."

Cranston's frown deepened.

"I fail to understand."

"That makes two of us," sneered the Funeral Director. "For, until now, I have failed to understand that you had no relative authorized to pay your ransom. So I have made other arrangements. Be advised that upon your release, you will tender to me the princely sum of one million dollars. In return, I will relinquish your lovely niece, Weltha Cranston."

Lamont Cranston made fists on his knees. "You have kidnapped Weltha, you bounder?"

The man in the monk's robes clapped his hands twice, and out from the side came two men holding a struggling woman.

"Weltha?" gasped Cranston.

"Uncle Monty!" sobbed the young woman. "Thank goodness you are safe!"

Another handclap and the two toughs dragged the woman from view.

The Funeral Director intoned, "You will be given your liberty. Make good use of it. Instructions will follow. Heed them to the letter. Or I will be forced to make final arrangements for Miss Cranston."

With that, someone stepped up from behind the millionaire and dropped a cloth sack over his head, tying it tight around his chest.

Lamont Cranston attempted resistance, but the familiar hardness of revolver muzzles gouging into his chest and back dissuaded him from further action.

The multimillionaire was escorted out and shoved feet-first into the back of an idling machine, laid down so flat he knew at once that he had been placed in the curtained rear of funeral hearse. A heavy door slammed shut, making the vehicle rock on its springs.

Cranston saw nothing of his surroundings as the crepe-curtained machine eased out into the spreading dawn, bearing him away.

LESS THAN an hour later, the hearse rolled up the circular driveway of the Cranston estate, slowed to a stop, and the driver and one other came out. They flung open the back of the machine, and unceremoniously dragged out the millionaire globetrotter, sent him sprawling across his own manicured lawn.

Reclaiming their machine, the henchmen roared off, leaving the erstwhile captive to struggle with his bonds. His muffled shouts for assistance summoned from within Stanley the chauffeur and Richards the valet, who fell upon him and quickly helped shuck off the ropes that held him fast.

"Mr. Cranston!" cried Richards. "Thank Heavens. You are safe!"

"Yes, safe," ground out the millionaire. He found his feet. "I am safe, but Weltha is in the hands of fiends."

"Shall I ring Commissioner Weston for you?"

"Not yet. I must speak with my banker at once."

The reunited trio pushed back into the palatial residence.

MORNING brought a fresh wave of headlines.

LAMONT CRANSTON FREED BY KIDNAPPER
Niece Taken in Daring Criminal Swap

That was one headline.
Another boasted:

CRIMINAL KIDNAP RING MAKES BOLD MOVE
Will They Collect This Time?

Predictably, not every sheet printed the story correctly. There was speculation that the two kidnappings were not connected, except for the famous name of Cranston.

The millionaire clubman and world traveler refused all interviews, leaving it to his friend, Commissioner Weston, to field all press questions.

The Commissioner's office released a statement that Lamont Cranston was holed up at his New Jersey estate, working on the release of his niece, Weltha, and that his detectives, as well as the New Jersey Police, were hard at work on the case, one of the most audacious ever to come to official attention.

By this time, thanks in part to The Shadow's radio broadcast the previous night, the name of the Funeral Director had made it into the popular press. The police refused to confirm that any such person existed.

Meanwhile, Manhattanites continued to succumb to sudden heart attacks, and this added to the growing hysteria. That most of these unfortunates were of the age when such distressing calamities strike was ignored by the general public.

As yet, no reporter had linked the wave of kidnappings to the plague of heart seizures among well-to-do individuals. But with the two stories sharing the front page, it was only a matter of time before someone did.

Among readers of the news, both were a hot topic of conversation.

The persons who read these newspaper accounts sent out for the next extra editions, which were issued within an hour, and got a fresh shock. Police investigations had been at work and had uncovered some startling facts regarding the most recent heart attack victims.

The supposedly honest banker had turned out to be a thorough rascal, and his bank was closing while an audit was made to see how much he had stolen. Fortunately, the new compulsory government insurance would protect the small depositors.

And so it went through the list of brokers, lawyers and the other banker and millionaire factory owner. Most of these supposed possessors of upstanding reputations were discovered to have been the blackest of scoundrels. There was an exception or two, but the police freely admitted that they expected to find some of these sterling gentlemen were crooks, too.

The one notable exception was attorney Sydney J. Palmer-Letts, who had represented the missing millionaire, Lamont Cranston, in his business affairs.

Here, the two sensational stories became entwined. But the police hastened to assure the public that Palmer-Letts had probably succumbed to natural causes, whereas the other deaths were being marked as highly suspicious.

It was a white lie, of course. But the authorities did not wish to create any more of a panic among the general populace than newspaper scareheads had already engendered.

One physician offered the opinion that an unknown disease was striking down prominent men. There was a great deal of uninformed speculation regarding this theory, with other medical men expressing doubt on the first doctor's suggestion. This first medico was a heart specialist of some renown, so the public did not know what to think.

Doc Savage was asked for his opinion. Since a reputable journal had inquired, the bronze man issued a short statement to the effect that there appeared to be no greater number of heart attacks felling New Yorkers than usual. The statement was slightly disingenuous, but it helped quell a restive population, many of whom were flocking to their doctors.

IN HIS office, Police Commissioner Weston was conferring with Detective Cardona.

"The New Jersey Police should have posted a detachment of plainclothesmen at the Cranston manse!" he thundered, pounding the desk with his fist. "Now, while we have Cranston back, his niece is in the hands of this unsurpassed blackguard."

"It's not our jurisdiction," Cardona returned calmly. "Besides, who would ever think a kidnapper would let his victim go before collecting his ransom?"

"The only reason appears to be the problem of releasing

Cranston's own funds for that purpose," said Weston, somewhat mollified. "His late attorney's demise appears to have made it a virtual impossibility. This stymied both his niece and the kidnapper, forcing the latter to change the game entirely. Now Cranston is in a position to pay the ransom, but not for himself."

"It amounts to the same thing," decided Cardona. Shifting his cigar from one side of his mouth to the other, he added, "Speaking of games, what does Cranston plan to do?"

"I just spoke to him. He has mustered together the stipulated sum. He only awaits a communication from this Funeral Director on the hows and whys of surrendering it."

Cardona frowned. "So what's our angle on this?"

"As you correctly point out, Cardona," Weston returned grumpily, "this is not our jurisdiction. We are forced to sit on the sidelines." The Commissioner looked up. "Unless you have a suggestion to make?"

"Last night over the air The Shadow talked about the Funeral Director like he knows something about it."

"Balderdash! The news broadcasters are having a field day with this confused mess. Why should that radio noisemaker not get into the act as well?"

Shrugging, Cardona picked up a newspaper from Weston's desk. "Interesting column about One-Ear Shawn by Clyde Burke in the *Classic*. Hints that Doc Savage knows something about Shawn's disappearance. You know, a lot of bad actors have been vanishing since Doc Savage came on the scene. Before, I had a hunch that it might have something to do with The Shadow. Now, I'm not so sure. Maybe you should ring Doc Savage up."

Commissioner Weston regarded his ace detective sternly.

"Cardona, I want you to get two items straight. I do not wish to hear a bad word about Doc Savage in my presence ever again, and I do not want to hear uttered any further mention of The Shadow. Is that clear?"

"It's about the only thing that is," Cardona admitted resignedly.

Chapter LII

THE SHADOW DIVULGES

THE SHADOW AWOKE suddenly.

Deep-set eyes snapped open and quested about. The white interior of a hospital room greeted his searching gaze. He lay on a clean hospital-style bed.

Long-fingered hands went to his lower face, encountered bandages. Then he heard the clinking of chain.

The Shadow sat up. He was attired in a black pullover jersey and matching pants—the garments he most often wore under his sable cloak. One wrist was manacled, and a long chain led to the iron posts of the bed's headboard.

A well-modulated voice said, "We took the liberty of repairing the damage to your jaw incurred during the war. The plastic technique is new."

"The same technique you employed on One-Ear Shawn?"

"Evidently, we know one another's secrets," remarked Doc Savage. "For example, the chemical preparation you employed to blind me during our encounter in your sanctum was known to me. Professional conjurors call it the 'Devil's Whisper.' I duplicated the formula with the idea of giving you a taste of your own medicine."

The Shadow said nothing.

"It is interesting that your fingerprints can be found in no official file," resumed the bronze man. "Repeated calls to Washington failed to uncover your identity. Either there is no existing record of your service as a wartime spy, or you remain on the rolls of active agents."

A weak laughed sounded. It was muffled by the bandages.

"Nor could I determine from your surviving facial features precisely what you had looked like in younger days. You remain an enigma to me."

The Shadow changed the subject. "I was expected," he said sibilantly.

Doc nodded. "You were. We have been eavesdropping on the Funeral Director's short-wave broadcasts, and learned that Vincent and Burke have fallen into his hands. It stood to reason that you would come here to rescue Cliff Marsland, in order to fight back."

The Shadow nodded. "A sound deduction."

"A great deal about your recent activities was recorded in your archives," continued Doc. "Enough for me to understand that you operate for the good, even if you do so outside of the law."

"You do not approve of my methods."

"Usurping Lamont Cranston's identity does not paint you in a very favorable light," the bronze man said dryly.

"I required a cover identity and funds for my campaign on crimedom. Cranston possessed both, and used them infrequently."

"He originally thought you were the Funeral Director, and went to Ham Brooks for help. Cranston, by the way, has been released unharmed. He is back in his home."

The Shadow whispered, "Now he must ransom his niece. For that is the Funeral Director's latest scheme. Unable to extract his extortion settlement from Cranston's family, he has set his victim free to reverse the game."

"We have found no trace of Weltha Cranston, although I have my operatives looking far and wide."

"Marsland?"

Doc said. "He is anxious to be released. I had planned to let him go, since quiet investigation has revealed that he has paid his debt to society—if he was ever guilty in the first place—and there are no charges against him now."

"And myself?"

"You will need a few days to recuperate from your surgery."

"Weltha Cranston may not have a few days."

"We are working on that angle. What can you offer toward that end?"

"Allow me to consider this request."

"You previously indicated that there was a clue to his identity in the Funeral Director's choice of occupation," prompted the bronze man.

"Have you unraveled that riddle?"

"No, but we encountered the Funeral Director passing himself off as a chemist named Ernest Coffern."

"So learned through Rutledge Mann. It is another clue. Can you puzzle it out?"

"The real Ernest Coffern was experimenting with toxic gases in hopes of concocting a more humane way of executing criminals than present methods," stated Doc. "The Funeral Director apparently took over his home and identity after doing away with him—much as you have victimized Lamont Cranston. Since the unknown criminal employs exotic gases in his crimes, it stands to reason that he learned how to concoct these potions from Coffern himself."

"There is more to it, Savage."

Doc Savage's aureate eyes grew more animated.

"Think!" hissed The Shadow. "The clue is in the last name."

"Coffern?"

"What device does the Funeral Director use to communicate with both his minions and victims?"

"A miniature casket."

"Technically, it is a coffin, a casket having six sides and a split lid for viewing, while the more costly coffin boasts only four sides. The arch kidnapper was attracted to Ernest Coffern not only because he experimented with deadly gases, but due to the similarity of their last names, which suggests the Funeral Director's mordant profession."

"Are you suggesting that this man is also named Coffern?"

"No! *Coffran*. Isaac Coffran. Twice before we have battled, and twice he eluded The Shadow's justice. In his last failed game, he played the part of a counterfeiter. After I crushed his wretched schemes, Coffran vanished. I have been seeking him ever since." *

"How do you know this?" pressed Doc.

"The Funeral Director is wise to my ways. Only one I had conquered before could divine that The Shadow sometimes played the part of a man named George Clarendon. I saw in the paltry sums he demanded for his victims a scoundrel of advanced years. All the rest was deduction."

Doc nodded. "How did you know Coffran would visit me?"

The Shadow's eyes gazed ceilingward. "Isaac Coffran feared The Shadow," came the sibilant response. "But The Shadow has no standing with the police. Not so Doc Savage. It stood to reason that he would attempt to draw you into a trap, sooner or later. For he realized that once you ransomed your man, Brooks, you would leave no stone unturned until you brought him to book. And the reach of Doc Savage is globe spanning."

Doc considered. "That might explain why his earliest victims were shady and unsavory men."

"It does explain it! Coffran did not wish to provoke The Shadow into fresh conflict, lest he meet deserved destruction. So he selected men who possessed suitable wealth, but persons who also dared not seek police protection. No doubt many paid. Others refused, and to them he delivered doom. Doom in the form of an untraceable gas. It was a scheme that appeared foolproof, but in his growing greed, the Funeral Director se-

---

* *The Eyes of The Shadow* and *The Shadow Laughs.*

lected a man who was not by nature a criminal. Lamont Cranston. That misstep proved to be his undoing."

"The Funeral Director is still at large," Doc reminded.

The Shadow chuckled softly.

"Why did Cranston's attorney pay you a visit?"

"The Shadow knows!"

"That is no answer," admonished Doc.

"Perhaps Sydney J. Palmer-Letts had skeletons in his closet, and The Shadow wished to warn him that he might be on the Funeral Director's list of intended victims."

"That is speculation, not an answer," Doc pointed out.

The Shadow paused. "As George Clarendon, I told a different story for public consumption. Here is the truth. The number of mysterious deaths by heart failure had attracted my interest from the outset. I battle what I style supercrime—misdeeds that often go unpunished because they are undetected. Seeing a growing pattern, I became concerned that Lamont Cranston might become a target of this superkidnapper, and for reasons of my own, I wished to forestall any stab in his direction. As it happened, I knew Sydney J. Palmer-Letts, for George Clarendon had secured his services once. Not wishing to alarm Cranston by a direct approach, I invited his attorney to visit me, where I intended to apprise him of my suspicions."

Something resembling anger came into the orbs which were like black coals on either side of the enormous hooked nose.

"Unbeknownst to me, the men of the Funeral Director had been watching him, suspecting that Palmer-Letts was blocking Cranston from paying the demanded amount. One of them, discovering that he was to meet George Clarendon, no doubt obtained instructions to do away with him by subtle means, leaving one of the diabolical caskets as a warning to Clarendon." The eyes of The Shadow clouded briefly, although his bandaged face remained immobile of expression. "A warning that backfired as badly as my invitation to poor Palmer-Letts. For it confirmed my suspicions and placed me firmly on the trail of the Funeral Director, whose existence I had hitherto only suspected."

"I see," mused Doc. The bronze man seemed to consider this new information. Finally, he said: "As Clarendon, you once offered to join forces. Does that offer still hold?"

"My agents must be redeemed from Coffran's clutches, along with Weltha Cranston. What conditions do you impose?"

"That there be no killing."

"The Shadow has his own ways, as do you," said the man on the bed, laying his dark-haired head back on the pillow. "I must rest, but I will consider it."

The Shadow closed his eyes.

"Ring the bell when you have decided," said Doc Savage, exiting the room. "But keep in mind the possibility that your men are to be put to death very soon."

Hooded eyes sprang up, glowing strangely. "What makes you say that?"

"Monk Mayfair and I were briefly prisoners of the Funeral Director," stated Doc. "Before he decided it was too dangerous to kill us outright, we overheard plans for our bodies being incinerated in a crematorium. We are investigating every such place in Long Island as seems likely to be the one to which he referred."

The Shadow sat up, came to his feet. Burning eyes bored into Doc Savage's frank gaze.

"The crematorium is not located on Long Island, but in New Jersey. I have seen it. Bring me my garments and my guns. We will go there together."

"Your garments, but not your weapons. There will be no killing."

The Shadow seemed to hesitate, but then he nodded solemnly.

"In a pocket of my cloak you will discover a vial containing a purple elixir of my own preparation," he intoned. "It is a restorative I employ in dire emergencies."

"I have already analyzed it," said Doc. "As a physician I would caution against resorting to this preparation too frequently but, in this instance, it should have you back on your feet for the battle ahead."

"Produce Marsland. He is why I came here. We will need his services if we are to vanquish Isaac Coffran, the Funeral Director."

The laugh of The Shadow pushing through the muffling facial bandages sounded like a soft knell of doom.

Chapter LIII

CONFERENCE

LAMONT CRANSTON WAS pacing his study, his ordinarily calm features fretful.

Upon his return, the millionaire globetrotter had discovered his mansion to be in a state of disarray. Servants had explained as best they could. They did not know how the exotic dagger came to split the library paneling. Nor could they explain the shattered stained-glass door window, or the broken lamp in his study—one that he had never seen before.

His town car was not in its garage. Not one knew who had made off with it.

The New Jersey Police did come, and had been sent away after taking furious notes.

Lamont Cranston had secreted himself within his study to be alone. Into an expensive valise that was securely locked, his banker had stuffed a considerable sum of money. Exactly ten thousand one-hundred dollar bills—the million-dollar ransom demand of the Funeral Director.

All that remained was for instructions to come.

Lamont Cranston was determined to deliver the money himself. Nothing less than that would be acceptable.

Going to his desk, he lifted the receiver, and checked for the sound of the wire. It was operating. Telephone workers had restored service, which had been severed by unknown persons.

The wait was becoming excruciating.

By this time, Cranston had come to a new understanding of

the chain of events that had brought him to this terrible state. He had been mistaken about The Shadow. That weird personage, whom he had encountered before, was not the author of his misfortune. It had been his leaping to conclusions that had made him think so, for he knew of no other who might victimize him.

Who the Funeral Director really was, ultimately was of no importance to Lamont Cranston. All that mattered was to rescue Weltha, his only relative of consequence.

As the afternoon wore on, the millionaire had refused all offers of food and drink. Had this been the African interior, and he were dealing with poachers, or stalking a lion, Lamont Cranston would know what to do. But this business of bounders who kidnapped young women for money troubled him deeply. The affairs of civilization, and its many complications, were one reason Cranston so often disappeared into wild places where the thrill of the hunt—or the expectation of danger—had nothing to do with unsavory sorts such as this so-called Funeral Director.

By afternoon, the wait had become maddening. Then Richards was knocking on the door saying, "Visitors, Mr. Cranston."

"Send them away!"

"Important visitors, sir. I am terribly sorry, but it is Doc Savage and some of his associates."

Cranston hesitated. He had met Doc Savage once, briefly. Both were members of the Explorers Club. Their acquaintance was only glancing, however.

"Show them in," said Cranston, changing his tone.

DOC SAVAGE entered and, so great was his size that the room immediately appeared to have contracted. With him was a man who greatly resembled a gorilla Cranston had once encountered in the Congo bush country. Two other men accompanied the bronze giant. One was a rather undersized fellow with a bulging forehead and sickly pallor, while the other was the familiar face of the noted attorney, Theodore Marley Brooks.

"I am damnably glad to see you alive and at liberty, Brooks," said Cranston honestly. "Please accept my sincere apologies for dragging you into my personal plight."

Ham Brooks dipped his head in acknowledgement. "The circumstances were obviously not of your doing."

Doc Savage said, "Commissioner Weston sends his regards. We have been on the trail of the Funeral Director since your abduction. Our aim tonight is to help you free your niece, Miss Cranston."

Cranston nodded noncommittally. "Who are these other men with you?"

"This is Monk Mayfair, the chemist, and Long Tom Roberts, the electrical expert," explained Doc.

Long Tom growled, "I'm the guy that planted that busted lamp on your desk."

Cranston looked perplexed. The lamp remains now filled the wastebasket.

Doc Savage explained, "This was done at my behest. We feared an attempt on your niece's life, so Long Tom slipped in to plant the lamp, whose light bulb doubles as a microphone."

"Well, there it is," said Cranston, waving to the wastebasket.

Long Tom peered down into the wastebasket, saw that the lamp was beyond repair, and frowned deeply. It had cost a great deal of money, and many hours had been expended in his basement laboratory to construct the eavesdropping device.

A fifth man, who had been hanging back, now entered the room.

Looking at him, Cranston's eyes narrowed. For the lower portion of his face was swathed in gauzy bandages.

"You seem familiar to me," he suggested.

The new arrival was tolerably tall, with pronounced features, and possessed deep-set eyes that seemed to sparkle with a strange light.

Doc Savage said, "This individual is working with us on this matter."

"You may call me George Clarendon," said the new arrival.

"I have heard your name bandied about the Cobalt Club," admitted Cranston, "recall once having the pleasure of meeting you. A criminologist by trade, if I am not mistaken?"

"I, too, have been on the trail of this nefarious Funeral Director," said Clarendon. "Indeed, before your unfortunate brush with him. An attempt was recently made upon my life, but I survived it. These bandages on my face are temporary. I look forward to this just reckoning."

Cranston nodded, not entirely satisfied. Then to Doc Savage, he declared, "I am awaiting the ransom call, or however the demand will be delivered. I will insist upon delivering the money myself, in order to ensure that my niece is freed unharmed."

"That is a sensible plan," said Doc. "But perhaps we may improve upon it."

The millionaire's eyebrows jumped. "How so?"

Clarendon interposed, "I have some ideas on that score, if you would care to listen."

"Anything that will expedite the release of my niece, Weltha," said Cranston sincerely.

"And, it is to be hoped," added Clarendon coolly, "punishing the perpetrators severely."

"We are of one mind, Clarendon," murmured Cranston.

For some strange reason, this remark caused George Clarendon to laugh softly in a way that made Lamont Cranston shiver slightly.

Chapter LIV

DEATH ORDERS

ISAAC COFFRAN SAT at the ham radio set that he used to communicate with his underlings. The set was warming up. He much preferred this method of communication to the sending-key radio set he had temporarily adopted.

Seizing the table microphone by its neck, he drew it closer to his thin lips. It was tuned to his special frequency, one he had refused to change even after the voice of The Shadow had spoken to him over it. It vexed the man who called himself the Funeral Director that his hated foe, whom he had twice eluded, had stumbled across the secret frequency. But Isaac Coffran was a stubborn man. He would not change it. No brain could possibly pierce his contrived front as the Funeral Director.

Of that he was certain.

Coffran did not suspect that the mocking voice heard over this loudspeaker not long after one of his underlings had slain Sydney J. Palmer-Letts and the subsequent failure to frighten George Clarendon off the case had not, in fact, been The Shadow, but the famous Doc Savage impersonating the master of midnight.

Nor did Coffran suspect that the voice that now suddenly jumped out of the loudspeaker was emanating from the same short-wave set, the one that was housed in Lamont Cranston's tower radio room.

For just as the Funeral Director was about to check in with his morticians at the crematorium he controlled—along with a half-dozen funeral homes and mortuaries scattered through-out Greater New York and New Jersey—an unfamiliar person began calling him.

"Calling the Funeral Director. Calling the Funeral Director."

"Who is this?" Coffran demanded querulously. "Who speaks?"

"This is Lamont Cranston."

"Cranston! What are you doing calling me? You were told to await instructions."

"I have grown weary of waiting," returned the firm voice. *"So I am taking the liberty of calling you."*

"How did you get this frequency? Who told you of it?"

"No one," returned Cranston, calmly. *"Your man Creece left my short-wave set tuned to this frequency. Since neither I nor my servants touched the dial, it could only have been him. Hence, my call."*

"Very clever. You have the funds?"

"I have. How would you like the money conveyed to you?"

"In person. Come alone. Alone, do you hear me?"

"I hear you clearly," returned Cranston, smooth-toned.

"Excellent. Now listen carefully. We will make our exchange at a place you should know well, for your ancestors are interred there. Do you know whereof I speak?"

"Yes," said Cranston. *"I know exactly where the family vault lies. If I am not mistaken, I have recently paid it a visit—much against my will."*

At that, the reedy voice of Isaac Coffran emitted a ghoulish cackle.

"Very good, very good. You have a sound head on your shoul-ders, Cranston. Shall we say midnight?"

"I will arrive at the witching hour. Do not neglect to bring along my niece."

"Of course, of course," snapped Coffran. "What would be the point of this charade if I did not keep my part of the bargain? Midnight it will be. Come alone. Alone, I say! Tell no one. Or

I will re-inter you, the living with the dead. Do not forget, I am your Funeral Director!"

Isaac Coffran snapped off his set, and waited exactly ten minutes. Then, with his eyes going crafty, he switched the short-wave set back on.

"Undertaker Desmond," he called.

"Undertaker Desmond speaking," came a distant voice.

"Have you disposed of the remains yet?"

"The furnace retort has not reached the required temperature."

"Hasten the process! Complete the procedure. There is much to be done! I will brook no further delays. I am your Funeral Director."

"At once, Funeral Director."

Again shutting off the set, he lowered the cover to his roll-top desk, concealing the set. Turning in his creaking wooden chair, he keyed an intercom.

"Yes, Funeral Director," came an obedient voice.

"Prepare the cars. Send the girl on ahead in the hearse. We will meet Cranston at midnight, but I do not like the confident and assertive tone he used upon me. I do not trust him. We will take no chances, not with The Shadow still at liberty. We will throw the niece in with the others. Fling them *all* into the crematorium. Cranston, as well. Their combined ashes will rest in the Cranston family vault, unsuspected."

"Fitting."

"Cranston has earned his demise," sneered Coffran. "Now let us be on our way. It is a long drive to the cemetery and I wish to arrive at least an hour before the doomed man."

"At once, Funeral Director."

Chapter LV

STRANGE ESCAPE

HARRY VINCENT WRENCHED at the handcuffs which secured his wrists behind his back.

"No use!" he groaned. "If only they had used ropes!"

The chamber in which he lay was very black. He was not alone. Clyde Burke had been placed beside him.

They had been awake less than an hour. They were relieved to discover that they could see—all but astounded to discover that they still dwelt among the living. Their brains still swam somewhat from the effects of the gas that had overpowered them both.

A low-wattage light bulb encased in a mesh cage above their heads permitted vision. The room in which they had discovered themselves was a steel cell. No windows. But one door, and that plainly locked. Not that they could get to the stainless steel handle lying on the floor as they were.

Burke, fortunately, had only been bruised and shaken in the overturning of The Shadow's powerful taxicab. Vincent himself was a bit battered, but not seriously so.

Clyde, as far as Harry had been able to see, was unharmed.

"Damn them!" Clyde growled spiritedly. "If I could get rid of this jewelry, I would— Say, why did you follow me?"

Harry groaned, "I discovered the phone line had been cut. That phone call was a trap. For both of us."

Clyde asked, "Have you any idea what they did to Miss Cranston?"

"None," admitted Harry. "A little while ago I heard some kind of a commotion in the passage. After they brought me in here. It sounded like a man being subjected to a grueling third degree. After a while, the sounds stopped."

The click of a key sounded at the door. There came a clatter. And the door swung ajar.

Harry lifted his head, and was nearly blinded when the panel opened and let reflected light in from the passage. Flashlight rays were dashed into their eyes, momentarily blinding them.

Blue-eyed Weltha Cranston was shoved inside. The door closed after her.

"Miss Cranston!" Harry exclaimed.

"I-I'm alright," the young woman gasped shakily. "Oh—I'm so glad we're together again! Being alone in that awful place was—was horrible, suffocating!"

"Where were you?"

"I do not know," she admitted. "But I was being held in a room where I smelled flowers—a cloying suffocating smell. Later, rough men came for me and I was handcuffed and placed in—" Her strong voice wavered, broke.

"Go on," urged Harry.

"A casket. The lid was closed over my face. Then I was driven here."

"In a hearse, no doubt," ground out Clyde.

"What will become of us?" Weltha wondered, looking about at the austere confines of her new cell.

"Something will turn up to enable us to get out of this," Harry told her, voicing an optimism he hardly felt. "Did you hear anything to indicate what they plan on doing with us?"

"Not a word," admitted the black-haired girl. "Do you think they'll—they'll—"

"I'm trying not to think of that," Harry told her gently. "You'd better use the same mental antidote."

The links of Weltha Cranston's handcuffs made a metallic rattle. She shivered. Then she gave a low cry.

"These terrible men all dress in black," she moaned. "I feel as if I have been waked while alive and all that remains is my interment."

"It is part of the Funeral Director's scheme to instill dread into his victims," advised Clyde. "The hearse, the mourning clothes and all that claptrap. That's all it is—claptrap. Don't let it get to you."

Weltha nodded and bit her red lips. Her lustrous raven-wing hair was disheveled, but still beautiful to behold.

Harry commented, "It's deuced queer they should put us together. But let's take advantage of it. Miss Cranston, have you a hairpin?"

"I can't reach my head with my hands," murmured the young woman. "But there may be one left."

With flippering movements, Harry crossed the concrete floor to her side. He managed to fumble in her fine raven hair, although the manacles held his wrists behind him. His fingers found a tiny, springy hairpin.

"I'll see if I can free your handcuffs," he told her. "Luckily, they are an old trunk key type."

Picking the lock of the cuffs proved to be a tedious task. But at last Harry was successful.

"Now, see what you can do with mine!" Harry requested.

The young woman went to work. Her fingers were evidently more supple than Harry's, because she had his wrist free in a very short time.

"That's fine!" he told her softly. He busied himself on Clyde Burke's manacles, freeing him also.

"You're the skipper!" Clyde told Harry. "What do we do? Rush them when they open the door?"

"We'd get our heads shot off," Harry pointed out.

"That's about what would happen," Clyde decided morosely.

He took a turn around the steel-walled cell. The space was entirely windowless, and boasted only one door. Air circulated through holes bored into one wall.

Harry thrust a finger in one of the holes to ascertain the thickness of the concrete. Almost an inch!

"I've got an idea," he said at length. "We will replace the manacles—"

"They've got spring locks," Clyde pointed out. "They'll lock when we close them and we'll be back where we started."

"Let me finish," Harry interrupted. "We'll tear off bits of cloth and cram them into the mechanism. That will keep them from locking. A single jerk will free our wrists."

"Wonderful!" Weltha exclaimed admiringly. "You think of everything!"

With fragments of cloth, they fixed the handcuffs so they could be closed without locking.

FIVE minutes later, the door opened again. A black-suited minion of the Funeral Director crowded in, stubby-snouted gun in hand.

"On your feet, prisoners! You're going places."

"What kind of places?" demanded Clyde, suspicion threading his voice.

"The girl is being ransomed in another hour."

"Oh, thank goodness!" Weltha cried.

Still suspicious, Clyde asked, "What about us?"

"You two are going where she is! Now come on."

Harry and Clyde swapped thin glances. They didn't like the sound of that, although on the surface the guard's words carried the hope of living to see another day.

Nevertheless, they struggled to regain their feet. It was no easy task, and the impatient guard finally jumped in and assisted them without being gentle about it.

They were marched out of their cell and down a concrete

corridor that twisted sharply and then turned again. The absence of windows made them wonder if they were underground.

The solitary guard toted a small, flat automatic. He walked directly behind them, holding it rather negligently.

The three prisoners followed instructions barked into their ears. "Go left. Now right. Straight ahead now."

Tight-lipped, Harry walked along, his mind racing. He happened to glance down. A glint on metal flapping against his chest caught his eye. He had not noticed it before.

It resembled the aluminum "dog tag" soldiers wear into battle in the event they are killed or wounded. Stamped into the metal would be the full name, service rank, and other identification. But this item was of stainless steel.

Harry could see the name stamped on his. It said:

WILTON G. BARGES

This alarmed him more than their predicament. Experimentally, Harry tensed his wrists against the handcuffs. An ounce more pressure would free them.

Hissing a single word of warning to Clyde, Vincent went into violent action.

Harry suddenly swiveled, pitched headlong into the prodding man. A wrench freed his wrists. He dashed a clubbed fist against the trailing guard's blunt jaw.

The fellow was shaken by the blow, but not rendered senseless. He poked a frantic finger at a wall button. Harry knocked his hand away. He hit the man again, then seized the fellow by the throat and banged his head against the solid concrete wall. The guard became loose-jointed and quivering.

Shucking his own handcuffs, Clyde Burke stepped forward and helped complete the job of making him unconscious.

"What the devil?" Clyde gasped. "Why did you jump him? Now we're in a pretty mess."

Harry beckoned the others close.

"Listen!" he breathed. "Here's how I figure it! All that talk of turning us loose was a trick."

"But that guard said so!" objected Clyde. "What was the idea of jumping him? We were getting away with our whole skins, weren't we? And now you've spoiled it!"

Harry shook his head impatiently. "You don't understand! Look on your chest."

Clyde did. Puzzled, he fumbled his tag into the wan light. As a newspaper leg man, he had visited countless morgues and mortuaries in the course of covering his beat. He recognized the significance of the tag, and even more the fact that it bore a name not his own.

Burke expelled his breath in a shocked gasp.

"What is it?" demanded Weltha, her oval face pale and strained.

Harry reached over and lifted the tag hanging from her neck by a delicate ball chain. "You have one, too," he said hoarsely.

"What is it?" she cried, seeing the horror on Harry's face.

"Let me tell it," said Clyde. "These fireproof tags are placed on bodies that are to be incinerated so that the ashes can be identified for burial, or after being interred in funerary urns."

Shock drained Weltha's features. "They—they—"

Harry nodded grimly. "They had no intention of setting any of us free. We were being escorted to a crematorium. The tags probably belong to bodies that are awaiting incineration. Our ashes were unquestionably slated for the graves of other people."

"We've got to get out of here," Clyde muttered. "Snappy, too!"

"Exactly!" Harry agreed.

They searched the fallen guard. Another small automatic pistol came to light. Harry kept his and gave the other to Clyde. They removed the magazines, found them full of reassuringly heavy bullets, then replaced the ammunition clips.

"We will have to move quick, now!" he warned.

They resumed negotiating the concrete passageway, not sure where it would take them, but mindful of the thin tags flapping on their chests, stainless steel tokens that reminded them of the horrific fate that awaited should their efforts falter or fail….

Chapter LVI

THE BLACK GHOST

OUTSIDE THE CEMETERY crematorium where the black hearse had carried Weltha Cranston to this rendezvous, three men dressed as morticians loitered, furiously smoking cigarettes in the Autumn moonlight.

They wore almost identically dolorous expressions, as men do when in mourning, and conversed for a moment in low voices.

"The Funeral Director ought to be along any minute," one warned.

Another looked at his watch. "Less than a hour to midnight. Once Cranston gets here, we can finish our business and clear out of this damned spooky graveyard."

The third inhaled deeply, then released a dry bubble of smoke from pursed lips. The smoky ball wobbled, began falling apart.

"Do you—do you think the Funeral Director will kill them first? I mean, before we gotta shove 'em into that damn furnace?"

"Hard to say," opined the first speaker. "I hear he's hoppin' mad over all the trouble Cranston caused. First, we go to the effort to snatch him, then we gotta grab up his niece—all just to collect one ransom."

"Well, in a way it was his fault. For putting that Cranston lawyer on the spot in the first place, what I mean. If he wasn't dead, he could've arranged the ransom, havin' power of attorney and all."

"Don't remind the boss of that," warned the first man. "Or maybe you'll get slid into that hell furnace with the rest of 'em."

"The mouth of hell might be preferable to what will happen if The Shadow ever catches up with us," grunted the third man. "We'll be pushin' up daisies for sure."

"I ain't afraid of The Shadow so much as I am of that damned Doc Savage. He's poison to crooks. At least if The Shadow croaks you, you'll get a proper burial. Guys that buck the big bronze guy just up and disappear. No one knows what happens to them."

"You reckon either of them devils are gonna give us more trouble?"

"We can handle 'em!" boasted the first man.

"Between Savage and The Shadow," complained another, "it's gettin' so a dishonest guy can't make a buck in this man's world."

A morbid silence followed.

"Aw, quit your bellyachin'," scolded the first speaker. "Cranston ain't the first. We've fed nearly a dozen birds the gas treatment, haven't we? Some of 'em tried to buck us, didn't they? Tried mighty hard. And where did it land them? In the boneyard. And look at us. Rollin' in dough. Keep your mind on that."

One guard—a burly, thick-necked fellow who looked like a down-on-his-luck-professional wrestler and obviously hired for his muscular attributes—was peering into a dark wall of trees that shifted and shook in the evening breeze.

For a moment, he thought he saw an elongated shadow pooled beside a tall granite grave marker surmounted by a forlorn-winged marble angel.

He was about to call it to the attention of the others when the moon, breaking through a ragged bank of clouds, threw silvery light down upon the spot.

There was nothing there, after all! The man relaxed. Just his nerves.

Finishing their cigarettes, two of the three went inside the crematorium building.

The burly guard remained outside. He noticed he had left the cowl lights of the hearse burning. He muttered a complaint and went over and switched them off.

A soft yet sinister laugh caught his attention.

Pivoting, he suddenly confronted a strange, towering shadow. It was such a shadow as he had glimpsed earlier—only it was more distinguishable now.

The guard's eyes bugged out. The shadow was alive!

He opened his mouth to howl for help. But the large shadow flung forward, enveloped him. A black-gloved palm stoppered his mouth, thumb and forefinger pinching his nostrils shut. The guard could not breathe or make a sound.

He tried to kick and claw the dark form which had seized him. But the thing seemed full of steel bands. They coiled about his legs, around his arms. He was held absolutely helpless.

Then a fist, one which delivered a harder blow than the guard ever felt before, struck his jaw. The fellow collapsed.

Lifting the man, the shadow carried him a few yards and lowered him behind several cars parked in the shadow of rustling trees. A black-gloved hand came close to the guard's nostrils and broke a tiny glass vial. The anesthetic contained therein trickled onto the man's face. It would make him unconscious for hours.

An instant later, the monster shadow was standing beside the door. It opened.

A voice—it was exactly like the tone of the unconscious guard—rang into the warehouse.

"C'mere, you!" it said.

"You mean me?" demanded a man.

"Sure. Who'd you think?"

Grumbling, the fellow approached the door. He came alone. Stepping through, he looked about—but could see nothing but a looming patch of dense darkness.

Before he could speak, the cloud of blackness was upon him.

It enveloped him, as it had the other guard. Again, a glass vial of anesthetic was broken in a black-gloved hand, with identical results.

Shapeless and bat-like, the shadow hovered over the prostrate form of his new conquest. The thin beam of a flash flicked out, racing over the features of the unconscious man.

The cloaked intruder lifted the senseless body, bore it over and placed it beside the other. As the phantom shape stooped, the rippling black cloak seemed to spread and cover both forms. Fully a minute passed before it fell away.

The form revealed seemed to be that of the fellow who had succumbed second. His face was that of the unconscious man.

To all appearances, the person who stood there *was* the guard—although the fellow lay senseless beside his comrade.

A master of impersonation and make-up, this phantom!

ENTERING the crematorium, the supposed guard closed the door behind him and crossed moth-like to the group beside a small office room.

"The dumb cluck!" he announced, referring to the guard who had apparently called. "Wanted to borrow a buck so that he could send to the diner for some grub."

The voice was exactly like that of the senseless guard!

The guard followed the others deep into the structure, coming to a great chamber filled with heat. There, on wheeled catafalques, four open coffins stood. They were simple pine boxes, lacking all funerary embellishments.

"Four, huh?" he muttered.

"Sure. One each for those two Shadow snoops. Another for the dame, and the last box for Cranston himself—once he arrives."

"Thorough," remarked the disguised guard.

There was a temperature gauge mounted on the great stone kiln of a thing. A man consulted it.

"Almost ready to bake our bread," he said gleefully.

His tittering laugh was not joined by the others, who were sweating, and not entirely from the intense heat of the chamber. This was a grisly business they were undertaking tonight.

The other man looked at his watch. "Jake should have brought the prisoners up by now."

"We startin' early?"

"Yeah. No sense trying to burn all four at once. We'll start with the snoopers. Max, you go see what's keeping him."

"I'll do it," said the disguised guard. "This heat is already getting to me."

"Be my guest."

The guard who was no guard eased from the room, making almost no sound.

He found a passage, saw that it led to a blank wall and an open manhole-type cover. Peering down, he drew from his clothing a trailing black cloak of astonishing thinness and a battered black hat. These he donned. They completely concealed his disguised features and purloined clothing.

A moment later, his mammoth figure slipped down the ladder, found a concrete floor and floated along it, casting a shadow so massive it might have escaped from some lower level of the netherworld.

THE MAN OF STEALTH explored, soon discovering that the low hill on which the crematorium proper had been erected was honeycombed with poured concrete passages, some of which ended in simple wooden ladders.

Coming to one, he climbed it, popped the ceiling manhole lid above. The noisome smell that greeted him made the cloaked one hesitate.

A flashlight came out, popped illumination, quested upward. The ray revealed aged granite walls, cobwebs and other evidence of charnel circumstances—the interior of a burial crypt.

Hastily, the interloper sealed the cover and continued on his careful way.

Moving soundlessly, he was able to detect the rattle of footsteps and hastened along, coming to an open area that seemed to be some kind of utility room.

Trying a door, he found it suspiciously empty. Evidently curious, he entered.

The closet into which the shadowy figure squeezed was unlighted. Gloom filled it. He had hardly disappeared through the door before his skilled fingers were trying the handle. It was unlocked. Out into the passage he went.

But almost instantly he faded back into the closet again.

Several men were striding along the passage. All wore the customary severe black suits of professional morticians.

The intruder, although he had moved about considerably in the last few minutes, had done so swiftly. It appeared he had crawled inside in time to intercept the group on their way to report to the Funeral Director.

A cadaverous-faced man leading, the picturesque procession passed the open door inside which the interloper crouched. Rather, all but one of them passed. The last man of the cavalcade happened to be trailing the others by a dozen feet.

As he came even with the utility closet, it fell open. A rowdy black cloud popped out of the door to envelop him. Fingers found his throat and shut off his attempted outcry more effectively than if he had been beheaded. He was carried, paralyzed by the unbelievable strength in the hands which held him, back into the utility closet.

But some faint sound attracted the attention of another of the morticians. One turned. Discovering his companion had vanished, his jaw sagged.

"Jake!" he called. "Where did you get to?"

Inside the closet, a black-gloved fist drove a short, terrific blow. The man called Jake abruptly became limp. The cloaked one crouched over him. The dark cloak, spreading, covered his form like turbulent smoke.

"Jake!" barked the man outside. Uneasiness had grown in his tone. "Is something wrong?"

From the utility closet came a muffled voice.

"I noticed this door open," it said. "Just checkin' for spies."

The words were hollow, rather unclear. But the man in the passage evidently thought they sounded thus because the speaker was poking around in a closet.

"Come on, you dummy!" he snapped. "You're holdin' us up!"

In the closet, the black cloak of The Shadow shuffled about, the crimson lining showing momentarily. Then it seemed to vanish, revealing a man who might have been a brother or cousin to the one lying on the floor—except that the fellow on the floor was no longer attired in his black mortician's suit. In fact, the senseless one was naked, save for his red union suit.

A man who looked generally like Jake stepped out into the passage. Thanks to the wan ceiling lights, many of which needed replacing, this fact was not immediately evident.

"What was it made you stop?" asked the fellow who had given the alarm. "Your face looks kind of funny. Did you see something?"

"Nah." Jake's voice was a hoarse, angry growl. He gave the other man a violent shove. "Call me a dummy, will you!" he snarled. "Get goin'! We gotta get topside. Cranston will be here any minute!"

The interloper knew his crooks! He had succeeded in guessing pretty near the sort of manners Jake had, for the other man was deceived. Turning, he followed the procession down the passage, taking care to remain far in the rear so that his lack of facial resemblance to the unconscious Jake was not evident.

It was also of note that the black suit was all but popping its seams on his well-developed body.

The procession made its way along, and each time it turned a corner, the man in the rear fell back briefly, and tested such doors and nooks as he happened upon. In every case, finding nothing of consequence.

Once, the group came to an open door and one man poked his head in.

"Empty!" he bleated. "Blackie musta pulled them out already."

"They—they goin' into the furnace?" chattered a nervous man.

"Yeah. Even the girl. The Funeral Director wants no witnesses, or bodies. The fire takes care of both."

"Cranston's kind of a celebrity. Won't this raise a big stink?"

"Sure. But once they're reduced to ashes, no one can tell who they are. No body, no crime."

Having hung back, the spectral prowler heard all of this. Swiftly, he performed another startling quick change.

When he popped around the corner, he was shrouded in a sepia cloak.

A great black hat, the brim yanked down, hid all the head and face.

This sudden flurry of fabric caused all heads to turn. Eyes popped wide and faces turned stark white at the spectral sight.

"The Shadow!" a man screeched.

A pale hand had been holding a tube, pinched between thumb and forefinger. When the tube hopped into the other hand, thumb and forefinger were covered with a substance.

The hand lifted, snapped its fingers once. Came a terrific report, followed an instant later by a blinding flash of light.

Blinded, the Mortician staggered backward.

In swept the mammoth figure, seizing two heads, one in each hand and banging them together. They collapsed, struck senseless.

Two others staggered about, hands clapped to their light-seared eyeballs. They barely felt the terrible hands that took hold of them, producing simultaneous concussions.

All four men were lifted into the steel cell that had formerly held the prisoners and the door was quietly shut on them.

With an eerie absence of footfalls, the phantom attacker continued on his prowl. The shadow he cast was gigantic, formidable, like a hulking demon which had escaped from the nether regions.

UNDERTAKER Desmond was nervous. As second in command to the Funeral Director, he was privy to his boss' plans and intentions. Matters were coming to a head. The big payoff was at hand. But now there was a hitch. Several of them, it seemed.

First, he had wasted the evening torturing a prisoner, who had been abducted by accident. This victim had died, without revealing any useful information.

Worse, an attempt to cremate the incriminating body had gone awry. The furnace fires had not achieved sufficient intensity to do the job. The scorched-black body had to be removed from the flames, for later disposal.

The sight of the charred corpse had so unnerved Desmond that he had repaired to his private underground room, and slept fitfully.

Once, he awoke and thought he heard wicked laughter in the darkness. Snapping on his light, he sat bolt upright.

There had been nothing there. Creeping to the door, he cracked it open and spied a figure ghosting along in the alternating zones of light and darkness. Carefully, he followed it until the black blot of a thing came to the room where the torture session had taken place. With a weird twist, it entered the room.

But when Desmond mustered up the nerve to investigate, he found nothing. The room was empty but for a shrouded figure in an open casket—the tortured man. The black thing might have been the wandering soul of the slain unfortunate.

Shaken further, he had gone back to bed, in a vain effort to purge his conscience of the screams of the tortured one and his memory of his blackened cadaver. Desmond had slept fitfully, but not for very long.

Since awakening and seeing the eerie black shade of an apparition out in the corridor, the Undertaker had not mustered sufficient courage to reenter the room where a burnt body lay. That sinister, terrible laugh seemed to ring in his ears still.

It was not long before Desmond felt the need for some artificial courage. So he went to a storage room, taking pains to turn all the lights on ahead of him and leave them on. He found some of the liquor kept on hand for medicinal purposes. He drank. It helped him so much, he drank again. He repeated the treatment several times, the process occupying nearly a half hour.

His courage replenished, Undertaker Desmond drew out a huge, ugly automatic pistol and made sure it was loaded. Then he left the storage room.

For a time, he paused in the corridor, his alcohol-stimulated brain doing its best to think. He finally reached a decision.

Shaky legs carrying his rangy body with an air of determination, he made for his quarters, slapping his automatic with an air of maudlin bravado.

"Just bring on yer black ghosts!" he scowled. "I'll handle 'em!"

He swiveled suddenly, whipping up his weapon, just to show himself what he would do in the event that uncanny thing of the darkness should return. His eyes probed the gloom. There were shadows aplenty about him. Some seemed darker than others. He stared at one in particular for several seconds. But it did not move.

Deciding he had demonstrated his courage to his own satisfaction, the Undertaker hurried on back into his quarters.

He warmed up the short-wave radio set, attempting to raise his boss, who was on his way to his cemetery rendezvous. He hoped that the Funeral Director had his portable receiving set turned on, as was his habit.

Very quickly, a familiar voice snapped impatiently, *"This is your Funeral Director."*

"I got something to report."

"Go ahead."

"I don't know if there's anything to it," muttered the other. "But you said always report anything that looked queer, so I figured I'd tell you this. I am not exactly what you call superstitious, or—anyhow, I never—"

"Get on with it!" rasped the voice of the Funeral Director. *"Quickly!"*

"I seen a ghost!" Undertaker Desmond blurted. "A big, black ghost with empty eyes like the hollows in a skull."

The Funeral Director was silent after the man paused. The underling squirmed and perspired.

"It sounds crackpotty, I guess," he muttered. "But that's what it looks like to me. Just a big, dark shadow—!"

"The Shadow!" The two words were a brutal blast, like glass shattering.

"Yeah, a shadow," mumbled Desmond. "And I heard a funny kind of a laugh. It wasn't funny, either. It was—!"

The underling groped among the few words he knew for an adequate description of that eerie laugh—and suddenly he did not need them!

For the terrifying sound was filling the very room in which he crouched!

Undertaker Desmond gave a frightened yell, and twisted to his feet.

Just inside the door loomed a tall form clad in black. It seemed a wraith of the night—a somber, sinister being who had materialized from some adjacent dimension. Across the floor lay the shadow of the figure, long and weirdly shaped and so black it seemed solid.

Desmond vented another yell and clawed frantically for his automatic pistol.

The black figure beside the door appeared to lose its human shape. Like a great, smoky cloud of sepia, it crossed the room.

Undertaker Desmond had hardly begun to draw his gun when the apparition was upon him. The terrified man half expected the weird being to flow to and through him, as he had heard ghosts do. But nothing of the sort happened.

What did occur was equally fearsome though.

Suddenly, great arms lunged forward, whipping off the black cloak. Like bat wings, the inky garment enveloped Desmond's head, blocking all light and all but smothering his cry of fear.

His hands became entangled. Despite his knotting, straining muscles, Desmond's arms were forced down as smoothly as though he were putting them there willingly. The terrible man in black was wrapping him up, tangling him the way a spider entangles a helpless fly in its web. For no matter how mightily he struggled, Undertaker Desmond was helpless to resist this monster who had ensnared him!

A powerful hand dug in, found his lips, and clamped them shut.

Then a voice that sounded amazingly like his own, said, "It sounded just like that, the creepy laugh, I mean." And again that horrible hilarity rolled out.

"Are you certain, Undertaker Desmond?" came the anxious voice of the Funeral Director over the air.

"Yeah. That was the laugh, all right."

"Inform your fellow Morticians that I am nearly at the cemetery gate. Tell them to shoot at any shadow that moves, no matter how innocuous. We will take our gains from Cranston and shove the lot of them into the fires. The Shadow, too, if he shows himself!"

The angry voice broke off, and the carrier-wave hissing was all that remained.

Undertaker Desmond felt the clamping hand remove itself and there followed the click of the short-wave set being shut off. He could not see if the fantastic phantom of the darkness still clutched him. Indeed, so terrible had been that frightsome grip on his wrists that they still felt as if they were being held.

"Lemme go, damn you!" he screamed. "Lemme go!"

A funereal voice demanded, "Where are the prisoners?"

"In a cell."

"The cell is empty."

"Then—then they musta been brought to the big furnace for—disposal."

"The men at the furnace are awaiting the prisoners," informed the voice. "But they have yet to appear."

"But they gotta be on their way to the crematorium," blurted Desmond.

"Take me there."

"If I do, the Funeral Director will incinerate me alive."

"If you do not," proclaimed the sardonic voice, "your fate will make the suffering ones in Hell be happy that eternal punishment was all they had to endure."

It sounded like bad melodrama, and no doubt it was sheer bluff, but the way the evil voice intoned that threat made Undertaker Desmond's blood run cold in his veins.

With a sinking feeling in the pit of his stomach, the chief minion of the Funeral Director understood that he had no choice in the matter.

"You win," he said dispiritedly.

A hand that felt as heavy as an anvil dug into his shoulder with fingers of iron, twisted him about, and gave him a forceful shove.

A hard round object dug into his spine. A gun barrel, from the steely feel of it. He had no inkling that it was in reality a human finger possessing the properties of tempered steel.

The entangling black garment was yanked from his head and the weird voice ordered, "Lead the way."

With knees of water and feet of lead, Undertaker Desmond started off, thinking that this must be how condemned murderers felt as they walked the last mile to the gallows and the hangman's rope.

Behind him, the sinister shade trailed like a guilty conscience.

Chapter LVII

GHASTLY DISCOVERY

HARRY VINCENT WAS leading the way through the underground honeycomb that constituted the Funeral Director's sub-cemetery lair and crematorium works.

The labyrinth was astonishingly complex. There were numerous blind alcoves and dead ends leading to ladders which, when climbed, opened into musty crypts and burial vaults.

From past experience, neither Harry nor Clyde Burke wished to attempt escape via those dreadful exits.

Pulling Weltha Cranston along with them, they retreated and sought other, less terrifying, means of escape.

Once, they heard approaching footsteps which forced them to double back, climb one ladder and huddle in the depressive dark of one such charnel vault until they felt it safe to open the floor hatch and exit below.

During this nerve wracking interval, they tried the steel vault door, but it refused to budge. They were not greatly disappointed, for they expected no better result.

Returning to the passageway, they made their way along, single file.

Almost at once, they came upon a door unlike the others. It resembled a medieval portal, of heavy wood and studded with iron trappings.

Going over to it, Harry gave the closed door a series of taps with his knuckles while Clyde Burke stood ready with his captured automatic.

It opened, framing a glum-faced man. Harry jammed a gun against the fellow's rather prominent nose.

"One peep and you're done!" he grated. "Search him, Clyde!"

Burke slapped ungentle fingers over the man's trembling form. He discovered no weapons. Then something caught his eye.

"Guard him!" ordered Harry.

Dashing past the fellow, Harry approached a sheeted form. The figure was held in a black casket by pairs of handcuffs and leg irons. A white shroud swathed it like a toga. The form was rigid, unmoving.

Harry's eyes discerned the fiendish purpose of the narrow coffin as he crossed the chamber. The thing was literally bristling with inward-pointing knives! By turning a small wheel, the points of the blades could be forced into the flesh of the victim held in the casket.

Harry noted also that electric wires were attached to the knife blades to permit shocking current to be induced into the body of any wretch in the torture casket. A fiendish instrument!

All that was impressed on his brain in a matter of seconds.

Harry reached the figure in the coffin, saw that the shroud covered even the individual's face. The cloth teepee created by the hidden nose did not stir, indicating a lack of respiration. Fearfully, Harry swept it away.

A yell of unutterable horror and anguish was torn through his teeth. His eyes glazed. His knees almost buckled. His heart seemed to freeze and lungs to cave inward.

Harry had just received one of the most grisly shocks of his entire life.

For the body in the coffin had been roasted in a fire! His face was a blackened joint of meat distinguished by a prominent jaw in which the gaping mouth displayed teeth that had been cracked and yellowed by tremendous heat. It was difficult to tell who the unfortunate man had been.

ATTRACTED by Vincent's anguished cry, Burke ran over. He, too, registered stark horror.

Both young men turned away, unable to bear the sight.

"Keep back!" Harry choked at Weltha Cranston. "It is—ghastly!" All the pep and desire to live seemed to have gone out of him. His feet dragged as he crossed the room.

"Dead!" Harry croaked. "Whoever he was…." Suddenly, he gave an inarticulate cry and pointed his gun at the other man. But he did not press the trigger. Sickened though he might be, Harry could not bring himself to shoot down an unarmed man, no matter how vile a person he might be.

"Don't shoot me!" he pleaded in a not-unpleasant voice. "I have never worked with the Funeral Director of my own will. I have been forced. I, also, desire to escape. Will you let me help you?"

"You killed—this man!" Harry grated.

The glum-visaged man shook his head. His sad face was extremely pale, almost bloodless. He said: "I did not kill him. He was tortured to death, his body shoved into the crematorium to test the heat. It was not hot enough to consume his mortal remains. Let me help you escape—please?"

"How?" demanded Harry.

"I will lead you out as though you were my prisoners," offered the man. "Perhaps they will not suspect. We may be able to reach the upper ground."

Clyde Burke frowned. "That's taking a big chance."

Harry studied the man's features. The fellow did not have a vicious countenance. His eyes were mild, but somehow haunted, too. He seemed very much in earnest.

"All right," Harry conceded. "But one misstep out of you, and it will be your last."

Harry unloaded one of the automatics and gave it to the man. He pocketed the other gun, which was loaded. They carefully secured the manacles to their wrists again so it would appear as if they were still prisoners.

The fellow led them out of the room. Several unsavory toughs loitered in the narrow corridor further along.

"I have orders to take these prisoners to the crematorium!" said the glum-faced man harshly. "Others will follow shortly. You will wait here for them."

The loiterers evidently knew the glum individual, because they grumbled surly acknowledgement of the commands.

The party reached a small open elevator, evidently for freighting purposes.

"It's working!" breathed the man as he pressed the button. The cage came down. They waded into it. The elevator mechanism carried them upward.

A pinch-faced man with eyes too close together stood on guard above.

"I am taking them to the crematorium," repeated the man. "Others will follow shortly."

But the guard was the suspicious sort. "Well, wait a minute!" he ordered. "This don't look right to me. I'm going to check up on it."

Suddenly, the hands of their escort shot out. They caught the guard's mouth, muffled his outcry.

Leaping forward, Clyde Burke shook off his manacles and brought his automatic crashing down on the guard's skull. The fellow gave a mad jerk and went limp. Clyde eyed his benefactor.

"That was good work!" he complimented.

The man nodded as if relieved.

Out into the tombstone forest they went, removing all handcuffs, which had not completely locked owing to the artifice of stuffing them with fabric.

Harry's heart was in his throat. It was incredible that they should just walk boldly out of the devil's nest! Yet they were doing just that.

The pinch-faced man calmly led the way.

Trying not to appear overeager, the others followed him. Harry and Clyde brought up the rear. Their feet were lead on the ground. They could feel little elation at their escape, for their hearts were torn by grief. For they had recognized by small signs the identity of the charred corpse in the coffin. This information, they kept strictly to themselves.

"Step lively!" breathed the man in the lead.

It was amazing how this fellow had taken charge of things, Harry reflected.

Clyde had the same thought. "Who are you?"

"My name is Paul Moran. I am the owner of the crematorium—or I was until a terrible man came into my life."

"The Funeral Director?" suggested Clyde.

"That is not the name by which I first knew him. When he entered my life, he was calling himself Isaac Coffran."

"Coffran!" exclaimed Harry.

Clyde looked at him blankly. The name was apparently unfamiliar.

Harry explained, "The Shadow battled him twice before. It was early in my service to him, before you joined up. Both times Coffran eluded capture."

Clyde frowned deeply. "He must be something to escape The Shadow!"

"Coffran is a damnable ghoul!" cried Moran. "He used my furnace to dispose of his enemies. Sometimes they are consigned to the flames—" his voice choked up—"while still living."

That thought was no sooner sinking in when the headlamps of an automobile swept in from the path to the cemetery entrance gate, making the leafless trees seem to writhe and strain, as if about to uproot their massive roots and stride about the earth like the Titans of old.

Moving swiftly, the group ducked behind such tombstones as would conceal them and waited the new arrival.

Chapter LVIII

DEADLY DEVICE

THE HOUR WAS eleven o'clock when the gleaming black flower car turned into the cemetery where the crematorium was being fired up.

Isaac Coffran was not driving. An underling designated as a Gravedigger performed that chore. He wore mortician's black, regardless of his lowly rank. All of the Funeral Director's men did.

Coffran was saying, "If The Shadow has tracked me to this place, it will prove to be his undoing. Mark me, Gravedigger. Mark my words. I will see his meddling bones smoldering in his own ashes."

The driver nodded. He said nothing. Isaac Coffran was easily agitated and quick to anger. Underlings who crossed him sometimes disappeared. It was rumored that the crematorium furnace took care of their bodies.

"Cranston will be here in an hour. Pull up to the crematorium entranceway."

The driver piloted his queer machine to the building on the low hill in a far quadrant of the sprawling burial ground, beside an assortment of vehicles ranging from touring cars to a flashy boat-tailed roadster that had last been seen at the Cranston mansion. Donald Hume's machine.

Braking, he exited the vehicle and went around to open the door for his passenger.

Coffran exited and paused while the door was dutifully closed after him.

"Where is Undertaker Desmond?" he demanded of the men loitering outside.

"He has not been seen since the failed cremation, Funeral Director."

"Desmond radioed me," snapped Coffran. "The Shadow has been spotted prowling hereabouts. Did he not alert you men?"

The worried-eyed underlings shook their heads mutely.

Coffran's smooth face gathered in tight, thin wrinkles, hinting at his true age.

"One of you find him! The rest of you, begin a general search for The Shadow. Shoot the interloper on sight. Show no hesitation. Cranston is due with the money at midnight. Nothing will prevent me from claiming it. Nothing!"

The men scattered while Coffran stormed into the crematorium proper. He went directly to the great furnace, whose tremendous heat could be felt through several insulated doors and walls.

Men were attending to the chemical furnace. The atmosphere in the room was intense, like a dry desert baking in the sun.

"Has the proper temperature been reached?" Coffran demanded.

"Nearly so, Funeral Director," said one minion.

"Where is that sniveling fool, Moran?"

"Below."

"Fetch him. He will be a witness to the disposal of the new bodies. Let it teach him that it is fatal to cross the Funeral Director, who controls life and death through his network of mortuaries and crematoria."

A stiff-faced embalmer went to find the cowed owner of the crematorium.

Isaac Coffran watched the furnace. His eyes were avid, not

merely with greed, but with the power of life and death over which he held sway.

"When Cranston and the others are cast into perdition," he mused, "perhaps we will turn our attention to fresh victims whose wealth is soiled. Men with guilty consciences pay more swiftly than the honest. Lamont Cranston is a case in point. He had nothing to fear from the law, so he thought he could balk my demands. Tonight, he will pay the ultimate price for his temerity."

The henchmen of the funeral Director looked uneasy.

"The girl, too?"

"Yes, yes, of course. There must be no living witnesses."

"Alive?" croaked a man.

The Funeral Director considered this grim question.

"No," he said thinly. "For she did not deliberately thwart me. I have no animus toward her. We will dose her with the vapor that stops the heart from beating. It will be a merciful death. Then her remains will be fed to the furnace, wearing a tag identifying her as another person entirely. Even if the authorities become suspicious and she is exhumed, who could distinguish one urn of ashes from another?"

At that thought, Coffran tittered reedily.

None of his men joined in the repellent mirth.

"Croakin' a jane," whispered one man. "I don't like it."

"Me neither," undertoned another.

Unhearing, Isaac Coffran went on, "Undertaker Desmond believed he saw a strange shadow. It may be that he did. But does this shadow live? That is the question. All of you men—be alert for shadows that lurk and skulk, and whose eyes burn malignantly. Should you see any such shade, kill it at once. No hesitation!"

With that, the Funeral Director moved on, going to an office where business was conducted, for this cemetery catered to the general public as a legitimate business when it was not serving the nefarious needs of Isaac Coffran.

In one corner of this office stood an old green filing cabinet, constructed of steel. Taking a key from a coat pocket, Coffran unlocked it and pulled open the top drawer.

From it, he removed a long Bakelite tube with a wooden handle at one end. The other narrowed into a thin nozzle. It was a sprayer, of a type employed to spray weed killer on plants, or insecticide on mosquitoes.

"Such a simple device," he clucked happily. "Yet how elegant in its ability to dispense death to the deserving."

"The death gas is in that tube?" asked the driver who had accompanied Coffran into the building.

"Yes, the very preparation Ernest Coffern devised as a more humane method of putting condemned men to death in the gas chamber. Coffern created many vapors before he stumbled across this noxious formula, for it is odorless and colorless. Death is virtually instantaneous. Almost, but not quite. As Sydney J. Palmer-Letts and others discovered—too late to do anything about it."

The underling's orbs grew uneasy. "Won't it croak the one usin' the thing?"

"Not if the Undertaker is careful. For only Undertakers are permitted to wield the heart-arrestor vapor. Undertaker Desmond used this exact sprayer on Palmer-Letts. He waited until the unsuspecting attorney entered the hotel, waiting on an upper floor.

"Pressing the call button on the self-service elevator, Desmond summoned the car carrying the lawyer to his assignation with George Clarendon. When the cage arrived, he made excuses that it was going down, not up, and declined to board the cage. As the door rolled closed, he pulled out this easily-concealed tool and inserted the nozzle into the gap. One push of the primer handle introduced the gas into the lift. By the time Palmer-Letts reached his floor, he was stricken. He managed to stagger out of the cage to Clarendon's door, where he collapsed, the apparent victim of a heart attack.

"Desmond hurried to the fire escape and managed to hide one of my casket wire recorders in Clarendon's room while he was called out. Clarendon! Of all men, only him do I fear. Or should I say his other self—The Shadow!"

"The Shadow can't touch you."

Coffran nodded. "No, I think not. During the interval since my last brush with him, I have studied The Shadow. Paid good men to look into his past. Little did I learn. But enough. Enough. I divined his method of communicating by radio broadcast to his agents. I learned that he sometimes called himself George Clarendon. Whether that is his true name, I cannot say. For Clarendon proved as elusive as The Shadow himself. But finally we may be in a position to rid ourselves of that cloaked interloper. For if The Shadow survives, he will never rest until he locates me."

"But The Shadow doesn't suspect that you are the Funeral Director."

"No, he does not. But since he has fallen on the trail of the Funeral Director, my peril is now double. It is my hope to vanquish him before the night is done and day dawns."

Someone knocked on the office door and Coffran snapped, "What is it?"

"A swanky limousine just pulled up."

Coffran pulled out an old turnip of a pocket watch, snapped open the face, and consulted the dial.

"He is a half an hour early! I told him midnight. Why could he not be punctual?" The old man's eyes narrowed. "Where is Undertaker Desmond? I want him at my side."

"He has not been found."

"Then find him, you dolt! It is highly important that you do."

The man raced away to do his boss' bidding.

Handing the sprayer to the Gravedigger, Coffran snapped curtly, "You will have charge of this until we need it. Take care you do not extend the handle, for that will prime the device."

Reluctantly, the minion took the deceptively common instru-ment in hands that trembled. "Yes, Funeral Director."

His voice trembled, too.

Chapter LIX

GRAVEYARD ASSIGNATION

THE TOWN CAR belonging to Lamont Cranston crawled carefully along the winding graveled road that wended its way in and out of the various sections of the cemetery until at last its blazing headlights illuminated a blocky granite crypt on which was chiseled a single name:

CRANSTON

The limousine glided to a halt, the engine died, but the headlights remained burning.

Behind the wheel, the chauffeur said, "I see no one."

The calm tones of Lamont Cranston issued from the rear compartment, murmuring, "We are early." For a man making a midnight rendezvous with a ruthless abductor, he sounded remarkably unworried.

The Autumn night was cool, breezy. In the cobalt of the sky, stars were like suspended sparks knocked from the lustrous disk of the moon. Only the trees seemed to move, shaking their heads and dropping dry leaves that rustled like snakes crawling, unseen, close to the ground.

Five minutes passed. Then ten.

The chauffeur looked at his expensive watch and remarked, "It is a quarter of twelve."

"Wait here."

The rear of the limousine stirred. A door opened, then closed.

Standing under the light of a nearly full moon, a tall, elegant figure hovered. The solemn features of Lamont Cranston were revealed. Eyes that swam in pools of shadow under hooded brows searched the tombstones arrayed all around.

The night was preternaturally quiet. A coolness had quelled the last crickets of the departed Summer. Only a few peeped. Somewhere an owl hooted disconsolately. Night-hunting bats wheeled overhead, but they were silent.

The steady deep-set eyes did not glance in their direction. They were fixed on the crematorium bulking up on a low hillock a fair distance away. They barely blinked, as if the brain behind those penetrating optics had focused his entire being on that building.

The grinding of an automobile starter came, followed by another. Headlamps flared into life. Throwing great funnels of illumination ahead of them, the machines crept forward, unhurried, almost majestic, taking their time, the way a funeral procession weaves its way toward its ultimate destination.

The lights of the approaching machines drove the deep shadows cast by bare trees and sere gravestones, making them shift and lengthen ominously, as if the dead were coming up out of their buried coffins.

Strange shadows crawled across the impassive features of Lamont Cranston. His expression did not flinch—or even change slightly—when he saw that the nearing machines were a funeral hearse and trailing flower car.

Reaching up, he lifted the collar of his Fall overcoat so that it shielded his lower features from the chilly night air, throwing them into deep shadow.

Chapter LX

FOUR YAWNING CASKETS

ISAAC COFFRAN WAS beside himself.

Undertaker Desmond was nowhere to be found. A search of the entire underground warren beneath the cemetery crematorium had been conducted, but to no avail.

When this was reported to the Funeral Director, he glowered angrily.

"Very well! We cannot wait any longer. Cranston is waiting."

"Funeral Director, there is no sign of the prisoners," the reporting Pallbearer added shakily.

"What!"

"Moran, the former owner, is among the missing, too."

The eyes of Isaac Coffran narrowed.

"Undertaker Desmond reported that The Shadow was seen, and he vanished, along with the others. We dare not tarry. Come! We will treat with Cranston and vacate this foul place."

They had piled into the black hearse and flower car, and made their way to the Cranston vault, driving with decorous speed, owing to the winding road.

When they came up on the limousine with its burning headlights, Isaac Coffran let out an oath unbecoming of a man of his advanced years.

"I see Cranston standing there. But who is that behind the wheel of his town car?"

The driver attempted to see through the blazing headlights.

He caught a glimpse of a shadowy head topped by a billed uniform cap. The man had thrown one arm across his face in order to shield his eyes from the hot glow.

"Chauffeur."

"I told him to come alone!" snarled Coffran.

The hearse braked, as did the flower car. All doors opened and black-suited men stepped out, faces hard, guns drawn, trigger fingers knuckle white.

Only then did Isaac Coffran disembark. Flanked by his underlings, he strode over to the limousine and raised his quavering voice in shaking anger, indicating the tall figure of Lamont Cranston, whose overcoat collar was lifted high to protect his lower face from the nippy air.

"Cranston, I am your Funeral Director."

"I have brought the money," the other responded calmly.

"I warned you to come alone!"

"I did. I did not think a faithful servant counted."

"When I say alone, I mean exactly that!" raged Coffran. "Was it too much to ask that you drive yourself to this rendezvous?"

"My apologies." Searching the array of hard faces, the millionaire added, "I do not see Weltha."

"She is safe," lied Coffran. "Now produce the money."

"I would prefer to make an equitable exchange—the valise filled with money for my living niece."

"You will be reunited with your niece shortly," snapped Coffran. "Show me the pelf."

With evident reluctance, a long-fingered hand opened the rear limousine compartment and shortly thereafter produced a valise. This was set atop the long hood of the limousine.

Snapping his fingers, Coffran directed a man to step forward and claim the valise.

This was smartly done, and the bag wrenched open for his inspection.

Under the spectral moonlight, it could be seen that the valise was crammed with banknotes of high denomination, individual packets held together by paper strips bearing the name of a reputable bank.

"It is all here," assured the calm-faced man. "The precise sum you demanded."

"Requested," corrected Coffran. "For these are for Miss Cranston's *final expenses*, which I will safeguard until her eventual demise."

"Now that payment has been tendered, I would like to take my niece home. The hour is very late."

"Eh? Oh, of course. Come, we will fetch her."

"I prefer that you produce her," insisted the other.

"And I insist that you accompany us to the crematorium, where she is being held. And bring your damned driver with you."

Quickly, the limousine was surrounded and a Gravedigger yanked open the driver's door and hauled the unresisting chauffeur out.

Another Mortician gave Lamont Cranston a thorough frisking, and grunted, "Clean. No guns."

"I did not think there would be," spat Coffran. "Mr. Cranston is a big-game hunter, accustomed to much more unwieldy weapons than concealed pistols."

After the frisking was completed, the pair were prodded into the back of the hearse and made to lie down on their stomachs in the long, crepe-curtained space in the rear.

"Stay that way until we get there," a rough voice instructed.

The hearse and its companion car got underway and slithered on back up to the hill. The beginnings of wispy grayish smoke had begun to rise from the brick chimney of the lonely crematorium, indication that the furnace was firing.

The passengers had no way of knowing this, since they had been made to lie flat on the steel bed where a casket normally resides. Besides, the chauffeur had kept his cap pulled low, as if fearful of having his face revealed to the gunmen. He did not peer out from under the bill of his cap.

A short time later, they were ordered out of the stopped machine and forced at gunpoint into the crematorium proper.

The aristocratic features of Lamont Cranston betrayed no worry, although the same could not be said of his chauffeur. He walked with shoulders slumped, cap visor pulled low, evidently fearing for his life.

HARRY VINCENT and Clyde Burke were silent observers as the long limousine entered the desolate cemetery.

They had been working their way to the entrance gate, clear on the other side of the sprawling autumnal cemetery. A tall fence of wrought iron encapsulated the remote place. It was impossible to climb without exposing themselves. Too, medieval-looking spear points topped the structure at intervals, making it dangerous to surmount, even if it could be accomplished safely.

Never mind the undeniable fact that to attempt a climb would be to expose them to being spotted in the effulgent moonlight. So limned, they could be picked off by sharpshooters.

So they crept along.

At one point, Moran the crematorium owner whispered, "There is a spot up ahead where kids pried the iron bars apart in order to sneak in and play among the headstones. It's thin, but we might wriggle through."

"Show us," hissed Harry.

When they came to the narrow opening between two bent bars, their hearts sank. It was wide enough for children, but husky Harry could never squeeze through.

"You try it," he told Clyde.

Wiry Burke inserted a leg, but his chest, thin as it was, could not be enticed to pass.

"I give up."

Weltha made an attempt, but quickly gave it up as hopeless.

Strangely, Paul Moran found that he could slip through. It took a great deal of effort, and once he gasped that he could not breathe when his chest became caught. But Harry gave him a shove and he popped through to the other side.

"I will go summon the police!" Moran assured them. Then he slipped away into the night.

They continued on, until they reached the spot where they spotted the limousine crunching slowly along the graveled pathway, and froze in silent surprise.

Cornflower-blue eyes dilating, Weltha Cranston exclaimed, "That's Uncle Lamont's town car!"

Clyde and Harry had the same thought, but it was Clyde who voiced it.

"He's come to ransom you!"

"Shouldn't we rush over to him?" breathed Weltha.

Harry and Clyde considered. They were a fair distance from the limousine, with plenty of open space between the headstones. Rushing the distance would mean poking their heads up above the granite markers, and exposing themselves to sniping fire.

If only Harry and Clyde's lives were at risk, they would have gladly charged in. But to bring Weltha Cranston along meant chancing her recapture.

Finally, Harry decided, "We will work carefully closer and see what happens."

They did, moving one at a time, from headstone to monument to sheltering tree trunk, phantoms in the midnight murk.

In this fashion, they got closer to the waiting limousine, but it was still a chancy thing. Guns bristled from the fists of the Funeral Director's underlings.

They were debating the wisdom of making a run for it when the black hearse and flower car came to life, and began making their way to the Cranston crypt.

Quietly, hearts beating high up in their throats, they observed the waylaying of the chauffeur and his passenger, and their removal at gunpoint to the crematorium.

"Double-cross!" breathed Harry.

"What do we do?" Clyde asked.

Harry said instantly, "We have one pistol each, with full magazines. We will rescue Cranston."

"I am going as well!" insisted Weltha.

"Not a chance," Harry told her. "It is much too dangerous. The back of the limousine is open. Hide yourself there. If the worst happens, you can drive off with your life."

Weltha Cranston showed stubbornness.

"My uncle is risking his life for me, and I can do no less for him!"

Harry shook his head firmly. "He would want you to live, no matter what. Into the limousine you go."

Reluctantly, Weltha did as she was instructed. Creeping along quietly, she made her way to the waiting limousine, eased open the rear door, and slipped inside.

The final click of the door lock was a signal for Harry and Clyde to check their automatics and move in the direction of the crematorium.

They did not entirely abandon stealth. But they moved with greater speed than caution would normally dictate.

Quite soon they reached the front door of the grim structure and Harry nudged it open with his gun muzzle while Clyde trained his automatic on the opening gap.

They were not challenged, and so managed to slip inside without incident.

The sound of voices rising in agitation drew them in a certain direction. They followed this commotion, weapons pointing ahead.

Finally, they came to a reinforced door leading to what appeared to be the central chamber, and the heat radiating from the walls told the pair that beyond this portal lay the crematorium furnace.

Drifting up to the door, they laid an ear against the insulated steel panel. It was hardly necessary.

The aged voice of Isaac Coffran, the self-styled Funeral Director, was rising to a fever pitch.

"Did you think that I would let you see my true face and live?" he demanded.

The voice of Lamont Cranston spoke firmly, "It was a chance I had to take to rescue my niece. Now, where is she?"

A silence followed this question.

The voice repeated, more sharply this time: "Where is Weltha Cranston?"

Isaac Coffran finally gave answer.

"Perhaps she has already been consigned to the furnace that you see before you. The very foundry that will soon absorb your mortal flesh and bones, giving back mere ashes and calcified bones."

"If you have harmed Weltha—"

"We have no time for such tender feelings," snapped Isaac Coffran. "These four coffins that you see before you were prepared for your bodies. Since we are missing Miss Cranston and two others, you and your chauffeur will have to fill them. Now I offer you a stark choice: climb into your own coffins, after which I will mercifully snuff out your lives, or, if you prefer, my men will simply shoot you where you stand and hurl your bleeding bodies into the flames."

A short silence followed that cold threat.

Then, from out of nowhere, yet seemingly everywhere, sardonic laughter rippled out.

Harry and Clyde exchanged startled glances.

"The Shadow."

"He's here!"

They needed to hear no more. Setting their shoulders, they prepared to charge the door, emboldened by the certain knowledge that their cloaked master was on hand!

Chapter LXI

THE HUSH THAT IS BLACK

HARRY VINCENT AND Clyde Burke burst into the furnace room, guns drawn.

The tableau that greeted them was arresting.

The henchmen of the Funeral Director were arrayed about the room. In the center stood the tall figure they recognized as Lamont Cranston. Beside him cowered his uniformed chauffeur, head hung low, his shaking hands held high.

Standing before the open mouth of the crematorium retort was a quartet of catafalques on wheels, and atop each, an open casket, bare of any lining. Obviously empty, they yawned as if hungry for human fodder.

Harry barked, "Hands up! All of you!"

The laugh of The Shadow continued rolling through the chamber, but there appeared to be no one to author it. For no sign of the spectral figure was visible.

Standing off to one side, Isaac Coffran was searching the space for the source of the mocking mirth. He could find nothing, for in the fiery chamber there were no shadows anywhere.

Angry orbs mere slits, the self-styled Funeral Director seemed oblivious to the entrance of Harry and Clyde, had eyes only for the mocker he could not see.

Then his gaze fell upon the face of Lamont Cranston, whose firm lips were parted. Cold eyes snapped wide.

"You!" he cried accusingly. "You are making that infernal laughter. I see the truth now! You are The Shadow!"

This pronouncement so stunned Harry and Clyde that they stood momentarily frozen.

This was a mistake, for suddenly gunmen swiveled and trained their weapons on them. Too many of them. Shooting back would imperil the others scattered about the hellish chamber.

"Drops them gats!" one snarled.

They had no choice but to surrender. Pistols dropping to the floor, the chagrined pair raised their hands.

Isaac Coffran stormed over to them. Pointing a quivering finger at Clyde Burke, he said, "I do not recognize you." Then his eyes stabbed in the direction of Harry Vincent. "But *you*— you have interfered with my schemes once before."

Harry said nothing. The memory of being tortured by the henchmen of Isaac Coffran months ago was burned into his soul.

"Your master is The Shadow?" questioned Coffran.

Harry set his jaw. Clyde studied the rage-filled old man. Neither made answer.

"Is that man The Shadow?" demanded Coffran, pointing a gnarled, fleshless finger, shaking in the direction of the stiff-faced individual they recognized as Lamont Cranston.

The young men remained silent. The same thought was in the mind of both. They did not know the answer to that question. But had they known it, each was resolved to give his life rather than reveal it. The Shadow commanded, and willingly received, the utmost loyalty from his agents.

"You do not answer—just as your accursed master refuses to show his face to me," stormed Coffran, his smooth features satanic in the incinerator glow.

Then, as if to fuel the confusion of the room further, a far door banged open.

In stepped Undertaker Desmond, slack-jawed, hands held high.

Behind him loomed a gigantic figure, greater in size than anything human could possibly be. A wide-brimmed hat concealed the features beneath. A flowing cloak draped the great shoulders.

Coffran turned and his jaw dropped sharply.

"No! I was mistaken. There! There is The Shadow!" Pointing, he screeched, "Burn him down!"

A jittery embalmer objected. "But Desmond is in the way—"

"Shoot through him!" Coffran screamed. "Slay The Shadow! Slay them all!"

That was the signal for a massacre. Gun muzzles shifted, fingers constricted on hair triggers. But no blasts of flame emerged.

For as the mocking laughter seemed to lift, the room went suddenly black.

As much as anyone else, Harry and Clyde were stunned by this development. Blinded, they could do nothing. Had they retained their weapons, they would have dared not shoot. Either way, they were helpless.

Not so the Funeral Director's men. Their surprise was one of fear. Their weapons had been trained on enemies, so they completed the started action.

Guns blazed, but no eye beheld the spiteful flashes. The kiln-like furnace, being electrical in nature, had abruptly ceased operating, its frightful heart instantly banked.

Grunts of pain followed as blind bullets found their marks. Curses filled the air.

In this weird impossible darkness, several things happened unwitnessed.

The black-cloaked apparition which held Undertaker Desmond flung him to the floor, doubtless saving his life.

Bullets struck the towering figure in the black garments, driving him backward.

In the center of the room, Lamont Cranston doubled low. A

black cloak appeared, as if by legerdemain, and enveloped his gaunt figure. The personality of Lamont Cranston vanished. For the individual who had presented himself as the globetrotting millionaire had been all along—The Shadow!

His mastery of make-up and voice mimicry coupled with his unbounded nerve, had brought him unsuspected into the crematorium. Cunning make-up applied with skill had concealed the marks of recent plastic surgery. The preparation was the product of the unsurpassed genius of Doc Savage, who had applied it.

The Shadow now had to find Weltha Cranston. Find her and wrest her from the morbid clutches of the Funeral Director!

Moving swiftly, he crossed the great chamber. Powerful hands seized Harry Vincent and Clyde Burke, and drew their heads together, enabling both to hear low, hissing words.

"Where is the girl?" he hissed.

"In Cranston's limousine," returned Harry. "Safe. But I can't say the same for—" And he whispered the name of the torture victim found in the electrical casket.

Rapid orders followed. "No guns! Retreat to safety. Leave this to us!"

There was no time to ask who "us" was. Unexpectedly, Harry and Clyde were released.

Fumbling for the door at their backs, they threw themselves flat.

Bullets barked and whined, some ricocheting off walls and digging into ceilings, making them crack loudly.

Pandemonium reigned all about them. Rushing, colliding forms seemed to fill the chamber. They grunted and swore at each other. Occasionally, a pair of assailants started an exchange of blows which lasted until a word from one of the combatants advised the other he was fighting a friend.

Harry Vincent crawled for the door. Something hard landed on his head.

Jeweled points of fire shuffled gory curtains before his eyes.

Gunfire followed. Clapping sound was terrific in the confines of the corridor. Lead-shoveled ceiling plaster erupted, judging from the sounds.

"Get him!" Coffran shrieked. "Great wealth to the man who kills The Shadow!"

Obeying the command, the attackers charged around the room, to no particular result. But the sound of Coffran's shrill voice served as a guide to a cloaked form who swept toward it like a winged creature of the night.

A weird whisper hissed, "I will take that!" And the valise containing the Cranston ransom money was snatched out of Isaac Coffran's grasping hand. With a swish, the unseen assailant withdrew.

"The Shadow!" Coffran shrilled. "He has stolen the ransom money. Stop him!"

But in the Stygian murk, that was a futile hope.

Someone came charging in from a fresh direction and tripped over Clyde's prostrate form, landing on Harry. Reaching out, Vincent attempted to throw him off.

Harry thought he recognized a familiar hair tonic, hesitated.

"Cliff?"

"Harry?"

"Where did you come from?" Clyde demanded of Cliff Marsland.

"I was hunkered down among the tombstones, in reserve if the plan went awry. Which it did."

"Who else is here?" asked Harry.

"Burbank. And another crowd. It's complicated. Explain later." And Cliff was up on his feet and plunging into the furnace room.

Wild bullets had felled some of the Funeral Director's men. One whistling slug bloodied an ear, causing Coffran to screech out wildly: "No guns! No shooting!"

All gunfire ceased. An unsettling quiet followed. Only the ragged sounds of men breathing hard were heard.

Then came the meaty noise of fists colliding with jaws. Men going down. Other sounds of close quarter physical contact.

"Oww!" a man yelled. "Something stung me!"

The man's final word trailed off eerily, and a body hit the floor with a dull thud.

More fighting raged. Additional bodies dropped. Hard voices rose in frustrated panic.

For the gigantic cloaked figure who had been garbed as The Shadow had picked himself off the floor, where wild bullets had driven him. Apparently impervious to wild slugs, he ranged about the intensely black chamber, seeking additional victims.

One floundering Mortician, stumbling about, discovered him. Or perhaps it was the other way around.

The man never sensed the approach of his stealthy attacker— had no suspicion of his presence until fingers like bands of tempered metal closed about his throat. The fellow was lifted bodily off his feet. One of the monster's hands held the man helpless while the other plucked his revolver from his fist, as if he were a baby being denuded of his rattle.

Irresistible fingers loosened on the man's throat long enough for him to speak.

"Wh-what are you going to do with me?" the fellow whined.

The silent one replied nothing. His fingers tightened, producing a sharp squeal of surprise from his captive.

Carrying the helpless one out at arm's length as though he were a mere fish he had caught, the invisible giant set himself. A sharp rap of knuckles against the fellow's jaw rendered the disarmed captive unconscious.

The laughter of The Shadow came again, high and taunting. It seemed to fill their ears like a thousand imps cavorting. It froze the blood of many.

Rising up behind that uncanny sound was another, at first not impinging upon their ears because it was so low. Then it climbed the scales, running as a melodic counterpoint to The Shadow's Satanic hilarity.

It was the uncanny trilling that only one human throat could produce. The sound of Doc Savage!

Had they been able to exchange glances, Harry and Clyde would have traded startled ones. Suddenly, they understood what Cliff Marsland had meant by another crowd.

Doc Savage and his outfit were on the scene!

Someone screamed, "The jig's up! We're surrounded!"

Panic overtook the minions of the Funeral Director. There was a general exodus from the building, in which some succumbed to crashing fists, but others made hasty, stumbling but successful flight, owing to the impenetrable darkness and general confusion.

Harry and Clyde were nearly trampled, but managed to reach out and grab fleeing ankles, bringing men down and pummeling them.

Outside, two motors ripped into life. The heavy engine of the hearse and the lesser one belonging to the stubby flower car.

In this confusion, the voice of The Shadow broke off his mocking laughter and called out, "Savage! The hearse and flower car are escaping."

A moment later, the light came back on. The great brick kiln roared back to life.

Harry and Clyde scrambled to their feet and cautiously inserted their heads into the chamber room. The floor was littered with bodies, some dead, but most wounded or unconscious.

They saw several things at once which they failed to entirely comprehend.

The first was the sight of a man attired in a chauffeur's uniform, brandishing a long, lean rapier. But this was not Stanley, the Cranston driver. Instead, the determined features of lawyer Ham Brooks surveyed the tableau of fallen foes, the tip of his sword cane dripping crimson.

Rugged Cliff Marsland stood with his broad back to one wall, his fists surprisingly empty of weapons, knuckles bruised and bleeding, but otherwise looking like a man who had gotten some much-needed exercise.

He waved a chopping salute in their direction.

In other part of the room stood an imposing figure draped in black, a sable hat atop its head. The darksome cloak rippled and shook.

Clyde and Harry were pleased to see their master. Until the tower of animated darkness turned around.

Instead of the enshadowed features and hawk-like nose they knew, the stunned pair beheld the metallic countenance of Doc Savage, the Man of Bronze!

"Where is—?" Harry blurted out.

"Evidently, The Shadow departed ahead of the fleeing machines," said Doc, stripping off the garments that had permitted him to pass as the dark avenger long before the arrival of the Cranston machine.

"Where is Cranston?" asked Clyde, looking about anxiously.

"The Shadow took his place, just as my aide Ham impersonated his chauffeur during the exchange for Weltha Cranston." The bronze giant's golden eyes flickered with concern. "Where is she?"

"We left her in the back of Cranston's limousine," Harry replied. "The Shadow knows this."

Doc Savage plunged for the exit door, Ham and the others following close behind.

The hearse and the flower car were fast departing. But the town car had already quitted the cemetery. They could see its red tail-lights clearly. The other two machines were dark. No tail-lights burned as they went howling away.

Harry and Clyde were dumbstruck. Their cloaked master was fleeing the fight, without capturing his enemy!

Chapter LXII

DEMISE OF THE FUNERAL DIRECTOR

THREE AUTOMOBILES STOOD parked a short distance away. The motors of two were howling as Harry and Clyde came into view. Gunmen were scampering into the machines like scared rabbits into their holes.

Headlights blazed into life. The rear tires threw fistfuls of gravel; the heavy machines swerved onto the winding drive with such speed that they skidded half across the thoroughfare. They took off at a high rate of speed, the last of the Funeral Director's henchmen following their leader to safety.

Harry lifted his reclaimed automatic. A thought hit him— where was Cliff Marsland?

One car, a costly coupe, remained at the curbing. Harry raced to it, reached in and twisted on the lights.

A man was slumped motionless in the seat!

Harry gave the unmoving form only a glance, then jerked back out of the machine, his automatic lifting. But he did not fire!

Clinging to the tire carrier of one speeding roadster, made visible by the headlights Harry had turned on, was a man. Harry recognized him instantly.

Cliff Marsland! He was making a valiant last-ditch effort to follow the abductors. Hastily, Harry cut off the coupe headlights, fearing that one of the Funeral Director's men would peer through a rear window and discover his clinging passenger.

When the machines had thundered around a corner, Harry

snapped the coupe's lights on again. Wonderingly, he examined the form of the man sprawled senseless on the cushions.

It was Undertaker Desmond. A bullet had caught him in the stomach. Bleeding profusely, he had stumbled out to claim a getaway car, only to succumb to his mortal wound.

"We have to stop them!" Harry told Doc.

The bronze man nodded. From a pocket, he produced a small flare, which he ignited with a striker. It sizzled angrily.

A moment later, a sleek gyroplane appeared. It settled to earth with a notable absence of clatter, pneumatic floats absorbing the shock of landing. The hatch popped open and Monk Mayfair stuck out his blunt skull.

"Worked like a charm, Doc. That Burbank guy shut off the black-ray gadget right on time."

"The Shadow has deserted us," Doc informed him.

Monk grimaced. "Remind me to paste him one in the snoot next time we tangle."

"He has evidently taken Miss Cranston to safety," added Doc.

"Leaving us to mop up on the Funeral Director's mob."

"So it appears."

"Swell!" beamed Monk. "More skulls for me to bust."

Doc climbed in, and said, "Take the controls."

Ham Brooks, minus his uniform cap, charged up and sprang on board.

Harry Vincent asked breathlessly, "What about us?"

"No room!" Monk guffawed. "You and Burke go peddle your papers."

Chagrined, Harry and Clyde withdrew as the great rotor blades increased their rotational speed. Autumn leaves were whisked about friskily.

Long Tom was already aboard. Doc said, "The Shadow previously replaced the tail-lights of both the hearse and flower car with ultra-violet bulbs. We should be able to trail Isaac Coffran to his ultimate headquarters, wherever that is."

"Right." Long Tom handed Doc a pair of the oversized goggles that resembled condensed milk cans and donned another pair for himself.

Monk sent the gyroplane climbing up into the midnight sky without benefit of much of a take-off.

"What made The Shadow fade out of the picture like he done?" Monk wondered.

"I do not know," confessed Doc. "At a guess, I would say he is trying to square matters with the real Lamont Cranston in some way."

DOC SAVAGE's gyroplane tore through the midnight air over the hills of New Jersey, making whispering sounds that could not be heard on the ground.

Monk Mayfair was saying, "Figure on that Shadow to run out on us."

Doc said, "He has his reasons."

Monk eyed Ham Brooks, still attired in the gray chauffeur's livery. He could not resist a crack. "If the law business ever goes stale, you can always hire out as somebody's driver."

Ham lifted his sword cane as if to crack the hairy chemist on his head.

Monk blinked, wondered aloud, "Where did you hide that thing?"

"At the small of my back," sniffed Ham. "The unsheathed blade is very flexible. I merely had to reach up behind my uniform collar to extract it. I accounted for many of the Funeral Director's men, I will have you know."

Monk snorted, "When we land, it will be my turn."

Peering down with his ultra-violet scanning goggles, Long Tom remarked, "I never thought we'd see the day when we would trail an enemy using someone else's gimmick."

Doc Savage said, "The Shadow had the foresight to exchange tail-light bulbs at two different opportunities. He also had clamped a radio transmitter to the flower car, but its batteries were soon exhausted. Otherwise, the machine would have been traced long before."

They were watching the ground carefully.

"What gets my goat," grumbled Monk, "is that this Shadow was on our side all along."

"Not exactly on our side," reminded Doc. "He fights outside the law, and his methods are often ruthless, even if they are unquestionably effective."

Monk nodded. "He mops up on those crooks what don't pop their heads up very high. Lotta folks don't know when he's operatin', or what he's done until after he's done it."

"All of this was revealed to me when I read his accounts stored in his sanctum," related Doc.

"Well, he's going to have to get himself a new headquarters, now that we know where he hangs his hat."

"Perhaps not," advised Doc. "No more than we will need to relocate our College, now that The Shadow understands its true purpose."

Ham remarked dryly, "I gather that we have a truce going forward."

"You might call it that," allowed Doc.

Then the cabin fell silent as Monk jockeyed the nimble wing-less gyroplane around, attempting not to lose the fleeing hearse and its companion flower car.

It was not an easy task. The area of this section of New Jersey was extremely hilly, and the tail-light bulbs were naturally tiny. But without them, following the fleeing machines might have proven next to impossible.

The machines were tearing along at a tremendous rate of speed, and several times they nearly lost their footing, skidding off the winding road.

Despite the silence of the gyroplane, they were evidently spotted. For the hearse suddenly doused its lights, the flower car shortly thereafter following suit.

Now the chase became even more interesting. Without the headlights to help guide them, the tiny ultra-violet bulbs became even more important.

As the short train of funeral machines, followed by a trio of henchmen cars, careened along, another vehicle came into view. It had been running ahead of the others, but now the gap was closing.

Long Tom was the first to recognize it. Doc Savage had been concentrating on the tiny fleeing tail-lights.

"Hey! Isn't that Cranston's limousine?"

All eyes turned toward the new vehicle. Running at a high rate of speed as well, its headlights drove twin tunnels before it like demonic horns of illumination.

"It is," advised Doc.

"I thought he took a run-out powder on us!" exploded Monk.

Doc said, "He may well have. But evidently Isaac Coffran and his men are not fleeing to some headquarters, but pursuing the limousine."

"But why?" demanded Ham. "That makes no sense!"

"When The Shadow, in his disguise as Lamont Cranston, departed, he managed to secure the valise containing the ransom money. That is what Coffran is so anxious to recover. That money."

"Jove!" breathed Ham. "The bally chase is on then."

It was on, but not for very long.

The Cranston limousine, despite its superior motor, was no match for the hearse, which relentlessly overhauled it. Soon, they were pacing side by side.

Small flashes of light appeared along one side of the hearse. Over the noise of their gyro rotor, they could not hear the gunshots, but that was what they were.

"Trying to shoot out Cranston's tires," Doc imparted.

Long Tom sent the gyroplane hurtling downward, as Monk unlimbered his supermachine pistol, growling, "About time I got in on some of the action." He pushed open a shielded firing port.

Doc Savage cautioned, "At the rapid rate they are traveling, a fatality would likely eventuate if you puncture a tire."

Frowning with all his homely face, Monk withdrew the muzzle. At this distance, the hollow mercy bullets would do little good anyway.

"How the heck do we stop 'em?" he demanded.

Doc had no answer for that, for his intention had been to follow the enemy to their lair. This new wrinkle created complications.

The bronze man reached back into a storage compartment, and removed with great care several large globes of glass. The shells were heavier than the small grape-sized gas pellets he carried on his person. Inside, sloshed a bilious liquid.

Monk said, "I get it! If we fly ahead of them, we can drop these babies in their path. They'll drive right through it and the gas will put them out of commission."

Doc nodded. "This concoction does not take immediate effect, so they will have time to brake and pull over safely once their brains are affected."

It was a sensible plan, and probably would have worked except that, down below, the driver of the Cranston limousine apparently grew weary of being shot at so relentlessly.

Suddenly, he braked his machine, swerving to one side.

The hearse overshot, and went hurtling past.

Headlights painting it, the limousine charged forward, and very quickly was pacing alongside of the black funeral hearse in an area where granite outcroppings bulked on their side of the turnpike.

Doc Savage rapped, "Lower, Long Tom!" His normally restrained voice was a crash of urgency.

For the limousine suddenly swerved, fenders clashing, and shedding sparks. Steadily, inexorably, the heavier machine pushed the swerving hearse into the soft shoulder of the road.

Spiteful flashes of gunfire showed that the hearse occupants were fighting back. But the limousine driver would not be thwarted.

With a final wrench, one that sent blue-white sparks flying, the limousine forced the long funeral machine off the road, where it went hurtling downward, caving in its ebony snout against a hard granite outcropping.

The other cars swerved to a halt, doors came open, and gun-wielding men rushed to the rescue of the damaged hearse.

By this time, the gyroplane was flying close to the ground. Doc Savage rapped, "Now, Monk!"

Gleefully, the homely chemist stuck an arm out the side window and opened up with his superfirer.

MEN fell under the withering bursts.

Immediately, the would-be rescuers dived back into the protective shells of their automobiles. There they prudently sat, as the gyroplane landed on the middle of the highway.

Up ahead, the limousine tail-light was disappearing, but floating back came a jibing mockery. The triumph laugh of The Shadow!

Stamping his feet in frustration, Monk complained, "Guess he got the last laugh, after all."

Looking to Doc Savage, Ham remarked, "You instructed him not to use guns; you said nothing about not killing anyone by other means."

"Something to remember when and if we cross paths again," the bronze man said grimly.

Long Tom and Ham took charge of the stopped vehicles, while Doc and Monk scrambled down a declivity to the battered hearse.

The passenger doors had not opened, and could not be opened.

Finally, Doc Savage managed to open the rear hatch, and the bronze man crawled into the casket-carrying space, and worked forward.

Behind the wheel slumped the driver, whose steering wheel lay shattered in his lap. Beside him sprawled the Funeral Director, Isaac Coffran. There was a bad bruise on his forehead, but when Doc Savage examined him with his probing fingers, it proved not to be fatal.

Reaching into the oldster's shirtfront, the bronze giant felt for a heartbeat. He found none. The same was true for the driver.

Then Doc discovered the Bakelite flit-gun sprayer, which had cracked open in the collision. Picking up the shattered pieces, his flake-gold eyes grew animated. And his trilling issued forth, low and doleful, a kind of funeral dirge of a sound.

The bronze man immediately deduced the purpose and nature of the simple device. It obviously had contained the heart-arresting vapor that the Funeral Director so liberally inflicted upon his victims.

In the end, Isaac Coffran had succumbed to his own diabolical death device.

Exiting the ruined machine, Doc Savage went back to the roadside, and instructed Long Tom to radio for a number of ambulances from the bronze man's private stock.

"These men are all going upstate," he explained.

Nothing more needed to be said.

WHILE they were waiting, a flashy open-top roadster eased up and the door opened. It was Donald Hume's machine, but they did not know that.

Out stepped a rugged individual who approached, knuckles bruised and bloodied.

"Marsland," grunted Monk. "Late to the party, ain'tcha?"

"Thought you could use a hand," Cliff Marsland returned gruffly. "I can see that you don't."

Ham noticed a man in a mortician's black suit slumped in the roadster's passenger seat, out cold.

"I hitched a ride on the back, climbed in and we had an argument over who would drive," explained Cliff. "It took a while to settle it, otherwise I would have caught up before I did."

Ham remarked, "I will add that one to the growing pile."

Cliff asked, "What are you going to do with them?"

Monk ran out a belligerent jaw, growled, "These boys are goin' to a place you already been to. Careful we don't make a mistake and include you in the cargo."

"I thought we were on the same side," Cliff said truculently.

"We do things a little different than that big noise you work for," retorted Monk. "Now beat it. You heard me. Go roll your hoop."

Angered, Marsland lifted his bruised fists and squared off against the hairy chemist.

"Maybe you'd like to go a second round, you slope-skulled gorilla," he threatened. "Without that fancy rod of yours."

Monk flung off his coat, and began rolling up his shirt sleeves, exposing thick, hairy forearms that bristled like coppery wire. Battle-scarred fists erected.

"I don't need my superfirer to take on the likes of you!" he snarled.

Doc Savage stepped in, got between the two combatants.

"That is enough, Monk," he said sharply. Turning to Marsland, the bronze man stated, "We have the situation well in hand. It would be better if you were not in the vicinity when the police show up, as they undoubtedly will."

"I get you," said Marsland. "By the way, Burbank cleared out with the ray machine."

"The next time you speak with The Shadow," advised Doc, "inform him that I would like a closer look at that device."

"I will. But don't count on any cooperation. Well, it was fun knowing you boys. See you around sometime."

Marsland returned to his roadster and went on its way.

Monk muttered, "We're lettin' The Shadow and his crew off kinda easy, ain't we?"

"No important laws were broken by The Shadow's men," advised the bronze man. "We have nothing with which to charge them."

Ham said to Doc Savage, "It will be easier to explain all this to Commissioner Weston if there aren't very many loose ends, at any rate."

"Exactly," said Doc. "As matters stand, we will be forced to leave out a great many angles pertaining to the evening's activities."

Chapter LXIII

THE BEREAVED

THE PRE-DAWN HOURS found Harry Vincent and Clyde Burke in the private study of Lamont Cranston.

They had gone there at the behest of The Shadow, where they explained the events of the evening to the waiting multimillionaire, who had remained at his mansion at the request of Doc Savage.

And there, they held vigil all through the post-midnight hours.

The jangling of the telephone was answered by Cranston. "Yes?"

A weird voice hissed: "Lamont Cranston. Switch on Station WNX."

The line disconnected.

Replacing the receiver, Cranston explained, "It was the voice of The Shadow, instructing me to tune in to the radio station over which he broadcasts."

Harry frowned, perplexed. "The station is not on the air at this late hour."

Cranston turned on the mahogany cabinet radio, but nothing emerged from the loudspeaker except the expected steady sizzle of static.

After a short interval, there came a violent electrical hissing, and an eerie, whispering voice broke through.

"This is—The Shadow! Stand by."

A pause. Then a familiar female voice came over the ether.

451

"This is Weltha Cranston speaking. I wish to say to whomever is within the sound of my voice that I have been rescued by the man calling himself The Shadow. I do not know who he is, nor why he took my part. But I am grateful. Eternally grateful."

Cranston listened with set expression, deep-set eyes sparkling.

"I wish also to state that Mr. Vincent and Mr. Burke, the two men who were also captives of the so-called Funeral Director, were instrumental in my salvation. They are blameless in this horrid affair."

Another pause.

Then the uncanny voice of The Shadow came back on the air.

"All that you have heard is true. But there is more that needs to be known. The criminal calling himself the Funeral Director was a scoundrel by the name of Isaac Coffran, who had long eluded the law. Coffran is no more. He forced The Shadow's hand, and so he perished. Doom he sought to deliver to many, but instead a just doom was delivered to Isaac Coffran.

"Two men who have been accused of being accomplices of The Shadow were, in reality, mere dupes. Vincent and Burke no more know the identity of The Shadow than does Commissioner Weston."

A ghoulish chuckle accompanied this jibe.

Harry and Clyde exchanged frank glances. They said nothing. But the same thought was in their minds. The Shadow was getting them off the hook with Doc Savage and the authorities, although whether it stuck or not remained an open question.

Finally, The Shadow intoned:

"I am The Shadow. Many believe me a myth. I prefer it that way. But those who know otherwise know also that I work to further the cause of justice, not to defy it."

Then the laugh of The Shadow pealed out in long, rolling waves that reached an infernal crescendo before trailing off into mocking chuckles.

The strange broadcast ended. Static returned. It was doubtful if anyone other than those gathered in the Cranston study had heard the words of The Shadow, the hour being so late.

After Lamont Cranston finished listening, he switched off the console receiver and sat down, a pensive expression roosting on his aquiline features.

It was clear that the millionaire was thinking about the mystery man who had saved his niece. His thought processes went on for a long time; finally, he broke the silence.

All Cranston said was, "I think I understand The Shadow now—even if I do not know who he is."

Harry remarked, "I imagine your niece will be home shortly."

"Count on it," added Clyde.

No more was said. It had been a long night and no one had eaten in many hours. Cranston ordered Richards to prepare an early breakfast. By the time they had finished consuming it, dawn was nearing.

A vehicle pulled up outside.

They went to the library window and saw that it was the missing town car of Lamont Cranston. One fender was still scraped up from its sideswiping collision with the hearse of the Funeral Director, but the bullet-shattered window glass had been replaced.

The rear door opened and Weltha Cranston stepped out, eyes brimming with tears of relief.

Harry Vincent, Clyde Burke and Lamont Cranston rushed to greet her at the front door.

As uncle and niece embraced in joyful reunion, Harry and Clyde slipped out to the limousine. They bent to see who had driven it home.

They were expecting to see The Shadow. Instead, the seat was empty!

Opening every door, Harry and Clyde discovered the town car was deserted. However, the valise crammed with banknotes that had been carried to the cemetery rendezvous rested on the passenger seat. Harry took it in hand.

Coming erect, he looked about in the dwindling pre-dawn darkness.

Surveying the street before he switched off the headlights, Harry saw no other machines.

"Only one person could vanish like that," remarked Clyde.

"Yes," replied Harry. "I wonder— *Uh!*"

The ejaculation came as something brushed his coat sleeve. Harry looked around, and seeing nothing, half concluded some flying night insect had collided with him. Then he chanced to glance down. An envelope lay at his feet. It was that which had struck his sleeve.

Harry picked up the envelope hastily. Retreating to the veranda lights, he opened the missive.

The two young men read:

> Surrender Cranston's funds with my compliments. Say your farewells. Return to the city and your usual routines until your services are again needed. There will be no further trouble from Doc Savage or the police.

There was no signature.

"The Shadow!" Clyde breathed.

A soft laugh filtered out of the surrounding shrubbery, uncanny and untraceable. No matter how hard they peered about, they saw nothing of its author. Nothing—but night shadows.

Harry crumpled the paper and tossed it away. He had no fear of anyone finding it and bringing the writing out by treating it with chemicals. The chemical formula of the vanishing ink The Shadow used precluded that.

A moment later, a modest four-cylinder coach ghosted by. But neither man noticed it. It did not look like the type of machine The Shadow might drive, which was precisely why the dark avenger had appropriated it.

Harry and Clyde returned to the house, and found Lamont Cranston with his niece Weltha in the baronial library.

"We found this in the front seat," said Harry, surrendering the valise. "I am certain that every dollar is there."

"Doc Savage assured me that it would be, when we made our special arrangements," replied Cranston.

Harry and Clyde, although naturally curious to know what had happened to Weltha, asked no questions. Not so Cranston.

"Where have you been all these long hours, my dear?" he demanded eagerly.

Weltha Cranston smiled faintly at the term of endearment. Then she glanced at Harry and Clyde.

"I can imagine you two can guess who I met," she said. "He is a most astonishing individual, a man of unbelievable resources."

"What do you mean?" Cranston questioned sharply.

"Just what I said," Weltha explained. "A strange man of the night who accomplishes unbelievable things! Why, I was never so much in awe of anyone in my life."

"But where have you been?" Cranston demanded. "I don't understand. What occurred?"

"I left the cemetery with this—this mysterious man," the young woman told him. "His whispered words reassured me. He took me to a broadcasting station. There I spoke over the air, emphasizing his role in my rescue. Evidently, he wanted the public to know of his good intentions."

"Didn't they know this fellow at the radio station?" Cranston inquired skeptically.

"There was no one else there," Weltha told him. "The station had closed for the night. This man—he was a weird shadow of a figure—turned on the power himself. Then he took me to an all-night chain drugstore, where I donned a uniform and pretended to be one of the clerks. The others in the drugstore acted as though I were one of the employees. They asked me no questions. Later, *he* returned and brought me home."

"You don't know any more about him than that?" Cranston queried wonderingly.

"He was unquestionably the most remarkable person I ever met," Weltha Cranston asserted. "There was something almost unreal about him. He made absolutely no noise when he moved. When he left me at the drugstore, and again when he came for me, he assumed the disguise of a taxi driver. It was astounding. His appearance was completely altered."

Cranston passed a hand over his forehead. "This sounds very queer to me."

Weltha eyed him levelly with her cornflower blue eyes. "Don't you believe me?"

"Of course I do!" Cranston insisted hastily. "It's just that, well—it all sounds so strange."

"He was a strange man." The black-haired girl glanced at Harry Vincent and Clyde Burke. "He kept me safe at the drugstore until he could be assured all of the Funeral Director's men were rounded up and the danger had passed."

That statement did not please Lamont Cranston.

"Aren't you neglecting something?" he said testily. "What about finding your missing fiancé?"

"My fiancé is no more," Weltha insisted. "He—the man of shadow—told me that. The men of the Funeral Director seized Donald, thinking that he was one of The Shadow's men. They tortured him cruelly and, when he failed to divulge information of value to them, he was—slain."

Harry and Clyde said nothing. They had suspected that the charred corpse they had discovered in the Funeral Director's torture room had been Hume's, but refused to divulge this information, wishing to spare Miss Cranston the horror of their discovery when she needed to keep her wits about her for their daring escape.

A somber silence followed.

"What will you do now?" Harry asked gently.

"I do not know. Everything has changed so rapidly. My brain is in a whirl."

"I have an idea," suggested Cranston.

All eyes rested upon the hawk-faced millionaire.

"Life here in the States has been alternately dreary and hectic. I yearn for the taste of clean air and the sight of open skies. I am considering a trip down the Amazon. Would you care to accompany me, Weltha?"

The thought struck an adventurous chord in the girl's mind. "It sounds like exactly the type of tonic I need."

Her blue eyes lanced in Harry's direction.

"I—I don't suppose you would be free to join us, would you?"

Harry shook his head heavily. "I am pledged to the—man of shadow as you call him."

A flicker of disappointment touched the young woman's comely face. "I understand."

"But when you return," added Harry, "I would be happy to take you out to dinner and hear all about your adventures."

Weltha smiled bravely. "I would like that. It sounds grand."

With nothing more to be said, they shook hands all around and the two agents departed the Cranston mansion, let out by Richards the valet.

Walking to a waiting rental coupe, Clyde asked Harry, "Were you sincere about taking her out?"

Harry looked back, his expression torn.

"I would like nothing better but, by the time she does return, who knows? I might have fallen in service to The Shadow."

Clyde nodded grimly. "Not to mention the awkwardness of not knowing if her uncle was himself or—the man of shadow!"

Harry laughed at the thought. Neither agent knew how close to the truth Clyde's jest had been, for they did not suspect that The Shadow's impersonation of the millionaire globetrotter was not a product of extraordinary conditions, but a habitual routine calculated to cloak the true identity of their spectral master.

Chapter LXIV

CASE CLOSED

THAT EVENING, A meeting was held at the office of New York Police Commissioner Ralph Weston.

Doc Savage was in attendance, as was Detective Joe Cardona.

"The Funeral Director was a man named Isaac Coffran," Doc was saying.

Weston turned to Cardona.

"Is this Coffran known to us?"

Cardona nodded. "A notorious counterfeiter wanted by the Secret Service. Never caught. They're autopsying him right now. Good riddance."

"The autopsy will show that Coffran perished of a heart attack," related Doc, "but in truth his own lethal gas, not the collision, was the cause of death."

"Funny how he lost his life—in a hearse, no less," grunted Cardona.

"Some of Coffran's mob may have gotten away," Doc said, neglecting to add that they had not eluded him, only official justice. Soon, the survivors would be undergoing the course of treatment that would transform them from lowbrow crooks into upright citizens.

"Coffran was on the run, and made the acquaintance of a chemist named Ernst Coffern," continued Doc. "From Coffern, Coffran learned of the gas that induced heart attacks. He did away with Coffern, and took over his home, which proved the perfect cover for his activities. Coffran then purchased a number of funeral homes and mortuaries as a way to further his schemes. Disposal of unwanted bodies was important to him because he and his underlings believed that without a *corpus delicti*, he could not be lawfully convicted of murder."

Weston nodded. "Mistakenly so, I might add. So Cranston instructed his lawyer to contact George Clarendon for assistance on the man blackmailing him, but this Coffran person learned of the rendezvous and did away with poor Palmer-Letts."

"Threatening Clarendon in the process," amended Doc.

"Where *is* Clarendon?" asked Weston in an exasperated tone. "No one has seen hide nor hair of him since the night of the attack upon his life."

Doc Savage and Joe Cardona exchanged glances.

"Perhaps I had better answer that," said the bronze man.

Cardona looked pained, as if expecting an explosion momentarily. The significance of this expression was not lost upon Doc Savage.

"He appears to have vanished," explained Doc truthfully. "The spectacular attempt upon his life may have rattled him."

Cardona eyed the bronze man with relief, but said nothing. To mention that Clarendon was an alias of The Shadow would be to invite scornful ridicule from his superior.

"Lamont Cranston is leaving town tonight," fumed Weston. "For the Amazon, no less. Probably gone for six months. Not that I blame him. He has been through a terrific ordeal, and his bravery in helping to set the trap that resulted in Coffran's destruction was noteworthy. Didn't think he had it in him to walk into the jaws of peril as he did."

Doc Savage quickly changed the subject. "Many of the recent victims of the Funeral Director were not victims at all, but ordinary persons succumbing to natural heart failures. The press seized upon these deaths and blew them out of proportion. With the exception of Lamont Cranston and his attorney, all of Coffran's other victims were clandestine criminals."

"I see," mused Weston. "This explains why his crimes took so long to come to light." The police official glowered like a thundercloud. "What I fail to understand is this: If this ghoul targeted men of unsavory reputations to start with, why did he turn his attention upon Lamont Cranston? The man has an impeccable reputation."

Doc observed, "Ferreting out perfect victims was a difficult process, and Coffran soon exhausted his list of such men. Still greedy, and confident that he could continue to get away with his crimes, he picked a victim who was unsullied. It proved his undoing."

Cardona spoke up. "We followed up on that radio broadcast Cranston heard, where The Shadow exonerated Harry Vincent and Clyde Burke."

Weston's frown grew deeper.

"It appears that I was in error regarding my suspicions about Vincent," added Doc.

Cardona nodded. "It checked out. Vincent works for an investment counselor named Rutledge Mann. Nothing shady about Mann. Burke is a solid police reporter, even if his paper is on the yellow side. Looks like they're in the clear."

Doc added, "My own private detective force failed to uncover any unsavory activities on the part of either man. They appear to be exactly what the radio voice claimed they were: dupes. Nor have my operatives been able to uncover any trail to The Shadow."

The Commissioner frowned more deeply.

"The Shadow!" he expostulated. "There is no such person."

"If there is no such person," Cardona pointed out, "then Vincent and Burke are doubly in the clear. You can't be accused of being an accomplice of somebody who doesn't exist in the first place."

Weston had no rejoinder to that.

"Incidentally," continued the detective, "the New Jersey Police are holding a man named Paul Moran as a material witness. He owned the crematorium where we found a few stiffs and wounded men who had belonged to the Coffran gang. They had forced him to operate the crematorium according to the Funeral Director's schemes. He's complicit in some crimes, but has agreed to turn state's evidence in any trial."

"Are there any survivors able to stand up in court?" wondered the Commissioner.

"Only smallfry," shrugged Cardona nonchalantly. "That seems to clear up everything." His swarthy features brightened. "Oh, there is one other item."

Weston's military mustache bristled. "Yes?"

"A witness at the Hotel Spartan described a suspicious character hanging around the neighborhood the night of that mob massacre. The description fits that underworld snitch, Spotter. We think he fingered Clarendon for Coffran's killers. So I had him pinched."

Weston looked intrigued.

"Spotter confessed," continued Cardona. "Claimed he had worked for Coffran in the past. That checked out, too. But there's more to his story. Spotter said he had a visit from The Shadow last night. The Shadow ordered him to go straight. Or else. It really rattled Spotter."

"Bah!" said Weston. "Is The Shadow everywhere?"

Just then the door opened and a tall, stoop-shouldered man barged in, carrying a mop and pail.

Cardona eyed him and said, "Can you wait until we're through here, Fritz?"

The tall janitor nodded vigorously and mumbled, "Yah, yah," then proceeded to apply his sudsy mop to the floor in one corner. His drawn features possessed a dull cast.

Cardona chuckled wryly. "That's just Fritz, our janitor. Doesn't understand English very well. Comes and goes when he pleases."

Doc Savage eyed Fritz speculatively, but offered no comment.

"Where was I?" mused Cardona. "Oh, yeah. So I pulled Spotter in and sweated him some. He confessed right on the spot, said he was ready to go up the river. That was the only place he could think of where The Shadow wouldn't get him."

In a corner, Fritz mumbled to himself as he sloshed a wet mop about with long-armed ease.

"Since Clarendon wasn't killed—at least that we know of—we don't have enough on him to put him away for a long time, but Spotter will do a couple of years in Sing Sing, at any rate."

One golden orb on Fritz, Doc Savage said, "In the matter of The Shadow, Commissioner Weston, you might consider keeping an open mind."

"Nonsense!" snapped Weston. "According to the facts you have laid out before me, The Shadow has been here, and there and everywhere, including broadcasting over the radio from a station that was not even on the air! I tell you, there is no such creature. Why, if there were such a being, he could be any one of us. Including Fritz over there."

At the sound of his name, the industrious janitor gave a nervous laugh of acknowledgement. It was nothing like the laugh of The Shadow. But that might have been a matter of interpretation.

Doc Savage rose to leave.

"I must be going, Commissioner, but I am pleased that we have resolved this difficult case."

Weston stood up, saying, "I would feel better about the entire sordid affair if I knew where George Clarendon disappeared to."

"Clarendon," advised Doc, "is a person I would place in the same category as The Shadow."

"How so?"

"A phantom. Nothing more."

"But I have met him in the flesh, as have you."

"This is only a hunch," returned Doc, "but I think you have a better chance of meeting up with The Shadow than you have of ever again dining with George Clarendon at the Cobalt Club."

Fuming, Weston turned to his ace detective.

"That's my hunch, too," said Cardona blandly, taking his cue from the bronze man.

In a far corner, Fritz the janitor was recharging his mop with soapy suds, mumbling, "Yah, yah. *Goot!*"

One dull eye bent in Doc Savage's direction, and their gazes met, locked. Briefly that dim orb flared up like a living coal. But the Man of Bronze said nothing.

He knew.

EPILOGUE

A RATHER SHABBY bus pulled into the gates of Sing Sing Prison thirty miles north of New York City on the banks of the Hudson River, carrying a cargo of sullen-faced individuals. These men were uniformly garbed in prison stripes, their wrists shackled and their ankles festooned in leg irons.

Lurching to a halt, the driver jerked the lever that threw open the door.

"Ossining!" he sang out with grim humor. "Last stop! Everyone out!"

Distributed among the rows of seats were gray-uniformed prison guards. These worthies stood up, began prodding the seated convicts with their blunt truncheons.

Reluctantly, the men rose to their feet and began shuffling off the bus, shoulders hunched, mouths slack, features dejected.

Woodenly, they began lining up as the captain of the guards stood inspecting them, backed by a cohort of armed guards. Some had rifles. Two brandished Thompson submachine guns. All had revolvers and truncheons weighing down their Sam Browne belts.

"Welcome to Sing Sing, you yard birds!" the guard captain hollered.

Grumbling and muttering, the new arrivals completed assembling for inspection.

"When I call out your name," said the captain, "sing like a canary."

More muttering was heard.

"Wagon, Blister."

"Here!"

"Ryan, Tim."

"Present!"

"Brown, Walter."

"Not guilty!" retorted the prisoner named.

"Are you trying to be funny, Brown?"

"No, boss. Just truthful."

"Well, cut the comedy. You'll live longer." The captain stared down at his clip board. He made a face.

"Spotter!" he barked.

"That's me."

"Step forward."

Spotter stepped out of line. He was no less wizened in prison stripes, and a jail-house shave had improved his pinched looks only slightly.

The captain of the guards glared down at the little crook. "I see you refused to give your right name every step of the way."

"Spotter's the only name I go by, Cap'n."

"Well, from now on you are Convict 3344. No more Spotter. Get me?"

"I was thinkin' of changing my moniker anyway," whined Convict 3344.

"Do that after your release. Provided you keep your nose clean."

The roll call went on, and finally concluded. After which the prisoners were marched in lockstep into the prison proper. The sound of their clanking chains was a rattling commotion.

Behind Convict 3344, a cadaverous prisoner whispered, "That took nerve, talkin' back like you did."

"I got nerve," growled Spotter. "And plenty of it."

"I like that. My name's Tapper. What handle are you going by now?"

Spotter considered that question as he passed out of the bright sunlight and into the tenebrous gloom of the great prison walls.

"After I get out of this joint, I'm goin' straight," he muttered. "But startin' today, call me Hawkeye."

About the Author
LESTER DENT

LESTER DENT WAS the young Oklahoma pulp writer who had relocated to New York City when Street & Smith editor-in-chief Frank Blackwell sent him three copies of *The Shadow Magazine* and invited him to submit a plot featuring the mysterious new character. This was in February, 1932.

Lester jumped at the opportunity, recycling a plot he called "The Golden Vulture" and submitted it to Blackwell. Although Blackwell declined Dent's first effort, Lester tried again, producing three chapters and an outline that were considered promising. The three chapters were immediately discarded, since they portrayed The Shadow in his discarded identity of criminologist George Clarendon.

Undaunted, Lester worked hard on the story, his first attempt at a novel, finally finishing it in July of that year. With the five hundred dollars he earned, Dent went on an extended tour of the Southwest, where he panned for gold. He may or may not have known it at the time, but Street & Smith had given him the project as a test to see if he could handle a new pulp adventurer they were contemplating. Not until the Depression year of 1932 was almost over did they call him back to pen the inaugural Doc Savage novel, *The Man of Bronze*.

The first issue of *Doc Savage Magazine* was released in February, 1933—a year after *The Golden Vulture* project had begun. Over the next sixteen years, Lester went on to write over 150 Doc Savage novels, but he never again penned a story featuring The Shadow. *The Golden Vulture* was filed away, resurfacing in 1938, when series originator Walter B. Gibson was given the manuscript to revise for publication.

With *The Sinister Shadow,* which was constructed from the unused chapters and leftover scenes of the early drafts of that manuscript, Lester Dent now has a second Shadow novel to his credit, over eighty years after he drafted his first, and a half century after his untimely death in 1959.

About the Author
WILL MURRAY

WILL MURRAY FIRST thrilled to the laugh of The Shadow hearing reruns of the old-time radio program as it was broadcast over Boston's WORL in the early 1960s. The character later popped up in an Archie Comics series he collected. Then one day in 1966, Murray stumbled across a paperback copy of a book called *The Shadow's Revenge,* by Maxwell Grant. He could not find the other novels in the series for several years yet, so he read this one two or three times over, not once suspecting that mystery novelist Dennis Lynds was the true author.

In 1969, Bantam Books released the seminal 1931 Shadow novel, *The Living Shadow,* followed by several reprints of the original pulp magazine stories—and the old modernized Belmont paperbacks certainly seemed like thin blood by comparison. Before long, Murray was collecting *The Shadow* pulps, along with *Doc Savage,* which he had discovered early in 1969.

It wasn't long before he met the true Maxwell Grant, Walter B. Gibson, at a New York City comic book convention and a long-term friendship formed. The year was 1975. Gibson was 79. Murray was 23. Murray interviewed Walter many times, eventually co-authoring a book, *The Duende History of The Shadow Magazine,* which included Walter's final Shadow story, "Blackmail Bay." Neither man ever suspected that Murray would go on to write the famous character.

The Sinister Shadow is the culmination of a dream Murray has long harbored, and which he shared with fans of both Street & Smith superheroes for a very long time—to team up Doc Savage and The Shadow in one exciting story.

With any luck, there will be more Shadow novels from Will Murray's pen.

About the Artist

JOE DeVITO

JOE DeVITO WAS born on March 16, 1957 in New York City. He graduated with honors from Parsons School of Design in 1981 and continued his study of oil painting at the city's famed Art Students League.

Over the years DeVito has painted many of the most recognizable Pop Culture and Pulp icons, including King Kong, Tarzan, Doc Savage, Superman, Batman, Wonder Woman, Spider-Man, *Mad* magazine's Alfred E. Neuman and various characters from World of Warcraft. Throughout, his illustration work has had an accent toward dinosaurs, Action Adventure, SF and Fantasy. He has illustrated hundreds of book and magazine covers, painted several notable posters and numerous trading cards for the major comic book and gaming houses, and created concept and character designs for the film and television industries.

In 3D, DeVito sculpted the official 100th Anniversary statue of *Tarzan of the Apes* for the Edgar Rice Burroughs Estate, *The Cooper Kong* for the Merian C. Cooper Estate, Superman, Wonder Woman and Batman for Chronicle Books' Masterpiece Editions, and several other notable Pop and Pulp characters. Additional sculpting work ranges from scientifically accurate dinosaurs, a multitude of collectibles for the Bradford Exchange

471

in a variety of genres, to larger-than-life statues and the award trophy for the influential art annual *SPECTRUM*.

An avid writer, Joe is also the co-author (with Brad Strickland) of two novels, which he illustrated as well. The first, *KONG: King of Skull Island* (DH Press) was published in 2004. The second book, *Merian C. Cooper's KING KONG*, was published by St. Martin's Griffin in 2005. He has also contributed many essays and articles to such collected works as *Kong Unbound: The Cultural Impact, Pop-Mythos, and Scientific Plausibility of a Cinematic Legend* and *Do Android-Artists Paint In Oils When They Dream? in Paint or Pixel: The Digital Divide-In Illustration Art*.

In regard to the creation of *The Sinister Shadow* cover, he writes:

> So far as I know this is the first authorized novel featuring Doc Savage taking on The Shadow. It is one of those cool times that you never would have anticipated as a kid. Though I am less familiar with Lamont Cranston than I am with Doc Savage, I knew of The Shadow long before I became aware of Doc's existence. Of course, I have painted many Doc covers for many projects, but this is only my second involvement in a project that featured The Shadow (the other being *The Martian Legion*, created by Buddy Saunders—which also includes Doc Savage).
>
> The multi-faceted Man of Bronze vs. the amorphous enigma that is The Shadow. Empirical science vs. the ambiguity of mysticism—it was an unusual pictorial problem to solve. From the beginning, it was decided to use what is perhaps the most stoic, monolithic pose ever portrayed on a Doc Savage cover. This was contrasted (after many alternate approaches) with the apparition of The Shadow, materializing out of nowhere within the safety of his own sanctum. Why does The Shadow take a shot at Doc and how could he miss at such close range—or does he? Did he appear and shoot out of reflex, surprised that anyone could even find his hideaway, let alone enter it so fearlessly? Was he testing Doc to see how far his fearlessness extended—or is there an undercurrent playing

out that only they are privy to? Doc's pose is a veritable classic that only heroic model Steve Holland could conjure from his incomparable ocean of Doc Savage body language. It anchors the composition, in stark contrast to its surroundings.

If the collision of opposites truly creates dynamic tension, all who read this book are surely in for a thrilling treat!

www.jdevito.com
www.kongskullisland.com
FB: Joe DeVito—DeVito Artworks

About the Patron
HENRY LOPEZ

AS A CHILD, I was always enamored by fantastic tales; from comic books to the *Star Trek* TV series, I just couldn't get enough. As luck would have it, my childhood friend had just returned from a family summer vacation and his parent had purchased a couple of Doc Savage paperbacks to keep him occupied during the long drive. Upon his return, he lent one of them to me and I was hooked! *The Monsters* became the first book I ever sat down to read outside of school and I devoured it. I was nine years old.

After forcing my parents to hunt down every single copy available within a few miles of my Miami home, I went through a dry period until I landed my first job at a used bookstore when I was 15. I was in hog heaven. While the pay was lousy, I had first dibs on any books that came into the store and would regularly blow my meager weekly salary on Doc Savage paperbacks.

To me, each new Doc was a joy to read, from the captivating covers to their thrilling stories. I was catapulted to phantom cities in one, while the next would introduce me to an underground lost civilization or the South China Sea.

Early in my used paperback commodities career, I stumbled across Steranko's *History of Comics* and discovered that Doc was just one of many other pulp heroes, with titles just as exciting and covers that were equally evocative. My eyes lingered on the Shadow covers reprinted along the top of the page in black and white and my imagination raced. I quickly mounted an expedition in my place of work to discover that there were a handful hidden away in the mystery section and there went most of my salary that week!

As I read the novels at a feverish pace, I wondered if Doc and The Shadow ever had a crossover adventure. Comics did it all the time and my pre-Google investigation uncovered that both characters had been published by the same company. It seemed like a no-brainer to me, but to my surprise, in the combined 506 novels published, not one ever featured the other.

And so, the titanic meeting between these two legendary crime fighters would be relegated to mediocre tales in the various comic books, which just didn't have the page count necessary to do the story justice. The chronicle of the first encounter and inevitable matching of wits between Doc Savage and The Shadow would remain in the realm of wild fan speculation and the inevitable half-hearted fan-fic.

Until now.

When Will Murray hinted at the possibility of writing this historic tale in one of his upcoming Wild Adventures of Doc Savage, I was overjoyed! Will had done such a superb job with his previous stories, that I knew he would be more than up to the task of penning such an historic story. I dropped (not) so subtle hints that I would be very interested in being that cover's patron. Months later, I was contacted by Will asking if I was still interested in commissioning the cover. Needless to say, I jumped at the chance!

Working with Will and Joe DeVito in designing such an important cover was a daunting task and a heck of a responsibility, but the two of them were very friendly, enthusiastic and patient as we tossed ideas back and forth until we had the cover you see gracing the book in your hands. I think Joe did a marvelous job of capturing the metallic immobility of Doc clashing with the fluid, unstoppable force of The Shadow.

Having the painting of the cover hanging on my office wall is the fulfillment of a childhood dream for me. Each time I look up from my desk and gaze at it, for a moment, I'm nine again and filled with the same sense of wonder I felt when I was handed that first Doc Savage novel.

Henry Lopez
March 8, 2015
Melbourne, Fl

Henry Lopez was an I.T. director for twenty years before deciding that starting a new career in law in his forties would be a great idea. He now wrestles with regulatory legal compliance by day, while spending most nights writing epic dark fantasy or swashbuckling horror adventures for his role-playing game company, Paradigm Concepts.

THE ARGOSY LIBRARY ™

SERIES 1 INCLUDES:

* DENT * KETCHUM * KLINE *
* MacISAAC * ROSCOE *
* ROUSSEAU *
* SELTZER *
* TUTTLE *
* WIRT *
WORTS

THE BEST FICTION
FROM THE FRANK
A. MUNSEY LINE

GENIUS JONES
BY THE CO-CREATOR OF DOC SAVAGE
LESTER DENT

WHEN TIGERS ARE HUNTING
THE COMPLETE ADVENTURES OF CORDIE, SOLDIER OF FORTUNE, VOLUME 1
W. WIRT

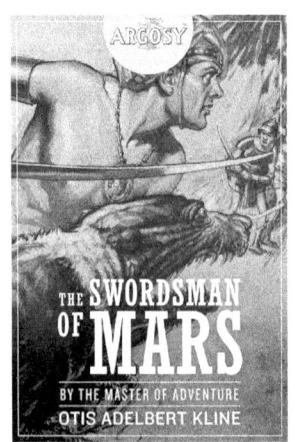

THE SWORDSMAN OF MARS
BY THE MASTER OF ADVENTURE
OTIS ADELBERT KLINE

THE SHERLOCK OF SAGELAND
THE COMPLETE TALES OF SHERIFF HENRY, VOLUME 1
W.C. TUTTLE

GONE NORTH
BY ARGOSY READERS' FAVORITE
CHARLES ALDEN SELTZER

THE MASKED MASTER MIND
BY THE AUTHOR OF PETER THE BRAZEN
GEORGE F. WORTS

BALATA
BY THE AUTHOR OF THE GAMBLER
FRED MacISAAC

BRET-WALDA
BY ARGOSY READERS' FAVORITE
PHILIP KETCHUM

DRAFT OF ETERNITY
BY THE CREATOR OF JIM ANTHONY
VICTOR ROUSSEAU

FOUR CORNERS
VOLUME 1 • BY ARGOSY LEGEND
THEODORE ROSCOE

SERIES 1 • AVAILABLE SPRING 2015

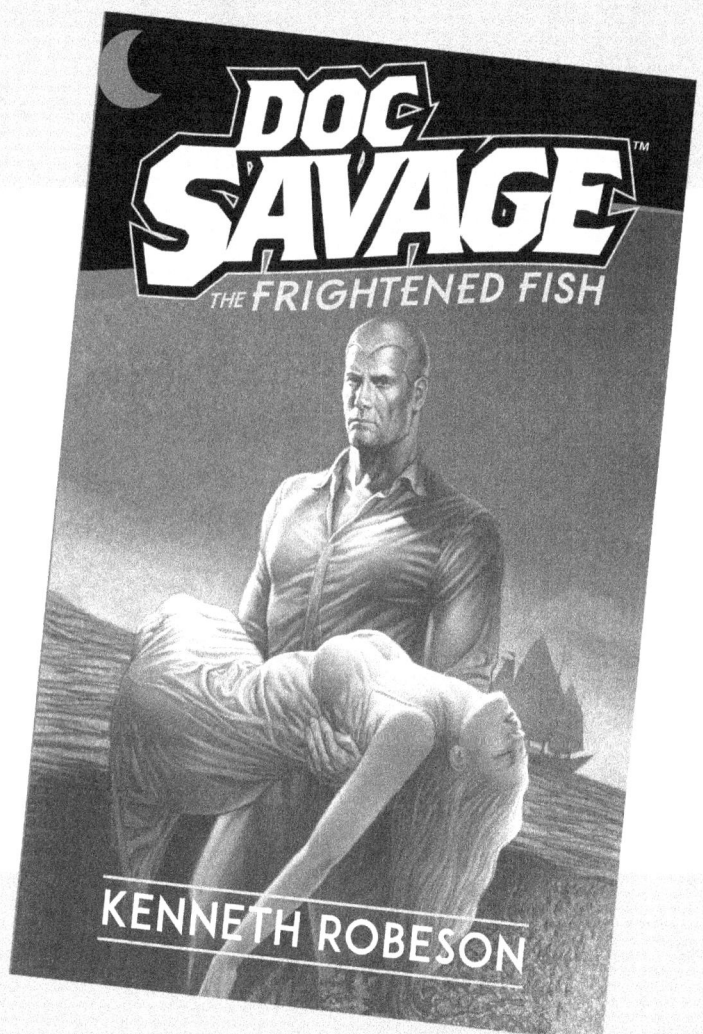

The Martian Legion: In Quest of Xonthron

- **An *Epic Adventure Novel in the Grandest ERB Tradition!***
- ***The Finest ERB Collectible Ever Produced!***

Written in spirit by Edgar Rice Burroughs with an assist from Jake Saunders.

- A quarter million words of high adventure! Like getting four ERB novels in one!
- Tarzan, John Carter, The Shadow, and Doc Savage battle the Holy Therns!
- First 100 copies signed by Saunders, Grindberg, Hoffman, Mullins, DeVito, Cabarga, and Cochran.
- Featuring 24 full color painting and illustrations, plus 106 spot illustrations by Tom Grindberg, Michael C. Hoffman, and Craig Mullins, including....
- Leather bound, full color, 11-1/4-in. x 12-1/4-in. x 1-1/2in., 423 pages.

Now available at TheMartianLegion.com!

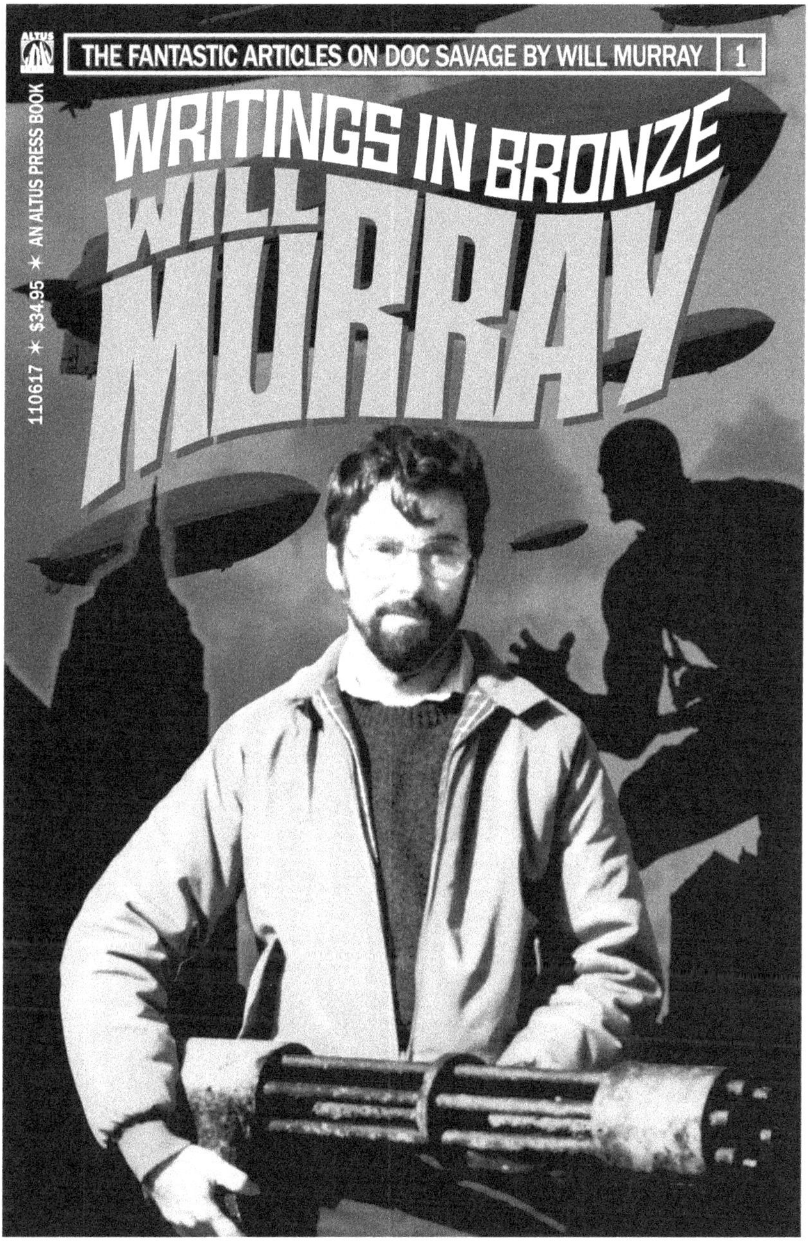
THE FANTASTIC ARTICLES ON DOC SAVAGE BY WILL MURRAY
1
WRITINGS IN BRONZE
WILL
MURRAY
110617 ★ $34.95 ★ AN ALTUS PRESS BOOK

.

www.ingramcontent.com/pod-product-compliance
Lightning Source LLC
Chambersburg PA
CBHW070541030726
47505CB00001B/112